I0525620

Pebbles

LOVE ACROSS THE MORECAMBE BAY

Printed in the United States of America

Ironmantle Books

LOVE ACROSS THE MORECAMBE BAY

By

STEVEN KAY

Ironmantle Books
Publishers Since 2012
An imprint of DonnaInk Publications, L.L.C.
17611 Aquasco Road
Annapolis, MD 20613

Ironmantle Books

Copyright © 2019 by Steven Kay.

Library of Congress Cataloging-in-Publication 2019947595.

Kay, Steven, author.
  Title: "Peebles: Love Across the Morecambe Bay" / Mr. Steven Kay.
    295 p. cm.
      Subjects: FIC027200 FICTION / Romance / Historical / 20th Century;
                   FIC027020 FICTION / Romance / Contemporary; FIC027000
                   FICTION / Romance / General; FIC000000 FICTION / General.

Identifiers: ISBN – 13 - 978-1-947704-45-9 (alk. KDP paper); 978-1-947704-11-4 (alk. BN paper) | ISBN – 978-1-947704-27-5 (digital eBook).

Printed in the United States of America
First Edition: 12 11 10 9 8 7 6 5 4 3 2; 2019. All Rights Reserved.

For more information contact:
DonnaInk Publications, L.L.C.
17611 Aquasco Road, Annapolis, MD 20613
www.donnaink.shop

Other Books by Steven Kay

For the Love of My Children
In Wordsworth's Shadow
The Satanic Court
You and Me

About the Author

Steven Kay was born in Lancashire and grew up in Hambleton close to the Morecambe Bay and the Forest of Bowland. His father introduced him to the great outdoors and his mother showed him how to make the most out of his life. His education started in mathematics and at university transitioned to languages. Steven leads a simple life as a health-food enthusiast, he loves to go lake swimming, cycling and camping. He maintains fluency in Dutch and intends to retire in Austria where the landscape reminds him of Cumbria but without continual rains. In Austria, he communicates fluently with locals, and meets up with many flying Hollanders, who appreciate the Low Countries rather than the Alps.

Finally, without a car and TV, Steven values the love of a bygone era and peacefulness it allows him to enjoy.

• • •

Table of Contents

• • •

About the Book

People and pebbles are similar; in many ways they are symbiotic, just as one person's voice on a still morning, a ripple from a pebble cast into a tarn and spread afar. Lancastrians Karen and Frank would, along with their children, play with pebbles. They swapped their gemstones throughout Europe, which were found in places as far apart as the Lake District, Canary Islands and the Alps with their loved ones. Their family considered the pebbles a kind of talisman and took them on their travels.

The most precious of all; was a blue slate pebble, given with love on the continent to Mark from his lover. A few years later, back with the mother of his first child; his gifted pebble was placed in a bedroom overlooking Lakeland Fells.

This good luck charm stayed with him, while the origins of her secrets; were carried to the grave by the man who was at home in Garstang with the love of his life who hailed from his hometown.

About Morecambe Bay

The Morecambe Bay lies in the Northwest of England and is the buffer zone between the Irish Sea and several wonderful places listed below and throughout this book.

The bay itself starts off at Rossall, a splendid north facing beach in Fleetwood, whereas in most shores up until the Cumbrian border, at Arnside, great views of the Lakeland Fells can be seen. Back in Fleetwood, just a few miles up the coast from Blackpool, this is the place where the Wyre empties herself. Going upstream through Garstang, the home of the Taylors, the source of the river is in the Forest of Bowland where the family had many fun outings, usually by bike. The next tributary of the bay is the Lune, which runs through Lancaster, an important city regarding the education of the Taylors, while further upstream lies the beautiful market town of Kirby Lonsdale, where one of the children would settle down. Silverdale, lying between the waters of the Keer and Kent rivers is the home of paternal grandparents and the source of this romantic tale.

From then on and along the shores of the bay the views are southwards, where on a clear day Blackpool Tower can be seen. The final river of the Morecambe Bay as we travel anti-clockwise is the Leven, whose waters are sourced at Lake Windermere and beyond at Rydal and Grasmere, and once again another important landmark in this saga, since almost every character in this book simply loved the charm and adventure of the Lake District. After the Leven the towns of Ulverston and Barrow-in-Furness where the bay ends, are hardly mentioned in this book, but both are connected by a railway service running through Silverdale and Lancaster, an important artery concerning the transportation in the lives of those in this book and their love of pebbles.

LOVE ACROSS THE MORECAMBE BAY

By

STEVEN KAY

Chapter One

Mark's parents were born into predictability; both were at least 5th generation in their respective villages in which they grew up. His father was born in Silverdale, at the extreme northwestern corner of modern Lancashire. His locale had more to do with the Lake District lying just 4 miles (6km) away (as the crow flies) and Beatrix Potter country than with the old Lancastrian metropolis of Manchester, which was still in the county of Lancashire; yet a staggering 53 miles (86km) away (just like his parents and their parents). Albeit somewhere down the line; since the Wordsworth family tree began, there was one off comer that was not even from Lancashire. Young Geraldine Davies came from the county of Westmorland. She was not foreign since she heralded from Arnside just 4 miles away by road. The terrain for these farmers was favorable, lying directly on the Morecambe Bay with rolling hills close by. Houses were made from slate and there was easy access to both Lancaster and Kendal. As with all Lancashire farmers leading up to his birth, they were selling much of their produce to Booths, where they would buy quality foods from the sales of their dairy, fruit, vegetables, and meat.

Mark's mother, Karen Jenkinson grew up with even more homogenous blood. The hilly terrain around Calder Vale; a village with Quaker origins between Lancaster and Preston, kept the village more cut off than Silverdale. Although small, the parish was completely self-sufficient with its mills, farms, butchers, fish and chip shop, local post office, and the co-op store that opened in 1915. As such, everyone from Karen's family came from as far back as Calder Vale's 99-year-old veteran, Nicola Sanderson whose mother was born in January of 1947. She came from pure stock of the parish of her birth - being Calder Vale, of course!

Before we look at Mark . . . we will cover the main events leading up to when his parents met.

Mark's father, Frank, named after the American crooner Sinatra, was born in 1943. A war baby, he was just like his two older siblings - Colin, born in 1939 and Beatrice born in 1941. The three of them grew up on a small farm in Silverdale between Lancaster and Kendal. On their small holding they had hens, six cows, and six sheep with an acre of land used as an orchard for selling fruit to Booths down in Blackpool. With a horse and cart and freight trains running through the village, life had not changed much since the advent of the railway one hundred years earlier. The family was on good terms with the owners of Booths. Once a week, as an appreciation of their business and customs - a hamper box arrived for the Taylors to collect from the local railway station. Also, of importance for Lancashire life, the centenary year of Booths, the grocers, and Karen, as mentioned earlier, were born in the very same year of 1947.

The Taylors supplemented their income with the advent of the new cycling craze, which at the turn of the 20th century brought in many tourists looking for a bed for the night at their guest house - either on the way to the industrialized parts of Lancashire or coming from it and on their way to the Lake District. Part of the land not mentioned was occasionally prone to flooding as it was lying on the shores of the Morecambe Bay. When camping became all the rage, they used this land for tents. Living in this area of natural beauty was a fortuitous place for those working in the holiday trades. The overnights on their site were as high as similar places in the lakes. Many of the campers had children who would collect pebbles from the shore and place them at the entrance of their tents, often taking them home as souvenirs from the Morecambe Bay. As such, they worked hard for their money and lived comfortably but were not rich.

Frank was the brightest in the family. He managed to get into Lancaster Grammar one (1) year earlier than normal, at just ten (10) years of age. A keen sportsman, he cycled to school every day. After leaving Silverdale Primary, he would cycle through the windy roads along the Morecambe Bay onto Carnforth where it was plain sailing along the A6 to Lancaster and his new school. With a mild climate, he rarely needed to take the train due to inclement weather. In school, he was popular. He was a member of the school's swimming team from the age of thirteen (13). He woke early at six (6) a.m. for breakfast and set off at seven (7) a.m. to cycle the twelve (12) miles to school. Three times a week, he would come home late due to swimming club. At just fifteen (15) years-of-age, he was already 6'1 (185cm) and weighed one hundred and seventy (170) pounds (77kg) and looked every inch a man. Every Sunday he met up with the Morecambe CTC close to the Lancaster Royal Infirmary for day trips to the Lake District, Forest of Bowland or Yorkshire Dales. He would cycle around ninety (90) miles (145km). Given they could find themselves having lunch in Grasmere, Settle, or Horwich they met other cyclists as far away as the Scottish borders, the northeast coast, or the North Midlands who like them were also out on round trips. As such, it came as no surprise when he decided to go to teacher training college, now the university, in Preston, to become a sports teacher.

As for Mark's mother, Karen had a modest working-class background in the country. She grew up in the Quaker Mill village of Calder Vale in a valley of the River Calder that powered the local cotton trade. She lived in a two-up two-down mid-terraced house. Her parents worked at Lappet Mill, which was a minute walk away. She would walk on her own. Later, with her younger siblings through Mill Pond, passing through the wood and sights of the tumbling stream below and going uphill to her primary school. Karen was a bright girl that excelled in her village school . . . St. Johns Primary where she became an A student at Garstang High. She was one of the first pupils when it opened its doors in 1958.

Being the eldest of the three children, she helped her mother look after her younger siblings; Beatrice, who was born in 1950, and Amy who was born in 1953. Being headstrong, and ambitious, she often took the newspaper off her dad and ordered him to help her mother with parental duties. Discreetly, she would go out leaving her parents to believe she was merely on a walk, but she was secretly visiting another villager. Using her academic skills as a means of making some money and progressing socially, the mill owners who lived a mile away from her family home were delighted with her teaching skills. So delighted, they opened a Furness Building Society account especially for her.

Although just fourteen (14) years of age, and only working a few evenings each week, Karen was earning as much as her mother. Of course, being the sixties (60s), her father earned nearly twice as much as her mother despite the fact he did the same work as his wife. But, then again, Karen's mother was paid to stay at home when their children were sick; and she was granted concessionary days during school holidays.

The Jacksons, another local dairy producer, prepared food hampers that were rather generous and included Lancashire cheeses. Karen often ate supper with them. At first, her parents were humiliated with what they saw as handouts, but Karen lied to them and said she had been offered pocket money that covered the cost. She knew, given they were relatives of farmer Jackson, this was a way she would receive more for her easy work, to keep her parents off the trail regarding the incredible money she was earning.

For this, she received the lion's share of her favorite cheese at home. During the summer of sixty-two (62), she went away with the Jacksons and stayed at their opulent summer retreat at

Fawe Park close to Keswick in the Lake District. The grounds went into Derwentwater Lake and had been the retreat of the young Beatrix Potter and her parents. It was here, her hosts advised Karen to study French and law at either of the prestigious Oxbridge Universities.

In September of that year, she was back at her parents', studying at Preston High for A levels. She walked two and a half miles (4km) from her village to the railway station at Catterall and would take the train to Preston. On the way back, she walked the same way.

Frank was in his final year at college at that time. He was in his final days of being a teenager. Although he had a room on campus in Preston, he often preferred the thrill and excitement of cycling thirty-three (33) miles (53km) each way in just over an hour and a half. The route from Lancaster took him along the A6 and it was when going through Garstang he would eye up the local talent. As a simple country boy, he found Preston girls who enjoyed the departmental shops springing around Fishergate too high maintenance for him. In the early 60s, Britain was still a class-ridden society. He looked down on those who lived in one of the back-to-back terraced houses, which constituted many of this urban town.

Maybe he had already seen Karen walking around Fishergate during school lunch breaks but seeing her as she got off the train at Catterall near Garstang, was a completely different kettle of fish. She had striking looks and dark hair. Yet, she resembled Hayley Mills. As it transpired; we learn, he simply ignored her when she smiled at him as he cycled through Fishergate the previous week. Back in Catterall, as she got off the train, with two friends of hers, he tried to talk, but she blanked him out. That night, alone in his room in Silverdale, he couldn't take his mind off Karen as he rehearsed a cunning plot over and over in his mind.

The following day, after a semi-sleepless night, he cycled to his college as usual and spent most of the day daydreaming about Karen. On the way back, he was more stressed than usual, the wind had turned into a northerly direction and he wanted to arrive at the railway station near Garstang five (5) minutes earlier than the day prior. Although he had given up on his preconceived timing, he decided to try with all his might to get to that fateful railway stop as soon as possible. He went through Broughton and Bilsborrow with sweat pouring off him as though he was in an Amazonian rain forest. As he arrived at Catterall, he felt as though he was about to pass out, and he arrived five (5) minutes later than the previous day.

Feeling lethargic, with a sprained right tendon, he decided to rest and as he started to recover the train arrived. Karen and her two friends from the day before were there, this time the prettiest one smiled at him. She was somewhat taller than Karen's 5 foot 4-inch (163cm) frame and had Lauren Bacall looks. Frank was able to swoon Jill at much greater ease than he could get Karen to even look at him. Within one week they had made love. Both virgins, Jill was totally under his spell and would do anything for him. As such, after a romantic session in one of the local barns he confessed to her she was simply a stepping-stone for Karen. Aged just 15, and madly in love with him, she agreed to help him find his way to the woman who had stolen his own heart.

While it had taken Jill just a few days to have full-blown sex with Frank . . . it took more than one-week for Karen to even agree to speak to him. When she found out in much detail through piecing together different parts of the jigsaw about the meetings between him and her best friend, which an embarrassed Jill and Frank told her separately, she felt quite disgusted. As such, after falling out with her friend Jill, Karen decided she never wanted to see Frank again. That night, she went to bed crying, her mind was full of every emotion and guilt started to set in. It was all her fault her friend's heart had been broken, because a young man who she had rejected wanted temporary solace with her friend. It appeared that man loved her enough to get her attention by sleeping his way into her best friend's affections.

As for Frank, he simply felt like an idiot. The girl he truly desired despised him. He broke the heart of a girl who, had he not set his eyes on Karen, would have been a consideration for the rest of his life.

The following day he didn't go past their bus stop.

Karen believed she would never see Frank again.

She went to bed thinking about how Jill was more attractive than she was and wondered if she would stay on the shelf for-ever. Luckily for her, she pulled herself together. It being a Thurs-day, she decided to think of a plan for the weekend before she went to sleep. The following day her mind was clearer. She called into her Furness Building Society branch in Preston and drew out 5 pounds. She begged her friend Jill to forgive her and to post a letter to her mother. Given Jill was so in love with Frank and had read the letter before Karen sealed it; she agreed. The letter stated Jill had been involved in an accident and was at Preston infirmary but fine and would come home the following Sunday since she was staying at another friend's house to be close to Jill. Of course, this was in the days before everyone had use of a telephone. After posting the letter though the letterbox, she carried on her way up to Oakenclough, where she lived with her parents.

After school, instead of taking the train through the usual platform entrance, Karen walked to unknown territory and entered the grand building of the railway station where she bought a weekend return from Garstang to Silverdale. All she knew from Jill was he was Frank from Silverdale. It was her first train journey beyond Lancaster. The excitement of boarding the steam locomotive was incredible. What was more exciting was she had a seat next to the window. The train set off and she watched in amazement how things passed at great speed as the train raced northwards. It was only her second week commuting by train and as she saw the small hill on the right from the train leading up towards Calder Vale, she felt as though she was a prisoner on the run fretting about her family. What if Jill hadn't dropped the letter? Karen was stressed. Who could have blamed her for the way she had been humiliated? From the train, a moment later, she saw the village of Scorton, which apart from one visit to Lancaster, was the northern limit of her previous adventures. When she went out on a big trip with friends on foot via Nicky Nook and just under 5 miles (8km) from her house. With the newly built bungalows there was a more delightful sight than the corroding bricks of her own terrace home, thanks to the plumes of smog from the mill. After a few more minutes with rolling hills around the northern fringes of the Forest of Bowland the train pulled in on time at Lancaster. She smiled to herself.

She had read in school about Lancaster and its prison. As she saw a policeman get onto the train, she froze. Not wanting to attract any attention, she took out a book for learning French. As the young copper walked by and noticed her book he smiled, attracted by her intelligence. He couldn't have been more than 21 years-of-age, but he was shy and, yes, he wasn't going to annoy a stranger who with looks like hers obviously spoken for already.

As the train continued through Hest Bank with the majestic views of the Morecambe Bay and Furness Fells in the backdrop, Karen was awestruck. As the train stopped at Carnforth, this well-read girl who knew about the film *Brief Encounter*, couldn't believe her luck in basically being in a film set. She looked at the young officer, he seemed to be in his own world, which was to her great relief.

Just a few minutes later, the train arrived at Silverdale. As she stepped off the train, she admired the beautiful scenery around her and the stiff breezes off the bay. She started thinking and quickly fell into the frightening reality of being in the middle of nowhere. Suddenly, she wished she hadn't done this - if only she hadn't fallen out with Jill and Frank.

Luckily for her, the police officer walked in a different direction from her. She made her way to the ticket office and saw a middle-aged man with a moustache that sat behind the desk smoking a pipe reading his newspaper. At 5 p.m. he wasn't expecting anyone to distract him from his leisure until the next train to Manchester arrived. She went up to the counter, "Excuse me sir." The ticket seller looked up surprised as he wasn't used to young strangers.

"Good evening young lady, what can I do for you?" He noticed from her accent she had travelled from a different location to that of his own dialect that was almost a Westmorland lilt. *She appears to be a rather exotic being*, he thought.

"Do you by any chance know of a fellow named Frank who rides a bicycle?" She asked rather hopefully, while feigning inside herself wanting momentarily to be back home safe and sound.

"I am afraid, I am of a different generation to you, young lady. I have no idea about young men from this village, nor any called Frank who ride a bicycle."

Feeling nervous Karen left the station. Basically, she had run away from home. She decided to walk around the village. In her present mind, being over half a mile away from the station, it seemed a world away – she felt paranoid that all the eyes in the village were on her – a silly teenaged girl. Her nerves were bad. She arrived at the local off license store after what had seemed like an eternity. She wanted to eat something proper - it was getting late and the shops were closed; so, she had to make do with anything on offer. In the store, there was nothing that really took her fancy. She needed something to comfort herself. She had never smoked a cigarette in her life but heard when under severe stress, this was one way to resolve it. Since this was the most nerve-wracking moment in the whole of her fifteen- and three-quarter years – she thought about buying a pack of smokes. Suddenly, the young police officer walked in. Karen was under-age and had she bought some cigarettes she would have broken the law. At that moment, she froze.

A few seconds later, and to what seemed like an eternity, trembling with fear, she blurted out, "I am looking for a young man called Frank." The room went silent. She was expecting the worst when suddenly no longer under suspense wondering what to do with this young beauty who had caught the officer's dream-y eyes, he simply looked at her fondly with a benign smile.

"I know all about you, young lady, come on follow me."

"Please don't take me down to the station," she begged.

"Whatever gave you that idea, you sat next to me on the train. All you had to say was you were looking for my former schoolmate Frank Taylor, who cycles to Preston and Bob's your uncle!"

She didn't ask any more questions. It was blatantly obvious everyone in town must have heard about Frank and his adventures. Perhaps the entire village was waiting for her, but not in this way of her just coming out of the blue, which was one out of character for her.

Together they walked through the village and arrived at the Taylors. Karen looked in awe at the livestock grazing around. The officer rang the bell. Being in uniform when Mrs. Taylor opened the door, she answered it a little shocked to say the least but suspected he had come around about her wildest child. The officer simply looked at her, "This young lady has been looking everywhere for your son." He said smiling before walking away.

Mrs. Taylor was gazing toward space. She was having a little bit too much excitement with the law regarding her son in what was their protected world in the wilds of Lancashire and Westmorland borders. In what seemed a lifetime, both women stood looking at one another. Frank had been looking out of his window when he saw Karen walking up the garden path with John. He appeared reasonably dressed within one minute of Karen's arrival, walked downstairs, kissed his mother and stated, "Mom, this is Karen, we are going out on a stroll together and will be back later."

The two lovebirds walked into his village and laughed and spoke about their respective schools before walking back to Frank's home hand-in-hand where a Lancashire hot pot meal was served for them. Karen was the first young lady who had come around to her house – with her son already 19 years of age - she was relieved to say the least. She left the room after a short but pleasant chat, and went into her living room. She looked at her husband and stated, "Frank has a young woman here for the weekend so don't go in his room."

Her husband smiled and went back to reading his newspaper. That night neither Frank nor Karen could sleep. She simply lay in his arms the whole night as he held her tightly. They hadn't made love. They hadn't even kissed. She said she only wanted to be right next to him as a way of getting closer to him and the trip was already a personal achievement.

The following day after breakfast, they went out with the two packed lunches, which his mother made discreetly as they shyly ate their cereals followed by marmalade and toast with tea. His father was out on the farm with his other two children who were older. Neither Frank, nor Karen, had brought home any romantic interests to their families before this. So, the Taylors were taken by surprise and that turned to joy for Mrs. Taylor who made certain not to be a nuisance to her son with his girl.

Frank took Karen along the shores of the Morecambe Bay where she admired the pebbles that lay dreamily in the sand. This was unusual for her. There were pebbles in her local stream, but she hadn't cared much for them back home. In the warm late summer sunshine, they walked onto Arnside, where they had lunch at the promenade. The railway viaduct lay to their right crossing Kent Estuary with views of Grange-over-Sands and Furness Fells of the Lake District, a little to the left and in the background, that simply left her awestruck having never seen anything like this apart from in books she had read.

From there they walked together hand-in-hand up the village hill passing all the villagers. All the nosey so-and-sos in this sleepy village were always on the lookout for the latest entertainment. Frank wasn't from the village, but he was such a handsome catch, girls in all the surrounding villages knew about him.

A little further out of civilization, the couple continued their ascent to Arnside Knott. At the end of the 500-foot (159m) climb, Karen thought of her favorite walk from Scorton up Nicky Nook, which was of similar height. She looked around in the direction of her home and then toward the fells around Kendal. When her eyes followed the Kent Estuary moving to Morecambe Bay she was spellbound. She had never experienced such a beautiful view with someone who took her breath away, as such . . . the panorama of the sea, bay, estuary, and inland mountains was settled into her mind now and would always be a part of an important turning point in her life.

By this time, Frank was a little nervous. He knew Karen was a good girl. Looking at her he stated, "I have waited a long time to bring a girl up here and show her the most beautiful place on earth." He moved his head toward her, kissing her on the lips.

At first in two minds as to what she should do, Karen believed Frank was a gentleman at heart, but he had made love to her best friend already . . . so she knew he wasn't as innocent and charming as she wanted to brainwash herself into believing in order to allow her desire to take over her mind. Karen spied a middle-aged couple walking by and felt a little more secure.

Frank began to kiss her with increasing passion. It felt like a wave with the momentum of a current of water escaping a basin when the plug is pulled . . . she felt the gravity of the potential of lovemaking that made her weak at the knees, and almost breathless. Unable to resist any further, she opened her mouth. The two French kissed amidst gentle Irish sea breezes that blew in their faces as the September mid-day sun beat down on them. As their kissing continued, her thoughts became increasingly amorous, combined with hints of jealousy as she thought about her best friend Jill who invaded her personal desires.

Frank showed her Arnside Tower. Although a ruin, it was an impressive sight. Walking through Eaves Wood, the couple re-turned to the Taylors farmhouse and went upstairs to Frank's bedroom. It was already after 5 p.m. He put on his gramophone player with some Elvis tunes. He started to sing in serenade. There was a knock on his door. He opened it to see a tray with two bowls filled to the brim with broth and sliced buttered home-made bread complete with cutlery, a teapot, and two mugs. He promptly carried their supper into their impending love nest.

"Your mother is such as sweetheart." Karen stated in admiration. In her dreamy heart, she knew this was going to be her future mother-in-law. The woman who had brought Frank into the world was to be revered. Karen was away from her home and feeling smitten.

"I am the youngest of my mother's children in our home. I guess she doesn't want to rub it in my siblings' faces they are still single. I see how happy my mother is, she likes you, Karen." He said, as they looked in each other's faces. They both felt a need for a little more reassurance.

"How can you tell your mother likes me?" Karen prodded.

"Oh, there is no doubt about it. I saw it by the look in her eyes when we left the grounds last night. Mother doesn't like everyone you know. She is always telling me about how the local bobby was taken to the cleaners for being too nice. When he came around and brought you here, she simply knew she had to obey his command." He worked on appearing more respectable to impress Karen.

"What do you mean he was taken to the cleaners? Was there something less than idyllic about this village?" She pressed for more information.

"Well . . . he had a girlfriend you know. She fell pregnant. He was as proud as punch. They were about to be married until he received a letter from his partner's lover. To be honest, it was damn awful. He hadn't written anything; it was simply a letter his girlfriend had written to the village stud with her being a former classmate of mine. He, the policeman from the year above me in school and a local, came up to me for some advice." He stated feeling proud of himself as she looked at him.

"What was in the letter?" she asked excitedly.

"She wrote as much as she could never love anyone else than he, her secret lover, she wanted to continue with her marriage plans since Tony (her lover) was still on the dole and living with his parents wasn't able to provide for her and her child a place to live. She also added had she not been with child she would have flown to the moon for him, but without much money, and as a responsible parent, he must accept what was best for his child. For the mother to make sure the baby is in an environment where it has a father figure who can provide all the required comforts." He said with a hint of disapproval.

"So, what happened next?" She asked, showing concern and affection.

"Well, this is the interesting bit. Being a devout Christian, I mean the copper, he called both the lovers into his office for an interview and simply read the letter to them. They both sat in silence. They were completely humiliated to say the least. The officer simply said the village wasn't big enough for all three of them. With that, the couple looked at each other and left the village. They took off for the Lake District where they both got a live-in job at the Waterhead Hotel in Ambleside. This happened this time last year. Since then, nobody has heard anything else about them. I think it fair to say they are still together and living in the Lakes." He hoped that was the end of the story.

"What about the policeman, isn't he sad?" Karen was showing too much concern about the story for Frank's liking since all he could think about was Karen and no one else but he answered nonetheless . . .

"Probably. But, he just got on with his life and focused on his job – isn't that what folks do? With this being a sleepy village and he wise for his years - more like a village elder than a man chasing criminals - his main campaign (his only one) remained to dish out fines to cyclists who didn't have lights on their bikes – like me. He would be of no use in Liverpool. I went there once, to see Everton playing. My main memory is of the city itself. I had read about London, and visiting Liverpool, with no idea as to what London must be like. It was like being in a space age. The women dressed differently, the buildings were ginormous, and when I came back to Silverdale it felt as if I went back in time."

He rambled almost out of control, seeming a little nervous and wanting to keep Karen's attention focused on him. She was bored of the monologue. She initiated a kiss, which was to his great delight. This time, and away from preying eyes, she let herself go a little more. He placed his chest on her bosom, and she started to get more excited and as he started to fondle her breasts, she suddenly turned frigid.

"I'm sorry I can't do this just now."

He understood and stopped his advances. He motioned to Karen with body language it was time to eat their solid broth. It had been long enough for their tea to have gone frozen. Once again, she slept snuggly in his arms. Thanks to their first kiss Karen was more relaxed. Frank was rather restless since he wanted more from her. He believed deep down; she wanted it too.

The next day, the entire Taylor family sat together for breakfast. This included Frank's parents, siblings, and paternal grandparents. Jack senior, so-called since Frank's father and grandfather were both called Jack, took everyone outside and got down to the business of harvesting apples and all the other fruits they could muster. The feeling of togetherness with family ushered in a new level of affection for Frank and his familial background, which was warming Karen's heart and her love for him.

Later in the day, the entire family had dinner together and as the evening was coming in, during the remaining daylight, the pair were left alone together. Upstairs they began to kiss once more as he tried his hand placing his chest on her bosom. Once again, she became breathless as she felt his iron rod of passion pressing against her skirt. This time there was no turning back. She simply threw herself with him onto the bed. Karen didn't expect it to happen this way, but equally, she had never met someone with whom she could trust, let alone consider spending the rest of her life with, and she knew she would never tire of him.

She felt from his touch he felt the same way about her. She knew she wasn't his first. She also knew he wasn't just about having sex with her. He made love to the woman inside her, who for him, was like no other. She felt special, and knew no matter what, the two of them were simply made for each other and nothing else mattered in the world.

• • •

The following day began with them making love like the evening just gone. It was all so natural and sweet but certainly full of great passion. After taking breakfast, they took the train to Preston. The main part of the day was no different to any other school day for either of them. That evening they both went to visit her family. For Frank, the walk was exciting, while Karen was nervous about arriving home with, as far as her parents would be concerned, some strange man.

As they arrived, Karen's mother was busy cooking while her younger siblings were doing homework. Her father was reading an old newspaper and smoking a pipe. She briefly introduced her father to Frank. She explained to both her gobsmacked parents Frank and she were an item; and that he came from good stock. She did so while he visited the only latrine situated outside.

Dinner was served. After eating, her family went upstairs earlier than usual, each to their respective bedroom, leaving the young couple in peace to sleep on the couch downstairs. It was obvious to Karen's mother she had spent the entire weekend with her young man. Her mother had been out of her mind with worry but knew Karen was not one to be told what to do and typically made responsible decisions.

During the mid-morning school break, a few hours later, Karen read the letter from her mother, which had been placed inside her lunchbox. "Dearest Karen, I have never seen you so happy in your life, I hope it all goes well for you both, but remember, me and your dad are always here for you." With that she felt sentimental regarding her family, but her need and attraction for Frank was too strong for anything to get in the way of her romantic desires. As much as she loved her parents, a new dawn rose, and she felt as though her life was now for her new love.

The next few weeks the couple would sleep between her parents' and his parents' homes. Most nights were together, but some nights were spent alone. They were in love, but both were young and naïve, even so everything was going perfectly well for them. On top of that, their romance was becoming infectious. Frank's sister Beatrice started dating. Amy, Karen's younger sister, as well. Being so happy, and lucky in love, they arranged a blind date for Jill and the policeman. This was only a few days after their own first date. Back in 1962, there wasn't much for the local village bobby to do and given the scandal his ex, created one (1) year earlier, most villagers felt sorry for this salt of the earth bobby. As such, when Frank's mother instructed Ethel, the village gossip, to let it get around John Watson wouldn't be patrolling the lanes due to his date, everyone held their breath and waited for his return. The secret was kept safe and sound on his watch.

For John and Jill, thanks to Frank and Karen, a weekend had been arranged at Slaidburn Youth Hostel and as was common at the time they all arrived by bike, which for the girls was just over twenty (20) miles (32km). The boys were in a dormitory of ten (10) and all beds had been taken, while the girls' dormitory again with ten (10) beds, had only Karen and Jill. The Friday evening, they cooked for themselves corned beef hash, followed by ginger cake from the village shop and went back to the girls' dormitory, where Jill, still reeling from being used by Frank earlier month gently seduced John.

During both Saturday and Sunday, they went walking and visited the quintessential villages of Dunsop Bridge and Newton on foot in addition to the beautiful Stocks Reservoir and a place called Wham close to Settle. It was here, in Wham, on the second official day of autumn, after their lunches had been eaten on their warm and sunny Sunday afternoon, the two couples wandered away from each other. For the first time ever, both couples, albeit a couple hundred yards apart from one another, made love in the open air.

Frank and Karen had been together for exactly one month and a half when November arrived. During that time, Karen hadn't menstruated. While this had been of great excitement to her lovemaking and with not being discomforted about being on the rag, which she hated; as each day passed, she felt increasingly nauseous and the reality of being with child was sinking in. Luck-ily, they already had been moving between the three dwellings during their love trails and both agreed while Silverdale was a long way from Preston. The extra time spent travelling would mean she wouldn't be hidden in Mark's room away from his landlady or intrude on the already overcrowded house of her parents. Silverdale was for the time being, the best option for them to make the most of things together, since their love chang-ed everything in their lives.

Christmas was spent between Calder Vale and Silverdale. They both experienced the coldest winter of their lives. Even so, with a warm glow in their hearts, they enjoyed showing one ano-ther their local childhood haunts - most importantly for this coup-le, who enjoyed their Christmas gifts and the company of their loved ones, was simply the love and passion they held for one another. After nearly four months together in came 1963, both sweethearts carried on normally with their respective studies and schools every day. On Karen's birthday, Frank gave her a pebble and card that read . . .

LOVE AND PEBBLES FROM THE MORECAMBE BAY.

He had another card for her from himself but wanted to show her how original he could be. With his efforts, she had been swooned. Their shotgun wedding took place January 12th, 1963. Four days after her sixteenth (16th) birthday, which was miracu-lously arranged thanks to a couple who agreed to postpone their wedding until spring. The wedding took place in Silverdale. Frank's family had more money and wanted everything at their home territory. Apart from it being a very beautiful church wed-ding, Karen's family enjoyed the fairy tale weekend and the stay in relatively opulent surroundings, in the guesthouse of Frank's family. It felt as if they were being treated like royalty.

With Karen conceiving during the early days of their court-ship, they were still getting to know each other during her preg-nancy. It was obvious to everyone who observed Karen and Frank's love for each other that their baby was being developed in the most harmonious of conditions. As for Valentine's Day,

Karen insisted on Mark singing, "Please Please Me." His voice, thanks to his desire to make Karen feel there was no one else like her in the world, was magical.

"Darling, I want you to sing softly to our baby."

Karen took off her top and looked at her baby bump. He kissed her belly and they shared a precious moment feeling their baby move together. With almost tears of joy in both of their hearts, he sang to both of his loves. As for Karen, she could take no more, and simply grabbed hold of him while he knew the desire which they had for each other was sending them into what they could only describe simply being one of pure heaven.

Spring came after more than two months of mostly a permanent freeze, which around the 6th of March had finally ended. Karen was thoroughly enjoying life on the farm, with it being surrounded by an area of outstanding natural beauty and her lonely nights at her parents were now a thing of the past. For Frank, he was still living with his parents - lonely nights had disappeared too. Frank was cycling to Preston again to save some money for their baby, of course, the main reason was so he could get some exercise outside of their mutual bed.

While Karen was quite impressed with Carnforth, their local town, she didn't have much money to spend there. In some ways it wasn't so different to Garstang and it was like her own Calder Vale. The area was steeped with connections of the Quakers and George Fox (one of the founders had visited the area in the 17th century). So, while Karen might not have been aware of this, she certainly didn't feel as though she was a stranger in her new home.

This happy and devoted couple didn't have much money, but for them they had everything they needed in each other. The Easter holidays came. Both of them spent a lot of the time with their studies. They provided some help on the farm and had time for themselves to walk hand-in-hand along the bay or inland in the countryside. As the cool spring got warmer in May, they enjoyed sitting on the beach with the sunset in their faces to make wishes and kiss until twilight when they walked back home.

● ● ●

They didn't go far. For them, the biggest excursion, apart from going to their schools, came during June, when they took the train to Grange-over-Sands. They spent the whole day during one hot Saturday at the open-air baths. Karen swam gently, while admiring Frank's swimming prowess. Before they went back, they took a gentle romantic walk along the promenade. By then, and largely because they were so in love with each other, they were ready for parenthood. Then they shared the joys of bringing up a child, their own baby, together.

Chapter Two

February: Pebbles in The Sands.

The birth, which had been due to take place on June 18th in the middle of the stressful exam period, had not arrived as expected. This meant Karen was able to sit through her end-of-year exams. By then, she lost regular contact with Jill, who like Karen, also fell pregnant at Wham but had given up her schooling. She was already 16 when she found out she was pregnant with her being two months older than Karen, and due to John's promotion in Ambleside, which he took on with relish, she moved in with him to the Lakes. They were now proud parents. Since the mutual due date of the expectant couples had seen the arrival of Jill's first child, right up until birth, Karen had been taking an active part in country life while Frank attended to her emotional needs.

On Tuesday, the 25th of June 1963, George Michael came into this world in a London hospital. The city where, even back in those days, one had 24 hours round the clock entertainment on their doorstep. Hustle and bustle, fast food, and plenty of shopping malls delivered people and experimentations with new things from all over the world, in cuisine, clothing, partners, drugs, and the Krays.

On this day, Lancastrian Mark Taylor also came into the world. In the home of parents in a sleepy northern village, where if you wanted to eat you had to cook for yourself, if you wanted to survive you needed a regular sleeping pattern to give one enough strength to work; and the main entertainment was from your partner and between the sheets after much talk to one another, and if she was lucky, singing some poetry from the heart.

Karen knew that one had to work hard in order to achieve one's goals, and although she had never once regretted her new role as a mother, it wasn't something, which she had planned. So, in love with Frank, she could have happily stayed at home while he went to work. She was living with his family and he was still a student. From September, he was about to start work as a teacher. Karen decided to take advantage of the fact her mother-in-law, who was on site when she needed her, was a woman who respected Karen's wish to have her own self-sufficient family and for she and Frank to get their own place. She was ready for some tiring times, but equally fulfilling times ahead.

The young mother bonded well with her newborn baby. Frank was around to share the tender moments with them. As a student, he had the entire summer off. Of course, he helped on the farm. He remained close at hand for his wife and baby. She, in turn, did her bit attending to guests so Mrs. Taylor senior could take time for herself. Of course, the other Taylor children helped too. Coming from a village where things were planned out generation after generation, the Taylors made sure the new mother and baby were living in a healthy environment and did all they could to make certain the young family was a success.

Together as they could, the couple made sure mother, father and baby in the pram, walked one hour each day covering the shores around their home. Then, into the village on an errand for the family who worked round the clock without a break, apart from feeding times.

By then, of course, Karen was performing the cooking and cleaning of the family home - basically a converted barn in the simplistic sense. Other family members brought in cakes and crumbles, so Karen could spend more time with her studies. While the barn had cooking facilities, beds, and heating, it wasn't much to write about since it had been built for hens and not for humans. Still, it was a free temporary steppingstone for a couple who had nothing to offer financially. Both Karen and Frank fully appreciated the help from his parents.

By the end of the summer, Frank was relieved to start work. Money meant savings toward a house. His new life of work and his first paying job meant a bike ride each day to Garstang. The journey was ten miles less each way than it had been to his studies in Preston, meaning about one hour each way or 22 miles. For Frank, this was a perfect commuting distance. Back then the roads were less busy. The cars were smaller. Karen happily took advantage of having her husband's family onsite. She was able to continue her studies at Preston sixth-form college.

The day began at 6. Karen would breast feed and make packed lunches for herself and Frank. He would make a cooked breakfast, which wasn't the best as it was too greasy for her - she stomached it knowing in time she could gently coax him into preparing something more palatable. With their demanding baby, her studies, and newly married life Karen was content with any help that came her way. At around 7, Frank's sister Beatrice came for the baby. Karen kissed Frank before he went off on his bike. She would leave a few minutes later to board the train to Lancaster. As the train headed south, she thought about her husband, who was probably not far away from her as he headed down along the A6. Frank could have taken the train too. This never came up as topic of discussion since as true country stock, they went on with their lives without endless analysis - a common feature of intellectuals. The station was 1.5 miles from his parents'. At the other end, it was 1.1 miles from his school. Using his bike directly, he saved 2.6 mile walk each way — meaning he saved time as well as money. In the train Karen used the 45 minutes or so for studies. This meant textbooks, pens, and a writing block and she would do this on her return journey as well.

Frank, as a sports teacher, had it many ways, easy, no homework to mark. He did find himself involved in after-school activities. This meant working with his pupils who represented the school in swimming and football - the main sports recognized at the school. In bad weather, he could, of course, take the train from Silverdale down to Catterall Station with his wife who then continued on to Preston. With all his activities he came home relaxed and happy to be with his wife and baby.

At lunchtime, they often thought about each other. They missed one another whenever they were apart. They both ate the same lunch and wondered if their other half was doing the same. Karen had prepared their lunch with love, only Frank's was of a larger portion. The lunch was packed in plastic lunchboxes. Karen placed sandwiches she made inside and added an apple and homemade cake. These were then placed into their back-packs. In Frank's case, this was a saddle bag since he was on his bicycle. Like Karen, he took his flask of tea to work. This enabled him to keep away from staff and gossip of colleagues who had been driven mad in the classroom. For him it was a role reversal since his pupils lived in fear of him.

As a sports teacher, thanks to his extremely active life, Frank pushed and pushed the pupils no matter how good they were. As far as he was concerned, there was always room for improvement. On top of that, he combined irony whenever he felt someone wasn't trying hard enough. Oftentimes, many felt humiliated. Instead of showing frustration at the boys who didn't try, he would call them, 'love' for the others to see how weak and effeminate some boys were in his mind. Equally, he didn't allow bullying. Whenever this took place on his watch, the bully was forced to perform some physical activity in front of the others, such as hard presses until they almost collapsed from exhaustion. As such, he wasn't very popular, but then again none of his colleagues were loved very much either.

At the end of his first-year teaching, his A class student wife had passed her A levels in French, German, and the law. Although they hadn't much privacy, they were thankful they had received so much help from Frank's family while enjoying the fresh air of the bay. At times, they felt rather suffocated, since they wanted to be fully independent themselves – but they maintained their gratitude.

● ● ●

During the summer, the village had a hoe down. For a few nights, Karen's sisters would stay over. At one of the dances, they found a brief summer romance. Their few nights turned into a repeat event. They were popular with the locals and had been asked to help out with a coffee morning. This was run by the church. Some pretty faces were needed to help serve the cream teas. While this became an event for Karen's youngest sister a few more summers, her middle sister, Beatrice (who also had the same name as the Taylors middle child) was about to enter a stable and secure relationship that would last the rest of her life.

In getting used to their routine, Frank and Karen managed to go away the impending summer. They didn't venture very far. They hired a caravan on the shores of Lake Windermere less than 20 miles away for two weeks. To get there, they had taken the train via Lancaster, which doubled the distance increasing the fun through the train journey. It wasn't very much different to Silverdale, but it was a holiday all the same without the responsibilities of their normal routine. Frank enjoyed his daily morning swim while Karen nursed toddler Mark, after almost freezing himself and going blue from being in the cold lake too long. Frank felt very relaxed after swimming from the east side to the west side of the lake and back a distance of more than one mile daily. He was content that even if they didn't venture far, he had more adventure than most of the others on holiday, who often spent the entire day lounging around the site.

Even so, they would walk each day - usually in the rain – and take turns pushing the pram. They walked through all sorts of valleys surrounded by the majestic Lakeland fells. They passed streams, woodland, farmland, and often sat in front of a tarn or lake if the weather was fair. To the amusement of their child, they would have some fun in one of the becks and brace the icy waters which came running down from the High Langdale Pikes into the valley. If it wasn't too cold they would place Mark in the beck, too to his initial horror, then later delight each time he went into the water. He enjoyed when his daddy picked up the pebbles and pretended they were large insects.

Garstang High opened in 1958. As Karen started then, and in October 1964, Lancaster University opened its doors up for the first time. A most eager, and fresh French law student was, of course, Karen Taylor. The first 16 years of her life, the start of the new school year made sure things in her own world in Calder Vale, just like those of her ancestors, weren't going to change. Now, things were different. Two years earlier, she fell pregnant and moved to Silverdale with a student, about to be husband, Frank. One year later her love started working to bring independence for the young family. This autumn, just two years since she met Frank, her life was full of subtle yet important horizons as she became a part of the student elite.

Karen decided since Mark was a little older, he was less dependent on her. As such, she decided to make some changes that would be of benefit to her. As such, she was no longer at Preston High for A-Levels. She was 18 miles closer to home in Silverdale with her new studies. She also decided to commute by bike to university. The 14-mile journey was a little bit too much for her on top of her other duties, but at just 17, she felt strong enough to manage anything - as did the majority of the youth in those days. Of course, for Frank this was music to his ears. Together they would cycle through the windy roads and reach the A6 at Carnforth, then cycle to the university. From there they would give each other a kiss. Frank would continue alone to Bowgreave 1 mile south of Garstang where his teaching post lay. Although Karen finished earlier than he, she agreed to wait for him in the university library where she could finish off her studies each day. Together they cycled back as two lovebirds.

For their child this was very positive. Mother and father had done something pleasant together each day. Mark although only a toddler, could sense this, and Karen didn't have to finish off her studies when she got home. As such, it was as if she was completely two different people. She was a full-time swot at Lancaster University while at home a full-time mother. University life was a joy. Unlike her peers who often moaned about how hard life was being alone on campus, Karen was proud of her incongruous path she had taken in the conventional student sense. As the months went by, the other girls started to feel stressed from sacrificing romance for study. Karen felt thankful in meeting Frank and his family. The weekends were certainly a time of family togetherness. Both parents felt tranquilized due to plenty of exercise and held plenty of patience teaching Mark to walk. They went out in all weathers as most people did back then.

Christmas was a beautiful affair. Mark was now 18 months of age. It was his first proper yuletide he was old enough to enjoy. They went to the Jacksons just before the New Year for three nights. This meant they were able to visit Karen's family, too. It was the first time Frank met the Jacksons apart from the wedding. He felt most welcome there. Although, he never had dared mention it, he felt Karen compared her own parents to his - especially since they took more interest in her academic life than her parents did. Of course, she had been prepared for this. She remained loyal to her family origins no matter how high she would climb socially she would always, to Frank's delight, remain humble.

During the spring of 1965, they found life much easier with Mark than the previous spring. Back in February of that year, on the shores of the Morecambe Bay, Mark hard started to enjoy picking up the pebbles in the sands for his mother. The best two were presented to her on Valentine's Day. Being able to venture around the love haunts of when his parents first met, brought joy to his parents. Mark was turning into a good little walker and he enjoyed going uphill. Of course, he needed some help and to be carried on Frank's back whenever he got tired. On warm days, the train ride from Silverdale to Grange was a fun day out. They had the foothills of the Lake District and important open-air baths. These made more sense than indoor pools as and when the air temperatures would climb into the mid 60's (17 Degrees). Many other families, like them, enjoyed the so-called Riviera of the north.

Summer arrived, Mark was two years of age, and they decided to go on a cycling holiday. The route contained seven (7) youth hostel destinations. Elterwater in the beautiful Langdale Valley. Patterdale on the shores of Ullswater Lake. Keswick beside the River Greta. Buttermere with views of the lake of the same name. Black Sail at the head of the Ennerdale Valley. Eskdale in the valley of the same name. Coniston high up in the old Coppermines. At each place, they would spend two nights enabling them to do whatever they wanted. On that day, they were not travelling to another hostel. Since they travelled by bike, they could easily buy groceries en route. The distances weren't so great, but they were extended with diversions. Mark enjoyed the day sitting on the seat and not worrying about the previous or following day when he was walking. Even so, he had plenty of fun and enjoyed going up Loughrigg Fell and scrambling up Haystacks.

Back home, one habit of Frank's was to leave a book in the toilet. Of course, as with all men, he had some strange habits. His was intentional as was perhaps true in many other cases too. Sensing she would be stressed whenever he was relaxing while she was studying, Frank invented a bowel problem. He told Karen, the book was there to help him take his mind of his intestinal problems. Reading a book would simply soothe him. As such, he read four books a year sitting on the toilet. In those days, books were thicker with much more to read.

September was a blissfully happy month for Karen. Things in her life were settling down. Although she yearned for a place for just herself, her husband, and child. She felt life was much better away from Calder Vale where the living conditions were cramped; her parents didn't always see eye-to-eye with her. The university year started again in October. Since she hadn't started her second year, she decided to cycle one morning with Frank to his school with Mark on the back of Frank's bike. From there she walked with Mark to her parents' house at Calder Vale. As she arrived, it seemed as if the whole village delighted in seeing Karen and her son. It was only 10 o'clock when they arrived at the mill. The receptionist immediately granted her parents 20 minutes to see their daughter and grandson. There, she could see in her parents' eyes how much the visit made their day and was thankful the mill was run by owners with a heart.

After the visit, feeling brave, she decided to follow the path close to the Calder and walked through the churchyard past her old school and went through Oakenclough. From there, she continued with her son in her arms up Nicky Nook, where they had their lunch and continued for Scorton before walking along the river onto Garstang. On the way, there at the confluence of the Wyre and Grizedale, Mark enjoyed playing with the pebbles and wanted to throw them at Karen who gently slapped his hand before he had the chance to do it. After a little play, they continued with Mark walking until they reached Frank's school. In total, they had covered 11 miles. In the warm September sun she nodded off to sleep on the school playing field with her sleeping baby who had already taken his nap. Frank knew where to find her since she had posted a note into his message box, which was simply one small compartment in his saddle bag. The couple had been together for three solid romantic years. After he aroused her gently from her sleep while playing with his son, they cycled back literally into the sunset since it was nearing 6PM. Just over one hour later they would see the changing hues of the sky. As they reached Warton, the sun about to set, they looked across the bay with the sky above Grange-over-Sands. It turned into a shimmering red. Karen felt she was the luckiest woman alive, while Frank looked on blissfully at her positive expressions, as his son would try to pinch him with love as he sat behind on his child's seat.

October came. The autumn gales brought storms into Karen's personal life. She enjoyed her first week back at university. Deep down, she enjoyed the cycle there the most. By the end of month, she was starting to feel the ride was becoming too much for her. She suspected she was with child but wasn't due for a period until the start of November. As a child close to nature and her own body, she felt things were changing inside of her. She continued with cycling, but after the first week in November it was time to confront her husband when she felt sure she wasn't fussing about nothing. Frank wanted another baby. He was 22 and she not quite 19 and he felt it best for Mark to have a companion. With Karen headstrong on not just her studies, but also her career, he worried they would never have any more children. She sensed he had done this on purpose to her. Then again, she knew it took two to make a baby. With her career being of great importance to her; she vowed to scream the truth out of him. Never once did he own up to the truth. Although she knew he had lied to her. She suspected she was starting to take things too far after rowing with him several times a day for one week. Things calmed down and the reality of living in their small former hen house with a baby on the way was sinking in. Frank realized he had made a big mistake but kept his secret intact. Even so, they were full of passion and still enjoyed kissing one another's lips before they made love in what was as romantic a display as during their early courtship days.

November was emotionally the reverse of October. By the start of advent, things were much clearer. Frank's dad, had kept a lot of money stashed under his bed. He didn't want to pay taxes so he hadn't banked it. Equally, he didn't know what to do with it either. As such, he wanted to give Frank 1,000 pounds to go toward a house, while his wife, Betty, sensed Karen was a little annoyed with her son over the second pregnancy. She approached her daughter-in-law woman-to-woman, "Must be difficult studying with another baby on the way." Mrs. Taylor said smiling.

"I think there are worse things than being pregnant."

"True, but it would be nice if you had your own place."

"Yes, but these things take time." Karen answered smiling.

"Those are wise words for a young lady." By then, both were smiling at each other. "Jack has just ordered me to give you some cash for a deposit to get your own house . . . we don't want any fuss, just for you both to be happy, and this money is only lying around with no home to go to!" After handing the envelope to Karen, she simply left the room before Karen had a chance to protest the wad full of notes. As she counted, she couldn't believe such an amount being provided. She felt positively overwhelmed with everything.

Karen felt stressed from so many changes taking place in her life in such a short time. She wanted to spend as much time in Silverdale as possible that Christmas. Partly, to show her gratitude to Frank's parents and partly because she was quite happy to relax. Of course, mothers then took things much more in stride than those of later generations. When on their house hunting rounds, they would often call in at her former family home. Frank was teaching in Garstang and she was studying south of Lancaster. She began to see quite a bit of her half of the family. As such, they were looking for a house between Lancaster and Garstang. By chance, and to her interest, they found in Scorton, after a few months of worry, a bungalow semi just outside the village centre going for 3,000 pounds. For the rest of the money, Frank took out a 2,000-pound mortgage. The house would be theirs from May. Of course, Karen was delighted, since it was close to her family, Mark's school, and her university.

Chapter Three

March: Pebbles at Home with My Family.

They decided to move in properly during the summer holidays. Karen was still relying on her in-laws' help so she could continue her studies. She was worried about how she would cope without them. From May onward, she no longer cycled to university but continued studies until the aca-demic year finished in June. In early July, about to give birth any day, the little family moved into their new house. Leaving Mark at Silverdale, since Frank was still teaching until the third week in July – on July 10th Karen gave birth to a baby boy, Matthew. Together, with her husband, they had 6 weeks off during the summer. It was during that time they got to know all the neighbors as well as getting their new home ready for immediate family members to settle in.

The summer of 66 ended very peacefully in the Taylor household. Mark didn't see anything to be joyful about. He had lost his extended family and now his mother was spending time with her new baby. Luckily, dad was doing activities with him, such as going up and down Nicky Nook, and playing in Grizedale Brook with the pebbles. For the rest, he missed his place of birth with the big grounds and freedom of the farm and doting attention he gained from the Taylor family. Frank too, missed living in a detached house. He was glad to have his own place for Karen and relieved his 46 miles round trip to school had been reduced to 12 miles. As for Karen, she had been brought up in a terrace, so living in a semi was a step up. On top of that she had got lucky, since the wife of a governmental minister lived in the village. She had three children whom she wanted to get into Oxbridge and offered to look after the Taylor babies while Karen was at university on condition she would help with their French and German.

From then on it became a daily habit for Karen to cycle to university and complete the 12-mile round trip by bike during her studies. Money was rather tight, of course. They managed having no car to run, no cigarettes to burn Frank's salary away, and not even a TV. One thing they had was dreams, which they shared. It turned out to be Karen's final year at university. It was a delight since she knew well in advance, she was on course to get a first-class honors degree in law and French. Normally, she was to take a year out abroad. She was a mum with two small children and the heads of both the French and law department agreed to give her an opt out on this. As such, for the following year she was offered a place to perform her MA and given hours to teach, which helped supplement the family income.

It was their first Christmas as the king and queen of their own little palace and they spent it quietly in their new house. They had more work to do than when they were living at his parents', but at least they were their own bosses. The following spring her youngest sister, Amy would come down for the local village hoe downs and stay over and sleep in the living room. During the summer of '67 with Mark, now 4, he was able to ride around the close-by villages. His brother would smile when on the back of either of his parents' bicycle. Other times, they walked around Nicky Nook. On hot days, before the package holidays were considered above 70 degrees Fahrenheit (21 degrees Celsius) they practiced swimming in the river. Once again, they took holiday in the Lake District. This time, they stayed again at Fallbarrow Park on the shores of Lake Windermere in a caravan for two weeks. Mark was old enough to fully appreciate the surroundings and would stare at the Langdales looming above the waters of Windermere.

One day they took the bus into Grasmere, and had a gentle walk to Easedale Tarn. Frank explained the water flowed into Easedale Beck before entering Grasmere Lake. Another day they took the bus again to Grasmere and followed the lake and stream flowing into Rydal before following River Rothay, which emptied into Lake Windermere. Back at the caravan site, Frank explained the lake would flow into River Leven. From there, meandering like a snake, it would lead down into the Morecambe Bay. Of course, only Karen fully understood what he was saying. It didn't matter, Mark enjoyed his daddy's tales as well as the walks. Matthew, although he was carried much of the way, understood almost nothing. He enjoyed listening to his father's voice just as much as the others.

In autumn, Frank was into his fourth year of teaching. Karen had become a part-time student and part-time lecturer. With both she and Frank able to enjoy the simple things in life, they found themselves managing nicely financially unlike those in the towns and cities who were blissfully unaware of things manufact-urers were pushing to sell. Since there were very few billboards and shops in their daily lives, they actually got more excitement from visiting the local village shop to buy a simple bar of choco-late than those who could traipse around the department stores all day in Preston. They believed the city folks were confused as to what they really wanted and had forgotten why they wanted to nip into town in the first place.

For Karen, Christmas that year was one of heaven. She had a nice house and was fully settled in. Her youngest child was able to take care of himself to some extent. As such, both she and Frank spent a lovey-dovey festive season together and trudged through the snow a couple of times visiting Calder Vale. On another excursion, they spent one night in Silverdale, both times with their boys of course.

As a French lecturer, Karen had been closely following the riots of May 1968 in Paris. She herself was just 21 and the same age as the average rioting student. She felt totally detached from the protests. Karen had a lovely family, lived in a nice part of the country, and was basically regarding her political outlook on life just like any other villager. This was nothing like many of the students she came into contact with. Politics at the time were calm. While she voted conservative and Frank labor, she had no problem with Harold Wilson. He found Heath benign enough. Fortunately, student politics of the UK were relatively peaceful in comparison to other countries. Karen started the new school with good intentions. Even so, reading about life in France was rather titillating to her at times – this combined with something that was about to shock her to the core.

Her boss in the French department was completely impressed with his young protege. He was, like Karen, happily married. He also felt a little cheated regarding the fact his wife put her career first. As such, he believed she left it too late for them to have children, which they never had. He was 41. His wife was 35. He would go home fantasizing about Karen. Equally, Karen found him unlike her husband. He was intellectually superior to her. Secondly, she hadn't forgotten Frank's dirty deed in making her a mother twice over when she was still only a teenager. Of course, she knew there was no one like her Frank, but even so she wanted to experiment. With the kids a little bit older her husband could take more care of them if her boss needed her to go away on a work-related trip.

Karen need not have worried, her marriage was almost perfect, and as for her boss, he too was in a rock-solid marriage. There was however one thing, he had his own office, which she often went in for a visit. They found themselves increasingly spending more time together speaking in French, making poems, and having great fun. One day, not wanting to look cheap, Karen burst out crying. She explained everything was fine, but at times she wished her life was less routine. With that her boss went up to her and put his arms around her before he gave her a massage to help her unwind. This, of course, led to the inevitable. It was nice, it was pleasant, and they were both very fond of each other but equally in their own ways devoted to their spouses.

As usual, the Taylors went away to the Lakes, staying once again in a caravan on the shores of Lake Windermere for two full weeks. They were able to be a little more adventurous, especially when one parent had the older boy to look after since he was already as able a walker as the average adult. On the way up there, they stopped overnight to Mark's delight at Silverdale and spent another two nights there on their return. So, they could have a day out on the Morecambe Bay sands, before going back home.

Before that summer, Karen's office frolics and more had become a regular event. As much as she enjoyed this, she became paranoid and this had somewhat marred her happiness over the summer. Meanwhile, during the recess her boss's wife conceived, and then he became the devoted expectant father. Now back after the summer upon seeing her boss, the father-to-be, Karen felt very uncomfortable with herself. She sensed too he was a little different. When he put his arms around her, she kind of resisted him. He never once annoyed her. She wondered if he was pleased, she was less strong regarding her previous affecttions. Maybe this was the real reason why he no longer tried to rekindle their adulterous liaison. In turn, she felt slightly rejected. As such, and feeling guilty, she decided on a whim to visit her husband at his workplace.

The day concerned came out of the blue. She had gone as usual to university. In solidarity with movements abroad, a day of protest had been arranged. Karen, being the well-known young miss goody, or traditional mother, was one of the last people to find out. As such, with the weather still fair, this early October day she cycled down to Bowgreave. On the way down, she called in at the Co-Op at Garstang to buy Frank some Bournville dark, his favorite. Then she excitedly continued on. Of course, she had no idea if she would find him; he might have been out at the swimming pool with his students, or he might have been busy, either way it didn't matter. It was the thought that counted. She wanted to do a good deed to the man she loved. With Mark in school, and Matthew being taken care of by the politician's wife; Karen was feeling as free as a bird as she cycled on her way to see the husband she was devoted to at his workplace.

It was in the middle of the school third lesson of the day when she arrived. Karen went around the back of the school with a spring in her step. As she walked past an office, she heard a gentle murmur, "Oh Frankie!" Her first reaction was to scream, but she knew it could lead to disaster. She decided to run away from the school. She was in tears but knew she couldn't say anything since she would have to admit her own adultery. In order to calm herself down she quickly gobbled the Bournville Bar like a man on death row eating his last supper just outside the school premises, before taking off again on her bicycle as though it was the end of the world, and that her marriage was over.

On the way back, she called in once again to the Co-Op and bought another chocolate bar for Frank. She went back home and baked a delicious cake for him. Part of her was living in fear in case her world would be shattered. The next few months they both wanted each other a little bit more than usual. She was a little more emotional since she wanted to keep inside her the affairs and not ruin her marriage. One night was to change things forever. As such, Christmas 68 was emotionally less balanced for Karen. Frank and the children hadn't suspected a thing. At her own request, they spent the festive time mostly at Silverdale where she felt her family would be safe under the auspices of the Taylors, the place on the bay, where their romance began.

Life in Silverdale was in this final year of the 1960s, a rather changed one to when the decade arrived. First, Frank had left, then his older brother Colin the previous year, since he went onto night school and now aged 30, passed his exams to become a solicitor. He had an office down in Blackpool. On the domestic front, things were settled. He bought a house with his wife he married secretly in a registry office that spring in Blackpool. They were living away from the hustle and bustle of the coast in a village called Hambleton. Thanks to the Wyre, it was cut off in many ways from the Fylde towns on the other side of the river.

The middle Silverdale Taylor child, Beatrice, was living on the farm with her husband from Warton. She too had a quiet but not secret wedding in the church at Warton that summer. They were taking over the farm as her parents were getting older. Calder Vale was changing too. Since Beatrice, the second child was now studying at St. Martin's College Lancaster and was dating a well to do man from Burneside near Kendal.

As for life in Scorton, the family went back to the Lake District. With Matthew then aged 3, and Mark already 6, they went to a youth hostel and covered 14 different overnight dwellings. Of course, both Mark, and his younger brother Matthew, were well looked after by both parents. With more money coming in, Karen was able to spend money on her children in a manner most mothers could only dream of. She gave her little loves a most wonderful Christmas time apart from books and clothes, she wanted them to have train sets and jigsaws as well as painting sets to keep busy. Of course, as much as the boys loved toys, the most important thing for them was the fact they grew up in a safe and loving environment with both parents whom they loved so dearly. As for Karen, she was relieved the demons inside her the previous Christmas were simply a distant memory. She saw no reason to jeopardize her beautiful life. She felt conscious enough of the fact for her marriage to work forever she would have to keep standing up her toes, which she knew deep down Frank was doing too.

When the 1970s arrived, Garstang was still a generation behind Manchester. Of course, Scorton, like Calder Vale and Silverdale, were subtly even further behind. Even so, Frank knew as a teacher with connections to the urban parts of Lancashire thanks to his away team matches for the school and the swimming competitions, domestic life in all social classes was changing, even in rural Lancashire. His own family with Karen the careerist being a testament to this.

It was mid-February early evening. Frank came home without his lights on his bike now that days were getting longer. Just after sunset when he had a little too much on his mind, Karen was happily baking, the boys were playing together, and she was looking forward to her husband coming home as usual. He looked a little pale as he walked through the door. He had been crying, but Karen hadn't suspected anything. A short while later, his subdued presence unnerved her somewhat. He sat down in the living room, watching, or more like gazing, at his boys playing together. "Are you OK love?" She asked him, but he hadn't heard her being so immersed in his thoughts. He then took out his newspaper, which was inside his daysack, placed it onto their coffee tablem and ran out of the room. Karen looked at the page about how the sports teacher at Preston High had taken his own life. She knew nothing about his personal life apart from the fact her classmates were in love with this guy who couldn't have been 10 years older than they were. Now, just a few years later, he was dead.

Karen knew Frank needed her. She looked at her boys making sure they were happy and walked upstairs to find her husband staring into space. She put her arms around him and he sobbed like a baby. "Just tell me what you want to tell me . . . " She pleaded softly and patiently.

"I don't know what to tell you." He said. There was a silence and then she thought about her own infidelities, uncomfortably.

"What did he tell you the last time you met?" She asked. "We met 6 weeks ago when my team was playing away against his. I think it was his way of saying goodbye . . . I have known him since 63. He was a young father married to this French stunner. She was a lecturer at Manchester University. She had been following events in Paris during the spring of 68. One day he came home to find a letter on the kitchen table, she basically wrote since she was a young Parisian, she felt it was her public duty to simply just run off from her husband taking his babies with her and to go marching on the streets of Paris. He caught a glimpse of her in a French newspaper and hasn't been the same since." He stopped talking. She wanted to know more. He was in code telling her he knew what she had done behind his back? If so, why wasn't he telling her? Was it because he too had slept with his boss, had he

STEVEN KAY

been bored with his wife, or was it revenge? She simply didn't know. They had as far as she was concerned as settled a life as could be. Anyway, she hadn't seen him with his boss and she might just be simply blowing things out of proportion. If so, she was the guilty partner and not he.

He then went downstairs with his wife. Feeling guilty he went over to his children whom he felt he had been neglecting. Then, as a family, they sat down for a meal together. As usual, he read some bedtime stories to his boys and Karen sat next to him with her arms around him. Then, he went to bed after kissing his boys goodnight. Feeling snubbed by him, Karen sat on the couch downstairs gazing into space, before going back upstairs. Karen was ready for an argument. They both had to come clean for their marriage to be saved. Maybe he was preparing her for a bombshell - being him shacking up with his boss. Nervously, she came to Frank who was delighted she was with him and without saying a word he simply took off her clothes. For some reason he made love to her with greater passion than normal. Of course, this satiated her but also made her feel guilty. Unexpectedly, he woke her up one hour later and was even more red-blooded, was he in competition with her former lover? As much as she enjoyed their lovemaking, she couldn't get out of her mind her feelings of guilt, she knew for some things at least she simply had to stay mum about. Then again, she was living in fear since she expected all of Frank's habits to be regular. Now, she was a little bit confused but even so she enjoyed the subtle changes in their lovemaking routine all the same.

That night she couldn't sleep. Everything connected with the affairs was going around in her head. As such, she decided instead of going crazy over nothing - not willing to confront Frank – she would take up teaching the children to swim as a priority. From then on, they made sure they would go together to the pool at least once a week. For the first time in her life, from the way he had spoken to her, the way in which he kept silent, she realized Frank loved her no less than when they first met. In many ways they were becoming closer and closer together.

• • •

Spring came, and Karen's younger and heavily pregnant sister, Amy got married to a milkman on her 17th birthday in the middle of May. She had met David the previous summer when staying over at Scorton for the hoe down. Like Karen, hers was a shotgun wedding and took place at Calder Vale in St. Johns Church. Both her sisters were bridesmaids. She had at first been dating him until someone better came along. Instead, she fell pregnant, and aged 16 and a half, she took him home to her parents in Calder Vale. They lived there rent free, albeit in rather cramped conditions, while he kept his milk round in Scorton. This meant a brisk walk through Oakenclough down into Grisedale Valley to Scorton, where he then went off on his daily milk round. After it, he would walk back. Sometimes, he would call in at the Taylors for one of Karen's cakes and a mug of tea. He was 19. Born and bred in Scorton. She was his first girlfriend.

Summer came. Karen was happy. Her other sister Beatrice was still away studying at Lancaster and her relationship with her boyfriend was going well. At least her younger and wilder sister who had just given birth, was under the watchful eyes of her mum and dad and seemed to be calming down somewhat. While David she trusted as someone mature enough to take on the responsibilities of domestic life, so Karen could spend more time thinking about her own family. Frank took both his sons' sporting achievements seriously. He was disappointed that now aged 7, Mark couldn't swim. They had previously tried everything, both parents had really tried teaching him. He had been on a swimming course in Garstang. Still, he couldn't do much more than simply float.

One day Mark suggested at the dinner table to his family that they should go to the open-air baths at Grange-Over-Sands and stay there until he had taught himself to swim. Off they drove early the following day on a warm summer's morning. Mark was happy the baths were quiet thanks to a less favorable weather forecast than conditions were. As they arrived at the pool, Mark left Matthew with his parents while he trained and trained and trained on his own. His father swam for just under one hour and

• • •

just over a mile and a quarter. Then it was his mother's turn to swim, while his dad was taking care of his brother. Still, no such luck came with his swimming. Lunchtime came, and he was forced to eat the packed lunch, which his mother had made. While his family rested, he sneaked off again for his training, and his mother gave up on the idea her son would be able to swim. Feeling a little bored she wanted to leave the baths, but his dad stepped in, which gave him a one-hour reprieve. After the hour, Karen was giving Frank an earful he should support her and it was time to move on. He just wanted to grin and bear it in the hope Mark would rescue everyone! Mark's mental tenacity paid off. When Karen calmed down and decided to see what Mark was up to, she couldn't believe it when she found him swimming unaided and looking very serious and simply couldn't take her awestruck eyes off him.

As such, and feeling very proud of him, Karen allowed him to stay until closing time. His achievement spurred her on in teaching Matthew to swim, who decided to be in competition with his elder brother. After it they called in at Arnside and had fish and chips along the sea front and a walk along the shores in search of the best sunset and pebbles to take back home before driving onto Silverdale for a surprise visit at the Taylors. They had all arrived like lobsters. This was before the days when everyone used suncreams. Instead, Mrs. Taylor senior placed sliced raw potatoes all over the bodies of her grandchildren and their parents, which wasn't a sight for sore eyes. The next day they returned to Scorton and just a few days later it was time for their Lake District holiday, which once again was spent in youth hostels.

Autumn came, and everyone was back at school. Matthew was already five. He had started attending the local primary school with his brother and they walked there and back together. A few months later, they had their typical Christmas, which was spent mostly at home in Scorton. With both boys now at school many of the presents were either connected with school through things, which could be learning based, or simply because they were the in thing as it were. Both boys felt that without the latest craze of Lego, Meccano, and Action Men that they would simply be missing out on life's necessities.

All in all, the early 70s were a peaceful time for the Taylors. In 1971, and at only 18. Amy gave birth to her second child, another girl. Beatrice graduated and went on to teach at a school in Kendal. She was, at that time, still going out with her steady boyfriend. Thanks to her new post she moved in with him, got engaged, and they planned to be married the following spring. That summer Frank and Karen were planning to stay away in youth hostels along with their children once more. Karen wanted to make sure Amy was fine and changed her mind to stay in a caravan where Beatrice could easily stop over for a visit and Amy would join them on holiday. As such, an 8 berth-caravan was booked. Frank was pleased that his Karen was happy.

The summer holidays came, and they went on their fourth visit to Fallbarow Park. Karen was happy to help Amy look after two babies. She was also torn between her loyalties with her immediate family and could see her younger sister wasn't enjoying herself much anyway. She put this down to the fact she was finding life difficult living with her parents. In short, Amy found Karen's piety a little too suffocating and simply wished she could have a sibling who would turn a blind eye to her flirtatious behavior. All in all, the holiday was pleasant. Beatrice and her partner Robert came around a few times. He took the three sisters out for lunch twice while Frank and the boys were out all day on their adventures and would arrive back boasting about their trips. Although Bowness was small and in a National Park, it had something of a seaside feel. Amy, who hadn't been much further than Garstang before holiday, enjoyed looking around the gift shops and watching the well to do as they walked around the resort. She would often wonder if she could simply run off with one of the gentlemen there. At times she wished she was on her own since she knew she had the looks to tempt. Of course, without much money, she wasn't able to visit tourist places. All she could do was wander around Calder Vale, where everyone

• • •

knew each other. No tourists ever came, apart from families mainly from Preston and Blackpool, who would go out walking after parking their cars in front of her house. Most of them were related to the locals. As such, given she wanted something else, which no one would have approved of, she felt she was constantly under surveillance by everyone, much to her dismay.

Christmas came. For the first time on David's insistence, Amy spent the whole day with her sister at her house in Scorton. She had, after all, a free holiday that summer thanks to the Taylors. One reason she hadn't visited was because she couldn't bear to see the difference between her own and her sister's fate. As she saw it. At the same time, she was happy to make the time and effort to visit Beatrice at Oxenholme where she was now living with Robert in a grandiose house. Even so, she managed to make the most of her trip to Scorton and put on her best in making a good appearance both visually and audibly, since of the three sisters, she was the most extrovert.

The New Year came in, and the proud Taylors of Silverdale organized a big event for the spring of 1972. They had the grounds to do it – their wedding ceremony took place at St. Johns Church, Silverdale. The Scorton Taylors arrived by bike. Karen and her family were there of course. Given Robert Taylor, Beatrice's husband was a second cousin of Frank, the farm was the ideal venue. With Robert heralding from Burneside, a village several miles to the north, and the Taylors around Garstang to the south, Silverdale was the perfect place for all concerned. Amy was there with her husband and toddlers. While David was well liked by everyone, many eyes were focused on Amy who simply didn't seem to be enjoying herself and was leaving everything to her husband. This meant him looking after the children and mingling with her family while she would wander off and go off for a quiet smoke, which wasn't very common in her family. Frank's sister, Beatrice, was enjoying herself and got on very well with Karen. Colin came up from Hambleton with his wife Vivienne, and their two daughters who were all dressed to the nines. As a solicitor he wanted his family to turn the heads of everyone.

● ● ●

Unbeknown to the rest of the Taylors, Colin was leading a double life. Although he grew up on a farm, Blackpool not only opened his eyes, but it also gave him new opportunities too. He found himself wanting to experiment. Like some of his colleagues he began sleeping behind his wife's back with men. At first, he didn't really enjoy sleeping with his colleagues; however, after some time he found himself enjoying it more and more. The woman inside of him was starting to feel more and more that his wife was good for less things than he felt when they first got together. Even so, although he could never love her the way he used to, he like many men he knew, wanted a family so much and were prepared to make the sacrifices. This simply meant they had to play the role of being straight husbands. This earned the respect of their clients. In Collin's case, the villagers too, since Hambleton on the other side of the river was a different kettle of fish to Blackpool, and virtually unknown to the people of the seaside resort. Hambleton, like the other Over Wyre villages, was strikingly way behind, the Fylde Coast, and like the place where he grew up, and in a time warp.

Once again, during the summer of 1972, the Scorton Taylors had their usual Lake District holiday. With both boys keen cyclists aged 9 and 6, the family organized two Lakeland tours that summer. The first was combined with a stopover at Silverdale for two nights. This enabled them to take the kids up Arnside Knott. Then they had some fun at Grange's open-air baths before moving on to Coniston. On day one of the trip, and with the children being small, they avoided the passes as much as they could. So they remained around the central lakes area combining Grasmere and Windermere before going back on the seventh night to Silverdale. Back at home they went on walks around Nicky Nook, had a stop-over at Hambleton for two nights enabling them to spend the day at St. Annes on the Sea where the boys enjoyed sand dunes and desert like vegetation, as well as the long soft sandy beaches and the views towards the Welsh mountains. For the Taylors at least, Lancashire and Cumbria had everything. When back at home they had a couple of walks to

Calder Vale, but obviously being cramped, they didn't stay over-night there. Mid-August came and they went on a walking tour of the Lakes, staying in youth hostels once again.

Late 1972 was also the tenth anniversary of Karen and Frank. She wanted to celebrate this decade as a celebration of her meeting her soulmate ten years earlier and getting married, with both exactly 10 years previous. As such, the latter part of 62 was in several ways, when things began. As such, not wanting to look like a complete show off and plan something big at Silverdale, she organized a tenth anniversary in her house for her immediate family and a few friends. A few locals came round and her parents walked over from Calder Vale. To Karen's horror, a big event had been organized at Silverdale that Christmas, partly as a surprise present from her husband. There were many guests and they enjoyed themselves all the same while the boys ate as many cakes as they could.

January 1973, the frugal Taylors paid off their mortgage and had been married ten years. Karen was now 26. Frank was com-ing up to 30. To celebrate paying off their debts, they decided to book a package holiday for the first time. That Easter they went on Gran Canaria as a family. Frank enjoyed swimming in the sea, in fact they all did, but while he could swim for hours, Karen found this type of holiday although pleasant and relaxing a little boring. They all agreed the dunes at Maspalomas were simply amazing and the food was better than what they had expected. On the final day, the boys collected a couple of pebbles each to take as souvenirs and to place in their garden back home. Other times, they would when they were back at home with their pebbles, decorate and paint them on rainy days or long winter ones, which they had been experiencing as late as March that season.

Summer was spent enjoying their own backyard and the free holidays staying at Hambleton courtesy of Frank's brother, who partly as a result of seeing the genuine love Frank had for Karen, felt a little detached from his brother. Back then, marriage life was very important. Colin rightly sensed as a man totally devoted to his wife, family man Frank would not approve of what his brother was doing behind his wife's back.

Thanks to the location, they had plenty of fun cycling along the Fylde Coast with one day out to Fleetwood, another to St. Annes and the sand dunes there, and yet another around Knott End and Pilling. They also spent a few days lazing around with the family and walking around the Stalmine and Out Rawcliffe. After staying at his brother's during the holidays they stayed at Silverdale and Oxenholme, both places were reached with their bikes. Both were close enough for excursions to the Lake District proper, especially at his sister's. The local train, called the Sprinter, could take them to the heart of the Lake District both cheap and prompt while traversing some lovely scenery.

Chapter Four

April: Amy, One Little Pebble in a Lonely World.

Visits that summer to Calder Vale were the briefest. Although her parents and brother-in-law David were very welcoming, Amy was becoming very closed. Karen wondered if she was rude to Frank, since she was often telling him how lucky he was. She herself wouldn't be following him everywhere on foot or by bike, since with all of their money they should be in possession of a car. Karen knew Amy didn't mean this and was unhappy with her own life and luckily, she didn't notice that her own sister was in fact in love with her Frank, her own husband, even so Karen felt that she had other things to worry about than her own younger sibling. Frank sensed Amy had a soft spot deep down for him and he was not at all pleased, since Amy was his sister-in-law, and he found her behavior disrespectful towards David too. While there, the Taylor boys played besides the stream, and the pebbles there with their cousins and got to know a few of the locals but were happy all the same when the time came for them to walk back to their home in Scorton.

Christmas came around, and Frank as well as Karen of course, was concerned about Amy, and they offered to take the whole family away to Fallbarrow Park for a second time. David although he didn't know Frank so well, got on well with him and they enjoyed speaking about the Lakeland Fells, which although he hadn't really visited, had read about them through the signed copies of Lake District guidebooks written by Wainwright, which

Robert had bought for him while on a previous visit to Calder Vale. While he was looking forward to exploring some of the fells thanks to both Frank and Karen, he apologized for not staying more than one night at the caravan due to work commitments the time his family holidayed there two years previously. Amy feigned excitement regarding the forthcoming holiday, but it was obvious for the others she wasn't exactly overjoyed with it or with anything else for that matter. She had been complaining about her cramped conditions and was none too pleased when Karen reminded her that one of the neighbors had seven kids with her husband to look after. In fact, Amy was feeling very much alone in the world since she had no one to turn to. Amy felt that looking after her husband and children was simply too much and simply felt as though that she was a slave. David expected a meal on the table, she had two small children to look after, and with her parents and their traditional ideas she kept all the frustration inside of her. Amy always felt ready to explode but because she was living with her parents, who were both fond of her David, she knew that she had no other choice than to grin and bear things and kept her problems to herself. Of course, her presence at home wasn't pleasant for the others, including for the children who could sense something, but that was their Amy.

The following year Amy had been seeing more of Beatrice, who lived outside of the county, than of Karen despite them only living at the other side of the local reservoirs, but Amy found that Beatrice had more to offer her. For the rest of the time, she show-ed very little interest in others. Sometimes she would walk toward her old primary school. On the way there she would walk to the stream and gaze at the pebbles thinking of herself as being one little pebble in a lonely world. During Easter of that year, it might have well been April, but for her felt as if it was the winter of her life. Later in May, Beatrice had been on one of her many flying visits by car to Calder Vale. She gave Amy some of her new and fashionable clothes she had bought while on a day trip to Preston. Now pregnant, she was getting ready for her new role of being a mother. She passed on her garments to a very thankful sister. That evening Amy stared in delight at the clothes and wanted to go out around Preston. That was, of course, only in her dreams. The reality was someone had to take care of the babies; the ones she conceived out of fun and wished she had never had.

The next day Amy told her parents she was off out to the local Co-Op to buy some bread. Her husband had already gone out, playing with the children. With a spring in her step, boosted further when she noticed villagers' heads were turning toward her – she continued with her errand. The shop, although small, was full of candles. Being the 70s, as the decade of the three-day week, power cuts, and winter of discontent. Her house was fully stocked up on wax, so she hadn't come for that. While waiting to pay for a loaf of bread and a milky bar for her elder child, she noticed the local brunette beauty at the till. An unfamiliar man walked in. He was tall, dark, and handsome. Seemingly around 35. She left the shop spellbound after paying for her things. She sat on the bench outside and placed the loaf underneath since for some reason it was an embarrassment for her.

Amy felt he was in the shop longer than usual for a customer. She was worried given the girl was single she might be flirting with him. Even so, a little later than expected, he left the shop and before she went into a sweat, he walked up to her. "Excuse me, could you tell me the way to Garstang please?" Of course, he knew where it was. He was used to hunting his women.

"I do. Actually, I need to get there myself." Of course, she was pretending too. She knew the game to play. She stood up and got inside his car. She couldn't believe she was sitting in what for her was the sexiest thing she had ever sat on. A leather seat inside a car she never thought she would touch, let alone be seated in. He smugly drove through the country lanes in his Mercedes down into Garstang. Amy was spellbound. While she had initially been attracted to his good looks, she already felt as though she was more excited by his shiny car than him. After a few minutes, while they were approaching the Royal Oak Hotel in the town center, he glanced at her, intensively. "Fancy a drink here?" He asked her confidently.

"I know a much better place, it is on the way down to Preston, in Bilsborrow." She smiled. She needed to get away from Garstang as many tongues would be wagging. She was, after all, still on home territory. Given she went to the local high school just 6 years earlier. Hugh was pleased since the further away from Calder Vale they were, the safer he was too. As such, they called in at Guy's Court, Bilsborrow - 5 miles down the road from Garstang. It was a nice buffer zone between being safe enough to return home if this man was a jerk, and far away from what she perceived to be the maddening crowd of Calder Vale. Together they went for a drink. Now was the time to get to know him. She already knew he was a nightclub owner since he had fliers in his car of his venues. The waitress came. He ordered a Babycham (a local beer) as well trout, chips, and salad for two. While waiting he smoked a cigar. Although she didn't yet know it - this was to be her final goodbye of Wyreside. She was never to be seen or heard from in this part of Lancashire again. As he took off down the M6 motorway from Preston she was looking forward to a new life.

Before the new couple had arrived at his home, a distraught husband and his parents-in-law decided to contact the local policeman. He told them not to worry, she was bound to arrive later that evening. The next day he came around to the house and explained Amy had been spotted getting inside a black Mercedes. With him not being in the house at the time of her leaving and the children too young to be used as witnesses, the Garstang police might wish to interview him. He agreed on condition he was there with his daughters who, now aged 4 and 3, were old enough to speak anyway. The young officer decided to deal with matters at Garstang. They were none too pleased regarding the officer's temerity. As they saw usurping his position, they decided to keep quiet for now at least and not to send David in for interrogation.

Amy's life was now incredible. She was staying in Belmont in her lover's country house, on a country estate, in the West Pennine Moors. Although she came from a similar geography it was, in fact, a far cry from her two up two down. She enjoyed going to some of the top nightclubs he owned in Manchester, such as *The Swinging Cat* and *The Gigolo*. She had arrived in her best clothes. For Hugh these were a little bit too plain. The next few days he took her to Kendals where he knew he could find some suitable attire for her. He then took her to Vidal Sassoon for her hair. He knew of the most exquisite coffee bars and this was in the city. It was the biggest place she had seen in her life. They ate in the most expensive restaurants and would drink wine and share a box of truffles. Amy was a little hurt that Beatrice's clothes were not good enough for the bright lights of Manchester but kept this inside her.

One thing she felt sure about was that she was no longer anyone's slave. She no longer had to worry about the children and be angry when her husband was sleeping with the excuse, he was too tired to stay awake all night. During the day she was left alone to bring up children, while he was out on his rounds. On top of that, he wasn't bringing in enough money for them to get their own place, yet he wanted to be treated like a king with his cooked meal ready for him on the table. Hugh simply wanted to eat out all the time, paid for a cleaner, and all he wanted from her was sex. She was never too tired for him.

After a few weeks, the excitement of everything was starting to wear off, but at least she felt safe and secure in the knowledge her previous life was dead and buried. Hugh thinking she was a first-year college student as she had told him, had no idea she was 21 and a mother of two babies. One thing she lived in fear of was his suggesting a day out in Garstang. There was no chance of that because of a dark secret. The day they met he had been round on a visit to one of his ex-girlfriends in Nateby, a small village two miles to the west of Garstang. The girl had told him she was pregnant. This poor young girl had no idea who he really was, or where he came from. Hugh, not wanting the responsibility of being a dad, never wished to return to Garstang ever again. As such both Hugh and Amy were simply two of a kind.

Just before she had a chance for the reality of her mistake in leaving her family behind in Calder Vale to sink in, Hugh took her to his apartment close to Lake Windermere. By day they would go up and down the lake in his motorboat. Amy had no idea as to whether her sister was in Windermere or not. She was pretty certain she was somewhere in the Lakes. Not knowing where her sister was, gave Amy the best of both worlds. Part of her didn't wish to see the Taylors, a part of her did. Another part wanted to escape back to Calder Vale. As such, when Hugh wasn't around, she called in a few times at the caravan park reminiscing about the time she was there with her family and with her husband and beautiful daughters going through with a serious bout of post-natal depression. She consoled herself when she realized nobody she might had met from that previous holiday recognized her. She was happy she was now away from her previous life of poverty. During the night she had an odd nightmare regarding her babies. After one week of her going through many mood swings, which increased through her Babychams, she drank in order to protect herself from her wild emotions concerning her choices in her private life. They went back to Belmont.

Karen had, of course, been shaken by the events surrounding Amy's disappearance. Understandably, the visit to the caravan had been cancelled. They lost more than just the deposit - Karen, feeling guilty, suggested they try camping. They booked them-selves in at a guesthouse in Keswick for one day at the start of the school summer holiday and arrived early after taking the bus into Lancaster from the Little Chef at Cabus. They then took the train to Penrith from where they took another bus into Keswick. On the way, Frank bemoaned about the closing of the railway from Penrith to Keswick, which took place just over two years earlier. The day they arrived the weather was bad, so as well as looking for new camping equipment they invested in some rainwear too. As they finished with shopping, the sun came out. They relaxed in the local parks where the children played while Frank and Karen daydreamed about the walks they would be doing the coming days. Everyone slept well that night. Being the

• • •

start of the holiday, they were relaxed but were tired from traveling and shopping as they were not used to so much.

The following morning after a hearty breakfast, they checked out of the guesthouse and walked to the nearest campsite next to the lake. A subdued and submissive Karen left everything up to Frank. Inside she was fretting about Amy. Unable to enjoy anything, she knew her family needed quality time alone together. She wasn't much joy herself and apart from being the good servant, cooking camping meals through groceries of her own choosing, she was happy for Frank to organize everything else. Equally, her libido wasn't exactly sky high. Staying in the cramped conditions of a four-man tent under the watchful eyes of two boys close to puberty was the perfect decoy for emotional distance between herself and her husband, which she had no control over.

While the Taylors were there, Amy and Hugh went back to the lakes once more and had a six-week stay in Windermere. This was interrupted two nights each week with Hugh having to go down the motorway to keep an eye on things at his nightclubs. This meant a round trip of 162 miles. While he was away, Amy stayed on her own at the flat. She couldn't keep up with the pace of moving so much. It was one such night alone, when she had one of her regular nightmares about her children missing her. She walked to the fridge and admired all the luxury foreign cheeses, which she had never seen before she met Hugh. She was playing with his state of the art Hi Fi equipment when he suddenly walked in with a bunch of flowers for her, unexpectedly. "You are so beautiful; I have really missed you." He said while thinking of the girl he had scored with a few hours earlier.

"I have missed you too." She said as though she wanted to melt in him as he went up to hold her.

"Things are going well in Manchester. I was wondering if we could go on holiday next year together to Aruba."

"Never heard of it!" She said excitedly and in awe of him.

• • •

"It is just an island in the Caribbean." He said looking rather smug and feeling somewhat sad since deep down there was something lacking in his life despite all the wealth he had.

The next day he decided to show her Keswick. While there, he bought some typical outdoor clothes from the exclusive George Fisher where, of course, he expected Amy to choose items for herself. Normally she didn't like this kind of shop but seeing it was the best of its kind, she couldn't turn down his kind offer. It was then she thought of Karen. She didn't know whether to feel sentimental or proud of herself. She knew Karen loved these kinds of shops, but certainly didn't have the money for such luxury. On the other hand, she knew Karen was practical and wore clothes for comfort when outside. In short, it didn't matter what she was thinking about her sister, the clothes were simply connecting her to her sibling. Strangely enough, it was Karen rather than Beatrice whom Amy missed the most. Hugh just wished he was with Agnetha Faltskog.

Back in Belmont she was delighted. She'd been tiring of her new life, but with his long-term commitment in the form of an up-and-coming holiday in the Caribbean, Amy started to feel some-what settled again. She even wanted to go out on walks. She soon gave up on the idea of walking. Feeling like a model, she enjoyed strolling outside. Many other rich locals noticed her, and with the clothes from George Fisher, Hugh was once again in awe of her beauty, as well as the prying eyes.

Now back into the new school year, Karen was getting stronger as her boss valued her professional work and achieve-ments in the French department more and more. On top of that his personal life was blissfully happy with photographs of the happy father, mother, and baby all over his desk. As such, Karen felt safe. She confided in the man who wasn't looking for any-thing with her but had bonded in a way no man apart from husband had. She never wished again for a repeat performance of her dark past, which she saw as something that could had easily ended in a tragedy. He understood her feelings regarding her sister and had met Frank on the odd occasion when he offered him a hot drink and chocolate biscuits. He decided that Frank was worthy of his assistant, whom he himself still secretly desired. He knew the worst thing that could happen in his life now that he had a family of his own, would be if his wife found out about him and Karen.

As such, feeling increasingly she was pulling herself together yet although still desensitized due to worry about her sister and her concerns about all the family members whom Amy had left behind in Calder Vale, Karen still had moments feeling amorous with fears of leading Frank astray. This resulted in them making love again. By Christmas, she was pleased she had managed to get through a year, which had been plagued with worry. That Christmas, although they spent it mostly in Scorton, was pretty much a Lake District affair. Several books had been bought about the northern half of the Lakes thanks to Frank. They imagined they were in Westmoreland as they spoke about their future holiday plans, on the cold winter days.

One thing about this family, which as the 70s moved on, was they appeared more and more as relics from the past. While it was mostly elderly villagers who were without cars, the Taylors were proud owners of their practical rucksacks they used on weekend walks into Garstang where they filled them with groceries before supermarkets, Co-Op, and Booths closed their stores at lunchtime from Saturday until Monday mornings. After shopping, they sat beside the river and fed the ducks. Then, they would head back on foot into Scorton. On top of that, as a student of French (although she hadn't experienced domestic life in France or anywhere else on the continent), Karen had been fascinated to learn how the Europeans. To the chagrin of visitors to their house (who didn't have carpets only special rugs and in the hall shoe racks for visitors) while the neighbors were busy cleaning cars and vacuuming carpets, the Taylors were having fun in the open air. Even so, they were the talk of the village. The offcomers were warned about this lovely, but incongruous practical family, who didn't allow shoes in their house. They still had cleaning to do as well as work in their garden, which often took place on Saturday afternoons but not religiously.

Sundays were often a family affair of the great outdoors. Apart from their usual walks to Calder Vale tying in Nicky Nook and Karen's family, they often went up Hawthornthwaite Fell. Cycling was a pastime pleasure of theirs too. They often cycled through the Trough of Bowland passing through Marshaw where they would often spend the whole day. Since the streams were of some delight for the boys, they would continue uphill through Hareden before stopping off for lunch at Dunsop Bridge. They'd continue mostly downhill through Whitewell and stop off at Chipping for an ice cream. Heading back home still downhill through Bleasdale which is old English for Blue Valley and probably had something to do with blueberries since there were plenty of them there. It it was the appropriate season, it might have been a stop off point so Karen would bake one of the easiest of cakes. The Blueberry Pie, after they had returned home and after a round trip by bike of 35 miles, as for the berries sometimes they were raspberries other times blackberries. It didn't really matter, everyone was given a tub to fill. There'd be no pie for the boys if Frank thought all the picking would be left to him and his wife as he saw it. The boys were secretly feasting in the bushes and leaving all the work to him and Karen. As such, the boys knew that if they wanted some pie, they had to pick some berries.

The opposite direction, and toward the coast, was more to Matthew's liking. He wasn't so sporty as the others - not just simply due to his age. The route west was of a similar distance to the one inland. This one reached the Fylde coast at Fleetwood via Winmarleigh, Pilling, and Knott End. They would take the ferry across and after a few hours on the sands, they would go over the toll bridge at Hambleton and visit Frank's brother where they often had dinner before going back home before dark via Out Rawcliffe, Pilling, Winmarleigh, and Cabus. One thing they missed without lights on their bikes was being able to watch the sun go down over the Morecambe Bay. Even so, both parents were satisfied they had done everything in making both of their boys happy.

During the summer of 75, Frank decided they needed even more adventure. Karen had forgotten how cold she was the previous summer in the lakes. Since she was emotionally and physically numbing with everything. Just before they set off on their holiday, her worries about being cold set in as everyone was sat at the dinner table one early summer's evening. "Can't we stay in a caravan or go hosteling this holiday?" Karen asked smiling.

"What for, we just spent a fortune investing in the camping gear." Frank was looking forward to their impending adventure.

"Yes, dad has some really cool things planned for us." Said Mark. She then thought about it calmly as she looked at her boys.

"Ok, but if I am cold like last time, I'm off!" She said half joking. The boys smiled at one another.

She needn't have worried. The summer was much warmer than the previous one. After going back to the same campsite as the summer before and storing much of their equipment in one of the campsite storerooms – they embarked with all their food minus water. Frank promised plentiful amounts of water with so many streams around for their three-night camping adventure. Frank knew the coming days would be hot and dry apart from the risk of a thunderstorm. Off they went along the shores of Derwent-water, following the path through Watendlath where they stopped for lunch, and continued on their way over Honister. They reached their destination of Blackbeck Tarn, which was an amazing setting with views of Kirkfell and Great Gable with a magnificent view of Loweswater, Crummock, and Buttermere lakes. The weather was sticky and very hot. Karen felt she had been walking on the moon. With nobody around, she dipped into the tarn naked and started swimming. The boys, after dragging most of the luggage up, were dozing off to sleep. Suddenly, the heavens opened-up, and a violent thunderstorm appeared. The boys had awoken and Karen was furious with Frank. Ten minutes later, the heavy rain stopped. In a flash, the sun came out. All the wet things started drying out in no time. Although it was early evening, the fierce sun kept the air temperatures close to 80 degrees (27 degrees centigrade) – even though they were 498 meters (more than 1,600 feet) above sea level. Karen was reeling since they had no tent and planned to spend three nights there but was getting tired. Although scared of another storm, she fell asleep quickly.

They slept well. In the early morning the boys went off on a swim to the other side of the tarn, after struggling with the sharp slate before the water was deep enough for a swim. This was a contrast with the pebbles down in Windermere that were less abrasive on the balls of the feet. Meanwhile, Frank and Karen, who were still young and in love, walked offsite 50 yards. It wasn't even 6 AM. There was no one around. They made love at the highest altitude of their lives. Later they did a lot of sunbathing and strolling around. That evening Karen was calm. The following day was much the same. They explored a wider range and the day after they walked back again through Watendlath into Keswick where they got loads of groceries before continuing with their next adventure on this holiday.

As for Amy and Hugh, the holiday on Aruba was cancelled due to his business commitments. That was the least of her worries. She found herself taking to drink increasingly. She was killing herself with the shame and guilt of destroying an otherwise honest and wholesome family. She thought about returning to her husband but it had been more than a year since her departure. She was convinced a good man like him had met someone else. Knowing he had settled with someone else would have sent her to further ruin. Accepting deserved love more than she did, she decided not to contact him since she felt humiliated enough from her reckless act. She would dream more and more about her safe life in Calder Vale. She hoped David would find her, take her back to her roots, and as a reward she would bear him another child - a son maybe.

It was up and down for Amy. One morning while alone in the state-of-the-art apartment at Windermere, wondering why Hugh had decided at the last minute to keep an eye on things down in Manchester, and in one of her moments of morbid depression, Amy picked up her pen and paper wanting her family to know she was alright.

Dear Karen,

Please tell the rest of the family I am ok. In fact, I am very happy. While I regret leaving behind my husband and children, it all happened like a whirlwind. I was too young to be a mother. My life is much better now. I am enjoying creature comforts, which I never even knew existed.

You have always been a good person, a role model sister and there is no need to worry about me. I am in a steady and loving relationship and free to come back whenever I wish, but I can understand how mad at me everyone must be. I am not yet ready to face up to what I have done.

Love, Amy.

She posted the letter and it was received the following day as Karen came home from work. She opened the letter, after looking at the postmark of Kendal, which she found a curious sight. She read it and waited for Frank's opinion. By then she was relying more and more on his opinions as her trusted confidence in things close to her heart. "I feel really sorry for David. He deserves better than this . . . As for Amy, I have no idea what she is saying, because I can't make head or tail of the message in the letter, I think she doesn't know what she wants out of life." Said Frank. After a few more days her parents had been informed about the letter. They were basically lost and confused. Since they only knew Calder Vale and maybe Garstang, they couldn't at all understand how someone could leave the place. Of course, the letter shook them to their core. While they had no idea as to what their wild child had been up to, in their eyes she had let them down. They both took their marriage vows seriously and believed in putting their children first. As much as they would have completely understood had David found a new partner - the fact he stood made them value him more than the child they had produced together. Amy was brought up in a world full of love and only let them down.

As for David, he looked ill and somewhat gaunt. For him, his wife was in a desperate state and needed him. Fortunately, as a man grounded as the origins of the River Wyre from whose currents had quenched the thirsts of several of his previous generational ascendants, he remained ever loyal to his Amy. He was convinced someone had to stay strong, watch the ship, and his beloved children until she came back home. For him, like everyone else around him, Amy was still alive. Now, there was the hope the children and parents would once again be a happy family again. Karen spent the next few days wondering if Amy lived near Kendal. Of course, Beatrice would have known. Did she go to the Lake District? If so, how often, or was it all some false trail set up? Maybe it was better to concentrate on her own family, who needed her so much.

Karen wanted to enjoy the Yuletide. Breaking up one week earlier than her boys did for the Christmas recess, she decided to give the house a thorough cleaning to surprise everyone over the festive season with her culinary experiments. While the men in her life enjoyed her chocolate, ginger, and orange tiffin and fruit crumbles - they ate her Gallic specialties at the dinner table. These included quiche Lorraine. Since, she was a professor of French, these were foods a cat from Cheshire might have tasted. She was still something truly exotic for those out in the sticks at the bottom of the Bowland Fells being used to cheese and onion pies and gravy. The boys enjoyed the smells and tastes of the heavenly recipes. They never once noticed how much cleaner and fresher their home looked. Karen accepted this because she was the only girl in the house.

On Sunday, the 28th of February 1976, Frank celebrated his 33rd birthday. Karen had been thinking about Amy. She wanted to show her husband her planned route regarding their wild camping trip the coming summer. The trip was to start and end at Keswick where somewhere along the middle they would spend 2 nights on the shores of Loughrigg Tarn. Of course, he agreed.

He was, in fact, delighted since he couldn't have arranged a more exciting trip himself. This, for him was the perfect birthday present she could have given to him.

A few months passed by. They arrived at Keswick where a new lightweight four-man tent was bought. Like the previous summer, the weather was hot. They relaxed and spent a lot of time swimming in Derwentwater. The following day they went up Skiddaw and then had two nights camping at Blackbeck Tarn. Once again when the boys were out of the way, Frank and Karen made love. It was time for Wastwater - the valley there had a couple of shops for groceries. They went up Scafell too. It was then time for a couple of nights at Levers Water. They carried over a two-day food supply from Wastwater since there were no shops en route. Then came the all-important, Loughrigg. As usual, they stayed at the destination en route for two nights and Karen explained she needed to do some girly things on her own in Ambleside such as looking at gift shops and visiting an attraction or two. Frank was pleased she wanted to do something just for herself. He would have found it boring anyway. The reality was, however, different.

While the boys went walking over Oxen Fell heading for Tarn Hows. Karen went on the south ridge of Loughrigg down into Ambleside. Her trip was not so relaxing as she made it out to be. She called the police station and took out the letter, which Amy had sent her. She handed it to the bemused policemen who could do nothing, since aged 23 she was old enough to do whatever she pleased. They kept the letter, which she had many copies as well as a photograph of Amy. Then, she went to Windermere by bus and visited some of the haunts she and Amy had been to 5 years earlier. Deep down she knew she was wasting her time. At least in her heart, she knew she had tried. If Amy visited any of the places, as much as the police would do nothing, the kind tradespeople of Bowness on Windermere had at least appeared helpful.

She arrived back at the campsite late that day. Frank was already busy with dinner. As things went quiet, the boys were nodding off to sleep. She whispered to Frank. "I need to talk to you alone." She said seriously as inside she was nervous.

"You want to go off for a stroll around?" He asked her gently.

"Yes." She said hastily. He kissed her on the lips and together hand-in-hand they walked down toward the tarn and she began. "I didn't want to worry you, but I just wanted to make peace with myself. I went into Bowness armed with photographs of Amy to the gift shops and asked them to look out for her, but I am not going to destroy myself over this Frank." She was worried in case he found her a little crazy. She was looking a little embarrassed as he was looking thoughtfully at her face, with love.

"Karen, you did the right thing. If I were in your shoes, I am sure I would have done the same."

"Darling, please follow me. I want to show you something." They stood up. She picked a pebble and threw it into the tarn. They both watched the ripples and Karen looked at him. "You saw how one pebble created a ripple that went around through almost the whole waters of the pond?" They looked at each other. Without speaking they both knew they understood each other well. Karen's lone voice in searching for her sister was enough to reach out all over the national park if that was what Amy wished. Karen was the pebble that would never turn to dust. The ripples she sent around the honey pots earlier that day would never be lost. With their feelings of closeness, they then sat down. Karen sat between his legs as they watched the scarlet sky slowly turn black after what had been a beautiful summer's day and a peaceful night followed.

The holiday continued at Grisedale Tarn after they called in at the Co-Op in Grasmere for groceries en route. From the tarn, the following morning, they went on a day trip to Ullswater, slept a second night at Grisedale Tarn, and the next day they walked over Helvellyn finishing off at Keswick. The holiday had done everyone a world of good. It had been one of the many things in Karen's life, which prevented her from worrying too much about Amy. As an adult who chose to walk out on her family and whose unfortunate actions had nothing to do with Karen. She felt as a wife and mother, her own home was her castle.

1977 came, and Karen celebrated her 30th birthday. She had enjoyed Christmas at Scorton. Both she and Frank had some good savings. She was happy with her job but didn't feel the need to go out on a spending spree. Even so, the money was there for them whenever it was needed. Amy was in her twenty-fourth year. Hugh assumed she wasn't a day older than 21 and she had no children. Three years and two children had been erased out of her life. When she met Hugh, she told him she was 18. Now, nearly three years later the crying, the nightmares, and the alcohol had taken their toll. In the mirror, she saw a woman closer to 30 than that of her real age. Three days before her birthday, which was bang on in the middle of May, she decided to write a letter during the afternoon. She wasn't sure what she was going to write. She had decided whatever she put into the letter she would simply have to carry out her acts before the letter would be received. This wasn't simply a rash decision. She had been thinking about her dilemma as early as her first season with Hugh. Now, knowing more about the kind of man he was, and realizing she had just fallen pregnant to him, the man who didn't want children, she came to a crossroad. Amy was in two minds regarding where her fate lay. She wrote two letters and decided she would walk out with both letters and post one of them. Firstly, she wrote a letter, which read:

Dear David,

I just want to let you know I am sorry. You were the best man I ever met. Our children are so lucky to have you. I can't bear the pain I have caused to three generations, my parents, you, my sisters and our children.

As you can see from the postmark, I am living in Belmont. It isn't and has never been my home. After the excitement of getting away from sleepy village life, I was somehow hoping you would find me. I was too much of a coward to return and see you with someone else. I regrettably stayed away. Of course, I could have returned. Soon after I left, knowing this is too much for me to bear.

• • •

When you receive this letter, I will already be dead. If I knew you would take me back, I would come back right now. I want to remember you as my doting and loving husband. I am too scared to see you with someone else, who is probably much better than me and someone whom you deserve so much.

Love,

Amy.

She then wrote her second letter, which read:

Dear Mum,

I have been such a terrible girl; I can't explain how guilty I feel about the pain and suffering I caused you and dad. I have been living a terrible lie for the last three years. Now I am going to take a chance. David has, is, and will always be the love of my life. If he isn't with anyone, please get him ready for me. Without my family and my husband, my life means nothing.

If David doesn't want me, I understand, it was my fault. I will take a chance. If the worst comes to the worst, I must sort out the mess I created myself. Of course, I hope to be with you as much as possible. As much as I have been a bad girl, I hope some of you in your heart will be able to soon forgive me.

Looking forward to being united with you all.

Love,

Amy.

While both letters had completely different outcomes, both meant Hugh would never see her again. After writing the letters, she walked to the letterbox holding each letter in each hand. She was just about to think about posting the letter in her right hand, the one about her return to Lancashire when the sun came out. She started to smile for the first time in ages. As the power of the sun became stronger, she imagined herself back in the humble yet safe setting of Calder Vale with her family. She was getting closer to the post-box and starting to become proud of herself. As for her pregnancy she would deal with that later. Maybe this time next week before she would be in her seventh week, her

● ● ●

marriage with David might already be consummated once more. As for an abortion, she couldn't go through with that. Besides Hugh had in her eyes noble blood. Just as she was about to post the letter, a dog ran up and ran off with the letter. This was yet another sign. Only this time it would wipe out many others. Since this one was the letter in her right hand. Believing David had met someone else and her parents had died from worrying over her. She burst into tears and posted the letter which poignantly prophesized her suicide.

Walking back, she had the whole world on her shoulders. She felt a little scared she had posted her fate and relieved it being a Friday night she had the whole weekend to kill herself before he would see the letter on Monday. Amy was an atheist. The church and its teachings, especially those regarding married life, had turned her away from anything connected to religion. Now she was by no means religious. She turned her thoughts to God even though she wasn't sure exactly what that meant. She called in front of the church and for her a synagogue, mosque, or temple were all the same since she wanted to connect with some divine authority. "Please forgive me." She left and continued walking on since her past was too much for her to bear.

Still continuing on her way, she thought about how much better her life was when her husband went to work. Quite rightly with him being out, she thought about their children. Her mother had looked after three children, how would she have felt if her own mother was too lazy to have looked after her as a child? With everything now so blindingly obvious she had failed as a wife and as a mother she hated herself more than ever. When she arrived back, she noticed Hugh was leaving and hid. She had no reason to say goodbye to the man who, at first, she saw as being exciting. Now, as being a complete and useless soul. She shamefully saw too much of herself in him too.

That evening, although feeling tired himself, Hugh went to the club on his own. She knew he would be surrounded by women, but didn't care. Later that evening she drank two bottles of his prized vodka and drank herself to death.

• • •

A few hours later a drunk, sexually satisfied, and exhausted Hugh came back and stumbled across Amy lying on the floor. He then telephoned the police who immediately came around from Bolton armed in a group of four and arrested him on suspicion of her murder. Knowing he would never see her again he wanted to make love to her but knew that thanks to the police he wouldn't be able to do that. Of course, it was too late since they had already arrived at the scene.

On Tuesday, the day after David received her letter, he called into the local store in Scorton while on his round. He noticed the early edition of the Manchester Evening News. It was all about his wife and her lover. He felt every emotion running through his mind, such as sadness since she had gone, anger for what she had done, regret he hadn't found someone new. Later he cried for Amy, he knew she realized too late, she wanted herself to be back in Calder Vale with her family where she would be safe and sound. Being the man he was he would have taken her back without any strings attached. He went back home armed with Amy's letter. He handed it to the village policeman who was on his rounds walking around the estates - keeping a watchful eye on several mischievous village teenagers. At the time, although adultery wasn't a crime; it was still frowned upon. He was already charged. The police were not in any great rush to release him.

Even so, a few days later Hugh was released thanks to David's intervention. All the charges were dropped. Being a celebrity in Manchester, the media including the prized Piccadilly and Granada interviewed him. He hadn't much to say. In short, he didn't wish to be known outside of his hometown of Salford and the Manchester club scene. He had been careful with the three women who had shared his house with him, but his dark past was catching up. With him nearing 40, he wondered if he should have had a child with Amy. He was starting to realize his money no longer meant everything to him. Amy was his love. If only she could somehow come back to life again.

As for his privacy, the media had other ideas. The suicide had taken place on Friday the 13th of May. The media wanted to cash in on this tragedy and anything connected with it. During the next few weeks, 6 women came forward from places as far apart as Rampside near Barrow-in-Furness and parted from Lancashire, Overton near Morecambe, Chipping and Whitechapel near Preston, Hornby had entered Lancashire and Cornholme which had moved into Yorkshire. All the young women were filing paternity suits against him. Getting women pregnant was a thrill and fetish of his. He didn't want the responsibility of bringing up a child, that's why his previous long-term girlfriends left him when they knew they would never have children with him.

By the end of the year, he filed for bankruptcy, fled to Amsterdam, and settled down with his new partner in Haarlem on the North Sea Coast. Together with Antje he claimed social security benefits. After some time, they had a family of their own. He didn't once miss the bright lights of Manchester. Hugh was a very lucky man. He had a young family in the 1980s and this was before the days when the media would hunt someone down all over the world. By the 1990s, his illegitimate English kids were starting to become independent themselves. By then, he felt safe and sound in the knowledge his past wouldn't catch up with him. By the time of his own demise in 2017, aged 78, he died of natural causes anonymously.

Back exactly 40 years earlier, the shock of everything surrounding the fallen mother and seedy nightclub king sent shock waves right across rural Lancashire and beyond. The most immediate effect was on those close to Amy. Karen took things very badly and apologized to Frank explaining she was going to need some time to pull herself together. She loved him and would continue with her job and role as mother and housewife but she wouldn't be any fun in the foreseeable future. Frank understood. Together they put on a brave face for their kids and anyone else they met through their families or publicly. Of course, the local tongues were wagging. People were blaming Karen herself for being the first of the Taylor gymslip mums. She had set a bad example for her youngest sibling and there was talk around the village they were going to separate, since their body language didn't look so cozy. As it had been previously. David carried on as normal. He and his in-laws had been sharing responsibility for looking after the babies. Now, his daughters were growing up fast and able to walk to school on their own.

As such, it was one of those times when Karen was glad she had been frugal. They had saved some money and decided she needed to try something new. As such, they would holiday in Switzerland. With her being a French professor it simply had to be on the shores of Lake Geneva in the French speaking part of the country. They flew from Manchester to Geneva Airport and stayed for three weeks as soon as the boys broke up for the 6-week summer holiday, they slept in an all-inclusive hotel next to the shores of the biggest lake in the Alps. Karen believed it really would be the holiday of a lifetime. The food was great, including the Swiss cheeses and desserts. The boys loved the Swiss chocolate. The weather was fantastic, even if it was a little too hot. Perfect swimming conditions were common and it was a complete change to staying in the UK. Even so, apart from the expense, the place was overcrowded and not the best for walking with major roads encircling the lake. The mountains were not so awesome anyway, but the most disappointing thing of all was they found the Swiss French a little too snobby for their liking.

Still after three weeks, Karen had recovered. After three more weeks she enjoyed the time spent in her own backyard and the boys had been busy drawing pictures of their prized garden pebbles. After they had placed the Swiss pebbles in their appropriate locations in the garden. By the end of August, all the Taylors were ready for the new school year, as such things were back to normal and everyone agreed there was no place like home. The next year it would be back to the Lakes as usual.

September came. Both boys were attending Frank's school. Karen was pleased to be back in the routine of the academic year. Meanwhile, tragedy struck again. Karen's mother Kerry suddenly took ill and died from the sadness over losing her favorite child that November. David, who had been totally indebted to his parents-in-law since Amy's disappearance, felt the time had come to move back to Scorton. He was rightly worried this would finish his father-in-law. That Christmas was a very morbid affair. Henry put on a brave face, after losing his daughter and then his beloved wife. He was a broken man and whenever his grandchildren called his attention. He would smile at them but was starting to look like a wizened old man.

The Scorton Taylors would often come around and visit on foot those still left behind in Calder Vale. Karen was always glad to get away from the place. She could see both David and her father were doing their best. Since her mother died, there was a stronger musty smell each time she went around to her former house. On top of that, although he appeared to be enjoying his time with his grandsons, it was blatantly obvious Henry was giving up on his life. His sadness was palpable for anyone who had a heart to see.

Aged just 51, he had recently bought a shotgun, went on a walk to his local church, he prayed it was Sunday May 14. He was there very early when everyone else was still asleep. His plan was to walk as far away as Nicky Nook to a discreet place. After two hundred yards of a painful and slow continuation of his walk from the church, he could take no more. He climbed over the gate into a field, which had a big bull inside, picked up the gun, and shot himself in the mouth. It was the year to the day of his daughter's own suicide. Now, he himself, was gone.

It was later the same day when David was informed by a very distressed police officer, the one who protected David four years earlier. The farmer who knew Henry telephoned the local bobby. As for Karen, she found out through a messenger of David's, via the neighbor's telephone since she herself didn't have a phone. Back in 1970, only 35 percent of households had a landline. Even in 1980, two years after this tragedy, 28 percent of households relied on the public telephone boxes. Things couldn't have gotten any worse. It had been one year since disaster had struck. She needed a push to get out of her misery. Geneva was her solution. Now, just one year later, she had lost both of her parents.

While she did her best to shield both the boys from her personal grief, with Frank being an adult, she expected him to be patient with her. As for Frank, he felt as if his wife had died. For him, in many ways, she was like some zombie. The times he tried to touch her with a hug he felt she was a million miles away from him. At times, he sensed she was angry with him. The mourning continued in bed too, with both far apart, wishing for this nightmare to somehow end.

One evening as she was preparing dinner, 6 o'clock arrived. She wondered where the hell her husband was. "Where is daddy?" Matthew asked. Wanting to burst into tears but knowing she couldn't ruin their lives, she put on a stiff upper lip.

"Oh! I'm sorry I forgot to tell you; daddy is away on a school trip with his pupils." It was the first big lie she had told her children. That night was the longest in her life. She wished her children weren't with her so she could search the local rivers, houses, and bridges for him. While, other moments, she hated herself in driving her solid rock away from her.

All alone in her bed, she thought about her unhappiness when he was with her the night before - compared to the depths of despair she was in. Those dark nights with the gap between then wide enough for a bridge over a river, now seemed as though they were a world apart. While financially she could support herself as an independent woman, if need be, she hadn't thought about this, since life without her Frank was one not worth living.

Chapter 5

The long night passed by. She got the kids ready for school, who were already old enough to look after themselves, but she wanted to feel useful. Later, she called in sick from work, by courtesy of the local telephone box, which was in front of the village café. Then she continued cycling down into Garstang. As she arrived at her husband's school, all eyes were on her. It was school break and Frank being a colleague was a news event for all the teachers. It seemed everyone, to her shame, recognized her.

Fortunately, Frank noticed her before she had time to feel embarrassed. He ran up to her. She fell to the floor and collapsed. "Please Frank take me home." She said pleading in desperation.

"Just wait here darling, let me tell the head I have something important." He then ran off to his boss before Karen had a chance to think about what he had just said. The head, who knew all about Karen's difficult times, still had a soft spot for him. He encouraged him to take the rest of the week off. Frank ran back to his wife. Together they cycled back to Scorton. With the kids in school, they made mad passionate love for the first time in 12 months. From that moment of passion both knew their marriage was once again safe and sound. Both of them were happy as if they were teenagers in love once more.

It was dark. The tears running down her face were invisible. "Why did you sleep away last night? Where you, thinking of leaving me?" She said as he was holding her in his arms. They were naked as usual and felt closer this way.

"No Karen, I wasn't. I just felt so helpless. I felt I was unable to make you happy. I have suffered too you know. I have been involved with your family over the years. I wanted to give you my endless support. I cried a lot for those kids. I don't mean ours. I mean Heidi and Ruth – it is such a shame!"

"Why didn't you tell me this before?" She asked confused.

"Like I said I am the one who is meant to be supporting you."

"You do, you do . . . Tell me Frank, do people think I am mad?" She said with her heart warming, wanting some reassurance.

"I think if this were in London it would be different. The capital is full of divorce, broken families and suicides, but here darling, we are cut off from the rest of the world. Family life is important here up north." He wisely stated as he held her tightly.

"It is not only London; it is the same in Manchester too."

"I know, any big place. We know from experience it can happen even here. On the whole, here in Scorton, and in Calder Vale despite gossip from certain quarters we could mention, you and David are known as being good family people."

"And so, are you Frank." She responded lovingly.

Well, I don't feel so because of me sleeping in my office last night." Which for him was the worst night in his entire life.

"Was it a cry for help, darling?" She asked motherly.

"It was, dearest. I would never leave you Karen. I'd kill myself before I'd ever do such a terrible thing." He was emotional.

"Don't say that." She was thinking about tragic deaths close to her heart in just one year.

Frank felt the time for talking was over. The only thing for him was to get inside her. The support they were sharing made both of them stronger and they made love a few more times before the sun rose.

Karen wasn't stupid, Frank's night away could had led to something worse. Who would have blamed him. There was only so much one could take. She didn't dwell on this - feeling she was responsible for the marriage too. She knew the important family matters would need to be discussed. As such, the subject of holidays came up again. Karen wanted to avoid the Lakes yet again. Frank understood. "I don't wish to go to the Lakes this summer, I am scared about the link with Amy and how it could trigger something off." She expected a reasonable and sensitive response from him.

"I know. I am not keen on Switzerland either, after last time." He gave a firm but benign smile. She felt safe.

"Neither am I. Have you an idea?" She inquired submissively.

"As it happens, I have indeed. On, and off, I had been doing research. It seems to me, 1) We don't want Switzerland, and 2) We want somewhere with big mountains and lakes."

"What do you suggest Frank?" Wanting him to open up.

"Austria." He smiled at her, as there was then a long pause as her mind was thinking about the *Sound of Music*.

"What have you seen there?" Well, there is a flight from Manchester to Munich. Then, there is a three-hour journey to the Austrian Alps where there are campsites next to warm lakes in sunny valleys surrounded by high-ridged mountains.

"No need to tell me anymore, we are going there!" She said enthusiastically.

For the Austrian trip two months' later they took with them mostly camping gear and after the hot weather in Geneva and the previous two summers in the lakes they didn't take anything other than summer clothing. A taxi took them to Manchester Airport where they then took the plane to Munich. From there a taxi took them to the nearest railway terminal – then two trains to Salzburg. From there, just like in the UK, they would stay close to lakes. Fuschl Lake was the first stop. They stayed at the camp-site on the side next to the nature reserve. While Austria in many ways looked just like being in the lakes especially when looking only at the natural geography, it still offered a different charm, the style of the houses, which were often wooden with balconies full of flowers. The language was German of course. The dress senses of the people with the men walking around in leather trousers and many women wearing dresses, which were more voluptuous than Karen would had dared to wear back home in Lancashire.

Armed with groceries they moved on and wild camped illegally but without the tent at Eibensee, a small mountain lake out in the wilds higher than the tops of Scafell. Other German speakers were camping there too. All were very discreet. The third site was at Lake Wolfgang in the quiet village close to the banks of the fast-flowing mountain stream Zinkenbach complete with views of St. Wolfgang across the lake. It was at Zinkenbach, where the boys were convinced, they had found the best pebbles in the whole world. It was here, and behind the backs of Karen and Frank, they sneaked into all the rucksacks pebbles they would carry all the way back home. They then moved on to Monichsee. Another tarn like Eibensee and just below the summit of Schafberg again a wild camp. Even at the higher altitude. The final and fifth site was Schwarzensee a basic campsite next to a beautiful lake. From there, they walked back down to the valley and took a bus from Strobl back to Salzburg and the train to Munich after 5 destinations and 17 nights. The holiday was a success apart from the scary thunderstorm or two. The time they got lost and ended up in Mondsee after the summit of Schafberg found themselves walking back almost in the dark back to Schwarzensee the day before their return. They cooked all their own meals and found the Austrians as being of a friendly and a lively race.

One thing they enjoyed about the campsites was, apart from the thunderstorms, which were a common feature of any summer alpine holiday, the nights were quiet. The campsite owners guaranteed a good night's sleep for everyone who stayed there. Anyone breaking the rules was thrown offsite to the benefit of those families with small children.

Now, back in Scorton, and fresh from their holiday, they invited David and his daughters over for dinner. When the girls went outside to play in the garden after eating, their own boys were by then somewhere around the village. Frank broke the silence.

"There is a semi going for 12,000 here. I thought it might be of some interest for you." He said seriously looking at David.

"Frank." Said Karen, who was none too pleased.

"I haven't got that sort of money." Said David somewhat sad.

"But you could sell the house in Calder Vale . . . Have you got any savings?" Asked Frank without beating around the bush.

"Don't be so rude, Frank." Karen stated annoyed and ashamed wanting to protect poor David from humiliation.

"He is my brother, I can ask." There were then a few moments of silence, as they all started thinking about the property. "Karen, Frank's right, this is just the kind of house I could do with."

"The only thing is, I have heard that the owners want a quick sale, anyways I have already thought this through, and if you like, I will give you the money when I visit the bank to the value of your house, and the deeds will be in mine and Karen's names for us to sell the property." With that Karen was of course delighted, they were able to help David without humiliating him further.

"What can I say, this is an offer I can't refuse." Replied David.

Within 14 days, David was then the proud owner of a semi-detached bungalow similar as the one of his in-laws. It was just one week before the new school year and granted under the circumstances the girls were transferred from St. Johns School Calder vale to CE Primary in Scorton, without any fuss. A removal van came, and the useful things were sent onto Scorton, while the rest were either thrown out or handed to Karen as heirlooms or sold as a means of making funds for the local school. After it, the house was put on the market. It sold for around the price and trouble including solicitor's fees ETC to the amount, which Frank had lent David. As for his girls, they quickly settled in the school and were happy to see more of their paternal grandparents, knowing their mother was dead. They were able to grieve over her and recover. They were sad about passing their grandparents. The loss of one's parent hits harder than that of previous generations. Since they had never forgotten their mother, who they missed every day, now she was dead.

Things were then back to normal in the Taylor household, and now aged 31 Karen was starting to think more and more about her sons' futures. As for Mark, he would have none of it, and his idea of the future was the school fancy-dress taking place during the first week back at school. The following week, on the first day back at school on Monday the 4th of September, he cycled to school as normal. On arrival in school, he ran into the ladies with Cathy, his girlfriend. She dressed him up, to the giggles of the other girls who were allowed in the toilet. Since the prim and proper prudes had been ordered out to the other toilets on the first floor, suddenly Mark and Cathy walked out together. They left school and made love not far from the school grounds on a path in the bushes. After it, they walked back into school late, but many more people spotted them than they realized. They had been seen walking out of the school during school times - even holding hands. There had been sightings from parents and from other children of them close to people's gardens kissing passionately in public. This was all too much for a sleepy country school to handle.

A totally embarrassed Frank was called into the head's office later that day where it had been agreed that Mark would have to be expelled and with help, he could go to her husband's school that being St. Aidans, between Garstang and Blackpool. Frank was relieved, he had seen so many things he didn't like in the urban schools of Lancaster and Preston and clearly felt that this was the best solution. Back at home later that day Karen would have none of it, and the next day she called in unexpectedly to see both her husband and his boss in school. The setting was the head's office, with to the consternation of his wife, a fawning teacher of the head: her own husband of all people. "We both feel it is really in the best interests of Mark." Said the headmistress a little embarrassed.

"Yes, we do," Frank answered. With that, Karen looked for the first time in her life as though she was going to hit someone. Being the headmistress, her demeanor changed as she looked as though she wanted to burst out laughing.

● ● ●

"Well, I don't . . . let me get one thing clear, if he is forced out of this school against my will, I will tell your husband about your extra marital affair with my husband!" With that she stormed out of the school and decided given she had the rest of the day off. She would go and cycle through the Trough of Bowland while Frank and his boss were shocked to the core. Both wondered privately how she knew about their secret affair, but the school bell rang.

"She is bluffing." She said waiting for Frank to support her.

"No, she's not, she can be as hard as nails." He said proud of his wife, at the same time feeling ashamed of himself for cheating on her. There was a few moments' silence as his boss thought about her position as a figure of authority.

"Well, there is only one thing we can do, he will have to be made an example, and give a school talk as to why we have school rules. And, that girl Cathy, of course, as well."

"Ok, I am sure he can do this." He smiled at her as they both stood up, left the office, and walked to their classes.

Upon arrival at Dunsop Bridge, Karen decided to revisit Slaidburn. The village took her back 16 years to the time she was there with Frank and her friends who were on their blind date and their blissful time at Wham and ate the packed lunch, which she had prepared that morning. Then she cycled back into Dunsop Bridge and after climbing over the trough it was downhill back home through Marshaw and back into Scorton. She felt better but was then worried that Frank knew that she had slept behind his back too. Feeling so ashamed of herself, she didn't wish to think about this, and merely trusted her feelings that she knew what she was doing, and that like Frank, it was all a part of her distant past.

She came home, Frank had already cooked dinner, and told her that their son was safe in the school as long as he didn't commit any more stupid pranks and of course he would have to give a talk, but nothing would come of the speech since the fuss surrounding the incident had put Mark and Cathy into line, if they hadn't been already and being busy, the headmistress had other things to attend to. He was already in his final year of secondary education and she knew that in staying at Garstang High he would now be keeping a lower profile. A few hours later she looked at her husband who was sitting quietly and reading the paper. "I am tired and am going to bed darling." He knew what he had to do. During the past few months Karen had been thinking about how she had lost out on being a mother through her studies and her career and her family had everything they needed. Was it really time to move into a bigger house as her husband wished? Then again ten years down the road and her sons would be leaving the nest, and what would she do with a castle with just her husband? In the end she decided that she wanted another child to make up for her lost motherhood.

Of course, with three kids a bigger house would come in handy, but on one salary she couldn't do with the stress, as such and hoping that Mark would be going to university in just a few years she decided to see which way the winds of love would take her. As such without any mention of her plans, she decided to get her own back on Frank in getting her pregnant with their second child. Of course, this was revenge, but of a sweetest kind.

Since several years Karen started around 9 at the University and generally stayed until around 2.30, while Frank began around 8 and worked until around 4. As such she was the one who cooked for her boys and cleaned the dishes while they were in the bathroom getting ready for school. Once they left, she had the bathroom all to herself. At weekends Karen wanted to lie in the bed, but Frank wanting to make the most of the free day would get up and cook a typical English breakfast for everyone, and prepare a packed lunch, which was fit for a king. Then they would go out walking, cycling, swimming and in the evening on both Saturday and Sunday he would cook a simple but healthy meal since Karen was too tired but happy to eat anything he made for her. So basically, this routine had been pretty much a part of their lives as soon as Matthew was old enough to take part in everything.

A few weeks later, towards the end of September, Frank came home. He could smell his favorite dish a lasagna. As he walked into the kitchen Karen looked at him. "I want just you and me to walk up Nicky Nook after dinner and we have some things to discuss." She wanted him in suspense to keep him guessing, and with all the chaotic things, which had been going on in their lives he was a little concerned. After dinner, as planned, Frank and Karen walked through the village hand in hand as usual and then up the lane and took the direct path to the summit of Nicky Nook. She was as pleased as punch but didn't want him to realize she had been plotting, while she wanted him to be happy. He looked at her wondering what was going on. "I'm pregnant." She blurted out to him as the sky over the bay was a deep and fiery red.

"I'm lost for words . . . I know you don't want any more children." He said half delighted and half scared with his eyes focused on her, since she was, after all the woman of his life.

"I don't." She said poker faced, which wasn't one of her usual expressions, and one, which was scaring the hell out of him.

"So, what now then?" He said worried that another storm was about to hit their private lives and he was wondering how much more he could take, since it was becoming too much.

"We'd better be more careful next time." She said with a hint of feeling in her speech and knowing he was her scared rabbit.

"Are you keeping the child?" He asked concerned.

"Of course, I am, I just think that three is enough."

"Wont we need a bigger house?" By then he started to feel a little emotional and was in fact blissfully happy over the baby.

"The boys will just have to move in together." She smiled.

"Do you remember when I took you up Arnside Knott?" He said sweetly, while he didn't agree with the boys sharing a room when they could afford to move into a bigger house, he was of course delighted that his beautiful and still young wife was carrying their third child and that being a parent was so important for them. "I do." She was then wondering from his last comment if he knew about her deed, since her own memory wasn't so crystal clear as she wanted to believe, and maybe things were better that way.

● ● ●

"That was 16 years ago, and now you are coming up to being 32, I wonder where we will be in 16 years' time.

She then placed her hands on his face, with her hair flying around; which was blowing in the wind, and then they started to kiss. A bit later her maternal feelings were coming on stronger and thinking about her nieces in Scorton, her parents, and her younger sister combined with her walks around Calder Vale, which she no longer had the strength to partake emotionally made the tears run down her face. Frank noticed her sadness. "Are you OK love?" He said he was enjoying being the one looking after her.

"I am, you know it is scary to think what one wrong mistake can cause . . . I am so happy with you Frank, but I am still grieving about my parents who died prematurely because of my stupid sister, I sensed she wasn't right, I should had known, I could had helped her . . . and of course, I miss that stupid cow too."

"Karen, nobody forced her to run away, but you know the old tale, the grass isn't always greener on the other side . . . The world is a changing, people just want to try out new things all the time, but at the end of the day; for me it is all the same wherever you go."

"I never said goodbye to her." She said regrettably.

"Look Love, just remember you can't be responsible for everyone, but my life, the kids" life and you that's my only concern, for me Karen, family saves the world, my whole life is centered around us, without you I would be nothing more than just a pebble.

"What would you do if I left you?" She asked protectively.

"I would just go back to my parents in Silverdale, take early retirement and help out on the farm." He said with a serious face.

"I would never leave you." She always found him her rock in stormy waters and now he was as philosophical as the best.

"What would you do if I left you?" He asked her seriously.

"It is just too awful to imagine, I don't have any parents to run to anyway, I guess I'd just stay here in Scorton and cry myself to sleep at night and die from my broken and lonely heart."

• • •

"It is going to be different again when we have a baby, I was wondering if the kids could either stay here for Christmas or go to Silverdale and you and I could go on a holiday on Tenerife."

"You mean like a honeymoon?" She said as a warm glow went through her heart with the deep blue sky turning black.

"Yes indeed, come to think about it, we never got around to that did we?" With nothing more to say they simply kissed each other. Hand in hand, like the teenagers they were when they first found themselves in a similar situation, they walked back down in the dark and into the valley, without any cares in their world.

As expected, when the boys found out there was another addition and the implications this would mean for them regarding the bedroom arrangements; they were none too happy. Frank sweetened Mark by offering him a free cycling holiday on the continent provided he did well with his O levels, the forerunner to GCSE's, which came out later that decade. The boys decided to stay at Silverdale, the younger son wanted to help on the farm, while Mark was happy being close to the Lake District.

Of course, there were some cruel tales in both parishes behind David's back such as how he had killed them off; Amy and her parents, this down and out boy from a barn in Scorton had got his hands on what he always wanted, a house of his own. Where the barn came from nobody could say it certainly wasn't true, he grew up close to the village center in the terraced house of which his parents were still living in. The gossip died down until within 3 months of his move back to his village a former schoolmate of his 2 years his junior moved in with him. Her name was Doreen, and like David, she was getting over a family tragedy. Ten years earlier she had fallen in love with a village boy, Richard, a lorry driver. They got married, moved into one of the village semis and would be seen together on his Harley Davidson and ride around the Forest of Bowland together especially during the long summers evenings where they would stop off midway around Whitewell and call in at the inn there for a pint and a smoke. Eventually they had a child together and were very happy together.

● ● ●

Sadly, during the spring of 1977 Richard one Sunday morning said goodbye to his wife and child aged just 6 months for the last time. It had been a pleasant breakfast, the weather was fair, and he went out on his own for a quick ride down to Knott End. From there he went out on the sands and down into Pilling. The sun was pleasantly warm, and he was planning to call in at The Elletson Arms at Stakepool for a pint, when suddenly and still out on the sands of the Morecambe Bay, his bike got caught in one of the quick-sands and he was none too pleased.

He tried with all his might to get his bike out, which sank deeper and deeper into the sands, as he ferociously fought for his bike. He couldn't give up, how could he? It was, apart from his wife and child, his most prized possession. Suddenly the sand sucked him in from the underwater currents and he couldn't get out. The tide was going out and never once did he worry, a passerby came over to try to ease him out, but a second good Samaritan ran over to the local telephone box in front of The Golden Ball in Pilling. The man went back to Richard who was still accompanied with the other fellow, they were laughing and chatting together, until the coastguards came over from Knott End. After a while they could see that they needed more man-power and better equipment, apart from that the tide wouldn't arrive for a couple of hours so there was no need to worry. On his walkie-talkie the lifeguards from Fleetwood were alerted, they were better prepared and arrived not just in a Land Rover, but by fire brigade. By then the tides were coming towards them like sharks around their bait, even so Richard hadn't given up. Had they arrived earlier, the equipment they had would have been suffice. Richard smiled until almost his last breath, the rescuers lifted his head as the tides came and were still fighting against the seas in vain, until the tide went above his head and he drowned. Without her son Doreen, who was so devoted to Richard, would have given up on her own life, instead she left her nice bungalow since it was mortgaged, and went back to live with her parents who were also living in the same village.

· · ·

STEVEN KAY

Life is full of strange coincidences and David had moved into her old matrimonial domicile and that was the reason why it took her 3 months as opposed to 3 weeks to get away from the suffocating chains of her parents and to move in with him. Once she moved in she was kind of happy, she felt that Richard was happy for her too, but at times when she made love to David she could sometimes see, feel and hear Richard and this was a creepy kind of lovemaking, which for her at times felt almost necrophilic and made her uncomfortable to say the least; as such one evening in their bed, and feeling ill at ease she confronted David. "I really can't stay in this house forever." Said Doreen a little too sharply for comfort.

"I understand, but I don't see how we can do this right here right now, I would if I could." He said sadly.

"Do you understand my feelings; I don't feel great at all about this?" She said even less softly and impatiently.

"Had I known I was going to move into the former house of the deceased partner of my new girlfriend there is no way, it is creepy." He expressed to her with great understanding.

"Why didn't you tell me?" She said relieved and lost.

"What for, just to hurt you?" He said calmly with poignancy.

"I feel better knowing you understand, I just needed to know how you felt too." She said in all her sincerity.

"Of course, I understand." And then he kissed her, but after a few seconds she pushed him away, as she became nervous.

"And you promise me we won't stay here for too long?"

"I give you my word Doreen." He said, as he looked straight into her eyes. With that she felt safe, and her passion came back knowing that she had a future with the man she loved like no other, apart from Richard the man who would never leave her thoughts.

While the Christmas turned out to be freezing cold at Silverdale, Frank and Karen were enjoying what was back then a luxury holiday for most couples and since they were outdoor types, the sea was warm enough for them to paddle in, and after a few moments for them to swim in too together. She was 4

85

months pregnant and while nobody had noticed a thing at her workplace the week before, now wearing summer clothes and bikinis on the beach, her baby bump was there for everyone to see. One elderly couple asked them if they they this was their honeymoon, they told them their background and the lady thought, "I imagined that you were young newly-weds on holiday before family life." Karen and Frank smiled at each other contentedly and lovingly.

"That was such a big compliment Frank." She said feeling like a teenager in love with the man she loved, who loved her too.

"Indeed; it is, but don't forget, in these modern times, it isn't so queer to be married at 35 and 31 like us and to start a family . . . The world is a changing love as I keep on saying." At the end of the holiday, they bought some souvenirs, which included Belgian chocolate, which was unlike in the UK easily available, but most importantly for their boys they bought back some pebbles, which they had found on the shores of the Atlantic Ocean.

Back in her workplace after a holiday, which had done her the world of good, Karen was wearing lighter clothes and plans were being made for her to work less with other colleagues taking on more of her student markings, but Karen would have none of it. Even so she decided to plan for life after work and then she checked the dates for the Easter holiday, and with it being from the 7th of April she decided that she would work until then happily knowing that the final term would be safe in the hands of the new PHD student, who like Karen grew up in a terraced house.

Easter was a very happy affair and they stayed away in a caravan for two weeks, but this time in Langdale. Some days they would go walking together on gentle strolls, while other days Karen would relax, read, enjoy the spring sunshine and feed her hungry boys as they came back to the holiday home. It was a beautiful time away and being even closer to nature than back home in Scorton brought out a more pleasant side to her boys, "Mum."

"Yes Matthew." She said curiously and tenderly.

● ● ●

"I just want you to know that Mark and I are really happy that we are going to have a little sister." Said Matthew

"Is that so, do you mean it?" She asked delighted.

"Of course, we do, it will be fine for us all." Replied Mark.

After the holiday, Karen gave the house a good spring clean, was still cycling into Garstang and for her it was a real holiday, since she had already given 11 years of uninterrupted service in the department of French and Law. This pregnancy was different to her first two, she was more relaxed, she had proven to the world that she had done well in her career, and now was the time to show her appreciation of her Frank by simply being a homemaker. As such during the last week in April, she had a GPO phone installed into their home and this had been arranged around the time of her birthday, as well as the baby things she would need, and had been up to Lancaster to buy four paintings depicting life around Lancashire: of her parents village, of Frank's childhood, of a day out at the seaside and of one area which made her feel so proud and was a big part of their history. As such, on the north-facing wall in their bedroom there hung a painting of Silverdale, with views across the Morecambe Bay to the Lakeland fells in the background. In the living room on the east-facing wall there was a painting of Slaidburn. Upstairs on the south-facing wall of her baby's bedroom was a painting of Calder Vale, while in the boys' room on the west-facing wall, one of the sand dunes at Fleetwood.

When Frank came home; he was spellbound. His wife had shown him in his eyes how much she cared about what he saw as the important things in life. "My God Karen, these paintings are incredible!" He said, as he wanted to hold her in his arms.

"I have never really sat back and thought about our nest so much as now with me being busy all the time, but now I want this house to be something like our own little Victorian country manor." They were stood in the boys' room, they would be out for at least another hour and under the view of the painting of the Fylde Coast he made love to her, gently as they thought about their futures.

"We have three more scenes to go." He said to his adorable love, while they were resting, who couldn't get enough of him.

"What do you mean?" She said with a pussycat smile.

During the next few days, they had made love under the paintings of Fleetwood, Silverdale, Slaidburn and Calder Vale, and there was a repeat of this innocent fetish of theirs, since they imagined their good times spent when glancing at the painting, which was watching over them as they climaxed together with their hearts full of content. Early May arrived and already 36 weeks pregnant, she wanted to walk up Nicky Nook for the final time before she would give birth, with Frank. As they reached the top, a smile went across her beautiful face. "Just like old times, isn't it?"

"It is, now the kids don't join us anymore . . . Just look over there to the right of Blackpool Tower, that's Fleetwood, turn around a bit more and there is Silverdale!" He said as he was gently helping her with his arms and body. "Turn a bit more." They turned around.

"Slaidburn!" She blurted out and he smiled, as they turned.

"Calder Vale." They said together in a harmonious unison.

"Now that the boys no longer want to be with us all the time, I am really looking forward to bringing our new addition up here." The romantic talk between a loving husband and wife about to become parents yet again continued: on this memorable, dreamy and fine spring evening for them. Back at home that evening they were admiring their pebbles from abroad, as they were thinking of themselves as though they were in their second courtship and were wiser and enjoying their lives ever more.

Right up until the birth, on the last day in May when she gave birth to a healthy baby girl called Amy, at Lancaster Royal Infirmary, Karen had kept herself busy, she had even been up Nicky Nook twice since the beginning of the month and visited the swimming pool in Garstang several times for a swim. She planned to spend the whole summer at home, and she had had two holidays recently anyway. As such that summer they had plenty of home- grown vegetables and fruits, but sadly no pets, due to the fact they went away so often, but then Karen decided that she wanted a kitten. As such she brought home from one of the villagers while on a visit as she was pushing her newborn in the pram and came back with a cat basket and a lovely six-week-old tabby.

During the school summer holidays, Mark went off on his travels around Europe, in fact he left straight after his final O level on the last day of spring. Once a week he would send a postcard, which would arrive one week later. Thanks to his previous day trips of cycling to the Lake District and back, with his furthest being from Scorton to Keswick via Ennerdale Bridge and back via Grasmere and a total of 179 miles (288km) in one day, he certainly had developed some good stamina and well-conditioned legs. As such his 6 weeks trip took him from Scorton to Hull, then the ferry one night to Zeebrugge from there through Flanders and across to Maastricht, then down through Luxembourg, into Alsace Lorraine, the Black Forest, Switzerland and over the Alps into Italy and then he returned via a similar route. While there he spoke German when people couldn't understand English and was seeing first handedly the benefits in having a second language. Mark also enjoyed seeing so many cyclists on the continent and at times wished he had more time in getting to know the people more, but at the same time he wanted to see all those countries on his travels, and with so much sport and to his great regret; he forgot to bring back enough pebbles as souvenirs to place into his garden.

Meanwhile, Matthew had spent the summer at Silverdale where he enjoyed helping and getting some good money for his labors, and unlike Mark who only had time to glance at women, he had a brief and pleasant romance with a girl from Arnside.

As for the other Scorton Taylors, Karen, Frank and baby Amy, named in memory of her sister enjoyed the feelings of togetherness at home. Before the end of the summer holiday, Frank had received a letter from his boss, informing him about one of the deputy heads' promotion to another school and asking if he would consider. Without any hesitation after handing Karen the letter it had been agreed that he should take it. As for the kitten, she was loved by everyone, and would walk around the village, and enjoyed sleeping at the bottom of the bed where she could simply lie above the sleeper's feet purring the night away.

September came, and Mark was at Lancaster Grammar studying for his A Levels, Frank was now the deputy head while Matthew was in his third year at high school. While Karen enjoyed being mum throughout the school week, she wanted to keep herself fit and all the men in her life took it in turns to keep their eyes on Amy. One thing for sure, the house was a little bit too small, one bathroom for 5, the boys had to share a bedroom, so Karen would have no talk of moving-house since she didn't want the stress of having a big house one day just for two people.

It was while he was at sixth form college that Mark met Stephen Hamm. He kind of looked at Mark and was relieved that their sad history of annoying the other children would lie dormant in the memories of their mutual junior school. Steve had smartened himself up and found Mark to have grown up a bit more too. The next day while both were in the classroom learning Politics, and both alarmed with the loud mouthed Elizabeth Taylor who was no relation of Mark's in fact she was a radical, lesbian feminist, who to the chagrin of the students studying German, was convinced that all Germans were Nazis, women were slaves of men and on earth just to rear their children, and that the world would be better off without men, this created one of Steve's famous sarcastic looks, as such Mark realized that it was indeed the Richard Hamm of old, who used to rollover Mark on the playing field as a result of Mark's; Ham, bacon and egg taunts. As such from then on, they would sit together; and while Steve had been lost as to why Mark kind of ignored him at the beginning, he was proud of the way he had camouflaged himself. After primary school, Steve moved with his parents to Galgate and as such it made sense for him to go to Lancaster High, as such they had lost contact.

After the lesson, Steve who had German roots; was still deep-ly offended by Elizabeth, and when the school had a fancy dress, he dressed himself up as a German soldier. Elizabeth went ballistic and started to insult an innocent Mark who had nothing to do with it, while Esther the only Jewish girl in the school was in hysterics, which only added to Elizabeth's fury. On top of that Elizabeth had a crush on Esther and was furious when after trying to get her to go out on a date with her, she was alarmed to hear Esther inform her that she and Steve were an item. Her hatred certainly helped to bond the new lovebirds even more as they often had fun together when Steve kept telling so many jokes to Esther about the woman; who believed that she had every right, in every way to take Esther away from her beloved Steve.

The next few days Mark, Steve and Esther had a few meetings and they decided to set up their own business venture in Scorton. The idea was that Steve and Esther would serve, "Rich Hamburgers," in village halls and that Mark would be the DJ entertainer, with his brother Matthew working on the door. Fridays they were at Scorton and Saturdays they were at Lancaster University and Esther lived close by in the city. She was already 18, should have been in the year above, but had taken a year out and had been staying with her distant relatives in Frankfurt for one year on a school exchange. As such her Vauxhaul Cavalier was used as transport and on Fridays she would come down with Steve, and together they would get on with the cooking and refreshments. They started the third week in September and on the first night they had over 125 teenagers who came down. The equipment would then be placed in the car ready for the next day, and during the afternoon it was set up on the stage. This was left to Steve so that Esther could drive down to Scorton and pick Mark and Matthew up.

The venue at Lancaster was equally a success, they had around 200 students every Saturday. Mark started off just playing records and giving the odd mention, but after a few weeks he started to sing one song, until by the end of the school year he was singing for up to 30 minutes or more. They did this for two years: Mark had decided not to take up a career in entertainment because he didn't see much future in doing this

● ● ●

kind of work as a career. His main problem was that although he was well known and managers from other agencies had heard about him, there was, however, simply one big roadblock.

While Mark was open-minded and had nothing against homosexuals, they were running the shows up and down the country. A former manager of a famous rock band wanted to piece a band together with Mark as the lead singer, all he had to do was to sleep with the manager, a male who as Mark was to find out ten years later died of AIDS. One man even offered Mark a contract for 800 pounds each week in Amsterdam back in 1980, and he was even considering giving up his college studies until the man who was with his boyfriend told him that he would need to be gay as a part of the deal. In total over this two-year career, which was run by him and his friends, he had 6 opportunities to make it big, but all involved him doing something, which for him was clearly a no-go area. As such knowing that Steve and Esther would move on to university; he saw no future in entertainment, and reluctantly moved on to university himself, and decided that life was too short to keep on banging his head against a brick wall in becoming a star and in turn being increasingly frustrated.

Christmas came, and with everyone at home, baby Amy seemed to be full of giggles, David and his new family members would come around a few times with his own daughters. Houses came up, with a discussion taking place about the fact that the Taylors might or might not had needed a bigger place, while the 5 members of the patchwork family formed as a result of Amy and produced two of her nieces were discussing whether they should stay in the house of Doreen's deceased husband.

As the 70s drew out and the 80s were drawing in Karen and Frank were very content with their lives. Just before the new decade Karen took out all her photograph albums, which she had been collecting since when she met Frank, since in many ways that was when her life began and was pleased that even her teenage boys were enjoying looking at the memories, which Karen cherished. The new year came in and since she went off on maternity leave the previous spring, Karen with more time for herself found listening to the radio more appealing, she would often wake up to Ray Moore have breakfast with Terry Wogan and clean the house with Jimmy Young. As a true romantic her favorite songs were, from Doctor Hook, The Detroit Spinners, and Fern Kinney and as spring began, she was finding herself partly from her newfound love of middle of the road music more sentimental than ever, and as such she hadn't noticed the hormones changing in her body as she was once again pregnant and this time a little unprepared.

As soon as she realized on the last day in March every emotion went through her mind, she then went on a walk with Frank, while the boys shared looking after Amy, and a bemused husband wanted to know why they were going up Nicky Nook without her wanting to speak. As they reached the top she began. "There is something I need to tell you . . . We can't stay any longer in the semi." They both looked at each other relieved smiling.

"I know, it was you who wanted to stay in the semi." Suspecting what was coming he continued. "So, what has brought this on suddenly?" He asked her innocently.

"You know, don't you?" She said as they were beaming.

"I think I do." He said delightedly and in heaven.

Karen was of course delighted, she had badly wanted this baby, while she felt that she had originally become a mother too young, she certainly had no regrets. As they walked back hand in hand together to their home, she felt a little bit of remorse. Her mind had gone back to when she fell pregnant the second time. How could she have blamed Frank? These things happened naturally, and it takes two to make a child. The third child wasn't of revenge either. While for the first two, she wasn't fully aware about baby making, and one could say they were accidents, she had made sure that she would have the third and fourth child. As such it doesn't take a rocket scientist to see that Frank was always ready for a child with her, and that how it happened wasn't worth analyzing since it was all just a happy and natural part of their happy lives together.

● ● ●

The next day a meeting with Frank, Karen, David and his new partner, who like Karen had just fallen pregnant was held. The Taylors informed David and Doreen of their intentions to sell their house and to move into a bigger house in Garstang and close to the banks of the River Wyre. As such having to lay out money for the more expensive house, the plan was for David, Doreen and their three kids to move into their house, and for them to be given the deeds for David's and for the builders to accept as part payment, Richard's former house, which would be of no use to any of them. The next day they contacted the builders who agreed, and within a few weeks the company had received cash from Frank and the rights of ownership to one of the semis. Also given the new house wasn't quite ready, the builders agreed not to sell the house until the two families had moved into their new homes.

In May they were now in their new houses. The Taylors now had a four bedroomed detached house, which was to the main benefit of Matthew and Mark, two bathrooms to everyone's relief but even then Mark found that there were times when he had to run outside since his brother could spend what seemed like ages in the bathroom, and Frank apart from his reading on the toilet could spend more time than Karen in front of the mirror. Of course, without a wall sharing a home Karen no longer concerned herself in case the neighbors could eavesdrop on the men in her house battling for the loos. With the boys now, youths and no longer interested in the pebbles, it was Frank who quietly got on with moving the gemstones from Scorton to Garstang, and while they had many of them, for him it wasn't so difficult to separate the native pebbles from those, which had been accumulated from the travels. As for that late spring the Taylors were looking forward to their three-week log cabin holiday near Loughrigg Tarn, which they had already paid for before she knew she was with a child again. Back in 1980 the village of Elterwater had a well-supplied small shop with groceries; and the boys were often sent there on errands, often for items such as bread and milk.

● ● ●

Unsurprisingly Karen was a little tired since she had conceived this time after just a nine gap since the birth of Amy, even so at five months gone she was as fit on the fells as any other woman of her age. Frank carried Amy who slept most of the time in a baby sling, which in those days wasn't a common sight, since prams were the norm; but this active family had every intention of walking around Loughrigg Fell, swimming in the inviting tarn and were rarely to be seen in the honey pots of Grasmere, Ambleside and Windermere during that late July and early August.

As for the kitten while they were away, well she had by then become an adult and had been running back very often to her old home as soon as the Taylors moved to a new house. In the end it had been decided that she could stay in her old house, and in the end she would on her own free will visit the Taylors, where she was happy to spend a few days there at a time, before going back to the home she knew best in Scorton.

Health was and had always been a very important issue for Karen. She had three rules for healthy living. Most important for her was food, she believed in all things naturally, good or bad. What this meant was that when her colleagues at the university were trying out the weight watchers' diets Karen, who was slim anyway, simply didn't get too involved. She was a great believer in the essentials in life, so she simply enjoyed her food, which was usually local produce, and with her living now in Garstang, she would shop at Booths, for all the things, which she needed for her family. As for milk, that was of course David's job, as such, the kitchen was stocked up with whole grain cereals and breads, fruits and vegetables, meats in the fridge, local cheeses. What she didn't buy was: artificial drinks such as coca cola, white bread, foreign cheeses or low-fat yoghurt. Without TV she hadn't been brainwashed into trying out new things so much as the other mums of her generation, and she enjoyed some routine in her life. Another important area was exercise; she loved the fresh air and being outdoors, and that was more important for her than sitting in a smoky pub, and as much as she could talk to people, she was most relaxed socially when at a garden party or on an organized picnic with other mums. As for sleep, when her body was tired, she simply went to bed, and generally this was around 9.30 and she would get up around 6 in the morning and help put a smile on the faces of her boys before they left the house for school.

Karen never understood the point of going out all night and being exhausted the next day from a hangover. At the same time, she didn't go around preaching her views; didn't think of herself as being lucky with her healthy body constitution, since she believed it was all down to her own making. As such she didn't need to read about psychology or about the pleasures of sex either. She had mostly a healthy sex life with Frank, for her it was natural, we had developed from single cell structures to human beings without analysis and she saw no reason to change, life was too short and simply she wanted to do things rather than just complain. There was however one passive pastime which she enjoyed to relax with, and that was reading, and over the years the bookshelf had changed, as each year she threw out the books she never wanted to read again, and only kept those which were in her opinion gems, and limited it down to 300 books, now in her new house and no longer sharing a book cabinet with Frank, since she now had her own and planned to gradually increase the amount of books to 500.

That autumn and now living on a new posh estate and being surrounded with all the other young mums; Karen didn't at first feel like a fish out of water. She was busy with her family duties and living in her own world, but obviously the neighbors wanted to get to know something about her. Karen was the kind of woman who took everything in around her, and when she met new people, she simply was a good listener, not out of shyness, but out of curiosity, as such despite being very different to most of the others on the estate, she got to know them all very quickly.

Unlike the others whose lives were to a certain extent dictated by Coronation Street, the real-life soap operas from her part of Garstang were enough gossip for her. Wife swapping parties were common, secret affairs a fact of life she often wondered if anyone knew about events close to her heart other than those of her youngest sister, and regarding those that took place in the workplace of she and Frank outside of their marriage. There were times when she wondered if she should come clean before someone brought it all out into the open, but instead she decided to take a chance; and given, it was all a part of her past, she saw no need in bringing it up, but at times she often wondered if someone outside of the four concerned had an idea. In fact, there was a lot of ignorance regarding her private life; neither the spouses of Karen, the headmistress from Garstang High or her boss knew what happened behind their backs, only she, herself was aware.

By this time as she looked back, she realized that there were occasions when she had been totally absorbed in her own world and was placing her life at the university as being more important than anything else. Frank worked hard, but at home he just wanted to enjoy his time with his family, and with Karen in the workplace being frustrated from not enough passion at home when her boys were small, and with herself now being older, she could see that Frank's unfaithfulness was a reflection on her own neglect of her nest. If she wanted to know the answer as to who had slept behind the others' backs first, she would have to confront Frank, since she really wanted to know the answer to this. One thing she knew was that they were both being true to each other, she had to trust him and of course no one was perfect in a marriage, simply for her there was no sense in her telling Frank that he wasn't the only one, and in finding out who committed the adultery first would had only led to a lack of trust and to marital disaster.

As for Frank, he had been so busy with his family that he never thought about how and why the children were conceived and wondered why in the modern world there much talk and fuss regarding the politics around parenthood. As for his one and only affair, he wasn't at all comfortable with it, and as much as he knew deep down that he had been feeling neglected at the time with Karen, he would always feel guilt and shame while at the same time pure bliss that Karen never found out and that he had what was the most important thing in his life; his own family with the woman he adored. For him the best he could do was to forget about the past, he had wronged Karen, but equally wasn't going to hurt her about something, which she didn't need to find out about.

One morning Karen went around to one of the neighbors who had invited her for a visit. She rang the bell and Jane opened the door. "Come in Karen." Said Jane, who was a well-dressed attractive lady with striking well-kept wavy brown hair.

"Hi Jane, this is Amy." Amy simply looked; Karen took off her baby's shoes, before moving onto her own feet. They hadn't come from far and the weather was still mild, so they didn't bring much in the way of outdoor clothes and Karen was wearing a simple dress as usual. They made their way into the living room and Amy was content since she had some toys to play with. On the coffee table tea and scones were being served, Karen's eyes darted around the room admiringly as her eyes fell onto the nice framed and enlarged family photographs. "Beautiful photographs." Said Karen admiringly as she then thought of doing something similar in her own home.

"Yes, they are, but my husband left me for a woman half his age!" She said seeking sympathy since she was still pining.

"What a bastard! I'm sorry Jane, I shouldn't have said that."

"I'm 43 he is 41 and he is living with a 21 years old university student." She said dolefully and with elegance and poise.

"Some people are so selfish." As a decoy from her own perfect life, Karen spoke about the tragedies surrounding her sister. As such Jane started to open somewhat more, but of course she wanted to anyway, and Karen wanted to listen to her friend in need.

"It all began last year, my husband runs a building firm, you know what it's like; they work away from home a lot." Karen then thought to herself typical, while Jane continued. "And well our younger child had just started secondary school, it can be very lonely; and I had an affair with one of his builders, I was desperate, I wanted to see what it was like with someone else . . . It wasn't any different, anyways feeling guilty I had to own up, get it off my chest and apologize." With that Karen froze inside, but felt that she was being watched, and carefully controlled her body language, and gave the impression of being just a sympathetic ear. "Anyway, he went cold, couldn't forgive, and left me for the woman he is with now, you know, I think he planned it all out this way."

Later that evening Karen told Frank about Jane, he was none too impressed. "I'd stay well clear of her, she's trouble!"

"What are you on about?" She said terrified in case He'd been sleeping with her, or some other unknown dirty woman.

"She only told you half the story. The woman he is living with now is a trainee solicitor, and it all came out when she was at work and read that Jane is divorcing him on the grounds of him not consummating the marriage and that she was worried that he was giving too much attention to their daughter, this was her dirty way of fighting to get full custody as well as the house . . . . Anyways the woman he is living with now, the solicitor, told her boyfriend at the time who was an employee of Jane's then husband about the letter, and he thought that the net was closing in on him . . . and so he confessed that he was the one sleeping behind both his boss and his girlfriend's back! The next thing is, this solicitor stormed round to his house, Jane's then husband, with her boyfriend and everyone looked on in shock as she read out the letter. The kids were even listening, must have been really embarrassing. Jane ordered the young couple out, but the girl simply said that she wasn't going anywhere until this was all sorted out. Things went quiet then Jane's lover blurted out, "She said to me that, she is allergic to him physically and that the kids don't love him and that they only want him for his money!"

Jane started going crazy, the boyfriend ran out, then Jane started screaming, police, police, I want the police. Then the solicitor replied quietly, "I am the law and I am not going anywhere until this is all sorted out." Jane then looked at the children and said, "Come on we are leaving." She said about to faint.

"Mummy we are not leaving our daddy." Said the son, while the daughter ran back to her room. Everything happened so quickly and then the husband offered his wife keys to any of the vacant new properties on our estate, of her choice; then on being given the keys she simply fled and left. The next day she went looking for her young lover, but he had simply gone back to live with his parents in Longridge. As for the girl, she was too scared to go back to her flat with her boyfriend and that is basically how they got together.

"How do you know all this?" She said gob smacked.

"Just come upstairs and I will show you." Together they walked upstairs and looked at the painting of Silverdale admiringly.

"People can see for miles in the country and are all ears to the surroundings." He said to her as she started to giggle somewhat.

"I know, the whole of Silverdale and probably the whole of the Morecambe had plenty to say about the silly schoolgirl who went off in search of you!" Said Karen sentimentally and dreamily.

"Well, we have shown everyone we were made for each other." He said. She then feeling breathless went up to his face kissed him, which with their passion led to them making love.

As for fashion, her hair had always been long: she wore dresses for practical reasons and to show off her womanly curves, and would usually go for colors, which blended in with the country, such as blue or green dresses. Outside in winter when it was cold she would of course add some layers, but not wanting to fuss too much spending hours going backwards and forwards to the departmental stores in Preston, she was happy being all woman, and unlike the other young ladies who would come as far away from the Fylde Coast, and with their partners drive up and park at the top of Scorton at Higher Lane wearing their high heeled shoes and dressed up to the nines and ready for the half a mile trek to the top of Nicky Nook and the ten minute rest before the walk down followed by the pub lunch and the drive back into Blackpool, she herself was a natural, and walked happily for miles. It didn't matter who she was with, she walked out in her country clothes from her house and although dressed simply, she simply stood as out as being a woman of a most feminine kind. Basically, her style hadn't changed since Frank first met her, and still turning most men's heads she certainly had no desire to change. Equally she found dresses to be practical too for her during her pregnancies.

Just before Christmas on December 14th and two peaceful weeks after her baby's due date, Karen gave birth to Kerry named after her dear mother. Christmas was of course one of sleepless nights, the boys coming into manhood were a little embarrassed as to having baby sisters, one would had been special, but two when their parents should in their view be thinking about middle age was a little too much for them, but neither would had offended their loving parents in any way, and were grateful for the protective environment they grew up in, and most importantly of all, they didn't have to share a room with each other.

The new year came in Karen was about to be 34 and Frank 38, and their children were aged 17, 14 years, and the babies 19 months and about to be 1 month. Karen was of course very tired, but thankful for having had a winter birth, so that she could enjoy the spring and summer with her baby. One of their favorite authors was Thomas Hardy. Both had read the novel, Tess of the D'Urbervilles several times, and both were looking forward to the debut screening of the showing of the cinema release at Lancaster. As such they decided to spend Easter at Silverdale. One evening they took the train into Lancaster and went to the cinema. While Karen had already read the book, seeing the film brought the characters such as Tess, Angel and Alec into a new dimension. Although Amy, her youngest sister was no poor girl like the character portrayed by Nastassja Kinski, or Hugh, the man she had only seen on the cover of a newspaper like the male co-star, she simply drew striking resemblances between him and Alec the seedy and creepy character in the film.

One thing for sure, the night out for them was a night to remember, unlike most of her contemporaries who were watching their TV a few hours a day and had no idea as to what they were viewing, the Taylor's felt that whenever they saw a film, that they were almost a part of it, and would remember with passion the screenings forever. On top of that as Karen thought more about Tess, she started to see more of this girl in herself, and when she thought about the time when Angel left her for something which she confessed to doing before they met, it would over time become increasingly an important sign in her life that she had done right in simply forgetting about the time when Frank and she slept behind each other's backs. Frank would have of course forgiven her, but what if some unknown pressure entered the family on top of her infidelity, with marriages starting to break down over silly little things, there was no sense in placing her marriage at a higher risk of divorce, which neither she nor Frank would ever want.

While neither Karen nor Frank were very philosophical regarding everything, deep in their hearts, they knew that they were showing a good example for all of their children and would quite naturally as parents hope that their children would one day end up like their parents and create stable and loving homes for their offspring since they knew only too well what Amy had caused.

During the Summer Mark came into adulthood, while Karen and Frank's lives were by then settled, they had done well, while they were not super rich, they were comfortable because both of them were careful and didn't waste their money, and thanks to both their love of the outdoors and country life, and great escapes into the wilds, they led very interesting lives, Frank would keep up with his cycling to work and going out with his wife walking around the fringes of Bowland, while Karen made sure that the family was well nourished as possible not just in calories and carbohydrate but also regarding vitamins, minerals and fiber. While of course they would always be lovers of the Lake District, they found themselves appreciating more and more the scenic beauties, which were right on their doorstep, and this in turn led to them wanting to spend more time in their garden and getting on with their flowers and trees as well as mowing the lawn. By then Frank was pretty much aware of where the prized pebbles' origins were, and in order not to upset his boys, who sometimes valued the stones, he made sure that Amy didn't move them away from their sacred locations.

Going away less, also gave them an excuse to get a dog, and they would often be seen walking with their sheepdog Bes, around the local landmarks in their lives such as: Scorton and Nicky Nook as well as Calder vale, which was no longer too painful for her to visit, for that, the baby slings were required since the pram although made for two, wasn't much use off road. As for the cat, she would continue to come and visit them since Bes was such a mild- mannered sort. On top of that, their newly acquired hamsters would continue playing a role as long as their children were still at home. In a short while they, Karen and Frank, are not forgotten in this novel but from now on the attention moves onto Mark.

Chapter Six

June: Mark, and His Lost Pebbles.

W hile waiting for his A-Level results Mark was working in Patterdale at a youth hostel in the Lake District. The wardens were from Fleetwood, and as cyclists they knew Mark's Garstang very well, but now busy running a place for 80 guests meant that they were too busy to visit Lancashire; and Ullswater was anyway for them their Garden of Eden. The work was a little repetitive, mainly washing up the dishes, serving the meals, helping prepare meals, tidying and cleaning the rooms, but Mark was happy. Since the place wasn't a hotel, the atmosphere was relaxed and although standards were high, they were not neurotic, the guests or more commonly known as hostellers, were usually down to earth walkers and cyclists after all, and were attracted to the homely feel of the place. It was in this environment that many romances had begun, when people would meet up on a walk in the Lake District and find themselves heading down the valley to the same youth hostel, or maybe they would meet at dinner, or in the grounds of the building, and meeting a new friend in what was for many people their hobby's, since The Lake District and hosteling was a good way in which to get to know the real person.

During his days off he would go cycling around the national park and stay overnight at different hostels. In total he was there 3 months and during his days off he managed to spend the night at all the hostels in the lakes for free, which meant a bed as well as three tasty and nutritious meals at each stopover.

Moreover, and apart from being lonely in the middle of August he received some bad news when he was still away in Cumbria. His grades were disappointing so as such he wouldn't be studying Politics and German at Lancaster. Fortunately, as a backup, he had applied to Hull, normally a university like Lancaster it acquired good grades, but for some reason it was more lenient in the Dutch department, of which he just scraped in.

Late September arrived, and he left his beloved lakes, and went to visit his family. While there he noticed that his sisters had changed somewhat and after just a couple of days with his parents and brother who was always out with his girlfriend this made for him life his own personal life frustrating. Even so he was pleased that his brother was in love with a nice girl from Dolphinholme. Mark went on to Hull, by train from Preston and with his bike. His accommodation was in Cottingham to the west of Hull and he shared a house with 6 other students. Anna and Alison were very snotty and together they took an instant dislike to the others since they had arrived there first and wanted to own the place. On top of that the others were couples and madly in love. Longing for love Mark wasn't exactly over the moon with this situation, so he would have to plan his leisure outside of the house.

There were many clubs at the university and Mark was spoilt for choice, but when he tried them out, he found them to be simply a place to drink alcohol and nothing more, but the best place to spend the night with a woman. On his nights out, he usually only French kissed although he wanted to go further, he found it pointless since he didn't really like these women who simply wanted to sit around and do nothing, and he decided that simply going out and meeting drunk women wasn't the best place for him to find true love. Equally whenever he went out cycling or swimming, he found himself very much on his own.

As for his studies, his Dutch course was basically easy enough. At the beginning of the course students were divided into two groups: those who were advanced learners and those who were beginners. The beginners were those who had no A-Levels in a Germanic Language, while the advanced were those who had at least one parent who was Dutch or Flemish. As for Mark he simply and clearly felt that he was in no man's land and would shuttle between the two tiers the coming semesters. Christmas was a happy family affair; he spent three weeks at his family home and his sisters enjoyed playing with him. Given the course wasn't so difficult there wasn't too much studying to do and he was able to spend a lot of time with his sisters, which was to his mother's delight, and his dad was pleased when everyone was happy.

While playing with Amy and Kerry his own childhood came back to him and he remembered how different his mum was back then. Simply put she was much more of a mother with her younger two kids since she wasn't putting her career at the same importance as before, even so her priority was always for her family and now living in Hull and seeing firsthand the social problems of broken families there, he knew that his childhood had been blessed. Even so with her more relaxed attitude to her career and with the children now toddlers she was doing some research work for her university department and Karen like Frank were simply managing to save lots of money, since although they wanted to live nicely, they didn't need to have the most expensive products.

At the end of his first year, Mark passed both of his semester exams easily and went back to the Lakes for the summer. Given he was well known throughout the hostels his position was as an assistant relief warden, which was no longer based at one hostel. Instead, he would help wherever they were short staffed, and this was to his great delight and was indeed a mild promotion. Matthew and Elizabeth stayed over a few times, and Mark managed a summer romance with a colleague before it finished as she started university down in Exeter.

Back at Hull things were tiresome, where he lived nobody spoke to him, and only he cooked food in the house, while the others simply dialed a pizza. By then he hated the course, but without a clue as to what he would do if he left, he had no intention of giving up on the course. He could of course have continued working in the youth hostels, but sadly he didn't see much of a future in that since the pay wasn't very high. The salary might have been low, but workers got free accommodation as well as food, but like the other students working there, they simply valued their worth by the rate of pay they were getting, and were dreaming about the highly paid jobs, which they all felt that they deserved.

That autumn something hideous happened as he saw it, he had by then become a good dancer in order to impress the women, even found himself dancing to soul from acts such as: Shalamar, James Brown and 2 tone bands, as such he was seen as a very open minded being who loved black music, but thanks to his housemates who had a TV he became well aware of Wham. He wanted to simply dismiss this pop duo as a pair of pansies, but all the girls on his course could think of nothing else other than Andrew and George. Now while back in Garstang it was absolutely fine to make fun out of Marilyn, Boy George and Soft Cell on the liberal university campus which had many promising future Labour activists, Mark's views were seen as bigoted, as such he vented out his frustration by cycling, and his love-hate relationship with going out at night would continue until he found the girl of his dreams, while he felt that he was languishing on a second rate degree course.

At the end of the year, he went back to his parents for Christmas, and after one night out in Garstang and seeing ghoulish teenage girls dressed like Boy George, he decided to simply walk around the area by day and sit with his family during the evenings. Spring came, and he saw some light from the fact that he would be away from Hull or Hell, as he called it at the end of his sophomore exams. That Easter, Frank celebrated his 40th just over one month after his actual birthday. Mark came over for

Easter as usual and was expected to entertain at home in celebration of his dad and to DJ, and even sing, which he did very well and received more standing ovations than his own father. David and Doreen came around for the celebration, but like Karen they were very busy with their young children and although they were very friendly towards one another they were not so often in touch with each other.

In June he went off to Belgium in search of some work and went to Nijlen in Belgian Flanders. Nijlen had a youth hostel, and was run by a young Flemish couple, they had two babies who were not much older than him and were grateful of his help. The wardens were Bart and Chantelle, both happy in love and wanted him to enjoy his stay with them. The site was in a forest not far from Antwerp, but with so many visitors he never needed to venture far, unless he wanted to go off cycling or swimming between shifts. Once again, the pay was poor, but Mark saw it as a steppingstone since he would have some work experience abroad and maybe meet some girls. As for the women, he met plenty, and this time he wasn't worried about how much he liked them and started to have sex with some of them during the summer, while receiving letters from home, mainly from his mother about how pleased she was to see Matthew in love. Mark, although he was still happy for his brother, didn't want it rammed down his throat, since he was becoming increasingly desperate for a steady relationship.

Summer started to fade and then it was time to go onto his year of foreign study at Maastricht University. This was to be the highlight of his studies, and there he learned more Dutch than the previous two-year put together in probably the same amount, of months. On top of that the girls enjoyed cycling, and as such he was a little bit spoiled for choice, but in the end, he ended up dating a brunette called Sandra. She was tall, slim and beautiful, together they enjoyed the Indonesian restaurants, visits by bike to Vaals and the "Drie Landen Punt," which literally translates at being the frontier of three countries, those being: The Netherlands, Belgium and Germany. Mark and Sandra enjoyed swimming together, but she didn't like the UK. As for pebbles, well given she wasn't in anyway romantic, while he was too afraid to show this modern woman, the sensitive and tender side of his colorful character.

Even so Mark had a bright idea for her to visit Garstang, so that maybe she would fall in love with his beloved neck of the woods, and she had never visited England anyway. The visit was to some extent an eye opener. Sandra decided that England was a strange place and wanted to lie in bed all day while Mark wanted to show her the sights. One day Mark wanted to take her out on a bike ride around the Trough of Bowland, in the end she decided to spend the day with Karen and his sisters. As such Mark decided to go out cycling on his own for the day. He was clearly enjoying setting off out on his bike when just after a few minutes a pretty brunette smiled at him, and he then slammed his brakes on to a halt. It was half term holiday, and she looked very much like a girl studying for her A-Levels, and for him there was something really special about her; but when he found out that Louise was not quite 16, he decided that he had better continue with the girlfriend he already had, and anyway he was going back to the Netherlands the following week. Back at his mums after his ride around the Trough, the visit that February finished a few days later and then he could forget about Louise and get on with his life back on the continent.

Back in Masstricht with Sandra, the first few weeks were pleasant enough, but with no sign of either living in the other one's country after the academic year, the relationship was going nowhere. In June, just before his departure he hadn't given her any pebbles, which for Mark with her would have been a waste of romance. As such when he left the following summer she simply met a wealthy man, who had been chasing her as soon as she got back home to her parents in Nijmegan and before she had a chance to decide who she loved, she fell pregnant to this older man who was desperate for a child and found herself trapped with a man whom she didn't like, yet she took it all in her cool stride.

● ● ●

One of Colin's partners in the law office, Neil, had decided to leave his wife for him, and had already left his family and was living in a bedsit since he could no longer live the lie. He felt so lonely and wanted Colin to move in with him, and when he saw that this was unlikely to happen voluntarily, he decided that, if Colin wanted to really stay with his wife, he would have to confess his double life to her. Knowing that the truth was about to come out, Colin took his wife, Jane, out for dinner. The setting was a posh Italian Restaurant at Lytham St. Annes; the Spanish waiter there knew about Colin but was very discreet and paid all his attention to the lady, when serving the meal so as not to arouse any suspicion, since he had slept with all the four closet homosexual solicitors connected with Colin. "Do you know I want to spend the rest of my life with you?" He smiled at her, as he held her hands.

"Yes, I do." But she found his remark a little strange.

"You have always been and will always be the woman of my life." He said as though he was eating his last supper.

"I know dear." But inside she was somewhat bewildered.

"I am through with my gay phase." He confessed breezily.

"I know darling." She didn't know, but simply felt that this was the best way in encouraging him to get this off his chest. She then kissed him on his lips, while he was left wondering how she knew, while just like him, she simply wanted her family intact.

Back in his office his business partner had fled along with the petty cash in their safe amounting to ten thousand pounds and while Colin spent the whole day wondering what was going on, he simply decided to put the past behind him and to spend more time with his wife and wished he hadn't mentioned about his past, but of course, Neil had since telephoned her but he would never know, since, like Karen, Vivienne felt the best way was to act as though nothing had happened, and since not many men were as wholesome as Frank she was happy enough with her own husband.

In the summer of 1984 and Matthew and Elizabeth got married and had recently moved into one of the barns on her parent's farm, as such aged just 18 they were quite an interesting couple for the other singles on the 6th form courses, since couples were settling down later than in their parent's day. The wedding was held at Garstang and this time Colin was behaving less arrogantly towards Frank, and seemed to be more possessive of Vivienne, his wife too. With Matthew no longer at home, his bedroom was re decorated from its boyish appearance to one fit for a princess, and as such his sister Kerry moved into it.

The wedding was the reason why Mark couldn't stay on the continent and instead found himself back in the Lake District. Once again, the big Taylor wedding event took place at Silverdale, and all eyes were on Mark, since he was the older of the brothers, yet there was still no sign of him settling down. He was then 21 years of age, then his father was already working in a job he liked, had a wife he adored and was saving money to get his own place. Mark also felt a little used, because had he stayed abroad he would had gone back to Nijlen, and with it being not so far from Nijmegan he might have had a few more months with his beloved Sandra who had of course by then called it off, and of course with him coming from a family who settled down very young he was a bit of a hot topic, until Frank reminded everyone about his two older siblings and while Beatrice smiled, the sweat was pouring off Colin and Vivienne tried to soothe him by holding his hand and smiling radiantly at everyone, and after a few moments he calmed down and bravely smiled.

As such Mark started his final year at Hull miserably, but at least he was able to pass the degree with upper second-class honors. Summer came and then aged 22, he knew that he had wasted 4 years on the mickey mouse course, which had he decided to go and live in the Netherlands, would have been at least of some use, instead he decided with it being the 1980s and he interested in politics, to go on a European Studies course for his master's at Hull. Once again, he was working in the lakes for the youth hostel association and as a summer relief warden he was once again moving around depending on where the demand was greatest, once again this suited him very well and he once again saw virtually the whole of the park. Just before the master's course began, he enjoyed walking his sisters to school during much of September, and thanks to Frank's teaching, they would enthusiastically explain to Mark where the pebbles came from. Karen, his mum, had also returned to work at the university, but made sure that she wouldn't be working too many hours, since her priority remained looking after her daughters, Frank and her boys whenever they needed her.

In October 1985 Mark was back in Hull for his studies and of course with his year spent on the Dutch, German and Belgian border two academic years earlier he brought in valuable discourse onto the course, and after one year spent mainly in his room, he passed the course. Mark was of course proud of his academic achievements, but if only he could swap his Dutch for German and European studies for Politics, then he would really be able to arm himself with a striking CV, instead he was after the summer starting a safe and secure job in the civil service as an executive officer and spent July and August working for the YHA once more. Meanwhile during early summer Wham disbanded, and Mark jumped for joy, knowing that the person whom he reluctantly shared his birthday with was no longer the topic of conversation in his circles, or at least that was what he hoped, made him smile. He could have taken on the same job 5 years earlier, and once again it turned out that his degrees were of no real use. As such on September the 1st he started work at Lancaster. The job was awful, he hated sitting in front of junior officers and keeping an eye on them all day making sure that they were filing correctly, but at least during the weekends he had some money to go out around the clubs in Lancaster where he would meet women on his one-night stands.

Around this time two girls he knew from his days as an entertainer contacted him. Both lived in Calder Vale and were at the time of his discos a little childish for him. Joanna was blond and very pretty, while Carole, also pretty, was rather shy, neither would have done for him, but both only went to his discos for some childish fun. Even so, Joanna wanted to visit him on her horse at his home one morning in Garstang but was offended when he asked her to meet him in the town since he wasn't sure as to what his parents might think. Another time he went cycling past her home on his way to Bleasedale and Joanna started screaming at him. The strangest of all was the first time they met. Joanna came up to him while he was on the stage, poked him in his eyes and told him that, he was a weird guy, that she was happily there with her new boyfriend, but that Mark was more attractive, but couldn't be with him, that being Mark, since he looked too much like a weirdo.

Now five years later, both girls were working and by chance while cycling and nearly smashing into her horse as she was losing control, they arranged to go out for a night out with Carole. As such they went in Carole's car to a disco in Morecambe where they started to French kiss, both were enjoying it, until Carole pushed herself away from him on the grounds that she felt that he went around shagging anyone and had no intention of settling down. Mark was offended and hurt and had no intention of being in the same venue as her until 2AM. As such before midnight he ended up walking back pissed off through the streets of Lancaster back home to Scorton at around dawn, after walking a distance 13 miles, and wearing clothing which was fine in the office but inappropriate indeed for walking through the streets.

Without a steady partner in his life, he very quickly felt that his life was going nowhere, he hated his job, had no romance, and just wanted to escape and felt at times like one lost pebble. As such he planned to leave on the first day of spring go to the Netherlands and to see where his life would take him, and from Christmas, he would save as much money as possible and take up loads of cycling at the weekends. As the days leading up to his departure were getting closer, his carefree self and friendly out-going personality were becoming infectious to those around him, even at work, but he was still viewed by all and sundry as a man who was too impulsive when it came to love, and no one believed that he could ever find what he wanted. Or was he simply the apple of his father's eyes? Didn't Frank on impulse sleep with Jill

• • •

in order to get his Karen? Of course the late 1980s were different and much more cynical than the early 60s and Mark believed that on the continent that things were a little bit more romantic than in Lancashire, and that Sandra was nothing like the other Dutch girls he had met, but had simply ended up with her partly because of the physical attraction, and before he had given the other sweeter and more submissive girls a chance, who like Mark, would go anywhere around the world for love.

Chapter Seven

July: One Pebble Searching for A Home.

The first day of spring arrived on March 21st in 1987. After having breakfast with his parents and sisters, who were very sad to see their big brother leaving; he brought his saddlebags downstairs and placed them in the hallway, while Amy and Kerry looked on at them with a little disgust. He then opened the door, placed the bags onto his bike and kissed his mum who was then wanting to burst into tears but knew she was being watched and decided to hold her breath instead. Frank put his arms around him, and then the girls wanted to hang onto him like leeches with all their might and prevent him from going. "Have a good time, Mark." Said his mother.

"Make sure that you have enough condoms with you." Said Frank, who wanted to lighten things up a little bit, to Karen's horror since her girls were listening in.

"Don't be so disgusting . . . and if it doesn't work out, you know where your home is." Said Karen, who was still holding back the tears, with the others looking somewhat sad too.

"I know that mum, I'll be back for college in September."

He then got onto his bicycle and set off and waved back to his family who were waving back at him too. Fondly he continued and went through his sleepy town. By now he was to some extent away from the gossip, since as he continued down into Bowgreave less people knew who he was, apart from those who went to the same local school as both himself and those of his family, which seemed to be just about everyone.

As he reached Catterall he was starting to feel that the day was becoming adventurous, but then he noticed the tall slim and attractive brunette called Louise walking along the pavement. She was then 19 and had just celebrated her birthday the week before, had spoken to him a few times when he passed by on his bike since that fateful day when they met each other three years earlier. During his final two years at Hull whenever he came home on a visit, he often met her when she was walking, cycling and once at the indoor pool. She was now a university student and like Mark came from a very sheltered background, she smiled shyly at him, as he pulled up towards her. She noticed that his bike was blatantly fully laden. "Hi Mark, where are you going?" She asked smiling.

"I'm off cycling all over Europe." He said manly.

"I wish that I was going there with you." She said to him without realizing what was coming out of her mouth.

"I wish that you were coming with me . . . look I just want you to know that I should have said yes to you, when I told you that I did not want to get involved with a fifteen-year-old I meant it, but when I get back, I want you to be my girlfriend." He said sincerely.

"Don't be stupid, you will find plenty of nice foreign girls, and you'll settle down there." She said, wanting to escape from him, and felt somewhat uncomfortable as he looked into her eyes; she then looked on passionately, and nervously preened her hair.

"And what if I don't, maybe I really like you Louise, and anyways college starts for me in September." He started wanting to show her he liked her, while at the same time he didn't want to come on too strong towards her.

"We shall see . . . But if you are serious, then you had better write to me, look my friends are coming and we are going out on a trip to Manchester." He then kissed her hand as they both looked on at each other quietly before kissing her forehead and trying to French kiss, but suddenly she pushed him away, as her friends arrived and she was holding back the strong emotions she had for this man she hadn't forgiven in turning her down when she was underage, since her dad met her own mother when he was 20 and she was 15. As such Louise was filled with both love and hatred for him as well as being besotted with jealousy. He didn't deserve her, but at the same time he was leaving anyway and the desires running through her bosom were getting the better of her.

Fortunately, the car arrived just in time to release her from her confusion and Julie pulled in at the layby and pulled down her window and in the back three other young ladies were sitting waiting. "Come on Louise you can see the traffic let's just get there!" Louise then walked to the car as Mark started to set off on his bicycle. It was her birthday treat and she was looking forward to buying some clothes with the money, which her relatives had given her.

"Where is he off?" Asked Julie, as the other girls who were from Julie's village, Quernmore high up and at the foot of the wonderful Clougha Pike, close to Lancaster, and not from Louise's college sat there quietly.

"On a bike tour." She said but the somewhat subdued tone of her voice sounded as though she wanted to change the subject.

"You let him go?" Said Julie, who although she was more impressed with cars, couldn't help but notice that she herself found him attractive. Suddenly Louise started to feel as though a panic attack was on its way to her, and it was now or never for her.

"I'm sorry I can't go to Manchester; I need to see him."

"Ok, I will pull in here . . . Good luck!" Said Julie who was excited and pleased that her friend had found someone nice. Louise then got out of the car, which drove off and as Mark was approaching his bike sturdily, she looked at him delightedly.

"Mark!" She called. He then looked up surprised and was slightly licking his lips. Before he had a chance to speak.

"Why don't you come back to mine for a drink?" He then without thinking slammed his brakes, nearly smashing into a bus in the process, which really frightened the living daylights out of Louise.

"I'd love to." He said completely unaware of his near, death experience. "I don't think that I will make the Peak District tonight."

"I don't think that you will be going anywhere tonight." As soon as she said this, she felt cheap, and wished she hadn't said such a thing, but after three solid years of on and off waiting for him, her mouth had erupted with a warm flow of volcanic passion.

"Yeah, sure I can just imagine the look on your parents faces." He also said out of control, as they both wanted each other.

"They won't be back tonight." Said Louise who was so excited and by then had almost forgotten that she had nearly created an accident and was a little ashamed of her behavior.

As soon as she had finished speaking the earth stood shatteringly still for them. That moment they both knew fully well what was going to happen; with them finding each other incredibly sexy after what seemed like a lifetime of longing for each other since when they first met. With her womanly curves the first time that they had met three years earlier; she had been the embodyment of all woman for him, if only she been just a few months older, they would as it seemed had been together for already three years. He met her since that fateful day when they first met on his return visits from Hull or Maastricht, but the feelings she had for him were never quite the same whenever they were together, since he turned her down to her dismay the first time they met and they simply just chatted briefly as he stopped off while he was out somewhere on his bike training. Even so she had spent lots of time thinking about him, as she walked along the canal or into Garstang where she would be hoping to catch a glimpse of him, and without any conscience of what she was doing on this early spring day, with the blossom in flower combined with temperatures, which made one forget that winter existed was enough to make her cheeks go red with sunburn, excitement, and shyness, as they walked slowly to her house.

• • •

STEVEN KAY

They then walked up through the driveway of her house smiling, he leant his bike against the wall. "Don't leave your bike here, I will open up the garage." The garage was then opened, he wheeled his bike inside as she waited outside, he then left, and she closed the garage door behind. Then she unlocked and open-ed the door of her house and they both walked inside together into her living room.

"What would you like to drink?" She asked him.

"Surprise me." He said and then sat down on the couch while she then walked off into the kitchen where she then peeled some bananas and apples, which were lying next to a jug of milk with dirty mugs lying all over a table, since her mum was away.

After a few minutes she then entered the living room, with two milkshakes, gave him a drink and sat down on the couch next to him as they started drinking a drink very slowly, which had been made full of passion. "Um this is delicious, what is it?"

"Don't be so nosey!" She giggled passionately at him.

"I know milk, bananas and some apples." Trying to impress.

"So why did you ask!" She said wanting to sound cheeky. He then started to massage her, she wasn't ready for this, she hardly knew him after all, but on the other hand she had thought about him for the last three years and had since them met him several times.

"Come on, drink up and let's go for a walk along the river." He looked at her she giggled once again and she then froze as they were eyes to eyes, face to face, nose to nose, lips to lips, hand to hand, and in no time at all they started to French Kiss, both were able to kiss for a long time, and with his amorous tongue she felt as though they had made love. He then tried to take off her clothes, but she had already decided that she wanted to enjoy something with him before they would make love while from his kissing on the couch for her this exact spot is quite simply where their love began.

They then left the house walking hand in hand together, it was a little muddy, but as a down-to-earth country girl she didn't care. They carried on walking off the beaten track as the vegetation became denser and soon, they stopped walking. "You really know how to French Kiss." She said when they were meant to be working out how to continue walking through the bushes. He then placed his hands on her cheeks as they started to kiss. She pushed him away gasping for air as they then sat down together, with Mark seen massaging her back, he then starts to gently lick the back of her neck with his tongue as he places both of his hands on her bosom as she starts to then become breathless. The sun comes out and then they simply lose control and run off towards a hillock and undress each other before making love with great passion. Still happily stunned with events they both got dressed and continued walking with a very tight grip on his right hand and her left hand as the two lovebirds walked back together, and what a sight they both were with their mud-stained clothes but neither of them gave a damn.

It was certainly a much more fulfilling walk back than neither of them could had anticipated in their wildest dreams just a few hours earlier than when they woke up earlier that same morning, for Mark his travels were completely out of his thoughts, while for her he was a romantic boy just like the ones she read about in her novels. As they approached her house it started to rain. "I think that we had better take off our shoes before we go inside, I'll come back with my dad's slippers for you." After opening the door, he gave her his shoes. She then ran into the shower; Mark knew that she was teasing him as he heard that she had the shower turned on and as such he banged on her bathroom window.

"Hey Louise, it is raining out here!" He said annoyed.

"When you are a bit cleaner you can come inside, just go around the back, and I will just throw you some soap through the bathroom window, after I have washed all of the dirt off me!" Louise wasn't so stupid as her moment of recklessness had made her out to be, and she knew that she had to wash herself properly inside and out. On top of that he had kept her waiting three years for him, so it didn't matter to her that he was waiting a few minutes outside for her. By then he was starting to shiver as he was starting to feel very cold and very wet and could simply wait no more.

"I am going to jump inside the shower!" He said.

"Go on then!" She said feeling turned on by everything about him. Clumsily he climbed in through the window and then slid down to the bathroom floor and walked into the shower, as they both had a water fight with a plastic tub, which was lying around filled it up with cold water and they started throwing the water around each other as they were fighting for the supremacy of this act. She knew what was going to happen, so then she left the shower leaving him there to warm up and just to make sure than to be sorry she filled up a large bucket with cold water opened the shower door and poured a bucketful of cold water all over his groins. As well as probably reducing the chances of conception he was embarrassed when his tool looked no more, but his insatiable appetite regarding his lust for her turned him once more into the machine, which sent both once more into heaven. Today was her perfect day, and that was all that mattered to her. Then as she was expecting he started to kiss her passionately and before long they were making love in the shower.

The rest of the day was spent as one would expect two love-birds to be doing and they slept cozily, and snuggly through the whole of the night. Louise woke up at the crack of dawn while Mark was still sleeping, as much as the day before had been destined to be one of joy, today would be one of hell. If her parents hadn't gone away, she wouldn't be feeling so guilty and ruined and found herself making love to the guy she might never be seeing again. If only her parents weren't coming back until tomorrow, then at least she wouldn't need to be feeling so broken. Had he been able to stay another day her chances of being with him until death do us part would had multiplied, but for now at least, she had one thing to worry about and vowed that in two weeks' time she would go out on a night out and celebrate her lucky escape from motherhood, which she felt that had she spent another day with him was inevitable.

They had breakfast together, the house looked a complete mess, but that was the least of her worries, after breakfast he got all his belongings ready, his bike and as he was sitting on his saddle Louise was standing next to him. "I don't normally make love so quickly . . . You do believe me that you are my second?" She said feeling cheap.

"Of course, I do, I know your background quite well . . . You come from good stock." Louise then smiled and then they started to kiss but not too long since his mind was elsewhere, she knew why but was hoping to hear something really tender from him.

"I meant what I said . . . I will be back for you in September."

"I know that, Mark." But inside she was very sad but tried her best not to intimidate him and looked away from him slowly and was begging silently for him to stay.

Mark wasn't sure how he would cope with his 76 Mile journey to Eyam, since his mind was on Louise, he was wondering why one of them hadn't simply told him to stay; as such he felt like a complete idiot and was ashamed of himself too. Despite his devotion to her, he managed the ride as planned on the day he left his beloved lady. Each day he would wake up at 6AM, on day 3 he woke up near Grantham while day 4 began in Saffron Walden, only three days since the Lancashire Plains, and he was amazed how much lighter 6AM was which was partly as a result of him travelling eastwards where the dawn arrived that bit earlier.

As he stepped into the ship at Felixstowe docks, he felt as though he had made one hell big of a mistake, if only he hadn't met Louise he would now be looking forward to his adventures, but then again he had to do this journey, to get this once and for all adventure out of his system before settling down with Louise, but then again wouldn't her parents expect him to support her financially and what could he offer her since he hated at what he saw as being the, "Civil Service brain cell death camp," based in Lancaster and this frightened the living daylights out of him.

That evening Mark met a 20-year-old student called Nathalie Rochard, she was with her friends and lived near Brussels, they spoke a lot, but Mark didn't feel in any way attracted to her as he had been to Louise. The next day while he was having breakfast in the ship's restaurant, she came up to him. "Here is my address, you are very welcome to visit me." She said smiling.

"How about Friday?" He said pleased that he wasn't alone.

"Fine." She then walked off after receiving a limp wristed kiss on her cheeks from him and wasn't sure if he was himself a gentleman or just a pretty looking time waster.

A while later he left the ship and as he came close to the customs post he slowed down, but the customs officer waved him on and so he cycled more quickly. That day despite being tired, he managed to reach Geraadsbergen 60 miles inland, a small, pleasant town with rolling hills around and the following day after a good night's sleep he continued through the countryside and arrived at the village of Wauthier Braine, near Waterloo after cycling 30 miles (48KM). He then arrived at a traditional country house, parked his bicycle, pressed the doorbell and Nathalie arrived and opened the door. "Hello Mark, come in." She said.

He then followed Nathalie into her home. As he walked in, he noticed a very sweet girl, her sister, Mireille, aged 18 and as he was to find out her birthday was two weeks before Louise's. Longing for love, she is seen at the dining room table where he is heading. Mireille looks at him sentimentally as his smile slowly widens, they are both seen looking fondly at each other. "Mark this is my sister Mireille, Mireille this is Mark." She said as Mark and Mireille both look into each other's eyes radiantly and give each other a firm handshake and both wish that they were left alone in the room. "Well, I am going to take a shower". Said Nathalie and then she left to take her shower, and Mark was pleased so that he could get to know more about this amazing girl who took his mind off England. "Have you really cycled all the way from England?" Said Mireille as he stared at her and both wanting to break the ice.

"Yes, I have . . . are these your cigarettes?" He was almost shaking with excitement and although he knew that she wasn't the type to smoke, was looking for some common ground with her. She simply shook her head. "I don't smoke either, it really is a disgusting habit." He said, she then smiled and in return he smiled broadly.

"My sister smokes, these are her cigarettes." Mireille suddenly jumps up, walks into another room and comes back a moment later with a handmade armband. "This is for you." She then passes it to him, as they both seen with their eyes firmly locked into each other, as they could feel the earth move between them.

"Thank you." He said graciously, for him the present wasn't important, he just wanted to make her happy in some way.

As if from nowhere and through the outside kitchen door, Mrs. Rochard appeared and knowing that Nathalie had met Mark on the ship, invited him over as some friend on his travels, who could hardly speak French was enough to put this protective mum on her guard, and she noticed her youngest child giving him too much attention for her liking and this unnerved her. On seeing Mark, she smiled at him and sat down with him and Mireille. "So, what are you doing in Belgium?" Completely uninterested but wanting to act the part of a sociable adult, she knew all about oral finesse.

"I have decided that I want to work here." He said in his own way of wooing Mireille, who had taken his breath away as he had taken hers, while her mum was busy putting them under scrutiny.

"That's nice." Before the concerned mother had a chance to think any more seriously Nathalie appeared from and is seen looking tense as she notices how interested her sister is in him.

"We had better be going now." Said Nathalie.

"Have a good time." Said Mrs. Rochard, relieved that Mark was now in the hands of her older daughter who was still alone.

Although Mireille was 18 and was just 2 years younger than Nathalie, she wasn't interested in following her sister on a girls' night out in the city. She knew full well from his eyes that Mark wanted to be with her, but apart from by way of making a scene in showing herself up with her desire for this unknown identity,

• • •

she simply felt powerless. At that moment she decided to wait and to seduce him regardless of whether he would be taken up by her sister that night the following day, since nothing else mattered.

Later that evening Mark, Nathalie as well as her friends whom he had met in the ship, Celine and Lourdes were seen in the disco. "Wow! You really are a good mover!" Said Celine, he then took her by the arms, and they danced together. Being able to meet new cultures made Mark give off more of a glow from within, since he was away from the gossip and the stares of his own backyard, even so his mind was often elsewhere, and that was on Mireille.

Just around bedtime Mrs. Rochard caught Mireille as she was on her way to her bedroom. "I hope that Nathalie is safe being with him, I've never met a foreigner before." She said.

"I thought you considered the Flemings alien mother." She said as she was feeling hurt that her mother was standing in the way of her happiness, and she was finding it all too much.

"I did, I still do, but at least they can speak French."

"Well, I wish I had a boyfriend like him." She then looked at her mother waiting for a response; instead, her mother was lost for words, and suddenly nearing a panic in case her younger daughter was really going to chase this seemingly Don Juan.

"I'm going to bed, it's getting late, and I'm tired." Said the daughter. Mireille didn't sleep, she heard Mark return earlier than expected, this gave her hope that he was still free, she kept her ears to the ground as she drifted in out of her sleep as she was waiting for Mark to surface.

A few hours later Mark and Mireille were sitting eating breakfast together, Mrs. Rochard suddenly felt as though she was going to panic. "Mireille." She said. Mireille smiled at Mark.

"Excuse me." She then stood up and went into the kitchen.

"What are you doing falling for some guy you don't even know?" Said her mother who was starting to age with worry.

"I am eighteen and old enough to decide." Said Mireille, and then it looked as though a storm of discontent was brewing

• • •

between both mother and daughter even though their guest was listening.

"He has no job, he is a foreigner, and for all we know he might even be a criminal." Said Mrs. Rochard who was deeply confused since deep down she quite liked the look of him.

"Don't be so ridiculous he seems like a really nice guy." She said pleading in vain with her stubborn mother.

"He does, but he will not be staying here another night under our roof, he may come from a poor background and want to rob us." The mother didn't believe what she was saying, but didn't wish to take any chances, since she was a little bit scared of the consequences of something bad happening to her daughter. Mireille wanted to run out, but with Mark still there she did her best to remain in control and was embarrassed by her mother's behavior.

As it happened Mark had heard and understood more than an embarrassed Mrs. Rochard realized, and she then walked into the living room where Mark and Mireille were sitting silently. "Mrs. Rochard, I would like to thank you for everything, it has been a really pleasant stay, but I must be on my way since I am staying at a youth hostel and must arrive there in time." He said kindly.

"Oh! That is a bit sudden, let me just make you a packed lunch." She said as she was starting to warm to him, and wondering if maybe he should stay another night, then again, her daughter was young and had to respect her and she had to retain her authority.

"Thank you, that would be very nice of you." She then walked off, and he picked up the pen lying on the table and wrote down something on paper before handing it to Mireille.

"Mireille it was really nice meeting you, please write to me."

"I am really sorry about this; I am eighteen and old enough to." Mrs. Rochard appeared at that moment with the packed lunch for Mark, and Mireille sat silently, but inside she was full of emotion.

● ● ●

"Thank you, Mrs. Rochard, this is very kind of you." He then stood up kissed her on her cheek, before moving to Mireille who moved her face towards him as he kissed her on her cheeks, but being full face in front of her mother he didn't quite go to a kiss on Mireille's lips, but she wouldn't have refused him since she felt that it had nothing to do with her mother in any way at all. "Goodbye Mrs. Rochard, goodbye Mireille." A few moments later and after saying goodbye to Nathalie who had just got out of bed he left. Mrs. Rochard was relieved that he was departing, but equally her daughter had sown seeds of doubt into her, that her own judgement which she thought at first was sound, since she herself was becoming fond of Mark. As he left, Mireille looked at her mother.

"I hate you!" She then ran upstairs to her bedroom and locked herself angrily in there for a few hours stewing.

Back in those days it was about 50 pence a minute to telephone the UK from the near continent, which was a lot of money those days. Mark was feeling a little bit lost and confused and getting over the shock of a very appealing young lady whose mother wouldn't allow him to get anywhere near her, and now without any romance in the warm sunshine and wearing his cycling shorts and sunglasses, he went looking for a telephone kiosk. He then dialed. "Hi mum." He said after she had picked up the phone curiously.

"Hi Mark, how are you?" She said hoping that he was missing home and planning to return to his home very soon to her.

"I am having a great time here." He wasn't but didn't want his mum taking pity on him and telling him what to do with his life.

"There are some letters for you from a Louise." She said hopefully as Mark's face broadens as he breaks it out into a smile.

"I will let you know when you can post them onto me . . . Anyways I must go it is very expensive telephoning."

Louise was very much on his mind, what did she want from him? What was in those letters? Had she met someone else? How could he read her letters when he didn't have an address for his mother to post the letters onto? Even if he had the money to pay for a call for his mother to read the letters, he didn't have the stomach for her to do such a thing, if he had, his mother could have of course telephoned him and told him what was in the letters, maybe it was time to go home. The night was spent in Flanders, just a few miles away from where he had been staying the night before and he was still tired from the disco, as such and confused about everything he spent most of the afternoon wandering around the grounds of the youth hostel, which was complete with its own mini-zoo.

The next day, still wondering as to whether he should cut short his voyage short, and knowing that Easter was on its way, a time when many would head for the coast, he decided to visit Sandra and his friends from Nijlen. This for him was a one-week trip, first he went to Maastricht and found out that Sandra had left, but no one had told him why at the university. As much as he wanted to look around Maastricht, he had to find Sandra. Then he cycled up to her parents' house in Nijmegan the following day, only to be told that she had left home and was 8 months pregnant. By then Mark was wondering if a third disaster would strike. His ride to Maastricht was in vain and so was Nijmegan, with the two disappointments he moved further onto Nijlen, but his friends were no longer running the place and so as he had deep down expected earlier that day, he was third time unlucky on his travels that week.

As such, it being a few days before the Easter Holidays he decided to cycle to the coast the following day. The ride was just over 100 miles (161km) and he ended up at Oostduinkerke on the Flemish Coast and would spend basically the next two weeks there and return home. The next day and still tired from the day before and not knowing anything about the local sand dunes, he decided to rest in the hostel grounds, and just before he was thinking about what he wanted to do, something or rather someone caught his eye. Her name was Sophie, a very attractive, intelligent and sexy looking brunette, who was dressed casually. She was seeking solace away from the city life, after not being able to cope recently with her tear-away daughter whom she had recently decided to send to live with the father. She then walked up to him, "Excuse me is the youth hostel open?" She said as he smiled at her, charmingly.

"No, it is not, do I look like that I work here?" He said as he was looking at her body, which was really turning him on.

"You do actually." She said, as he then felt proud since he felt as though he had something about a native from the place.

"Where are you from?" He said trying to gently entice her.

"I am from Brussels." She said knowing that she was under his spell and feeling that he could sense this from his manner too.

Sophie, not wishing to look cheap decided to gently keep a distance from him, but he was constantly in her thoughts as she was in his. A few hours later, close to the reception area, she was hoping that he would walk by; and after a few long minutes he approached her while she looked as though she was immersed in the brochures on display. "Have you found something interesting?" He said to her as she almost jumped out of surprise, and a little timidly.

"Yes, I have actually, there is a walk along the sand dunes."

"Can I join you?" He said confidently and somehow gently.

"If you really want to." She said trying not smile too much.

"I would very much enjoy that." The conversation continued a little more, Mark didn't want to overwhelm her and as she got tired it was late and he simply let her get ready for bed.

That night in their respective dormitories both had been thinking about the other, she was pleased with the interest he had shown her without appearing too aggressive, but little did she know that just two days earlier he had been pining over another woman while he was on a kind of rebound of his own making regarding Louise. Then again would this woman had cared? Since she herself needed some carnal pleasures, which were a little bit too elusive for her. Sophie was in fact very romantic, but her loneliness, sadness and regret over her loveless situation made her rather desperate, she knew this and as much as she felt that she should steer well away from Mark she simply had no control over the forthcoming events, and like him she played with herself as they were both thinking about each while in bed in their separate dormitories during that long warm spring night.

The following morning, they met up with each other at the hostel dining area and after eating they both agreed to meet up in front of the building. The sun was shining, and they headed to the coast and went walking through the sand dunes. At first her own intuition had to some extent been right, but her own love life had been one hell of a roller coaster, and maybe all that she needed was just a short and sweet summer romance. They were speaking about simple things until Sophie popped a serious question.

"Have you got a girlfriend?" Though she felt he had no one.

"I have had girlfriends but nothing serious," He said.

"So, do you still live with your parents?" She asked as she started to feel as though she was on some romantic path with him.

"Yes, I do if I had the money, I would have my own place. In September I am going back to college. What about you?" His words about his plans that September disappointed her, but even so something was simply for her better than absolutely nothing.

"My parents are divorced, and I got thrown out of my mums at seventeen when I fell pregnant." She said sadly.

"Where are the child and the father?" He asked.

"That is a long story, he comes from a very poor, uneducated family, and he has been in and out of prison . . . Still, he didn't have much chance, his mother like his sisters was a prostitute and his elder brother Charlie got thrown out of school . . . Guy was very attractive when I met him, but his weight problems soon got out of hand and he went over 100kg (15 stone)," she said.

"I am listening to you Sophie, what if we sit here where it looks nice and eat our packed lunch and carry on talking here?"

Sophie was pleased, the setting was romantic with the high sand dunes towering above the beach with the sea behind and he was listening to her. They sat down and were eating slowly as they continued with their conversation. "How did you end up with someone like that?" For a moment she had to think about what he was speaking about and then she continued-

"He lied to impress me, I fell pregnant shortly afterwards, by then it was too late. My mum didn't care about me either . . . She was too busy with her men friends . . . If she cared about me, she would have made me have an abortion, but she didn't." She said as she was starting to fall into one of her black moods too prematurely.

"So where is your child now?" He asked a little shocked regarding her personal baggage, which sounded a bit wild.

"She is with him, he set a very bad example for her with his thieving, and I could no longer control her," she said in dismay.

"How old is she?" By then he was certainly listening.

"She is ten years of age and looks just like him."

"You don't look old enough to have a ten years old daughter." He said kindly but in all honesty.

"Well, I am 28, in fact next year in September I will already be 30." She said proudly and pleased with his flattery.

"I am coming up to being 24 this June... I bet you are glad that this is all in the past." Mark was a little surprised about her background and she was five years older than he and didn't want her to dwell at this stage about his age, as such his question was either some innocent decoy or delaying tactic.

"Yes, I am, still Guy's mum is still nice with me when I see her, mainly because she hopes that we will get back together."

"So, you left him?" He said curiously.

"Yes and no, he kept having affairs behind my back, so I left him." She said rather defensively and somewhat dismissively.

The walk back after they both paddled in the sea was a pleasant affair. That evening Sophie was feeling sorry for herself as she was then thinking about her previous relationship with Guy, while Mark was feeling sorry for her too, and part of him wanted to protect her, equally she couldn't understand him, since he came across as frigid, but little did she know that he

● ● ●

found her too much in her own sad world and that he was capable of making love at first sight. The next morning, they were together outside the youth hostel with them both looking very relaxed. "Why don't you come and visit me in Brussels?" She asked him warmly.

"Yeah sure, sounds like a very good idea, but I don't have your address . . . When should I come around?" She then looks through her handbag and then takes out a pen and a piece of paper.

"Saturday." She said and then she had to make her way to the railway station, and he was free to go off cycling.

It was only Tuesday, and Mark wasn't going to see her for four days, still it meant cutting his holiday short, and maybe post-poning his return to Garstang. The next few days he enjoyed cycling along the coast with the odd day trip to France just 7.5 miles away. Saturday morning came, a day which was a little daunting for him with the 100 miles ride ahead of him, what was more he would finish off the day in a big city, and although he had never been there, this country boy knew that this French speaking city had nothing apart from Sophie for him. Just before he arrived at her house a few streets away he asked a driver for directions and arrived efficiently on her doorstep just before 9PM and around sunset, complete with a magnificent scarlet sky.

The omens looked good, he had heard many stories about Brussels and was pleased to see that the neighborhood had many trees and was quite pleasant. He rang the doorbell and a very happy-looking Sophie answered the door. "Come in." She said excitedly. He followed her into her home, which was a part of a big three floored house, and she had the ground floor. They were now in the living room. "Well, this is a surprise to see you." She had in fact been a little nervous since she had given up on him arriving so late.

"Well, we did say today." He said, pleased with her welcome.

"Oh, with it being so late I thought you were coming tomorrow. I have a lasagna, ready, are you hungry?"

"Thanks, that would be lovely." By then he was sitting on the sofa, she walked off to re heat the lasagna, and came back with jug of water and glasses. Mark was delighted with the meal. "This lasagna, is really delicious." For Mark this wasn't the melancholic soul he met at the seaside, instead it was a warm and sultry Sophie Marceau lookalike.

"My father does not think I can cook." Mark was a little surprised with her negative response. A bit later Sophie wanted him to rid himself of his sweaty smell so he took a shower at her sweet request and when he came back Sophie was in ecstasy. That night she was so delighted to have him in her own home, yet at the same time she didn't wish to throw caution to the wind and had no intention of going with him to her bedroom. Instead, she was happy to kiss him, and to spend the rest of the night on the couch with him, and to imagine what she wanted from him later.

They had breakfast together and then they went on a walk right to the edge of the city, which had country lanes and signs which reminded him of home, the place was known as the Neerpede and there they ate French Fries, which Sophie proudly informed him where from Belgium and under no circumstances French. Sometimes the conversation was strained due to the language barrier, since neither of them spoke Dutch as a native language and in many ways, this was a plus since they would have less to argue about, or so it seemed to them. They had had a lovely romantic walk and once back it was time to relax and spend the evening kissing, which she had so been looking forward to.

Mark enjoyed running his fingers through her hair, this turned her on and when they started to French Kiss, she started to become breathless. "I think it is time for me to cook some-thing." She then walked off leaving him lying on the couch she was a little surprised seeing him behaving as a lord, but she knew that he hadn't lived with a woman before. They ate and on this second day together she introduced him to her bedroom, where they made love together for the first time. For both, the experience bought them closer together and this was a good sign that they were more than just a conquest for each other and that maybe he would stay.

The next day Mark and Sophie had been invited to visit her father upstairs in the house, and he lived on the second floor. Thierry was a nice man who was happily married and with four children until his wife got bored and ran off with a man half her age and younger than his eldest child, which wasn't Sophie, since she was the third child. Although Thierry was the one who had stood by his family, all his children went on regular visits to his ex-wife, but only Sophie remained in touch with her father. When his first two children were naughty, he had been known to slap them and this was often at the command of his then wife, but when she wanted to leave him, she would remind the children of his disciplinary action against them without a mention of their previous and unruly behavior. Thierry was family orientated, very sociable and had a moustache and was very much looking forward to meeting Mark and showing him round his well-decorated apartment.

Sophie and Mark knocked on a door and waited in front of his flat, he then opened his door. He smiled at Mark who smiled back, "Come in," he said to his guests. They all followed him to his dining room table, he then put out his hand to give Mark a handshake. "Nice to meet you, Mark," he said smiling.

"Nice to meet you Mr. Charlerbois," smiled Mark.

"Thierry to you." He then proudly walked off leaving Sophie and Mark together while he went to check his home cuisine. A few minutes later dinner was served, it was a very hearty one in fact, since four courses were about to be served. He was pretty obese, and his main conversation was generally around food.

"This soup is delicious." Said Mark relieved, since Sophie had warned him about her father's food being far too rich and fatty.

"It is." Said Sophie rather humbly and rather relaxed.

"I am glad that you both like it . . . In Belgium we eat like the French." They continued eating and during the next hour he would return to his kitchen until the fourth dish had been served.

● ● ●

They spoke for several hours, and Sophie was pleased that Thierry and Mark had got on so well and surprised at the same time.

The next week was fine but then when she went back to work, she was feeling a little bit more insecure, since at the back of her head was his desire to go back to England. Mark was in what was by then their home when she entered the house with chocolates for him. "Hi Mark." She said she was delighted to be back home.

"Hi Sophie." He stood up, walked towards her and they started to kiss. She then took the chocolates, which were then lying on her table and passed them to him, to his delight.

"I have bought you some chocolates," she said.

"Um that is great thank you," he said, appreciatively.

Sophie was happy to make him happy and seeing him delight in the chocolates gave her so much in the way of satisfaction, as such the chocolates became a regular event and given, she worked for Godiva she got a big discount of their products and would bring them home for him too. Mark was as usual waiting for her when she arrived, and he handed flowers to a delighted Sophie. "These flowers are great, and I have got you some chocolates." She said kindly and feeling so much younger, since she was in love.

"Thanks Sophie that is really nice, but I do feel guilty with you spending all this money on chocolates for me." Mark was feeling guilty since he planned to go back to Lancashire, this he had already told her, and was worried that she didn't respect this.

After a few days and during early May, Mark found work in a restaurant, the interview was in Dutch and the young girls wanted to know more about him. The first week there was great, some of the ladies could only think about this exotic being from the other side of the channel. Mark unsure as to where his amorous feelings lay, expressed nervously that he was already spoken for, and this in turn dampened his favorable position some of the Francophones had of him and were by then alarmed and disgusted with his poor command of French. Equally Sophie herself was worried, since with him out at work all day, she was dreading the moment when he would leave her and go to live with one of his younger colleagues.

After just two weeks at work Mark was called in to see his boss in an office. "You speak very good Dutch." His boss said.

"Thank you." Said Mark fully appreciatively.

"But your French is bad, so I am going to have to fire you."

A few moments later Mark was, with his head low, leaving the office before cycling home. As he arrived at Sophie's he placed his bike in the hallway and walked into the living room and to his great delight he noticed a new bicycle. "Sophie I am home." She then walked up to him, they then put their arms around each other and kissed. "Is this your bicycle?" He said rather dreamily as he was thinking about some bike rides which they could do together.

"Yes, it is." She said happily, knowing he was pleased.

"This is great." He said and then walked up to the bicycle smiling, before looking serious again. "I have been fired because of my lack of French." Sophie's eyes then light up delightedly.

"Well, that is okay, you don't need to work, I earn enough money for both of us . . . I am sure that you will find work elsewhere, and besides I am off tomorrow, so we can go out cycling together." Mark was delighted that they could now go out together but equally he was shocked regarding her flippant attitude regarding his work while at the same he was relieved that she wasn't going to give him a hard time over it. One thing that Mark appreciated regarding Sophie was her regular sleeping routine, which meant early to bed and early to rise, and this probably accounted for their high rates of sexual activity, simply put they had more energy for making love than those who stayed up all night watching the television.

The next day they went off on their bikes and approached the canal cycle path without a care in the world. He had arrived in Belgium with some savings and as a treat he wanted to take Sophie away on holiday. While cycling, two elderly cyclists passed by and Sophie burst out laughing. "Hey Sophie, that could be us one day."

"I don't think so; I have no intention of being old." She had already decided that she wanted to be dead at around 70.

"What about if we go away on a cycling holiday?" He said trying to change her morbid thoughts, which he didn't like.

With Sophie having the whole of July and August off since during the holidays the factory preferred cheap labor in the form of students, Sophie was very happy with the holiday idea, especially since just a few months earlier she had no idea if she would be able to go anywhere. A few days before they were to depart, Mark arranged his 4 pannier bags. Two for the front, two for the rear, plus a front and a back saddlebag, there would be plenty for them. One evening while Mark was reading and Sophie packing dresses, she looked at him. "How many saddlebags can I have?"

"We will share it darling, half for me and half for you." He said relaxed, while noticing her deep concern.

"But I have more clothes than you." She said in dismay.

"Sophie my half has bicycle repair kits and things for us."

"But you only wear summer clothes." She said annoyed.

"Can't you wear summer clothes as well? It is around 30 degrees." He said firmly but at the same time wanting peace.

"No, I can't, I want to look nice for you." She said starting to sound somewhat aggressive. Mark had had enough, but decided it wasn't worth an argument. In the end Sophie crammed in a huge and large number of things including; her Praktica analogue SLR camera outfit, which weighed half a stone. As such although it was July and he was looking forward to his holiday, he often felt as though he was once again one pebble looking for a home.

Sophie was delighted the day they set off on what for her was going to be a holiday to remember. It was her first cycling holiday, they had a full two weeks and a day more, and they took the train from Brussels went through Luxembourg and arrived at Saarbrucken, with their bikes so that they could enjoy both Alsace and the Black Forest. They stayed in youth hostels and cycled up to

50 miles (80km) daily, which was a lot for Sophie, since she hadn't ridden a bicycle in years. After a few days they had reached the lakes of the Black Forest and spent a week there and really got to know the lakes: Titisee, Schlusee and Feldsee. Normally the lakes were cold, and around 3,000 feet (900 Metres) above sea level, but they were lucky and with days around 86 degrees (30 centigrade), the lakes surrounded by magnificent landscapes were full of swimmers including both Mark and Sophie. Then it was time to return roughly the same way back through Alsace and the old town of Saverne before taking the train back from Saarbrucken.

While they both enjoyed the holiday together there were times when Mark found things about her, which he didn't like. On one occasion a group of French students were staying at a youth hostel in the Black Forest, and Sophie had nothing but contempt for them, but the most embarrassing incident for him was when a middle-aged overweight couple came to sit on a bench where Mark and Sophie were sitting. While Mark greeted them, Sophie ignored them but went on complaining about how fat and ugly they were in Dutch to Mark. Mark knew that the Germans understood and after a few moments the harmless couple suddenly left in disgust.

After a few days since their return Sophie was preparing a special pizza, while Mark was studying some French and sat in the kitchen to be near her. "When are your friends coming?"

"About 8 o'clock." She said relaxed and happy he asked.

"That is any minute now." He said. The doorbell rang; Mark remained seated as Sophie went to welcome her guests. She then arrived back with a couple aged around 30. Mark smiled at Jean and Monika, but they didn't make any eye contact with him.

"Monica, Jean this is Mark . . . Mark, this is Monika and Jean." She said doing her best to make everybody feel at ease.

"Hello." Said a very uncomfortable Monika who then looked away from him while Jean put on a very brave smile. They then sat down, and everyone enjoyed Sophie's delicious and wholesome potato pizza, but the conversation was rather drab to say the least for Mark, suddenly his ears picked up after an hour or so.

"We are thinking of going to England." Said Jean.

"Mark is from there." Said a delighted Sophie, since now the two guys had finally made some connection with each other.

"Oh . . . Monika where else are we thinking of going?"

"Austria." Said a relieved Monika who was smiling again.

"That's right." Said Jean in agreement with her. By then Mark felt very uncomfortable to say the least and decided to simply stand up and arrive back reading a book about anything.

Fortunately, they hadn't stayed until late and of course he was glad when they had left. Mark really wanted to have sex with Sophie as usual, they kissed and made love and within a few minutes he was aroused again to Sophie's delight since although tired she herself couldn't say no. Once again, she enjoyed it, "I want to make love to you again before we sleep." He said.

"There's no rush said a tired Sophie." After a while his gentle touch by way of lying next to her with his arms around her turned to one of a more passionate massaging and once again they made love and for the third time that evening and Sophie, like Mark was exhausted. Even so the more that Sophie got of him, the more that she wanted to make love and the more she enjoyed it.

A few hours later Sophie couldn't sleep, she needed it one more time, and he was a man and she needed him to look after her. Sophie then started caressing him, but it seemed almost impossible to arouse him, his body was tired from so much physical activity, and not just from sex but from cycling and swimming too. Eventually he woke up. "Sophie, I am tired we have already made love three times this evening, can't we wait until the morning?"

"I once had an Albanian thirty years older than you, he had a family and two jobs, but he was never too tired to make love when we met secretly." Said a lady who felt slighted since she had used up so much energy in trying to arouse him to no avail,

Mark was annoyed too, and felt he had to show her that she was not his boss.

"I am not him, and this is not at all romantic from you." He then turned his head away from her and fell asleep after a few moments of disgust; while Sophie thought about the passionless nights she had spent before she met Mark and decided to be more careful with her speech, since deep down she knew that he was still weighing up whether he wanted to stay with her.

Around this time Mark had found some factory work, it was simply stacking on a conveyor belt. With her day off work Sophie cycled there with him one morning and came back later and was seen standing outside his workplace as he left the site with his colleague Luke. "There is Sophie." He said rather proudly.

"She is very beautiful." Said a very impressed Luke.

"I know." He knew that she was beautiful, but was he in love with her, since he didn't reveal much after all. Luke walked off on his own way, as Mark approached Sophie and they kissed. He then unlocked his bicycle, which was near Sophie's meeting place and cycled off together along the canal. Just before they returned home, they decided to visit the local park so that they could enjoy the late evening sunshine together without a care in the world.

Back at home Mark was lounging on the couch as usual. "Is it okay if Luke comes around for a visit?" He asked her politely.

"No, because it is my house and Guy used to invite too many friends around." Mark wasn't at all pleased, at his parents all his friends could come around whenever they wanted, and now he wasn't allowed to have any social life at all, still he didn't argue, but immediately sensed some strange presence coming out of her, and equally he found her insensitive to say the least.

The following evening, they went out on a walk through the neighborhood Mark was singing to her and she was enjoying his lyrics specially tailored for her, when suddenly she looked up on hearing music from a band inside a house, and with that, a strange smile went across her face. "Why don't you see if they need a singer?" She said to him sarcastically, while inside she was afraid.

● ● ●

"Do you know, I think I will, why don't we go there together?" He said pleasantly and apparently pleased with her.

"No, it is okay." Sophie wished that she hadn't made such a facetious remark and was totally shocked and horrified that he was serious. Mark was not stupid, he knew that she had been ironic, but while he wasn't a man who thrived with confrontations, he wasn't anybody's fool either and although he wasn't really bothered about the band, he felt compelled to pay them a visit. As such he approached the house on his own after Sophie walked off in a huff on her own while he rang the bell and a few moments later Bruno, a friendly-looking guy around 30, arrived opening the door.

"Hello." Said Bruno, pleasantly and surprised.

"Hello, my name is Mark and I am a singer from England." He said oozing with confidence, as Bruno puts out his hand and they give each other a firm handshake of respect.

"My name is Bruno; come in." And Mark followed him inside.

Mark is now starting to feel excited, as they are both seen walking up the narrow staircase of the large, terraced house. They then enter a room, which looks very versatile since it has: a bed, table and music equipment and is quite large too. Sonia, his girlfriend aged 25, is seen smiling. "This is my girlfriend, Sonia; Sonia this is Mark he is a singer from England." They all then simply smile.

"Nice to meet you." Says Mark sporting a charming smile.

"So, tell me, what is your background?" Said Bruno while Sonia herself had a very similar question ready and waiting for him.

"I am from a small village in England and I used to hire out the village hall run discos there with myself as DJ and practice singing too while at school and college . . . What about you guys?" Sonia had been all ears and was clearly enjoying the moment.

"I am just a normal guy who wants to be a rock star."

"Can you, ad lib?" Asked his girlfriend excited.

"Come on let's go!" Said Mark hiding his nerves. Bruno smiles as he picks up the saxophone, while Sonia picks up the drumsticks. After a couple of songs Sonia looks on admiringly.

"You can sing!" Said Sonia, and Bruno was delighted since they both had the same opinion. Mark then looked at Bruno, since he didn't wish for him to think he was chasing Sonia.

"I would like to join your band." He said enthusiastically.

"Tomorrow night we will playing at the Heisel, can you join us?" Mark was now really excited since the venue was huge.

"What time do you want me to come around here?" Mark then feels as though he is walking in the air and was delighted that unlike the days when he was just a village entertainer, now it seemed that he really might be about to hit the big time in Brussels.

"Is 7:30 okay?" Asked Bruno, waiting for a response.

"That's great I will see you tomorrow at 7:30." Mark was then led out of the house by Bruno and after a few brief and pleasant exchanges he continued his way looking virile to say the least.

With his key he then opens the door to the house, walks inside, takes off his shoes before closing one door and opening another. He then walks into the living room where a sad-looking Sophie is seen; he then puts his hands on her shoulders before giving her a kiss. She is in two minds about this, because by giving someone else his attention he has hurt her. "Because of you I went to see the band." He said, putting the blame on her.

"I was only joking." She said almost in tears.

"Well anyway I am singing tomorrow night at the Heisel." For Sophie this was now becoming too much, the Heisel of all places, there was no way he was going to turn this down, at the same time she felt that their relationship was doomed. "I thought that you would be pleased, why don't you come along?" He then walks over and tries to kiss her but seeing visions of him in her thoughts kissing someone else she turns her head away from him.

The next day she woke up feeling better, in fact she was rather ashamed by her behavior, at the same time she blamed him for making her feel insecure since he had told her that he will be going back to college. Sophie wanted to be with Mark as much as possible, she was in love, had been alone for too long, and they would both go shopping for the groceries together as usual.

While walking through Delhaize supermarket and passing through the wine section Patricia, the younger sister of Sophie notices them she was with her smug and wealthy boyfriend Steffen and on seeing them she gave off a haughty smile, on noticing them, Sophie froze and marched Mark out of the supermarket. "I'm sorry, I forgot my credit card." Said Sophie, she was relieved, nervous and ashamed of her manner, but she was without any control.

"Sophie no worries, I have money." Said Mark calmly.

"I must make sure that I haven't lost it." She hadn't even checked to see where it was since it was just an excuse in order to get away from her sister. Back in the apartment she pretended to look for her card, and then they went back out to the supermarket, after a drink of tea and enough time to allow Patricia to leave the shop. She was relieved that he had taken everything she said.

That evening Mark went to Bruno's they then drove in his van with Sonia to the Heisel. When they arrived most of the equipment was set up and they had enough time to rehearse and then at 9PM they basically played songs, which Mark could sing, he had forgotten most of the lyrics, but he was in Belgium where not everyone understood English and the fans were delighted to have a British singer on stage. The four-piece band received lots of standing ovations at this very large and famous venue.

While Mark was out Sophie was at first distraught and then she picked up a pen and paper and put on her thinking cap. There were four possibilities,

1. He would continue with the band and then they would be done.

2. If she said nothing he would be with the band and share everything with her regarding his intentions.

3. With the band he would soon run off with one of his many fans.

4. Without the band their relationship would be safe a little longer.

All that she could do was to wait, and hopefully he would be back that evening, since deep down she realized that her choices weren't making much in the way of any sense. On top of that she had her emergency packet of cigarettes and started to smoke them one by one, she knew that Mark hated them, but he had upset her and needed comforting right then and he wasn't around to soothe her.

The drive back was magic, the spirits were very high, and while Bruno was driving Sonia couldn't stop speaking and inside, she was dreaming about a beautiful house in the country. Mark then dropped off, he then walked home, opened the front door, closed it and then walked into the living room which was full of smoke. He then left the room after almost choking and went into the bedroom. Sophie then followed him, he was a little less relaxed since he didn't like cigarettes and when Sophie arrived looking very sullen, he was prepared for some conflict. "How much did you get paid?" She asked him rather rudely as his mind was elsewhere.

"I did not get paid anything, but it is still early days."

"I am not having you using this place as some free hotel, it is another thing if you are getting paid, but you are not . . . Do I make myself clear?" She knew that she had gone over the top, but she wanted to take a chance and not waste time with him.

"But Sophie the band could do well one day," he said.

"That guy Bruno is a jerk, he is nearly thirty years old and he still lives with his parents, if he were going somewhere, he would have his own place." She was lucky since he wanted calm.

"Well, I had better tell him tomorrow." He said, disappointed.

"Do what you want." She said dismissively and put the onus on him. That night they felt very lonely in bed together, she wanted him so badly, but knew that there was no way he would get close to her with her smelling like an old and dirty chimney.

The morning was a little quiet on top of that Mark's temporary factory position had just finished, and he was wondering what the hell he was doing with his life, but equally didn't want to upset Sophie. As Sophie left for her work, she kissed him on the lips. He then went into the city, looking for work and dropped his C.V. off at W.H. Smiths in the city center, where he caught a glimpse of the British news headlines. Back at home he plucked up enough courage to walk round and visit Bruno in the street.

He pressed the bell and a delighted Bruno opened the door. "Hi Mark! come inside." He said excitedly, they then went upstairs together and sat down, with Mark feeling nervous inside.

"I have some bad news; Sophie won't allow me to carry on with the band." Bruno looked a little upset, but made sure that his voice was composed, while Mark felt somewhat bad inside.

"I know what women are like, look if she changes her mind, and as long as we are without a good singer, we will take you back."

"Thanks Bruno, thanks for the understanding." They continued speaking a bit more and Bruno was relieved that Mark left before his beloved Sonia came home to see him.

Weekend came the weather was warm they had made love quite a lot at home and decided to relax in the local park. They sat on the grass and Sophie was smiling and looking at Mark. Patricia is seen walking by, upon noticing her Sophie puts her arms around him. "I am sorry that I have been a bit difficult the last few days." She said so to distract Mark away from Patricia.

"I am glad that you have noticed." He said relieved, and then she looked on nervously at him with the sun shining on her face.

"The other day while we were in the supermarket, I noticed my younger sister with her partner, and I felt ill at ease."

"I never knew that she lived close by, anyways don't worry."

"She has never forgiven me. When we were children, I used to idolize the Nazis. As such I would not allow her to sleep until she prayed to Adolf Hitler. So, she no longer speaks to me. Obviously, I am ashamed of what I did." By then she was feeling very nervous.

"Sophie that was many years ago, and I really feel that your sister should have forgiven you by now." Mark was no supporter of extremism, but equally he felt that no one was perfect, including him.

"I love you, Mark." She said, feeling both happy that he was kind towards her regarding her dark past and nervous since she needed to hear how much he loved her too right then and now.

"I love you too Sophie, but there is something that we need to discuss." He said worried that she might lose it with him.

"Go on Mark." She said in terrible fear of what was coming.

"I will be going to college, like I told you when we first met, and besides we have very little in the way of money," he said.

"How can you say that you love me when you are planning on leaving me?" She said as she was feeling very upset.

"Sophie, I don't speak French, what job do you seriously think I can find here? I have tried three different jobs and have been fired from all of them, because of my lack of French."

"Well at least the end of my life has been the best part."

"What exactly do you mean?" He said in horror of her.

"When you leave me, I will kill myself." Tears then start running down Mark's face as he starts to feel very ashamed.

"Sophie this is not fair, you knew about my college plans when we first met." He said as he started to compose himself.

"I am sorry I did not mean what I said . . . The last few years I have thought about having a second child, but I never thought that I would find the right person . . . I guess I could bring one up on my own." She said merely dropping a hint that if she can't have him, she felt that it was high time for child number two, especially since her child wasn't with her and her motherly instinct was high.

"Do you mean that you would bring up a child of mine so?"

"Yes, I would, because then I would have something to remind me of you, when you have gone." She said sweetly.

"Well, I don't believe in bringing up a child without the father." Sophie smiles and puts her arms tightly around him. She then feels that his fate has been sealed and trusts that he will stand by her if she falls pregnant, although what he meant and what she didn't understand; was that he had no intention of getting her pregnant since he had no desire to stay with her.

The next day he called into W.H. Smiths it was already early September, he hadn't left her, so by then his talk about going to college must had sounded a little hollow to her. He was by then a little bit known by some members of staff and the deputy manager recognized him. The book unpacker had gone crazy and walked out the day before and Mark who was still planning to leave Belgium, with college starting in a couple of weeks, couldn't resist the idea of spending the whole day in a bookshop and getting paid for it. As such he felt flattered that he had been asked to take on the job.

Of course, Sophie was delighted since it really looked like her patience with him was yielding a promising future full of love. As for Mark he was a little concerned since for him he and Sophie were not right for each other, even so he loved her, and his escape route was of course his parents. As such, knowing full well that Sophie had already used up her holiday leave, he planned to tell his new employers that he had already booked a trip to visit his family just before Christmas. When Sophie heard about his visit, she quite rightly feared that he wouldn't be coming back as such and it being September, she had just 3 months for her plan to be a fait accompli.

The deal in the bookshop was for Mark to unpack three pallets of books each week. This hadn't been managed by anyone before, but he was able to do it and would take many breaks walking around the shop and looking at books. On top of that he played tapes in order to improve his language skills. He went there and back by bicycle and given that this was until then the best job he had experienced since working in the youth hostels he was very content. Of course, he missed Garstang and the Forest of Bowland, but for now at least he had a job, with which he felt at home.

Of course, Sophie was delighted with the job, but was angry regarding his Christmas visit to the UK. Still, she knew not to rock the boat too much. One evening mark was tense while Sophie was reading and equally tense. Mark then started looking around the room, looking inside and out of cupboards and Sophie was none too pleased. "Don't make a mess!" She ordered him abruptly.

"I am looking for the condoms." He said obediently.

"We must have used them all up." She said deceivingly.

"No Sophie that is not true, I can't believe that we have used the new box of thirty that I only bought last week," he said.

"I had to throw them out because they were out of date, and I am allergic to plastic, anyways I am on the pill and it is more reliable." Mark went to the bathroom and Sophie deliberately placed the strip of pills on her table, from which she took each day one pill out of the strip and threw it in the bin. Sophie knew how lucky she was with him, since it was obvious that she was taking him for a ride, but Mark was just a typical naïve country boy, not looking for trouble and too trusting to say the least and to her advantage.

Things were calm at home and Sophie, although a little nervous about his departure, was certain of his return. In front of her door, she kissed him goodbye and then looked at his fully laden bicycle. "So back in two weeks?" She said holding back the tears.

"I am." He said with emotions combined of compassion for Sophie while he also felt sorry for her, and relief for himself since he felt that living in her dark flat with her at times black thoughts was enough for him to simply wish to escape from her.

"Why are you not leaving all these things here?" She said gently so as not to frighten him away from her completely.

"At my parents there is plenty of space to store things." Mark then rode off as Sophie waved at him. Mark was a little nervous thinking about his things, since he hadn't decided whether to come back or not and was wondering how he could bring the things back, since his books of the Black Forest and Belgium were precious to him as where his prized pebbles whom he wanted just like himself to be fixed in one home, with one woman as one

● ● ●

heart. Equally he felt bad for Sophie, he genuinely loved her, there were things he didn't like about her, felt that she was trapping him but equally he didn't want to upset her either. He then took the train to Bruges, a place, which he loved, then cycled onto Zeebrugge and boarded the boat for Hull. That evening as he was alone, he sensed that he was a changed man since his last ferry crossing. Back then he was happy to flirt but now, it seemed that he was genuinely missing Sophie, and he had emotionally grown up somewhat. After breakfast and a good sleep, he disembarked the ship and cycled on to Hull Railway Station, from where he took the train to Manchester and then onto Preston.

Chapter Eight

August: Without A Grounded Pebble
And Falling Off the Wings of Love.

lthough he had never been a fan of large towns, as he left Preston station with his bike, he felt so good and was looking forward to enjoying his ride through the countryside and had a glow in his heart. From Barton he wasn't only enjoying the ride as expected, he was then feeling homesick, and thinking if only he had found work in a bookshop in Preston or in Lancaster. A bit further on around Bilsborrow, Louise noticed him pass her bus which had stopped at the bus stop and was delighted to see him, she had just been out shopping in Preston and seeing he had lots of luggage she felt that he had finally come back to stay in her beloved Lancashire. She wanted to get off the bus to meet him, but like him, she was loaded up with things, and she would telephone him later instead.

As he arrived home his mother was delighted as was his dad, and his little sisters who were jumping for joy with glee. It had been so long since they had seen him. They took him into one of their bedrooms and he read them lots of fairy tales; and they were listening to him attentively. Karen then arrived in Kerry's bedroom. "Mark there is a telephone call for you." She smiled at him as she looked at him with her daughters and feeling that it was time for him to settle down, she was delighted and hoping that this Lancashire lass would snare him and bring him back home. He then ran downstairs wondering who the hell it was so suddenly.

"Hello, Mark here!" He said curiously and friendly.

"Hi Mark, it is Louise here." She said warmly and tenderly.

"How great to hear from you, when can we meet up?" His heart was almost pounding since this was the woman of his dreams.

"Tonight?" she said equally with her sweet pheromones also running into a heavenly overdrive of expectation for him.

"Super, can I come around, when my sisters are in bed?"

"Not too late please." She said as she was starting to yawn "Is 9, OK?" Not wanting to upset her in any way.

"For you sweetheart it is." She said kindly and relieved.

After the telephone conversation finished, he then went into the dining room and dinner was then served. His sisters then got ready for bed and then he continued with reading them both stories. Sometimes they were distracted, since Mark had brought back some pebbles for them from the Belgian Coast, and Kerry would often be giving more attention to holding them in her hands than using her ears and listening to his words. In order to maximize his time with Louise he set off at 8.30 and arrived in just ten minutes.

He rang her bell very excitedly, she was wearing a large pink nightdress, and the first thing he noticed was her beautiful face as she opened the door, which although it was dark he made out that it was looking very rounded and he then looked down and obviously very quickly he noticed that she was heavily pregnant and he was gobsmacked, from seeing her beautiful face to her baby bump it had taken him less than a second, but it was one event that struck like a ball of thunder. His first impression was; what must her parents think? He simply stared in shock at her. "Have you never seen a pregnant woman before?" She said to him more, motherly towards him than she had been the last time they met together.

"I'm sorry I was in a daze." She smiled at him and he walked inside behind her. They then walked into the living room. She then walked to the kitchen and arrived back with a milkshake, just like the first drink she made him with bananas and apples. She then sat closely next to him with the drinks on the coffee table. She wanted to see his reaction to her and their baby. "This is my child." He asked her as he gently placed his hands on her belly. He then opened his bum bag and took out a pebble. "This pebble comes all the way from the Black Forest of Germany, I want you to keep this for good luck Louise." She then looked at him and they started to kiss and a little while later he placed his hands once more on her belly. "And this is where it all began." He said as she smiled at him, since the last time they were in this room she was about to embark onto her journey into motherhood as she fell pregnant to him.

Oh, if only they could go back to the last time they sat there in her house and play things the same way again only this time there would be no waiting for each for the next 8 and a half months until his return, since knowing what they know now he would simply cancel his trip and with her being pregnant they would have had every reason to set up home together. She then gave him the drinks, and for them the previous visit of his at her home had come back to life. He then to her great delight lifted her nightdress and placed his hands on her baby bump, and then they kissed on the lips sensually. "Where are your parents?" He asked.

"They are on Tenerife." The last time they met they were full of passion for each other, oh how they had missed each other since those early spring days, as such she wasn't thinking that she was due to go into labor any day, like him the long absence and the longing for each other which had been constantly on their minds paled everything else into insignificance; it was as if the previous spring was only yesterday. Mark enjoyed the extra fat on her, since for him it made her with her fleshier lips look even more feminine. He then ran his fingers through her hair and after taking off her nightdress, he kissed her all over and very gently and slowly he made love to her. Knowing she was carrying his first child since just ten minutes or so earlier, made him feel so alive, oh if only he hadn't left her, if only he knew, but now just in time before he was about to be daddy, he was back with her. Being with her made him feel so masculine, as being with her made her feel so feminine.

A few moments later her mind went elsewhere as she started thinking deeply about life. "I'm sorry I couldn't control myself." She said to him feeling dirty, and Mark was a little confused as to why she said that she was sorry but felt satiated to be back.

"I love you, Louise." He said sensing her insecurity.

"So, you didn't get those letters, did you?" She expressed in a more serious tone as her mind was becoming too thoughtful.

"I just arrived back today, but I will ask my mum to give me them when I get back . . . When are you due?" He asked.

"On the 12th." She said: as she was feeling nervous again.

"That's exactly one week from now." With the reality sinking in, she wanted him once more and all her thoughts filled with sadness were once again put on hold and with nothing more to say, they drank their milkshakes. After it they both went her bedroom, she was tired, she was happy, he was there, the love of her life, and she had to make up for lost time and forgetting that she was about to give birth, they made love again, while Mark was in heaven, she too was walking in the wings of love, but if only this night would last forever as both slept like the lovebirds that they truly were.

The morning dawned they had made love three times since he came the night before, and still recovering from the journey from Belgium he continued sleeping. She looked at her sleeping prince, she wanted him so badly, but with tears running down her face, for her, dreamy yesterday was gone and today was her unwelcome reality. She then went downstairs and decided to make him a cooked breakfast in bed. This she was doing out of love and out of guilt. She placed two Weetabix biscuits into two cereal-bowls, placed Lancashire cheese, bread, butter and marmalade on the tray with two mugs and walked up the stairs to her bedroom. She then walked back down and took the toaster and kettle upstairs. How could she wake him up? How as

● ● ●

a mother to be could she wait and wait for her breakfast for two when she was so hungry, and equally she couldn't bear to eat alone. Mark woke up as she was seen staring at him. "Darling it is time for breakfast." He then smiled looking lovingly at the feast, which she had prepared for them.

"I am just going to the bathroom." He said lovingly to her.

As he left the room she came back down to reality and when he arrived back the smile on her luscious lips was somehow more strained. "Thanks, gorgeous." Why did he say this, was it because she had called him darling and if so, why did she say this? They started to eat, the atmosphere wasn't like the night before, and Mark put it down to the fact that she was about to give birth and that he had let her down by being away so long and without any hope for them.

"I'm sorry, I don't know how to put this . . . I had no idea that you were going to come back, and it is not much fun being all alone and pregnant . . . So, I got married to Peter Bateman."

"Of all the people in the world, why the hell did you marry that tosser?" She felt bad, maybe in choosing Pete, she had let him down, but then again nobody could be good enough in his eyes for her apart from himself, and it was simply all Mark's fault anyway.

"I don't know, but he is away in the army a lot." She sighed.

"Louise, I came back here for you, can't we just get back together?" He looked on tensely at her, as tears are seen running down her face, oh how she had longed and missed him so much, but now she as a married woman an adulteress who was with her lover, the father of her child, and one big hell of a mess. Why had she broken her marriage vows and contacted the man who had turned her down and used her while on his way abroad, and why had she not got hold of the father of her child before looking for a daddy for her child? Everything was simply just too much for them.

"Look I'm sorry, I can't get back with you, I'd love to, but you know what my parents are like this would just finish them off." His mind went back to his grandparents from Calder Vale, they had been finished off thanks to Amy, and he had no intention of doing this to Louise's parents. One thing at least, she had at least used her senses and not told Mark where she was living with her husband and still in shock, he hadn't thought of asking that either.

"I need some time to think about this . . . Look I'm just gonna have to go, I have got college soon, and I'd better be prepared for it."

"Look I'm sorry, I'm really sorry." Mark then stands up and is seen walking away as Louise holds her composure, following him slowly. He then turns around and tries to kiss, but her jaw is locked and all he manages is one simple kiss on her lips. She would do anything now to stop him from doing what she wanted so badly from him. He then leaves her house and cycles off, while Louise runs up to her bedroom and cries herself to sleep.

Back at home Karen could see that he didn't look happy, but at the same time she wasn't going to force herself on him. Later that day he cycled off to Preston College. After looking around the place and calling in at the admissions department he met up with a female college adviser. "Well quite frankly, it is a little bit odd, that after gaining a degree you now wish to study here but you are old enough to decide." She said, as she wanted to get rid of him.

"The thing is, I don't know what to do with my life; the qualifications I have won't help me get a decent job." With that the adviser wasn't going to be responsible for making a mess of his career and helped him sign onto a course starting after Christmas.

As Mark was cycling along the A6 past her home, Louise was sitting with Julie. Mark glanced into her garden, but she wasn't there outside for him to innocently catch her attention, instead she was sitting inside with her friend Julie. "Are you sure that you want him back?" Asked Julie, who wasn't happy, that he had basically run off after getting her pregnant and so she found him irresponsible.

"Yes of course I am very sure about that." She said dreamily.

● ● ●

"Just don't rush in, remember he kind of left you, I am sure he really loves you, but he has to sort his life out. Just give it a day or two, there's plenty of time now that he is back for college." Louise very grateful of her friend's support felt better but decided not to continue speaking about the men in her life; and felt that Julie not being in this mess herself wasn't really the one to fully understand everything, on top of that she was to give birth any day. Her husband was away until Christmas and she wasn't going to call him back and given he wasn't the child's father, her mind was more on Mark, who of course meant much more to her anyway.

Mark then arrived back at his other home of his; that being with his parents, all he needed was Louise and then he would take on any job to be with her, even the dreaded, "Brain Dead Civil Service." At the same time, he wasn't going to be respon- sible for giving a mother to be, the one carrying his baby, un- necessary stress. Even so, she had hurt him in marrying an old school rival of his, he knew that his emotions were getting in the way of his rationale, but there was simply nothing he could do about it. He arrived home, had his dinner with his family and went upstairs and saw a card had been waiting for him. Karen being the practical person she was had placed the card there, so that he would eat his dinner first, before reading it. Mark certainly enjoyed his dinner, and this gave Karen so much joy, and after eating he rested before going upstairs.

As he looked at his table, he noticed the envelope and then looked at it nervously, he could see it was from Sophie and then he opened it. Inside the card was a picture of two lovers, a big heart and a baby; and Sophie had written. "Congratulations you'll be daddy soon." After a few seconds of shock Mark was feeling very weak and vulnerable, his life was a mess, but he had no one to turn to. How could he tell his mum that two of his women were expecting? For him the power was in Louise's hands; she was in this mess just like him, and only she could help him and sort out their fate. Worried about his family noticing how troubled he was, he decided to read a book about the Forest of Bowland and to plan a bike ride there for the following day.

After calming down thanks to the countryside scenes of his roots, his mum knocked on the door. He then ran to the door. "Louise is in on the phone for you." Karen was delighted, her son had found a local girl, he almost knocked her as he ran downstairs to catch Louise's phone call, which almost sent his mum into stiches since there was nothing more than she wanted than for him to settle down in Garstang and for him to be happy.

"Hello Louise." He said with his heart pounding and almost about to faint since it was up and down all the time between them.

"Would you like to call round tomorrow at 11?" She said.

"I would love to." He said with great passion.

"Do you know 37 Pennine Gardens?" She said kindly.

"I do." He said, feeling totally weak at the knees.

"It is where my home is." She said casually.

It was a long night for him, he hadn't slept a wink, and hadn't told anyone about his dilemmas, which in his own troubled mind were many, yet in fact they weren't so complicated as he thought. Being alone, his mind became too complex, and since he had been away much of his adult life; he had lost contact with many of his friends back home who were also settling down.

He arrived at Louise's looking very pale from his sleepless night, while she was feeling very happy and in control of her emotions and wanted to help her man, who looked as though he had just seen a ghost. "Are you all right Mark? You look very pale." She said, as she was feeling guilty about the pain, she was causing him. He then followed her into the unromantic setting of her living room, which she shared with her husband and had her framed wedding photograph on the window ledges, making him feel somewhat rather sick inside and uncomfortable.

"No, I am not feeling very well, Sophie is pregnant." He blurted out, without thinking as he looked at her in terror.

"Who the hell is Sophie?" She said seething inside but wanting to get to the bottom of this scandalous news.

• • •

"I had no idea you were pregnant, and she deliberately got herself into the family way." He said regretting his honesty.

"What's all this rubbish you came back to England for me then? You promised me September . . . I heard nothing from you, apart from receiving the odd postcard. I suppose you think I fell pregnant deliberately too . . . And you are just the poor baby." She said as she looked at him full of anger and disappointment.

"Louise, I love you." He said desperately and in vain.

"Just fuck off! And leave me alone." She was madly in love with him, but at the same time she found him weak, since this was the best way for her to somehow look up to the husband she could never love. Mark not wanting to make a scene left, and not wanting his parents to ask him too many questions about his day, not that they would anyway, felt that all eyes would be on him, making him feel uncomfortable; as such he decided to cycle round the whole of the Trough of Bowland and visit Slaidburn, just like his mum did when his dad had stressed her out several years earlier.

At first, he felt weak, but as he approached Chipping, he was starting to enjoy himself, and as he climbed uphill on the way to Dunsop Bridge there were some frost patches, and he decided to take lunch at the local inn. When he left the sun had gone and was relieved as he went through the pass in the trough itself, where the maritime air was more in abundance and the temperatures had risen further still so that the slippery roads were no more a danger for him, and so he simply enjoyed freewheeling down into Wyre.

Back in Scorton he called into the priory and bought himself a notebook in pink with symbols of love. From then on with still one more week at his parents, he would pen poems to his beloved Louise. With just 40 pages, he wrote everything from his heart in just a couple of days. He spent a lot of time with his sisters and his parents, and they went walking together around Nicky Nook. One day they visited Calder Vale, and Karen as they were stood in front of her old house, walked off on her own down to the fast flowing stream and Frank followed her, she had been crying and they kissed and walked back hand in hand together, for Mark seeing his parents so happy and in love almost brought out all the mixed emotions in him, but somehow he managed to control himself. He was already 24 and a half, at the same his dad was when he was settled in Scorton with two sons and a stable marriage, even his younger brother had settled down and had a young family of his own and he himself two women up the stick; one married to someone else, the other he didn't love. They then walked back down through the village, the place of so many memories, but for now at least Karen, his mum, had managed to move on in her life.

As for Louise, she had some feelings of hatred towards him. For her it seemed as though he had messed up her life. She was studying English Literature at Manchester University and gave up at the end of her first year because of her pregnancy. She was a highflier, but Peter didn't encourage her to continue with her degree course, and under the circumstances she felt at the mercy of him. While she got on with Mark like a house on fire, she felt that her relationship with him was one of bad luck, and was by then having mixed feelings about him, but as much as she felt that Mark was in many ways stupid, there was no one else like him who had the magic and chemistry which she longed for in a man.

Mark had expressed in a letter he was thinking of posting that Christmas; that he only got the letters when he had arrived back, of course Louise knew this, but obviously neither of them could see things clearly. Mark decided to post the small package containing his letter and gift to her parents, since he was paranoid of Peter not giving it to her. When it arrived the day after he posted it, Mrs. Jones put it to one side ready for Louise when she came around later that day. Sadly, she forgot to give it to her, still two long days later when she went around to visit her daughter who was one week past her due date; she finally gave it to her.

When her mum left, she immediately opened the small package, inside she looked breathlessly at the book and read the 20 beautiful ballads of poetry he had written for her.

• • •

Time doesn't always rhyme in my heart.

Had I met you one month earlier would our lives have been so nearer?

I felt the power of love the moment I saw you.

I saw in you a most heavenly lady.

Time was our block one stupid month.

The light in your eyes: those fleshy lips.

Were blindingly obvious what could have been.

If only I had put love before all distractions.

And walked into the sunset.

And been truly on the wings of love with you.

This poem struck more than a chord with her, it was poignant to say the least, she could feel that he was going through lots of emotions when he wrote it, and that it had everything to do with their lives since that fateful day almost nine months earlier. She wasn't stupid: she knew full well, she told him in a letter just under a month after his departure about their child. What a difference a month can make to one's life, but at least she could see that he hadn't used her as much as she thought, in fact it was blindingly obvious that he was madly, truly, and deeply in love with her.

Around these precise moments in time Mark was leaving his parents' house, Frank had already gone out hiking with the little girls, while Karen wanted to see him off personally, and privately since she could see that he didn't seem overjoyed to be leaving. "If it doesn't work out, please don't just stay because of the baby."

"I know that mum." They kissed and off he went on his bike.

He had told her the night before about Sophie's pregnancy and she felt relieved to have expressed herself, but he found it all so creepy that his mum appeared to sense his unease and was relieved that he hadn't told her about Louise's condition. Of course, he hadn't thought of the fact that as a woman herself she could have helped him, advised him to wait a little longer for Louise after telling him off for letting Louise know about Sophie.

● ● ●

Louise meanwhile lay down on the bed, and before long she went back downstairs picked up her phone, which was in the hallway and dialed. "Hello," Said Karen, by then a little curious.

"Hello, Mrs. Taylor is Mark in?" She asked politely.

"No, I am afraid you have just missed him." She said.

"I will call back later." She said very pleasantly and respectfully to her, if only, she was, her mother-in-law.

"Oh, he just set off about ten minutes because he is going back to Belgium. Can I take a message?" She said disappointedly.

"No, it is okay Mrs. Taylor, I just wanted to catch him before he left." She too was disappointed, but it was worse for her, and sadly she didn't cry her sorrows with Karen, but then again how could she under the circumstances anyway, how could she explain to his mum that she was also with child and married? As such the phone conversation ended gently. Karen sensed that something wasn't right, maybe she should have helped her but then again Mark had to grow up and accept his responsibilities with Sophie.

Louise then left the house and decided to somehow find him along the A6; as such she threw on some clothes, and within five minutes she was waiting for him. Every time a cyclist passed by southbound her heart skipped a beat but after twenty minutes or so she gave up. As it transpired, she had missed him by about ten minutes. Louise was distraught but before she had time to fall into a depression, her labor contractions started, she was relieved since Peter, the safe man providing her with a home for her and the baby wouldn't be around as she gave birth and in turn had her mind was taken away from her other problem, Mark. Luckily, she gave birth on the same day, December 19th, 1987, to a healthy baby girl called Sarah who came into the world late that evening, weighing a healthy 8 pounds (3.6 Kilos).

Mark who was feeling devastated over Louise, was looking forward to being dad in Belgium, even so when he arrived back at Sophie's den. He was nervous, and even though she had a sweet smile, he knew that as he followed her that he was going into unchartered waters with her. That evening they had a special vegetable soup, which was followed by a homemade pizza and finished it off with a fruitcake, all made and prepared with love from Sophie. While eating Sophie seemed very happy. "So, you will be a daddy." She said happily and waited for his reaction.

"So, you weren't taking the pill?" He asked merely wanting to know how this happened to him twice the same year.

"I never had any intention of taking the pill." She said.

"What! You told me that you were on the pill." He wasn't pleased that she had trapped him in such a way.

"You can't spend the rest of your life with your mummy."

"When is our baby due?" He said changing the subject after taking a deep breath from her highly provocative tones.

"August the 20th." She said proudly and dreamily at him.

"So as soon as you knew you contacted me." He said.

"Of course." In fact, she hadn't really known when she had posted him the card, she just wanted to make sure that he would come back, and now she was in her 6th week of pregnancy and had just visited her gynecologist two days earlier; as such everything was in her mind going to her highly devoted plans.

That evening, they made love, but for Sophie something wasn't quite right, his caressing and his kissing were less passionate, while the actual sex was fine, his less sensitive side made her feel less secure. Of course, his mind was on Louise, part of him was angry with Sophie, equally he was too scared to tell her about his other love child, since he sensed that Sophie could turn nasty, and unlike Louise whom he could tell everything, he felt less open in Sophie's cage and desperately wanted to run back to Louise.

Back in work his colleagues were pleased to see him he had just been invited out to the staff party and he was happy to read not just the British Press, but also the Flemish and Dutch ones too. As such he felt that being back in Brussels wasn't so bad after all. After work he then cycled home and promised himself that he was going to be as kind to Sophie as he could; without her taking too much for granted and feeling that he could survive a year with her.

● ● ●

As he arrived home, he was surprised to see Sophie looking very depressed. He then put his arms around her, but she did not respond. "Darling my boss has just invited me to the Christmas staff party, I know that I never go out, but I told him that I would ask you first." He knew this wasn't very diplomatic but felt that with her it was the best way to appeal to her better judgement. "So, what's for dinner?" He asked without thinking to her annoyance.

"Nothing, I'm not hungry and I didn't feel like making anything." She said provoked by his night out and his manner.

"Well, that's okay I will cook for both of us." He said.

"No, I'm not letting you mess up the kitchen . . . You will have to make yourself a sandwich." She said, regaining her composure.

"Sophie I'd prefer something cooked, so if you are not going to, I will cook it myself." He wanted to shout at her, had it been Louise he most certainly would have done, but he rightly sensed that there was something a little bit dark and sinister about Sophie.

"Okay I will have to cook something myself." She sighed and was relieved that he was acting like a man for once towards her.

While waiting for the meal Sophie is seen staring at some keys, she then walks downstairs into her cellar, looks around, smiles to herself and takes down some measurements. As she walks upstairs, she notices that Mark is in the living room and so she goes into the bedroom and measures the bed quietly.

She then walks back through the living room into the kitchen, opens the oven and then takes out a dish with leek, cheese and potato. Mark then goes into the cupboard and places two plates on the table and they eat together in total silence, which made Mark wish he had never mentioned Sophie's pregnancy to anyone, since he could have had just stayed in Lancashire and got on with his life there, but now this was maybe the best he could get out of life, the one being with Sophie. They then sat and ate together. "I have decided that I am going to the Christmas staff party." With that she fell into a deathly silence and carried on eating as though it was her last supper while morbidly mulling over things.

After dinner Sophie sensed his unease and together, they sat on the couch and looked at photographs together. There was a harmless one of him and Nathalie, but when Sophie saw it, she started to go hysterical. "I don't believe this, after we met when you were cycling to mine you had this photograph taken, this is terrible!" She cried at him.

"This is a harmless photograph, taken before we met so there is no need to be jealous." He said hoping to calm her down.

"I am not jealous; do you think that if I were to go upstairs and to show this to my father that he would be pleased? Answer me!" She then starts to cry, he then puts his arms around her, but she pushes him away. "You don't care about me . . . Tomorrow I am going to see a doctor about having an abortion!" She screamed.

Sophie knew that she was out of control but blamed everything on the fact that he was only with her because of the baby. She sensed deep down that had she not told him about the baby that he would still be in Lancashire and this made a part of her hate him too. As for Mark, he was thinking that as soon as the baby would be born that he would be off and in search of someone else, but for the meantime if she kept the baby he would look after for as long as he was able to stand her. On top of that his mind was going around in circles and wondering as to how things were going with Louise and his baby and knew that the only way to keep himself sane was for him to make sure that he would keep up with cycling, swimming and of course with making love to Sophie.

By then she had stopped going to work, now pregnant she used her condition as an excuse for staying at home more. As for Mark, his daily routine was fine. Twice a week after work he would come home one hour later so that he could swim, he had also encouraged Sophie to meet him there since he felt her being pregnant that there was no better exercise for her. Equally Sophie saw the benefits too of getting fitter. She made him tasty meals, she loved him and was starting to do things together with him; as such in many ways he was happy with her, for the time being at least.

One evening together they sat on the couch; he had his arms around her while he was also busy studying French. Sophie was watching a film. "What is this film about?" she was delighted that he had asked since she wanted to share her dark secret with him.

"It is about a man who was locked in the cellar by his girlfriend to stop him from leaving her . . . I have thought about this myself," she said. Sophie felt relieved in telling him the truth.

"What." He said rather shocked to the core, and afraid.

"I was only joking." She said sinisterly, but neither of them was sure as to whether she meant it or not and kept it quiet.

After the film she went to bed, it was only eight, but Mark decided to join her after he had finished off a little reading, he then brushed his teeth and went to their bed. Sophie was very depressed, but she was in want of him so much. He caressed her, but she lay as though she was unconscious, in fact she was hurting very badly inside and wanted to punish him, even though she was punishing herself in doing so. Mark then fell asleep and a confused Sophie spent the whole night tossing and turning. The alarm clock went off and Mark tried to caress her. She simply wanted him to know her feelings. "You know why I am in a bad mood, don't you?" She asked him with a face like thunder, as he stared at her in dismay.

"I have no idea." He said tiring of her childishness.

"It is because we didn't make love." She was still confused because as much as she didn't want him to have any pleasure from making love, she needed him if he were to fulfill her carnal desires.

"Well, I tried to caress you." He said to her in dismay.

"I never felt anything." She said. He then went up to her, he was aroused as was she and they made love. Sophie was happy,

● ● ●

but she knew that he needed to get ready for work. "What time will you be back from the staff party?" She said changing the subject.

"I don't know." He said wondering where this was leading.

"You must have some idea." She asked him impatiently.

"I have never been out on a staff party before." He said.

"Well, I think you must have some idea." She said.

"Before midnight." He said knowing she would be angry.

"What!" She bawled showing him how horrified she was.

"Probably before eleven." He said sadly and feeling trapped.

Mark wasn't so bothered about going to the staff party, he knew that had he stayed in with Sophie that he could have had lots of pleasure with her. They both had a very healthy sexual appetite, but Mark wasn't going to do everything she said, and equally he believed that he had rights too. As such and despite knowing the trouble it would cause between them, he still went out for the evening and felt he was well within his rights too.

The food in the restaurant with his colleagues was simply excellent, and one or two staff members who didn't particularly warm to him in the workplace became human beings during that relaxed evening. There was laughter, and everyone was pleased that he had gone out with them in a much more relaxed setting than at work, just as they had expected with everyone else in what they wanted to believe was a close-knit working community. After a few hours and with great difficulty Mark left since he was enjoying himself more than he had expected, and his colleagues were doing their best for him to stay longer while he was nervous about the lady who was stewing.

Sophie was usually asleep well before 11 and when he arrived back at around 11:30 he was hopeful that he would arrive back to a calm place. He got into bed and sensed an eerie silence. "You said that you would be in by 11 o'clock." She hissed at him.

"Sophie, you kept asking me what time I'd arrive if you are not happy, I am off!" He then left the room and slept on the couch.

In his own mind, he had finally decided that as soon as his baby was born, he was going to leave her on her own as a single mum. Of course, had Louise contacted him, then now was the perfect timing, equally given he was in Brussels he was just 14 miles (22KM) away from Mireille, surely given Louise was in another country, wouldn't it be better to go and visit someone he wanted to run off with who was on his doorstep? On the other hand, he had no intention of going to try Mireille after the last visit where he felt very uncomfortable thanks to her mother. For him this was a confusing situation, his mind was in great turmoil, and given he knew nothing as to his chances with either Mireille or Louise he was in many ways simply at the mercy of his Sophie.

The next day Sophie went to visit her father. Being a rather reclusive woman, who didn't have many friends and not being able to go around telling all the women she knew about how much Mark was destroying her psychologically was having a negative effect on her, since she really needed to let off some steam. At her father's and before she had even a chance to complain, her dad asked her why he often heard her shouting at Mark when he was doing the best that he could for her, and that if she continued, he would leave her. She then explained that she was terrified of losing him, and that was the reason for her jealousy; as such he put his arms around his daughter and begged her to be happy with Mark.

As such she decided that given; she knew how much Mark wanted her to look after her health, that she would just act in a submissive way and let him decide what was best for them both. This made her feel all woman and knowing that she wanted Mark to be the man of the house she felt that she was working hard on their relationship. There was however just one problem; Mark had disobeyed her by going out for the night, and she felt betrayed, on top of that she had no idea what happened there as such she spent an hour or so out of her mind with worry that he had met someone else, maybe he had even made love there too, maybe he went to work to make love, oh it was all so frightening for her, but what could she do without any proof? She then nodded off to sleep.

A few hours before he was due to return, she then decided to pick up the book from England, which he had specially bought for her, it was a forty-week diary and now she was in week 6 she decided to write things and make up things as she went along and to make a story of which their future child would be proud.

Mark arrived home pleased that he would be off work for the festive season and hoped that it would be one full of love between him and Sophie. As he walked into the house Sophie approached him and helped him with his outdoor clothes to his delight. He then walked into the living room. "I have decided that I want to get healthy." She said, smiling at him, before they kissed.

"A pregnancy isn't an illness." He said gently after their kiss.

"I know that, so I want you to guide me." She said to him.

"Of course, I would love to be your personal trainer . . . In fact, I would take up swimming." He said to her caringly.

"The baths are old and dirty." She said to him concerned.

"Not in Dilbeek, that's where I go as you know, you have been there with me a few times . . . You could join me when I go there from work on Tuesdays and Thursdays." He said to her.

"They say it is the best exercise for pregnant women."

"We can also go cycling together again when the weather gets warmer, also what are we doing for our holidays?" He said smiling at her. Sophie was delighted, holidays that meant that he wasn't planning on leaving her in the foreseeable future.

"Yes, what do you suggest?" She asked, kissing his face.

"Easter it will be one year since we met, so why don't we celebrate our meeting anniversary there at the coast?"

"Yes, what a great idea." She said excited and happy again.

"As for summer, well August is out, July is a bit risky, why don't we go away in June, somewhere special?" He said.

"Where to?" She asked curiously and in awe of him.

"Austria." He said. Since he knew it there quite well.

"Where in Austria?" Feeling as if she was in heaven.

"I went near some lake close to Salzburg when I was a child with my family, it was fantastic." He said looking very dreamily.

"Wouldn't it be better to go away in May?" She said as she was starting to lick her lips in great delight.

"Might be a bit too cold at night then," he said.

"Yes, June is also when the days are the longest," she said.

"You say you want to be fit and healthy, so one month next to an alpine lake surrounded by mountains with plenty of fresh air would be great for you and the baby, and for me too!"

"Yes, sounds great." She said as though she was climaxing.

"Of course, one month is a long time so we would need to go and stay at a campsite." Sophie was a little bit shocked with this idea of his, but equally she knew that one month away before the birth could do wonders for their relationship, and she had also been reading in the diary about this kind of holiday for the expectant mother too. "Also, I would like us to go away on weekend and visit your mum; Dinant is a very nice place, and I would like to see it."

"I'm sorry but we can't go there because my mum doesn't want to meet you." She said sadly, and uncomfortably.

"Really, she hasn't even met me." He said bewildered.

"I know but she has heard some bad things about you."

"Well, then it is up to you to sort that problem out, since you are the only person who has been speaking to her about me." By then she felt rather humbled to say the least. Sophie enjoyed attention, but didn't know it, while she wanted sympathy from others, as such she could never be happy, even if she had her man. She wanted others to feel sorry for her; it made her feel better since she was so used to life being unfair that she wanted him to do more and more for her, even though she felt that he couldn't make her truly happy, since she was always looking for some new problem.

The New Year came in peacefully for them both and she was taking her pregnancy diary very seriously although certain things listed there, she only wrote down in her head since she knew Mark would be reading about everything too. Sophie was suffering from morning sickness, which seemed to be getting worse and worse, and she wanted to take some medicine against it, Mark was against on the grounds that it would increase the risk of a miscarriage and told her it is a natural part of the body's changing hormones, and she took his advice to his fatherly delight. As promised, she met him at the baths at least once a week and was showing him by then how much she wanted to please him and would swim 1KM on each visit.

February came, and her morning sickness was easing, and she was still wearing the same clothes as before, but when she got on top of him in the bed, he could see her body changing and they had a wonderful time of making love since there were no worries about becoming pregnant and she knew that Mark preferred her bigger breasts. Also, with the longer days they started to do some cycling together at the weekends. Valentine's Day was a big celebration of love that Sunday in Belgium. The day started off very private, with them both opening their cards and chocolates for each other, as well as the flowers he bought for her, and ended up at a Thai restaurant, which like all the other restaurants in the city was full. Not everything was beautiful for them that month. Sophie's daughter Gisele came around to stay over, it wasn't the first time and on previous visits she had stolen Some of Mark's things. On the day she left, he inspected her satchel and found it to be full of Sophie's photographs and jewelry, and while she felt guilty regarding the way Gisele was behaving, and her own treatment of her own daughter, with her new baby inside her and love flowing deeply she wanted a new life and as such she agreed with Mark sadly that Gisele wasn't welcome inside their home anymore.

March came, and she was starting to feel wonderful, but at times she was worried that since she was starting to get big that he would find her less attractive, but with both wanting each other as much as possible there seemed to be no danger of that. After contacting her mother and telling her how nice Mark was treating her, and that there had been some silly misunderstanding, they went away to her mother's in Dinant. One evening after work she met him at the railway station and from there; they took the train to Dinant. Mark enjoyed walking along the river Meuse and Lesse in the warm spring sunshine and the rocks close to the bank were for him magnificent. As for her mother, well she wasn't overly kind to him, but equally she wasn't very demonstrative to Sophie either. All in the visit during that long weekend had been a success, apart from the fact that Mark couldn't understand why her mother had left Sophie's father for such an uncharismatic and boring man.

April came, Sophie was now in their eyes big, wearing maternity wear and they went away to the coast for Easter and stayed at the same place as they had agreed and took their bikes with them too. They did the same walks as the last time they were there along the sand dunes, which reflected the sun's rays onto their faces and burnt them gently and both felt that their first year together had made them happier, while this were true, there was no denying the fact that had Sophie ended up with a less exciting man who would never leave her, she would had been even happier; while for Mark, Louise and Mireille were the ones who had the right energy for him. Sophie enjoyed breathing in the sea air, which she was convinced their child was enjoying too. They also managed two bike rides and she enjoyed the terrain, which was even flatter than in Brussels and both were sad when the trip ended.

May came and she looked of course pregnant, but at the same time very healthy thanks to her healthy diet, exercise, plenty of sleep and the fact that she had stopped going to work completely the previous month. They were still very passionate with each other; but Sophie still worried that she was ballooning and wanted to make sure that he was still happy in the bed with her, and in turn the more that they made love, the more they wanted each other, as everything seemed so lovely for them both.

On the last day of May after work, Mark met Sophie at the Railway Station and from there they took the night train to Salzburg. They slept well in the couchette and they woke up refreshed around breakfast the following day and ready for their bikes, which were waiting for them at the station. From there they cycled with Mark carrying all the camping equipment to Fuschl. While there, fond memories of his visit 10 years previously came flooding back to him. They stopped for their lunch, which she had made the previous day and managed a swim too in the tranquil waters of the turquoise lake. Sophie wanted to stay where they were, but Mark persuaded her that the short ride to the next lake was worth the effort. In total they had covered, 24 Miles that day, Sophie was tired but immediately fell in love with the path after St. Gilgen which went running through forests, and in Abersee which had stunning mountain views, and was completely flat. Given that she was 28 weeks pregnant she was unable to cycle as much as the holiday the year before, but since the setting was so perfect, she was motivated to do as much as she was physically as well as psychologically capable of.

Sophie had never been to such a pretty setting before and after pitching the tent together at the same campsite as on his previous visit; they went into the welcoming waters and swam together for the second time that day. After a while she got out, while he continued for some strokes more. Then they cooked a simple camping meal before going to bed. Of course, this highly sensual couple made love a lot, but given they were close to families in their tents little more than a few feet (1metre) away they were more discreet. The next day they relaxed and borrowed some books from the village library and Sophie studied the local places of interest. First on the list was Bad Ischl, and the following day before the intense heat they followed the old railway line which had been converted into a bicycle path to Strobl and from there they followed the River Ischl. Sophie was delighted to visit the town, which was the summer residence of the former Habsburg Emperors. Another day they cycled to two other lakes: Mondsee and Attersee. Basically, it was one day of a trip the next day of rest and so on, while the bike rides were usually around 25 miles.

The second week they bought a Lake Wolfgang ship ticket for the week. They visited Black Lake, which Sophie fell immediately in love with, the waters moody look and wished that they could have spent the night there, especially since Mark had already camped there, but as he explained he wanted a holiday which wasn't too adventurous given her condition. Two days later they even managed Monichsee, and with its 3000 feet (900m) climb it was quite a feat. By then Sophie had seen four of the previous places he had camped at with his family: Fuschl, Lake Wolfgang, Black Lake and Monich Lake. There was just one place left, that being Eibensee and once again Sophie marveled, and wished that she could spend the night there. As such Mark suggested that given that the weather was so perfect, that they could spend the night wild somewhere and in the end; she chose Eibensee, the pretty tarn.

Their return trip to Eibensee was a most wonderful and romantic time, they took the mid-morning sail as usual, stopped off at St. Gilgen, and then walked up with views of Mondsee and Attersee to the tarn. As they arrived the place was busy with walkers en route to or from either Fuschl or Wolfgang but as early evening arrived the day-trippers had already returned to their cars in the valleys, and with it being the middle of June the sun was still high in the sky. Sophie couldn't imagine a place more beautiful, the water despite being above 3500 feet (1050m) was around 20 degrees, and with Mark leading and checking for logs which had fallen into the tarn, she followed him devotedly to the other side, where the sun was still heating the rocks. From there they got out of the water, and with nobody around they made love and groaned so much as if to make up for their quiet heavy breathing of the past two weeks at the campsite. Then they swam back, and Sophie was less concerned with the meal that they would concoct somehow, than with the passion she was begging for, since it was the new moon and for Sophie the perfect setting and perfect occasion for her to celebrate what was still after all; her new life with Mark. They then went back after a semi restless sleep combined with all night long passion before going back to the campsite down at Lake Wolfgang. She was now 7 months pregnant and the time had come to sit back and relax during the second half of the holiday.

Even after having such an adventurous time behind her Sophie became obsessed with the next full moon, which would take place on their final night in Austria and she wanted something special. Sometimes they would walk around the local area or visit Strobl just 2.5 miles away by bike and get their groceries. The late June heatwave was also making her at times breathless, but she made sure that she had plenty of dips and swims with Mark. The month had been one of bliss for them both, never once did she think about her previous life, and never once did he think about Louise. Life was so beautiful for them and their unborn child. On the final night; as Sophie had been expecting was spent under the full moon. The setting was less than about a mile away and although very close to the bright lights of Saint Wolfgang, at the other side of the lake, their side of the lake was very secluded, and they walked around the field which followed down to the lake on the north side and down to the mountain stream on the east. To the west towards their holy Eibensee they watched the sun go down. A short while later the full moon rose and, after wanting him so badly and after he had fulfilled her; they walked slowly back to the campsite, arrived inside their tent and fell ever so deeply sleep. At the end of the holiday, Mark had collected some pebbles, which were no longer for him, but largely for his sisters, and one for good luck, which he would give to Louise if he ever met her again.

Back in Brussels, the weeks leading up to the birth were peaceful, Sophie reduced her visits to the swimming pool in the hope that Mark would do the same too, but he insisted on it so that his back wouldn't give up from sitting around too much, basically he wanted his back muscles to stay strong as such Sophie knew how much the swimming was good for her and was thankful that Mark had given her this push to keep herself in

• • •

shape and was prepared not to complain for the time being at least. Sadly, in many ways that August, Sophie didn't compare herself in being a grounded pebble, and often thought of herself as being off the wings of love, since nothing could ever truly make her feel content.

Their big day arrived, and Sophie knew as soon as she was going into labor, they immediately took the metro, just a five-minute walk away to the hospital in a western leafy suburb of the city. Everything was fortunate, it being a Saturday and the 20th of August 1988. The birth was quick, was it because it was a second time birth being supple from the swimming or a combination of both? Either way Sophie was pleased that everything had gone so smoothly. As soon as Axelle appeared Mark picked her up into his arms, and he wasn't for one moment thinking about the other child of his whom he had never met. So, determined was he to move on in life, to accept there were things in the past that he couldn't change, and that he simply wanted to be happy with his new family; and most importantly he trusted that Sophie was a good mummy.

After a few days in the hospital Sophie came home. She was relieved to be back. Both Mark and Sophie had sleepless nights due to the baby and both had their responsibilities. Mark was working all day, and Sophie was with the baby all day, but after a few weeks Sophie started to feel that her life was meaningless, and she wanted Mark to help her. Even so she knew that Mark wouldn't be able to solve this, and that she herself didn't want to go to work but someone had to bring in the money, and knew that she was a mother, as such she kept things to herself knowing that in time looking after Axelle would hopefully get easier.

One evening a few weeks later Mark had had a stressful day in work, and just wanted to relax. He enjoyed watching Sophie bathe, clean and feed Axelle picked her up and sat with her, until Sophie put her to bed. Sophie didn't speak to him and just before he fell asleep, he left the living room, wondering what was wrong with her.

After a few minutes Sophie arrived, and they made love and he fell instantly in sleep. Sophie wanted him to understand what being woken up is all about and was furious that during most nights when Axelle woke her up that he just slept through it all, as such she started to shake him. "Why have you woken me up?"

"I am fed up with being responsible all the time for Axelle."

"But Sophie, you were already awake, and I have got work."

"Look if you gave up your job you would be able to devote yourself more to family matters like I do." She said scornfully.

"And what about money?" He asked her commandingly.

"You can sign on." She said not knowing what she wanted.

"Sophie I am not going to do this." He said in shock.

"Ok, but I want us to move away from Brussels and to move to somewhere in the country, it would be better for Axelle."

"I agree, but how can we move there without any money or work for that matter?" He asked her in great frustration.

"Well, we could if you would sign on there." She said.

"Sophie, this isn't going to happen, if I don't sleep, I can have an accident in work." He said and turned his head away from her.

Sophie wasn't at all convinced that he was playing fair to her, if he was tired, he would give up his swimming, true it was now once a week instead of twice since the birth, but she needed more commitment from him. Even so Mark had gone to work in reasonable spirits, he was tired as usual, maybe a little more thanks to Sophie, but was feeling positive all the same, and simply put down her unreasonable behavior to her post-natal depression. It was a Thursday he hadn't yet been to the swimming pool that week, and although this meant he seeing Axelle less that evening, he had to keep up with his healthy routine. He arrived at the pool with a slight ache from sitting in a poor position, but after his forty lengths in the pool he felt as though his whole body had been massaged. Then it was time to go home quickly and catch his daughter before she went to bed, and hopefully Sophie would be kind to him as he arrived home feeling relaxed and happy.

He arrived in the living room, which was in the dark, turned on the light while tidying up the mess from his pockets; Sophie then came in while Axelle was waiting in her baby chair. "I have spent all afternoon making the dinner, and you have arrived home late!"

"Sophie it is not late, I always go swimming on a Thursday, and it is just for one hour each week." He said tensely.

"Well, I think that it is time that you gave it up." She then left the room, Mark then followed her into the kitchen and ate his meal in silence, which she had made grudgingly for everyone earlier.

They then put Axelle to bed together, Mark had said his peace, didn't wish to continue making a fuss; but had no intention of giving up his swimming or his job for that matter. The weekend came, and they had been invited to visit her father for dinner. It was a relief for them. Neither had been speaking properly to each for a few days, and to Sophie's horror both Mark and Thierry had a lot to say to each other and were enjoying their conversation. In the end Sophie gave way and instead of looking as though she was constantly busy with Axelle, she moved towards Mark and made sure that she was showing some physical contact since she couldn't face being lectured again by her father again.

The rest of the weekend was fine, they made love and things were looking rosy for them. Mark hadn't forgotten her bad moods and as he saw unreasonable behavior but wanted to enjoy his time with his loves. Sophie meanwhile knew that she had been wrong, regretted what she had done and would while Axelle was asleep ask herself why she was doing something, which could easily send the man she so desperately wanted, to leave her.

Over the next few days, it was obvious to her that Mark was drifting away from her and she was thinking about how she should respond until one evening when he came home with some news. He came in through the door looking more confident than he had been for some time, he certainly didn't look at all hen-pecked and she went weak at the knees with lust on seeing him. "Hello darling." She said as he walked through the door more upright than usual.

"Hello darling, have you had a good day?" He asked her.

"I have thanks love." She wasn't sure as to whether she had had a good day, but his positivity made her want to show him the good girl she was. He then sat down, after picking up Axelle and placing her on his knee while she was delighted being with him.

"As you know, I have had a bit of back ache recently."

"Maybe you need to take it easier." She said happily.

"No, quite the opposite, exercise strengthens the muscles."

"I would love to do something, but I have to look after Axelle all the time." She said exasperated with his selfishness.

"No, you don't, just arrange an evening to go swimming and I will look after her while you swim." With that she smiled while he walked up to her to show his appreciation of her looking after herself by simply kissing her and smiling at her.

The rest of the evening was calm, but Mark had already come to an important decision and when Axelle was in bed he began. "As you know I need to get away sometimes and unfortunately Axelle isn't ready to go away just yet, so I am planning on a weekend away cycling as far as I can around the Ardennes." Sophie was hurt and shocked since she didn't want him to be away from her but realized that she had driven him to this.

The next few days she spent mulling over in her mind what had gone wrong between her and the fathers of her two children. Sadly, she couldn't pinpoint out where the problems lay. Sophie was in fact still in trauma from her ex; He had deliberately as she saw it got her pregnant in order to keep her 12 years earlier, and he had cheated on her several times too. Once when Gisele was already born, she went around to his parents and found him in bed with some young woman. Guy had even broken her nose, but she hadn't gone around to the police this was around the time when she wanted him to leave her, he didn't , so she basically insulted him until he could take no more since she had decided that a divorce was the only solution. As such she couldn't decide who was at fault, he for sleeping around behind her back or she for insulting him because of what he had done. She had discussed this once with Mark, who immediately decided that Guy was a twat, but for Sophie things were not so black and white. Equally she knew that Mark wasn't anything like as bad as Guy, but she was a little bit afraid of him, since the more she thought, the more she realized how her ex had been violent towards her and was confused as to what kind of man Mark really was. She then concluded that she knew that she was bad to Mark and needed him to lay down the law.

That evening she was waiting happily for him, and she just wanted him to take the lead in the relationship and to basically be the man of the house. They had just made love then Sophie wanted to get a few things off her chest. "What would you like to do this weekend?" She asked him and hoping he would take the lead.

"I don't know, I am just happy for us to be together relaxing and taking Axelle out." He said, while Sophie wasn't happy and wanted him to do something about her state of mind.

"I would like you to decide something, you are the man."

"Look Sophie I don't know." He said a little bit exasperated.

"What do you mean that you don't know?" She said annoyed.

"I decide quite a few things, you are swimming now, we are going away to the coast, and to England for a month, so for this weekend I am letting you choose, this way is fair too."

"It doesn't work like that." She said as her voice pitch lowered, and she spoke slowly and was sounding rather menacing.

"Sophie, I believe in equality." He said tired of her as usual.

"Well, I don't, either you are the boss, or I am the boss." Mark decided to ignore her as he put it, "Childish behavior," but instead the anger and frustration was fermenting deep inside of her. A few hours later she woke up in a cold sweat, she was thinking about the men in the Middle East and how the women knew their place, and honored the demarcation lines between the sexes, which made men men and women women. It wasn't

Mark's fault, he was right, but for women like herself equality wasn't right and in her confused mind she wished that she was living in Jeddah in spite of the fact that she hated Muslims, while at the same time his ideas on equality were driving her insane and were in fact polarizing her needs and dislikes in a volatile and schizophrenic way.

The next day was weekend and they basically did their usual winter things, braving it outside with the pram, eating and relaxing together as well as playing with Axelle. With the week-end gone, she was feeling disappointed and when Monday came, and he was out at work all she could think about was how he was hurting her so badly and then how she was hurting him too.

Another evening came, they went to bed, they made love, and then she couldn't sleep, her dark presence made it difficult for him to sleep too, and that was of course her intention, since with no one to support her when she wanted others to feel sorry for her, when deep down she knew that she had all her basic needs she felt a little confused. A while later, he looked at her after a nap and although it was dark thanks to the light from outside, he could make out her eerie look. "Why are you looking at me frightened?" He said. "I am frightened that you are going to hit me." She said.

"Sophie, I have never hit a woman in my life, and I have no intention of starting now." He said completely sick and tired of her.

"Well, I think that it is time that you did." With that Mark was disgusted, but he had work; the next day and wanted to sleep.

As for Sophie, she needed him, but he had shown her once again how weak he was. By simply falling asleep when she felt: as lonely as a cloud, was enough for her to wish that she had had a child with her former Albanian lover, and maybe living with Guy was better than the hell Mark was putting her through. At least the other men didn't pretend to be nice, while Mark wanted to be liked by everyone, she felt that he was simply a fake, since his love for her wasn't so deep and meaningful as she would have wished. Even so she herself was madly in love with him, and to her great dismay; she knew that Mark, who didn't deserve her love, was aware of this.

As for Mark, regarding his two children he felt like a complete failure and was tormented with the fact that had he not got further than Garstang; that he would now be blissfully happy with Louise and embarking on a family in the same and idyllic way as his parents, but instead he had failed in many ways as a responsible parent and was ashamed of himself.

Chapter Nine

September: The Blue Slate Pebble of Love.

W eekend came; in fact, it was a rather long one for him. His work was such that each week, he and his collea-gues, due to the nature of the job, were working four hours overtime and as such were given two days off in lieu each month. As such, the Friday morning he set off on his trails to Namur and beyond. On the way he decided to call in at Wauthier Braine and to pay a visit to the Rochards. The ride was pleasant enough, he wasn't expecting Mireille to be around, but given she had been on his mind on and off for two years, and more so recently due to Sophie's crazy antics, he simply followed his heart, he wasn't planning on leaving Sophie, but he was certainly open to some uncomplicated fun. The ride along the canal to Halle was pleasant enough and then he entered rolling hills and was glad to get away from Brussels and Sophie's den.

As he arrived at the Rochards, a little nervous, he rang the doorbell of the house and a smiling mother was seen answering the door. "Hello Mark, come in." Said Mrs. Rochard, who was delighted to see him. He followed her into her house and then into her dining room next to the kitchen. He sat then sat down as she left the room and went upstairs and stood in front of a bedroom door.

"Mark is here." She said delightedly to her child.

"I'm coming." Said a Mireille who was reading a romantic novel on her bed and almost jumped out of her skin, she then quickly brushed her hair in front of her mirror. Mrs. Rochard then entered the dining room along with her proud husband.

"So, what are you doing now?" Asked Mrs. Rochard.

"I am living in an apartment in Anderlecht and working in a bookshop in Brussels." He said to the delight of everyone, and they continued in French, and smiled as they got to know him more, after a few minutes of Mark speaking, he was interrupted.

"We are really sorry about what happened when you came to visit us last time, but things are different now, you speak good French and have a good job." She said apologetically and delighted with his presence. Mireille then entered the room as both she and Mark put their arms around each other while her parents were seen looking on delightedly. Her mother then made a tea, and after two years of wondering what had happened to this nice man who came to her house, she wanted to help her dreamy daughter in getting the man of her dreams and then and only then could she forgive herself for ruining it for them. Mark and Mireille were smiling at each other a lot and a few minutes later, Mrs. Rochard arrived with a tray full of homemade cakes and tea. "Help yourselves." She said.

"Thank you." Said Mark. He was then thinking that the previous visit was before he met Sophie and then he felt much more an innocent man, but that was because he was unaware of Louise's condition, as such he was feeling a little ashamed of himself, but so in need of love was he that he simply had to charm Mireille.

"You are very welcome to stay here this weekend."

"Thank you." Said a very surprised and delighted Mark and Mireille almost collapsed with shock and happiness.

"I am going to show Mark around." She said dreamily.

They were glad to leave the house and to spend some time alone. She then gave him a wristband, which she had made. "Thank you." He then leant his head toward her, and they started to kiss. They then walked around her large garden and she told him about her last boyfriend whom her parents didn't like one little bit, and how much they liked Mark. It was music to his ears.

● ● ●

Mark had been carrying close to his heart a pebble from Austria the previous summer, and by then he had given up on her, but then felt that Mireille was the one, as he took out the pebble inside his bum bag, kissed it, placed it on her lips as she kissed it too, and placed into her left hand as she was touched by his sentiment. Luckily for Mark, he still had two black pebbles hidden in his drawer, and one was for his first child if he would ever meet her. He then told Mireille about his domestic partner Sophie, and his daughter Axelle. Sadly, Mireille wasn't so magnanimous to him as he had been to her.

"I know it was all my mum's fault, but I don't wish to get involved and to ruin your daughter's world." She said sadly.

"You want me to go?" He said calmly, deeply and slowly.

"I don't know, my mum is expecting you here and I don't wish to tell her everything, since she would feel guilty." She said simply wanting the whole earth to swallow her up.

"I didn't have to tell you so soon, but all this could had been avoided." He said hoping to make her realize he was being honest and gentlemanlike. Mireille was then feeling so unhappy, she still wanted him as he wanted her, but she couldn't give herself to him since things had changed, and she knew that, so long as she didn't know what to do, she couldn't just throw him out after her mother had invited him and he graciously accepted. It was all just one hell of a big mess for her and for him too, since he just wanted to make her happy, and she was all confused.

Things became less tense and after speaking about life and their dreams, dinner was then served, which was then followed by a family movie. Bedtime came and with Mireille in such a great turmoil and against her will she took him to her bedroom. Although almost ill with everything she knew that she had to put on the false act of being in bliss with her beau, since although she hadn't created the mess, she didn't want to hurt anybody. They then went to her bedroom. "You understand my dilemma?" She said as he nodded, waiting for her to continue. "I really want you to go because of your family, but I really want you to stay because

• • •

I like you." She said, giving the impression that she was really infatuated with him.

"Mireille if it is of any help to you, as we are standing between no man's land and love, all I ask is to kiss you, goodnight." She was then relieved, and under his spell so much that she hadn't thought of a compromise between her other desire to get him out of her life as such she wanted a kiss and that was all. As he kissed her, he was kneeling lower below the bed somewhat, hoping to show her how aroused he was. That she didn't doubt but was ready to snub him if things got out of hand. It was simply going to be a kiss on the lips and nothing like the passionate and juicy one she had enjoyed with him earlier in her garden that day. He then started to kiss her on the lips, she reluctantly gave way, but when she could feel the force of his mouth pressing against hers, she lost control opened her mouth and they French kissed with so much passion that all their saliva could had easily been mixed and replaced with one an other's. They went to bed together, he kept on his underpants while she wore her pink nightie. She wanted him, he wanted her, but how could they get together? She kept thinking about how close to making love they were, all it took was for him to have kept mum just until they got to bed, and as much as she felt they could never be, she respected his honesty, as painful as the truth might be. Eventually, just before dawn they fell asleep after tossing and turning for much of the night.

After breakfast, they went on a walk together with a packed lunch; she simply wanted to spend as much time with him away from her family and to discuss everything in detail with him. Instead, she just wanted them to kiss each other. But when he started to kiss her breasts, she was shocked with herself since she hadn't given any protest whatsoever against the man who had promised not to go further than to French kiss her. He was soft, he was gentle, and at the same time his passion was causing her one big headache, because it wasn't right to be doing such a thing, he had a baby and there they were not far from a public footpath. After fighting with herself she protested, by moving his

• • •

head away, and she knew she had tamed him, while at the same time, she didn't know what to do.

Dinner was served, they both had an appetite, and this time as they kissed on her bed; she almost collapsed and lay down, waiting for him to repeat his kissing of her breasts and no more. Instead, she was disappointed, he wasn't going for her bosom, instead he was kissing and kissing her not just mouth to mouth but all over her neck, licking her as though she was some aphrodisiac and her breasts could take no more, they were almost tingling with pain, until finally she took control and pushed him away. She then looked at him, grabbed hold of his face to safety away from the rest of her body, until she became breathless and took off her top so that he could kiss her chest and her breasts, which by then needed caressing, as if that weren't enough her body was pumping, as for his, it had been pumping as far as she was concerned since yesterday but he seemed to have great control, however his physical prowess had seduced her to the point of no return. Luckily, she pushed him away ran to her drawers and took out a condom, it had been so close a call, since she hadn't expected to go this far, it was a spur of the moment thing, and she knew had he had not mentioned that he was already a daddy, that in the heat of moments like this that anything was possible. Suddenly she remembered the dream she had the night before, it was simply of him on top of her and kissing her all over and she knew that it was time for him to make her dream come true, and for him to get inside of her.

The next moments were crucial and she wondered how good it would be to have him inside of her, how long he could manage, but with them so aroused it didn't matter and as soon as he went in her, these two young lovers climaxed almost immediately. That night they managed to make love five more times and finished just as it was getting light. It was a Sunday, so they had nothing to worry about the prying eyes from her family. They woke up around lunchtime, and when they went downstairs to the dining room, they were greeted by Nathalie who had herself just surfaced since she had been to the same disco as the last

• • •

time he had visited, but now the roles were different, since Mireille was the one who had the night to remember, which was more than just simply dancing with him. Everything had come like a streak of lightning and was a bolt out of the blue for them.

The following day they spoke about when they could meet up with each other again, Mireille was busy for the next few weeks, Easter he wasn't around, so they planned to meet up again two months down the road. As for Mr. and Mrs. Rochard they were both delighted, he was a good man and was making their daughter happy. Fortunately, they had the sense to give them both space since they knew how they messed things up for her two years earlier and she ended up with a total nightmare of a man who neither of them liked and were relieved when it all ended and hoped that Mark was the answer.

On his way back, Mark formulated his route that he had taken, in case Sophie wanted to know where he had been. As such he thought about the train to Liege and a stay at Malmedy, and since he knew the route from his days at Maastricht he could simply speak about this previous trip as though it were in the present and that he must also take into account that the weather was completely different but was confident that he wouldn't get caught out.

Back at home Mark and Sophie devoted their time to a delighted Axelle, they ate together and then bathed their baby before putting her to bed. Mark described his weekend, which was based on the one which he had formulated cycling back earlier that day. Sophie was seething with rage inside, she hated him because she felt deep down that he didn't love her, while Mark was angry too, she had trapped him with a baby, and now she was his roadblock between himself and Mireille. Even so they drank fruit juice and ate chocolate together, went to bed and made love. Unlike the other night, once was enough for Mark, and deep down she knew it too, she could tell that it was simply a part of his routine for her and sadly nothing more, but poignantly better than nothing.

A few days later everything seemed calm, Mark was sleeping and then suddenly Sophie woke up, got out of bed, walked round and belted him across the chest, Mark woke up instantly, her punch was quite a blow and it hurt. He looked at her and she started to look worried. "I'm sorry." She then tried to caress him gently.

"Fuck off!" He said and wasn't impressed; it was the first time he had sworn at her like that. She then started to cry, he ignored her safe in the knowledge that she wasn't going to attack him in the foreseeable future, but at that moment he felt that he could never love her again and fell right back into his deep sleep.

Fortunately for them his family were coming over, and this had been arranged just before Christmas behind her back and was between her father and Thierry. The reason was simple, he sensed that Sophie would have made a big issue out of this and knowing how kind Thierry was he told him about his family. Thierry immediately offered one of his bedrooms and immed-iately sent an invite to the Taylors. It came at the right time since Karen had been thinking about the fact it was one year since she had seen her eldest child. She immediately contacted Thierry in French and everything had been arranged like a dream. Sophie had been told by a delighted Thierry, who given he was in direct contact with Karen knew before Mark, thus putting him in the clear, she was dreading the visit but felt that there was nothing that she could do, and to make matters even worse she felt that her own father was watching over her, and in many ways he was.

On Saturday the 18th of March 1989, the Taylors, Karen, Frank and their two girls aged 9 and 8 were feeling excited. From their home they took the early morning bus down into Preston and from there, the train to Leeds where they enjoyed the views of the Pennines on the Lancashire and Yorkshire Border. From Leeds a second train took them to Hull. Arriving just before lunch they had plenty of time to look around the city, where Mark went to university. Towards the early evening a shuttle bus took them to the harbor, and from there they boarded the ship to Zeebrugge along with 1,400 or so passengers. They slept in comfortable berth cabins for four and enjoyed a wonderful evening buffet before walking around the decks and getting themselves ready for bed.

After a good night's sleep, they went into the restaurant where they filled themselves up with the delicious English and continental style breakfast buffets. It sounds rather luxurious, but back then the price on the boat for the night half board was equivalent to what one would expect in a B&B. After breakfast the ferry shuttle bus took them to Bruges, and Mark had arrived with Thierry. The Taylors marveled at the medieval city, especially the little girls who delighted in the old, cobbled streets, canals and gift shops. Karen was so happy to see Mark enjoying the company of his father-in-law and everyone got on very well together. Mid-afternoon they took the train to Brussels and the metro to Veeweide, close to where they lived. After meeting her third grandchild, and Sophie too, Karen was pleased to see that all her fears about her boy being trapped in some strange lands were completely unfounded. That night they slept in the guest bedroom, which had a four-poster bed for the parents, and two matrasses were set up for the children but seeing as Karen and Frank weren't able to have some sexual activity with their kids in the way, they allowed two awestruck girls the opportunity to sleep in the four-poster bed together to their great delight.

The following day Mark was at work, so Sophie, Thierry and Axelle showed them around the sights of Brussels including the Mannekin Piss and the Great Square. Just before lunchtime they went to visit what was the largest W.H. Smiths the Taylors had ever seen, and Mark joined them for lunch at a Vietnamese restaurant. Tuesday came and just the four Taylors on holiday went up to Antwerp by train for the day. First they went to the zoo, which was next to the railway station and then for lunch they had a light snack in one of the restaurants in the Hassidic community, Karen who had read, The diary of Anne Frank, really wanted to enjoy a hearty meal, but knowing that Thierry had been spending the weeks leading up to their stay with his gourmet preparations she knew that she had to compromise.

After taking just a snack it was time to visit the city for a couple of hours and to return by train to Brussels and to come back to Thierry's, where the meal he had been preparing all day was enjoyed by Mark and Sophie, who joined too.

The next day was a restful day, and they spent the whole day thanks to Sophie hanging around the haunts of the courtship days of Sophie and Mark when she was showing Mark the rural parts of Brussels. They all loved the ponds and the French Fries at the Notelaar Restaurant. That evening a very happy Mark came home and was ready for the Easter break.

After an early breakfast the next day they took the train to Oostduinkerke and stayed in an eight-person chalet at the seaside, which suited them all perfectly. The Taylors slept in the four-bedded room, Mark, Sophie and Axelle in a two-bedded room and Thierry had a two-bedded room all to himself. During the day Axelle had to stay in the pram most of the time while the Taylor girls were literally jumping for joy and running around the giant sand dunes and playing on the beach, where to Sophie's shock and Thierry's surprise all the Taylors went in the sea for a paddle with Mark going one step further and swimming with his dad. At other times, Amy and Kerry were picking up seashells, and most importantly of all were looking for some prized pebbles to take back home.

Back in Brussels the Taylors had a relaxing day around the neighborhood and then they had a day out and this time to Maastricht. In many ways the city reminded them of Bruges with the canals, cobbled streets and horse-run carriages. The next day was relaxing and a Friday. The Taylors wanted to visit W.H. Smiths but of course FNAC was more to Karen's taste since there she could choose from as many of the French novels as she could imagine.

They left Belgium on the Saturday, and this time they were sent off with Mark, Sophie and Axelle. It had been an eye opener for Sophie, seeing how happy and in love Mark's parents were, who were both grandparents and parents of young children and not much older than Sophie herself. Well Karen was just 11 years older than Sophie, but in many ways, she was younger, and seeing the love between Mark and his family made her have some more respect for him and pushed her into working harder on her relationship with him. She also realized that Mark missed his family and she too, since she came from a broken family and had certainly enjoyed the effect that the calming influence of the older Taylor couple had on her own family and was thankful for this.

Back in the routine of things, life was calmer for Mark and Sophie, but now it was Mark who was starting to feel depressed. Given he no longer loved Sophie, his enthusiasm for staying in Belgium wasn't very high to say the least, while Sophie was happy that she finally had a healthy relationship or so it seemed to her. Mark certainly loved Axelle, and his face always lit up whenever he saw her, and Sophie felt that the love he had for their child was being directed towards Sophie too. His other reason to stay in Brussels was of course for Mireille.

During the long weekend off work in May, Mark again as arranged went to stay at Rochards. This time he arrived with flowers for Mrs. Rochard and a book specially written by him full of poems for Mireille. He had been writing the works of love at W.H. Smiths so that Sophie was kept in the dark. As much as Sophie didn't want him to go away, she felt that Axelle was still too young to go away too often; as such everything seemed normal to her.

Mark's third visit to the Rochards was again full of surprises. The beginning went pretty much expected: Mireille answered the door almost throwing herself at him to his great delight. Mrs. Rochard and her husband saw wedding bells in the air, while her older sister felt as though that she was being left on the shelf and started to regret going out to discos and meeting weirdos.

Like Mark, Mireille had waited all the minutes since they last met to meet each other again, and both had at the back of their minds their plans for each other when they would be alone together in her bedroom that night. During the day Mark helped with some gardening and then Mireille wanted to go walking with system STEVEN KAY

just the two of them. They were simply in love and hadn't much to say, but plenty of excuses to open their mouths and to kiss each other. Their mouths were also unlocked for the packed lunch; which Mireille's mother had made for them too.

Back at her home the dinner was fine Nathalie then went out to the disco as she had promised to go there with her friends, the parents decided to leave the scene which prompted an early night for Mark and Mireille. Given they had already made love together, there was more of a calm between them than during the previous visit and they felt more experienced with each other, on top of that their desires and longing for each other made this night simply one to remember and met both of their had great expectations.

The next day they eventually woke up completely exhausted; the house was empty and together they took a bath together, before going back to bed for an hour. They were simply madly and passionately in love, and all Mireille wanted was to hear his songs from his heart and to hear more of his poetry, especially for her. The weather was good the sun was shining, and their love for each other chimed well with villagers of a previous generation, since both Mark and Mireille were romantic lovers from the days of Victor Hugo and Alexandre Dumas, since for them; all that mattered was their feeling of desire, passion and longing for each other, which meant for them more than anything else which money could buy. That evening in bed she looked at him. "I spent hours and hours searching high and low, and in the end, I found this incongruous blue slate pebble, especially for you." She said to him dearly.

"Mireille this is so romantic, it is just like me, I come from near the Lake District, and there we have these blue slate pebbles everywhere." He said as he looked around her bedroom and spied on the pebble he gave her, which was lying on her window ledge.

On the third day and with Mark leaving the next day, the serious conversation about their next meeting took place like last time and after it, Mark began, as they were walking hand in hand in the aromatic woods which were carpeted with the bluebells of a typical day in May. "Dearest Mireille, we both love each other, why don't we live together?" He said dreamily into her ears.

"Oh! How much I want this Mark, but with me studying now it isn't the time." She said sadly and wanted to run away with him.

"I can move to Liege for you, then we can live together."

"Liege, I only study there, it is not a very nice city, and besides what work would you get there?" She wondered.

"It doesn't matter; I just want to be with you." For him it was so ironic, since if Sophie were in Mireille's shoes she would have jumped at this opportunity, and this filled his heart with pain.

"As I only want to be with you . . . Why don't you leave Sophie and move into a flat of your own?" She said to him.

"Darling I am only in this country for two reasons, and you know what they are." He said, trying to cover up his disappointment.

"Go on tell me." She said dreamily and knowing fully well.

"You and my daughter Axelle." He said romantically to her.

"You are saying that if you lived in Brussels on your own just waiting for me and for Axelle that you would feel very lonely?"

"Yes, indeed I am . . . Seeing Axelle reminds me of you."

"How can this be?" She said as she had suddenly frozen and wondered if he had completely lost all his marbles.

"I often wonder how things could had been . . . Basically Axelle is the child who we should have had together." He then paused and wanted to embrace her, but she resisted, to his worry.

"Go on tell me more." She said as she was starting to think about how her mother had got them both into this mess.

"When I first met you, my heart almost skipped a beat and all I wanted was you, OK, I didn't know anything about you, but I wanted to, my intuition told me that you were simply a girl country who knew how to be loved and to love someone too."

"And this is what I saw in you, Mark, but life is not so easy, it could have been so beautiful, but now we have to wait for each

● ● ●

other . . . So, what is the plan then?" He was shocked, since he didn't want a plan just to move in with her there and then, and forever.

"The plan is we must wait for each other, I will stay living with my daughter until your studies are over; and each time we meet, we will arrange our future rendezvous." She then smiled.

"Are you happy with this?" She herself wasn't happy.

"Modern life is full of obstacles, but hopefully things will work out well in the end." He said resignedly to her.

"You mean you have some doubts?" She said worried.

"I just wish that we could be together all the time, but I respect your studies and all that we can do is to simply wait."

Mireille wasn't at all happy with his response, since she simply wanted some miracle to happen; still they arranged that due to her year abroad in Quebec that they would meet up before the following month. Then she would be gone that August, the day after his arrival back from England. Sure, they met in June, and with her going off for one year, plus another two months since in July he was in the UK meant a more poignant visit. The love, making was less potent, with thoughts at the back of both their minds of how easy it could be if they could only follow their hearts. Although it hadn't been said; they both knew that things had been struck when the iron was hot for them two years earlier that being so naïve, so simple and dreamy, they would have been so happy as they were now miserable. After the visit Mireille shed many a tear, while Mark devoted more time and energy towards Sophie, who in turn showed more of her better side towards him.

The next big event for the Taylors in Garstang was the arrival for the first time in their home of Sophie and Axelle. Mark travelled with Sophie and Axelle, by train, and ship to his parents. They went there with their bikes, on August 1st the month when the baby would celebrate her first birthday and so it was considered safe enough for her to sit at the back of the bike, which she loved, since they had already had some trial rides the month before. The day they left the ride to the station was only 2 miles, then just another mile from the end station to the ship. The following day after an exciting night on the ship for everyone, they had to cycle to the railway station in Hull, which wasn't a very pleasant ride, with heavy traffic and ugly roads, the five miles seemed like an eternity, it was of course no wonder that Sophie wasn't too pleased. The train ride through the Pennines was spectacular enough and then they had an eleven-mile ride along the A6 to his Garstang. Once again this wasn't the friendliest of rides for a family to take, but at least as they reached Catterall the traffic calmed down, and Mark's heartbeat rose as he passed Louise's old family home.

Sophie marveled at his parents' home, it was in such pleasant yet down-to-earth surroundings, and almost next to the river; it was comfortable but at the same time somewhat modest. They spent one week there, and Karen although she was surprised by her son's choice of partner who wasn't the most of expressive of women did everything to make her feel as comfortable as possible. With Axelle in a baby sling they covered the historical haunts of the Taylors: Calder Vale, Nicky Nook and Scorton on foot, as well as a day trip to Hambleton by bike. One-day Frank who was still only 46 went on a bike trip with Mark around the Trough and started reminiscing about old times, while Mark confessed to his dad about Mireille, and he simply listened; since he found it all so complicated and could feel his son's confusion and promised to keep it all a secret, and Frank being Frank gave his son plenty of support.

A large 8 Berth chalet had been hired out in Langdale for everyone complete with two bedrooms; both four bedded and Sophie was pleased to be staying in what was simply for her of luxury and enjoyed the holiday. Amy and Kerry were in awe at the many of the pebbles they encountered, and Sophie joined in with helping them find some, which in many cases were simply gemstones. As for the walks, they simply covered the usual Taylor Lakeland haunts. Sophie felt that the area was even more beautiful than Austria, and she loved buying Beatrix Potter

● ● ●

souvenirs and toys for Axelle, while Langdale was simply heaven on earth for her.

One day back in Lancashire, Sophie was left with Amy and Kerry as well as with Axelle and Mark went with his mum and dad on a bike ride to Arnside; before calling in at Silverdale on the way back home. The day was perfect, he loved the beauty of the area so much and it was the perfect setting to tell his mum all about Louise, but what could his mum do, and what was the point of making his parents feel sad anyway? As for his other half, although everything was being done to make Sophie happy, she simply felt that her privacy had in her eyes been invaded and although she knew that she was unreasonable she had no control over her emotions and was unconsciously looking for something to complain about. Even so, Amy and Kerry were proud aunts: who both wanted to make Sophie feel at home as the mother of their niece and took Sophie around the garden to show her their collection of pebbles, which to the girls were simply grounded and secure on their land.

On the final night in Garstang before they left, Karen wanted to surprise Sophie with what she believed to be a beautiful present and had spent many hours since her visit to Belgium knitting. While they were in the kitchen alone drinking tea Karen looked at Sophie, "I will be back in a few moments." She then went to her bedroom and took out loads of baby clothes; then walked back to the kitchen and was in great anticipation of Sophie's joy. She then proudly handed the modern style baby clothes, which her own daughters had helped their mother to make, to Sophie. "The past few months I have been knitting quite a lot for you and Axelle."

"My mother is really good at knitting, but she doesn't do it anymore." Karen was a little shocked by what she saw as Sophie's abrasive nature, and after a few moments she decided to leave the kitchen and innocently go outside into her garden, she wanted to pace up and down her garden but didn't wish to make a scene, while there Sophie felt slighted; all of her demons started to fester some belligerent cocktail inside of her while she sat there stewing. A short while later, Karen walked back inside and sat down. "Does it bother you that your son is with a foreigner?" Said Sophie. With that Karen was shocked, her world had been one of protection and love and didn't know how to respond to this unexpected attack.

"Don't be silly, my only complaint is that you live far away." With that Sophie felt unloved and wished that Karen was dead. The fact that Karen hadn't shown her annoyance was a sign that she wasn't worthy of any respect; Sophie knew that she was acting like an errant child and wanted to see her mother-in-law showing her exactly where the borders lay.

Basically, the month away had been one great disaster for her, and she needed her strong man: who had no idea about Sophie's problems between him and his mum, and as soon as they boarded the train the next day she began, "You could have stuck up for me more in front of your parents." She said annoyingly, as Mark's jaw simply dropped deep down into the gutter.

"Sophie what the hell are you on about, I never saw a problem, why are you looking for some problem?"

"Well, you wouldn't think there's a problem, would you?"

"I have no idea at all with what you are on about." He said.

"It doesn't matter." She hissed at him violently.

"Sophie if my mum had done or said something wrong to you, I want to know . . . If your father upset me, I would tell you."

"Leave it, leave it alone . . . and as for my father he has never done anything to upset you!" She said as other passengers were listening and looking at Mark in case his partner was suffering as a victim from some of his psychological abuse, while Axelle didn't seem very happy either listening to her parents feuding.

Back in Belgium, Sophie was relieved to be back in charge of things, after living under the rule of the Taylors. She wanted to boss Mark but was scared that he would take off and go away more frequently, of course she didn't know the reason why he kept going off, which was for Mireille, and miraculously this jealous woman hadn't suspected a thing, thanks to Mark's well-planned organization and using his love of sport and youth hostels as a decoy. Mark wasn't overjoyed to be back in the dark flat, which had no garden; as such he insisted on them getting out on their bikes at the weekends. One weekend they went to Dinant and stayed at her mums, and another time they went to Nijlen, which was nostalgic for Mark. It was Sophie's first visit to the kempen, the ride was easy, around 35 Miles (55KM), and the route was flat, which included following a bicycle path along the Nete Canal from Mechelen to Lier. The following day they walked through the sandy forests and on the way back the next day, they called in at Plankendael Zoo and all three of them enjoyed drooling at many of the animals.

Home life appeared to be on the up too. Sophie would meet Mark some evenings at the swimming pool, give him Axelle so she could swim, as all three of them were benefiting from some aqua fun. Life wasn't so bad together but a few times Sophie had mentioned that she wasn't ready for another UK visit, and Mark not wishing to use his holiday leave up just at his parents quietly agreed. He wasn't so dogmatic regarding his annual leave; that was until Sophie welcomed him home one evening with madness and mayhem over him placing a cup in the wrong cupboard earlier in the day before he left for work. Mark was in total shock and was understandably thinking more about his family in Lancashire; as such he was ready for a battle. In between he had met Thierry and told him how thankful he was regarding the time he looked after his family, while Thierry instantly seized upon the chance to entertain with his French cuisine some grateful guests and without asking Mark, he invited Karen by way of letter.

The real struggle began a few days later when Axelle was put to bed. "What are you doing behind my back with my father organizing your parents coming here?" She screamed at him.

"Oh, this is some good news for me." He said smiling with unexpected delight. She was then lost for words, since she knew that if her father was involved that she would look stupid since she knew that he understood Mark's needs better than she did.

"I'm sorry she said." She said feeling rather stupid.

"I think given you behave the way you do; I want to see more of my family, and while we are on the subject of holidays; we are not rich and one month away there is a hundred times better than here in this dark cave, which you fondly think of as our palace."

"I'm not going." She said humiliated with everything.

"If you don't go, I will stay there." He said knowing he was taking a risk, and felt that although it could backfire, that if Mireille still loved him, surely, she would go and live with him in England. There was then an eerie silence between them both.

After a few moments Sophie had by then calmed down, but she felt badly beaten and bruised psychologically through the humiliation of it all. She wanted to punch him for everything, but knew if she did, that he had many reasons to leave her already. As such she decided to insult him, not immediately, but as time went by; he would become more dependent on his happiness with Axelle, and by then she would be in a much stronger position from which to dominate him and emotionally blackmail him with Axelle.

As for Mark before the argument, with his parents coming over that would have been enough for him, and he certainly was very partial to the idea of going on holiday in the Alps; that was until Sophie had behaved with such contempt and hatred for his family that he decided that he needed to be near them for quite some time. Luckily, he knew that it was best not to inform Sophie that he only chose another visit to the UK due to her madness, but then again there wasn't much he could do to please her anyway.

One Sunday evening after a passionless weekend, Axelle was playing in the living room with a proud father, while an angry looking mother started screaming. "You really are a disgrace, it is no wonder that everyone in this neighborhood thinks that you are bad, you go out all day and leave me on my own with Axelle." Axelle then looked frightened since the tempers were rising.

"I work all week in a dark cellar, and I am not prepared to stay in all day during my days off doing nothing when the weather is nice, and I want to take my daughter out." He said with utter contempt for her, and simply walked out of the room while a sad Axelle was looking on wishing to be held gently by someone.

Other times to amuse herself while Axelle was taking a nap during the afternoon and Mark was at work; she would draw strange pictures, including one of Karen suffering in some way since this was a way in which Sophie could make herself feel better.

There were also times when she behaved in a rather desperate way, and she would sit next to him after she had made him his favorite meal and then with her arms around him as they were relaxing on the sofa together, she would begin unexpectedly with, "Were you really serious about leaving me?"

"Yes, I was." He said rather coldly. Since although he appreciated her delicious dishes, he found the price to pay with her insults and tantrums simply too high a price to pay for.

"Well, I can't understand this . . . I am very attractive."

"I know that you are very attractive, but I want you to be nice as well." He said knowing fully well he was wasting his time.

"You don't love me . . . You are only here for Axelle." She is bursting into tears while he stood up and walked out of the room.

Once again Mark felt that he was justified in thinking of leaving her, he was also scared of her becoming violent but was looking forward to the return of his beloved Mireille. As such he decided to lay down the law and to her horror; he walked back in the room with a cassette tape. "Now before you think of damaging this recording, this is simply a copy and I want you to listen to it." He was in fact bluffing since there was nothing on the tape.

"Please, please, I can't live with myself, please I promise you from now on I will treat you with more respect." She begged.

"OK, I really didn't want to do this, and I hope that you are right." Feeling cornered she had listened to him but felt as if he was killing her. She was scared, and she was frightened of herself.

"Please Mark, what have you done with the other copies?"

● ● ●

"All I can tell you is that they are not in this house, and they are simply my insurance and evidence that you are at times insane if I or someone else will ever need them, on my behalf." He said confidently, but equally somewhat nervous in case she really had the guts to kill him.

In desperate times one will go to any length to appear strong in the face of hostility. Once again, she felt castigated and that his haughty manner was destroying her more than ever, as such although she wanted to kill him, she knew that she was being monitored, watched, and most depressingly of all she needed and still loved him. He had of course tamed her, but what a life to be living with some detective watching over her, when all that she wanted was for him to beat the hell out of her miserable existence, with his fists, and if he killed her, she didn't care since she felt that she didn't deserve his love anyway. Equally she knew that Mark would never lay a finger on her, and this made her feel even more hopeless and depressed and afraid of what she was capable of.

On the continent Christmas is celebrated on the evening of the 24th. Axelle was then 16 months of age and able to enjoy opening her presents with relish. As usual Thierry served as waiter, chef and dishwasher whenever he had guests and offered the couple his four-poster bed for the night, which Mark felt was very romantic, especially for his partner who was a woman after all.

Sophie knew at times that she was crazy, and during her moments of reflection she put the blame on her mother who left her father, and tried to alienate the children from him, while later when Sophie fell pregnant to basically some good for nothing, she received no help from her mother. Later she would suffer a most tumultuous relationship with Guy who would later influence their daughter negatively, and as much as Sophie said her past was behind her, in many ways she was still living her desperate past.

This was also the time when Mark felt proud of his master's degree in European Studies. There he was on the continent, and

● ● ●

the newspapers had been covering the events not so far away: in Poland, Hungary and then even closer to home in Germany and Czechoslovakia, regarding the fall of communism. Mark hated the Berlin Wall and the division of the families on both sides of the Iron Curtain and while he felt it was right in defeating Hitler, he felt that the Germans in the East had suffered enough, and he had equally the same compassion for those of the Slavic Nations, who had suffered just like those in Berlin at the hands of Hitler and Stalin.

As for Karen she ended the 80's just under 43, was already a grandmother of 3 kids, (A fourth she knew nothing about) but was still young with having Amy aged 10 and Kerry aged 9 In short she felt that the last decade had blessed her, while she had embarked on her journey with Frank in the 60s, achieved so much with him in the 70s, the 80s it seemed was the decade in which they enjoyed the fruits of their hard work together.

Without Mireille around Mark knew he had to keep Sophie sweet at least until his sweetheart returned, and this wasn't dependent on how much time he spent taking care of Axelle because Sophie wasn't bothered as to whether he looked after her or not, since all that she wanted was for him to do everything for her. Had his home life in Brussels been more settled he could easily have swapped Garstang and the Lake District for somewhere on the continent to visit, but equally he felt that a yearly visit to his parents and sisters shouldn't have been too much to ask for. The coming summer holiday had already been arranged but in order to soften her up a bit he came home with some holiday brochures from a few travel agents one evening. "What are these?" She said curiously.

"I picked them up from Neckermann and I thought that we could go away this Easter." He said kindly towards her.

"Really . . . How?" She said both delighted and surprised.

"I have a bit more money than I thought, and my boss said that I can take up two weeks off as unpaid leave." Feeling once again loved by Mark, Sophie made sure that she would do everything she could to make him happy, since now, she herself was happy inside.

The holiday was on Majorca and they stayed at a hotel in Soller in the north of the island, where with the pram they enjoyed gentle walks around Soller and up to the orange grove paradise of Fornalutx. Axelle enjoyed looking at all of the sights, which were usually beaches, coves, bays, the sea and mountain passes just a few miles inland at the foot of Puig Major which was around 5,000 feet (1,450metres) above their hotel which was more or less next to the sea, and the weather neither too hot nor too cold, while the accommodation though far from luxurious was comfortable enough and the cuisine although simple, was tasty and healthy enough.

Back in Brussels they enjoyed the weekends together and continued in going outside as much as possible, pushing the pram, but usually cycling, since it was more exciting for all three of them and easy regarding mobility with a small child. Sophie remained positive at home, Axelle was getting easier to look after and summer was on the way and the living was easy.

So, impressed with Garstang for walking was Sophie that she wanted to travel without the bikes. Mark too fancied a change and given he hadn't used his bike much there the previous summer he agreed with great pleasure. This time Karen, being Mark's mum, compared Sophie's standoffish manner with that of the sweet lady who telephoned him, that being Louise of course but she kept mum about this. They enjoyed the same walks as the previous summer; only this time with Axelle being a bit older they were able to be a little bit more adventurous in both Garstang and in Langdale. With many hot summer days like the previous visit, they spent a lot of time playing in the River Wyre locally, and in Blea Tarn in the lakes. This time Sophie was better behaved and managed to communicate somewhat more to Karen and even showed some interest with Mark's little sisters, also for the first time she met Mark's brother Matthew as well as his wife and two children. After the visit the Taylors went back with Mark, Sophie and Axelle since they were spending another month with Thierry and once again, they visited the seaside and there they were joined with Mark and his girls.

September came, and Thierry went back with the Taylors to visit Lancashire for the first time. Of course, for Thierry food was very important, he had heard so much about English food and was a little bit wary. As such he came over with plenty of food-stuffs from Louis Delhaize: wines, cheeses, and chocolates of course. After a few days his prejudices waned and before he left, he simply had to fill as much of his free baggage allowance with delights from Booths and given he loved Lancashire cheese so much he simply decided to store some back home in his freezer.

Late September came, and this was the first time Mark had been with Mireille since she left for Canada, both were pleased to see how little they had changed and were pleased to be rekindling their undying love for one another, and she was delighted to see that he was always carrying, "The Blue Slate Pebble of Love." On top of that they were planning to move in with each other at the end of the following summer, while her parents were secretly looking forward to a wedding event. Mrs. Rochard had certainly changed her tune, with Nathalie two years older and still left on the shelf; she was looking at Mireille as the child who would have a family very soon thanks to the man, she thought was a Don Juan, and was now thinking of him as someone who was of fine family material.

In Garstang events were taking place, which were close to Mark. One day and out of the blue, and shortly after Thierry's visit, Louise went around with Sarah to visit Karen. Karen then opened the door. "Hello." She said curiously as she saw a pretty young mum.

"Hello." Said Louise. "We haven't met before, but I thought that I'd come around and introduce you to your granddaughter." Karen was shocked, she then invited them both inside; while Louise made sure that the two of them would bond well together.

With Sarah already nearing three years of age, it wasn't so easy for the mothers to engage in conversation, which they found necessary. As such Louise arranged to come over again at a time when Frank or the girls could look after the child so that Karen and Louise could get to know each other better, but at least they had already communicated by the telephone to some extent, and on this visit, Sarah was of course the center of attention.

The first Saturday after Louise's visit to Karen's she returned, dropped Sarah off with Frank, who was wondering about how many other skeletons that his son was keeping in his closet, while along with Amy and Kerry, Louise went out the whole day with Karen. Karen felt so at ease with Louise and as they went up Nicky Nook towards Calder Vale, she told her everything about her life. In turn Louise told a dumbfounded Karen all about her feelings for Mark and how she was merely using Peter. She had gone around partly because she was having a difficult time with Peter, but after Karen gave a positive impression to Louise's ears about his life in Belgium, she in turn had given a more positive shine regarding her own story, when in fact she was disappointed. Little did Karen know anything about Mireille who was one of the main reasons with Mark keeping up his spirits, and had she known this; it would have been too much for her, since one mistake was fine, but having a love square as opposed to a triangle was irresponsible. Even so she really liked this wholesome local girl and would have been proud to have Louise as a daughter-in-law whom she got on so well with. The visits continued with Louise making sure once a week that the Taylors met their granddaughter and niece.

Christmas came, and Sophie had her best Christmas with Mark and Axelle, and even spoke about her desire to have another baby. Given he was secretly only going to be with her another eight months, there was no way he was going to lose control, and even if she fell pregnant; he had no intention of keeping Mireille waiting after his summer visit to England, but obviously her feelings towards him made him feel once again guilty and uncomfortable.

• • •

Spring came, and Louise came around to Karen's for a last time. She was moving to Scotland to live on a farm with Peter in the Scottish Highlands, but she promised that they could occasionally send letters, which wouldn't arouse too much suspicion, and Karen who loved both Sarah and Louise with a heavy heart understood.

Mark had arranged a most romantic weekend for Mireille at his home in Brussels. Sophie was away, Thierry too; in fact; he was in England visiting the Taylors. The doorbell rang; and Mark opened the door to an alluring Mireille. He then took her into the living room. "You came just at the right moment, dinner is nearly ready, make yourself at home, whilst I bring the food over." Mark then left, and Mireille then went around the room observing the photographs on the wall, while Mark took the pizzas out of the oven along with two jacket potatoes as well as the peas and sprouts. After serving up the meal onto two plates he came into the living room, went back into the kitchen and came back with two glasses and a jug of water. He then kissed her on her lips. She smiled as his gentlemanlike manner was making her simply go utterly weak at the knees.

"Sophie looks very nice." Mireille said as she noticed a sweet and loving family photograph, and inside she was feeling nervous.

"On the outside she is a very beautiful woman." Mireille didn't know what to make out of his comment, he had admitted that she looked great, but only hinted that something was wrong. They then picked up the cutlery and started eating together.

"This is a very nice meal that you have made for me."

"It gives me a great satisfaction knowing that I have cooked you something nice, which you are happy with." He said.

"Your daughter looks very sweet." She said a little lost as to what her feelings were with regards to everything around her.

"She is . . . without her, I wouldn't be with Sophie, and without you I would no longer be in Belgium." Her heart started racing, as she could feel his pain palpably in her own heart.

"One day we will have children of our own Mark." She said lovingly as he was of course touched by her sentiment and she was certainly behaving as some aphrodisiac in his otherwise, at times gray existence with Sophie. Feeling no longer used by him, he was looking after her, and planning to make an honest woman out of her and all she could she see was her prince riding with her on a horse and chariot. They had of course made love in her bedroom, now things were more private, and she could imagine her life with just the two of them. As such she went wild with passion as he wanted more and more of her, until after five times that night they were both almost dead from exhaustion, but so much in love.

They slept through much of the morning and when Sophie and Axelle arrived in the bedroom, Sophie upon noticing the two lovers shoved Axelle into the living room, walked into the kitchen opened a cupboard and picked up a small carving knife. She then walked into the love nest brandishing the knife. "Had a nice night together?" She hissed. A terrified Mireille and Mark woke up. "You have just ten seconds to get the fuck out of here!" There was then an eerie silence as both Mark and Mireille were seen getting out of bed naked. Sophie then followed them pointing the kitchen knife at the back of their heads, as they exited both the bedroom and the house. "Go and carry on fucking in the bushes!" Sophie said haughtily just as they fled the house and ran down the street.

"What are we going to do now?" Asked a terrified Mireille as they entered the local park as if they were insane exhibitionists.

"Let's just go and hide in the bushes." They then went there waiting for something, of which they had no idea, since sooner or later they would have to leave. No one saw them, but after about an hour someone went close by and had a wee in a bush about two yards away from them, and the smell was simply overpowering since it re ignited the odors of a previous and smelly activity.

After what seemed like a lifetime but was only a few hours, they both realized that they had to get back to Mark's home somehow. As such when a policeman walked by Mireille called him over. She explained everything that had happened, and he told them to wait there while he went to pay a visit to Sophie. He walked off smiling and was in fact enjoying the scene and went to Mark's home. After visiting Sophie, he came back laughing and told Mark and Mireille what a dirty pair of scoundrels they were and that he fully understood Sophie. What was more, Sophie had offered to give the policeman their clothes, but the policeman felt so sorry for Sophie that he wanted to humiliate them further. As such he escorted them back through the streets as they were still naked and all the onlookers in the street were simply astounded to see Mark in such a revealing and embarrassing state.

Sophie was delighted, she now had morality on her side, she was the strong faithful woman who had been let down by her husband, who had totally and quite rightly humiliated a disgusting couple, who had paid the price for their affair. She didn't need to go away telling people what a bastard he was, since everyone knew that Sophie was the victim. Equally the neighbors didn't bother with her anyway. As such when the lovers came home, she had to smother them both with love, and this was her own way in having some power over them.

"Miss Charlerbois, your guests are here, I have bought you the dirty scoundrels!" Said the policeman as he smiled at her.

"Thank you, I think they have paid their dues." She said smiling. The policeman then left he had more important things to attend, there was talk of a local drug addict and his pusher meeting up in the park, and the policeman was satisfied that Sophie, the victim was a well-balanced lady, a wife and a mother who put her own family first. As for Mark and Mireille they were no longer scared, since the policeman was involved, but felt humiliated all the same, especially Mireille, who was a simple rural girl at heart.

"Well, we can't have you both walking the streets like this, so come in and sit down while I bring back your clothes." After looking at each other they followed Sophie into the living room, and she left them both with Axelle, and Mireille started to feel as guilty as hell. As for Mark, yes, he had been wrong, he had committed adultery but equally there had been events leading up to it. Sophie then came back with the clothes. "I am sorry for this; we haven't introduced ourselves properly . . . My name is Sophie." She said, gently.

"My name is Mireille." She said shyly, forcing a smile.

"Why don't you join us for lunch before you leave?"

"Yes, why not." Said Mireille trying to look reasonable.

"Well get dressed and be my guest." Sophie then went into the kitchen as Mark and Sophie felt humiliated that his own daughter was seeing him in such an uncompromising situation, and he was devastated by the way in which Mireille was warming to Sophie. Meanwhile Sophie was in the kitchen and with a strange smile on her face she poured something into the jug of water and still smiling she sprinkled something onto one half of the main dish. "Lunch is ready." Axelle ran in with Mark and Sophie following. Everyone then sat down, and Sophie served her guests. They then started eating and the atmosphere was relaxed to a point.

"It is a little spicier than normal." Said Mark suspiciously.

"It is absolutely delicious." Said Mireille who couldn't compare anything else which Sophie had made and was grateful.

"Thank you." Said Sophie. After eating Sophie looked at them. "As you can imagine I am pretty upset about everything, could I ask you both to write me a letter?" They both found this request strange to say the least but didn't want to make her angry.

"OK." Said Mireille after a long pause of more than a few seconds and was starting to show some empathy for Sophie.

"Please follow me." Sophie stood up and then as they followed her, she took them into her bedroom, gave them pens and writing blocks from her bedside table and left the room. As she left, she made sure that the door at the front of the building leading outside was locked and kept her ears close to the ground in case they left through the window. She then put a video on for Axelle as a means of distraction. She needn't have worried, since everything was going to plan, and they had fallen asleep on the bed.

After making sure that Axelle was happy Sophie then appeared in the bedroom and started undressing Mireille. She then after several minutes stood up and Mireille, who was naked, slowly woke up and in her blurry mind and saw a naked Sophie leaving the room. Still waking up and confused, she then looked at Mark who was still fully clothes and started to shake him. "Um." He groaned, to her dismay and horror.

"Mark, I need to ask you something . . . Did you undress me?" She asked in two minds, wondering if another act of adultery was worth saving their relationship, or if Sophie was right to punish her for damaging her secure and modest world.

"No, I didn't undress you." He said confused, Mireille then started to cry and then a silence fell over them for a few minutes.

"There is something I have to tell you . . . there is obviously something wrong with you for being with that woman, and I never want to see you again." She said with tears running down her face.

"What about us?" He said as he still had some hope left.

"There is no us, and I think you have a beautiful woman and a lovely daughter." She said confused about everything, deep down she couldn't understand why he was still with her if she was so bad. In short, there was no way in which he could turn. Sophie was either; a victim and they had done wrong or he was a complete idiot to have put up with so much from Sophie. It had been one hell of a strange event, too much for Mireille who then left the bedroom.

"Where are you going?" He asked her in a helpless dismay.

"I want to thank Sophie for the meal." She then walked off into the kitchen after walking through the living where Axelle was still watching the video. All it took was for Sophie to make one mistake and she would be his again, and although wary of finding out the truth she had to make sure that she was making the right decision. As she walked in Sophie smiled at her.

• • •

"Please sit down." Said Sophie while Mireille who was feeling exhausted with everything sat down as she was told.

"I just want to apologize for everything . . . I won't be seeing him anymore and I have told him that he should work on his family." She said relieved to have got everything off her chest.

"Thank you." Said Sophie, who although accepted Mireille's remorse and appeared very welcoming wanted her partner's lover to as quickly and as possible to leave her home.

"I am sorry, but I am deeply ashamed and embarrassed with the pain I have caused you, thank you for everything. I will just tell Mark it is over." She then walked back through the living room; Sophie then followed unlocking the main door, while inside she felt delighted knowing that she had won one big battle. "Mark, I am sorry, but you have a child to her, no one is perfect, please stop fantasizing about us, and anyways my mother wouldn't approve of us as you know under these circumstances, goodbye." She then walked out and left without a scene, feeling as miserable as she was happy when she arrived the day before. Mark was left shell shocked and fell asleep and was still tired from the mystery substance that Sophie had drugged him and Mireille with.

Mark woke up thinking about how cruel life was, if only he had tried a bit harder with Mireille before he had met Sophie, then again who in the right mind would have stayed with Sophie who had belted him across the chest one night while he was sleeping, after she had deliberately trapped him into staying with her? Equally it was his fault, since he should never have left Louise in the first place, for him there was no escape he was simply making one complete mess of his life when now at his age he should be settled in his personal life. In the living room Sophie and Axelle looked calm, "Where is daddy mummy?" Asked Axelle caringly.

"He is tired, but he will come here later darling." Sophie was feeling calm, things were going her way and she was ready for round two, and that concerned the fact that Axelle needed a brother or sister. It was the late afternoon when he went into the living room and started playing with Axelle, Sophie then turned off the video and joined them both, placing her hands around Mark's waist.

The rest of the weekend was typical for a normal family, and while Mark was starting to hate himself, Sophie felt a spring in her step. On top of that he was still intent on leaving the woman he could no longer love, but the big question running through him was when, how and know even why? In short, he was looking very sad, he had something about the submissiveness about him and Sophie wanted to mother him. She had got him where she wanted him to be and for her it was no longer a problem to her if wanted to take up more swimming.

A few days later a letter had arrived for Mark. He didn't recognize the sender's writing, it was however postmarked Nivelles, so Mark assumed that it was from Mireille. In great anticipation of every outcome running through his tortured mind he opened her letter.

Dear Mark,

The times we have spent together have been of the most romantic occasions, which most people never experience and will always remain a cherished part of our lives.

I have never told you, but I have been seeing another boy after we first met. He is very good to me, but I had such a romantic perspective of us, that I was torn between two lovers. I had been a little bit too idealistic about us, and this other boy I have known since school and is the son of a friend of my father's friend.

Our experience has helped me to develop and I now feel ready and strong enough to be happy with someone who cares for me, and I will be accepting his hand in marriage.

My parents always knew about my double life, but I have since told them everything about you; and as such they fully respect and support my choice of partner.

Sophie obviously loves you, and she is a devoted partner and mother of your beloved Axelle. What more can you honestly ask from in life?

● ● ●

With my sincere and best wishes.

Mireille.

Mark felt as though he was going to faint, luckily for him, Sophie wasn't at home, she had left him a note informing him that she had just gone out to do some shopping with Axelle. Mark quite rightly suspected that Sophie was doing everything to make him realize how badly he had treated her, and he simply burst out crying. He then washed his face and fortunately Sophie was still out.

Sophie then arrived back home with some of his favorite chocolate, which Axelle gave to him lovingly and the three of them sat together with their arms around each other. Weekend came around again, and Sophie woke up early after they made love, and asked him to get the bicycles ready as well as the outdoor clothes for the bike ride, and together they cycled to Geraadsbergen. For Mark it was all a little bit uncanny since this was the place he stayed on the way to Mireille's, but Sophie had chosen the destination, and not wanting to make things any more complicated all he could do was keep quiet and enjoy the ride and the feeling of togetherness with his partner and his child if he had any common sense.

The weekend was one of bliss for Axelle and Sophie while Mark feeling paranoid had visions of Mireille getting married and staying over at Geraadsbergen, but he needn't have worried, she hadn't met anyone else, and was still grieving over him. All it took for him was to have called around to her house, and her parents would have been delighted, instead Mireille planned to tell them that she didn't wish to speak any more about it, and that her parents had ruined it all since he had a child to a woman he met after her. This was her way of warning her parents not to make the same mistake again. Even so, her mother blamed herself and would simply have accepted Mark in open arms if Mireille so wanted, since in her eyes there was nothing, he could do that was wrong. Even so the blue slate pebble would remain his good luck charm and memory of a beautiful girl, whom he still loved.

* * *

Chapter 10

October: Pebbles All Over the Place.

A
s for Sophie, things were not going to plan, she wanted a second child and could tell that Mark was being careful in not getting her pregnant, this of course disappointed her and in her case was bringing out the darker side of her character. As much as she was feeling dissatisfied with her life, she felt that then was not the time for her to go out onto the battlefield and simply wanting peace with him and to be happy, she was hopeful that things would all work out well in the end for them.

For the third summer in a row, they visited England and this time, Sophie wanted to take the bikes with them. Axelle was nearing three and quite able to walk, but equally still small enough to sit happily on the back of Mark's bicycle. When they arrived back in Garstang as planned one late July day, Frank would take Axelle on the back of his bike and go cycling with Sophie as well as with Amy aged 12 and Kerry aged 10 and they cycled around the Trough of Bowland on the usual Taylor circuit. The reason was so that Karen could put the pieces together in the jigsaw regarding Mark's affairs. As soon as mother and son set off together through the footpath leading along the river towards Scorton she began. "Why didn't you tell me about Louise?" She asked him gently but directly.

"I just wanted to block it all out." He said rather dismissively.

"You still have feelings for her, don't you?" She said caringly.

"I do." He said almost in tears since she was the one.

"Why didn't you tell me?" She said exasperated with him. "I made a mistake and I just wanted to get on with my life."

Karen's mind then went back to when Louise hinted that she wasn't happy. "Louise asked about you . . . and I told her that you were happy." Mark's jaw dropped, and Karen felt uncomfortable. "You didn't tell me anything." She said feeling sad for her son.

"How could I have known . . . Is she happy?" He asked.

"I sensed that she wasn't as happy as she seemed."

"What do you mean exactly?" He asked her.

"Women's intuition I guess, we sense things."

"I was so stupid, what a mess!" He said regrettably.

"Mark, everything in life is a risk, there's no point in crying over spilled milk." She said with a heavy sigh as she looked at him.

He then told her about Mireille, Karen was shocked. "I'm afraid this is life." She said poignantly as she thought about her nice son who could have ended up with someone sweet such as Louise but instead, he was going through with the trials and tribulations with a complete and utter nutter.

"Should I stay with Sophie?" He asked her like a little boy.

"You mean because you have no one else? With your situation there are no easy answers . . . But Louise and Sophie are the key players in your life . . . Fortunately, your dad and I have kids with only each other . . . There's no point in me telling you what you already know, is there?" She asked him.

"No, there isn't . . . Why didn't you mention that you had seen Louise, earlier?" He asked with pain in his heart.

"What in a letter for Sophie to read for herself!" She said.

"Thanks mum you did the right thing." He said with a smile.

"And besides you don't have a telephone there."

They continued with their walking and as they reached Scorton they stopped for what appeared to be a rest. They sat down on a bench, Karen then went inside her handbag and took out some photographs of Louise and his baby, she was 10 years younger than Sophie, and Sophie who didn't look younger than

Karen could had passed as being Louise's mother. He simply stared at the photographs one by one. After a while his mum took back hold of them gently. "I am keeping these pictures safely for you."

"Can I have them?" He asked her almost desperately.

"Where would you keep them?" She asked him surprised.

"I don't know; I guess that you are right." He said.

They continued walking and in Scorton center they called in at the barn and bought delicious Wallings ice creams, which were so large they managed to keep on licking them until they were well on the way up towards Nicky Nook. From there they walked into Calder Vale and then it was Karen's turn to tell Mark about her sadness over his aunt and grandparents, and why she doesn't want to dwell on it too much with his dad since they are so settled and happy, and that she just wants the fairy tale romance of hers and of the past 27 years with his dad to simply continue.

A few days later, as was becoming usual, the large eight berth lodge cabins were hired out in Langdale. The Taylors along with Axelle took the train, while Mark and Sophie went there on their bikes. They stopped off at Silverdale for tea and scones, and it was the first time when Sophie had met Mark's grandparents. The grandmother liked Sophie and went on telling her all about how Karen ended up with Frank. After an hour they continued for Arnside, where they stopped off for their packed lunches. Then they continued through Lythe Valley, dropped down into Bowness and took the car ferry, which enabled them to reach Hawkshead and Coniston. Then after a long day they continued for Langdale where a large sumptuous three course dinner was waiting for them, thanks to Mark's parents.

The holiday was a success. Frank enjoyed showing Sophie and Axelle: Blea Tarn, Little Langdale Tarn, Elterwater, Loughrigg Tarn, Stickle Tarn, Codale Tarn, not forgetting Grasmere and Rydal where he explained how all these bodies of water flowed into Windermere, which in turn went downstream into the Morecambe Bay. Mark and Karen were proud of his lecture, while Amy and Kerry were still taking in his geography lesson,

Axelle listened in on delight, but Sophie was jealous of Karen. Even so this time Sophie enjoyed the holiday and was delighted to change from going out on the bike or walking and even swimming, which Mark made the most out of with Blea Tarn close by. Axelle enjoyed being passed around various members of her family and for Mark the best day was his bike tour around the lakes with Frank. They set off early went up to Keswick via Grasmere, then stopped off for a swim in Buttermere before moving on and passing the fringes of the western lakes around Crummock, Loweswater and near Wastwater before going through Eskdale and the Hardknott and Wrynose passes back into Langdale. The ride was 77 Miles (125KM), and both of them were pretty exhausted after it and were served dinner by their ladies.

At the end of the holiday, Mark and Sophie cycled back this time via Grange-Over-Sands and from there they took the train across the Kent Estuary into Arnside and from there they were able to call into Silverdale and were surprised to meet the rest of the Taylors who had decided to take the train from Lancaster back up to Silverdale. Sophie felt relaxed in Silverdale and an overnight stay was arranged for the Garstang Taylors. The stay turned into a two nighter, so that Karen could lead the walk along the bay into Arnside and from there walk up the Knott before coming back into Silverdale, which turned out being a real walk down memory lane with plenty of commentary from both Frank and Karen.

Mark and Sophie stayed at his home on their own, and Sophie couldn't take her eyes off everything. She felt that life had treated her so cruelly, and wondered why she wasn't living in a house like this and when she noticed photographs of Karen around the same age as she herself was and looking so much gentler than she, Sophie was starting to hate Mark's mother who had simply no understanding of what any kind of hardship was all about. Even so, Sophie was able to hide her true feelings and the day his parents went up the Knott, he and Sophie cycled to Beacon Fell. Sophie was in awe of the views there and enjoyed looking out towards the Irish Sea. Later they picked up loads of Bilberries and after it, Sophie enjoyed the easy ride back downhill into Garstang. The following day Sophie baked with Mark, blueberry cakes, pies and crumbles for the Taylor's return. Once the family came back, Sophie was on guard making sure that she was on her best behavior.

Back in Belgium after staying in Garstang, life went on as normal, and Mark finally decided that he was going to spend the rest of his life with Sophie. For added security, Sophie wanted to get married, and a wedding was planned for the following September 12th, 1992, a Saturday and one day before her 34th birthday. Things had certainly turned out propitious for Mark and Sophie; it was a complete turnaround to one year earlier when he was counting the months down to his departure from Sophie and sadly his beloved Axelle, now the family was living under auspicious circumstances.

Christmas 1991 Amy was 12, and Kerry 11 and Karen was enjoying the fact that she was no longer looking after small children but missed having her grandchildren close at hand. Frank was of course a very contented creature, coming up to 48 and still enjoying being a sports teacher. While Mark, still only 28 was less excited about life than his dad was, since although his life was secure, he often missed Lancashire, and although Sophie was doing her best, he hadn't forgotten the hell which she had put him through, even so he made the most out of his sad situation. He was hoping that by the time of their wedding that he would be able to trust Sophie and to love her once more, and he was certain that all would end well since for him time was a healer.

The following year was Election Year fever in the UK, and although the Taylors were not very political, Frank voted for Labour because he was a John Smith fan, and Karen voted Conservative because she liked Michael Heseltine. Interestingly Frank didn't like Neil Kinnock found him too much of a wild card, and Karen found John Major a wimp. As for Mark he simply didn't care for him at best; they were all useless anyway.

Easter, they went away again this time they stayed on Gran Canaria and Mark concentrated on teaching Axelle to swim. Sophie mentioned again that now aged 33 that she wanted another baby, and Mark promised her after the wedding, which kept Sophie sweet on the outside, but even if she fell pregnant straight away she believed that the wedding wouldn't have to be called off, but with her biological clock ticking away she was wondering for how much longer she could stay patient towards him, and at times was very close to breaking point.

Summer they went away to the Pyrenees and stayed away with the Nature Friends for the whole of July. The holiday was cheap, and the air there did everyone a world of good, on top of that a cold mountain stream ran through the grounds of their holiday home, and Mark took care of Axelle a couple of days taking her to the outdoor swimming pool so that Sophie could go on longer hikes. Sadly though, towards the end of the holiday Sophie was falling back into a depression. She was frustrated that Mark wasn't so sure about having baby number two and knew that she couldn't fall pregnant like she had done the time before when she tricked him. Equally Mark wanted to make sure that the relationship between him and Sophie was one, which would produce a healthy environment for his third child. Sophie had planned to be married and to have a child, and as each day drew closer to the wedding and her 34th birthday, she was becoming increasingly nervous.

One evening at around 8PM Axelle was getting ready for bed, and Mark was reading in the bedroom because the night before Sophie felt neglected when he went into the common room for a read. This time he decided not to upset Sophie. "I'm tired, I want the light out." She said a little arrogantly, she then with Mark put Axelle to bed. Mark then took of his clothes, he got into bed with Sophie and started to caress her, but she didn't respond. Feeling bored he then stood up, got dressed and left the room. Sophie was depressed since she wanted him to suffer, but could hear him laughing with the other guests, while Sophie, who was as jealous as hell, couldn't sleep a wink.

The following day from morning until the evening Sophie kept going on about how he was neglecting her and telling him over and over that he had upset her in preferring the company of others to her. Had Axelle not been there he would have walked off allowing Sophie to calm down, while he continued walking on his own, sadly he didn't. As such Sophie was becoming angrier with him until eventually, he started to have a headache. As soon as he told her this she was delighted, since then she felt that she was in a stronger position than him. "Sophie, I have heard it at least a hundred times today here in this beautiful place with wonderful mountains that you are angry with me for speaking to guests yesterday evening . . . As such I have a headache too." He said desperately as Axelle looked on sadly.

"Good, so now you know exactly how I feel." She said with venom, while inside she was feeling satisfied.

Back in the holiday home later that day, they ate and around 8 it was Mark who went to bed, while Sophie was playing games with Axelle, a short while later they both put Axelle to bed. "Mummy please turn out the light." Asked Axelle sweetly.

"I need to read a bit longer." Said Sophie kindly.

"Sophie, darling I have got a really bad headache, could we have the light turned out please?" Said Mark calmly.

"No." She said firmly full of anger inside.

"I had to turn out the light for you last night when you were tired." Sophie then went into a cold but seething rage and then picked up her walking stick, with the metal end pointing towards Mark's groin by that time a terrified Axelle who was listening to everything, since the commotion had woken her up was now watching her mother as she was about to attack her father.

"I am going to kill you." She said with her beady eyes, he then jumped up out of bed, and was ready for a fight.

"Don't think that I am just going to sit back and do nothing."

"Well, perhaps it will be better if both of Axelle's parents are dead." She then lunged the stick just missing his groin and thanks to his quick movement he was struck on his bottom. He then screamed out in pain, and one of the guests with whom he had been speaking with the evening before burst into the room and saw the sight of blood dripping from his bottom and he had arrived just in time to have recognized that Sophie attacked him with the walking stick, while a terrified Axelle was hiding underneath her bedsheets.

"Madam, I am an off-duty police officer," He said firmly.

"Where is your ID then?" Said Sophie full of contempt.

"Follow me." He said with conviction. This time the officer wasn't so friendly towards Sophie as the previous one was, when the incident with Mireille had taken place, but luckily for Sophie this was in the pre–European Interpol Database days, as such she knew that once back in Belgium, she would be safe and sound in her country of origin. Even so she was shaken, and this humbled her somewhat since she realized that the law wasn't always going to be on her side. A short while later she returned to the room and Mark was summoned into following the officer. He bought him a drink, and Mark, who hadn't forgotten all of Sophie's bad deeds, let everything out. The officer told him that his life was in danger and that he was living with a very unpredictable woman who was highly manipulative and that one day she would kill him.

Once back in Belgium at the start of September Mark decided to leave Sophie and to give her time to get her act together and to follow him to the UK on top of that he postponed the wedding on the grounds that then wasn't the right time, she reluctantly agreed with everything on condition that he found work and accommodation for both her and Axelle. It was a very emotional time for them. Sophie still loved him, while he knew of no other woman, so deeply as she. Apart from Sophie he had never spent more than a few nights with a woman, he had never got to know someone really, truly madly and deeply, while with Sophie he had spent a few years with her and she was deeply ingrained inside his heart and his soul.

As for Sophie, as much as she wanted a baby, she wasn't so sure if things would work out the way she wanted. Deep down she didn't want to stay at home looking after two children if he was out all day working, and she simply wanted them to move out to the country and to have some Bohemian way of life.

Back in England in the home of his parents, Mark arrived psychologically numb. The thought of no longer being with Axelle was breaking his heart, and whenever he heard songs which for him resembled the love, he had for his child such as "I will always love you," or "Stay," he would burst out crying, so long that he wasn't in view of anyone, such as at home while listening to the radio in his bedroom. Being away from Sophie he was able to reflect on his life with her, true they had done so many things together, and his bonds and links to her were killing him when he thought about himself as being just a boy and living back with his mum, dad and sisters and not the man he used to be. Of course, he loved his younger sisters dearly, but they could never replace the feelings, which he had for his own daughter, the one whom he had produced, and the one he so dearly cherished, even if he didn't miss Sophie. On top of that, he wanted to have the love of a woman.

One night he started screaming in his sleep and shouting and Karen immediately woke and ran to his bedroom door. "Sophie, please don't kill me!" he was pleading in his sleep. Karen then walked into his room, she managed to get him to sit up and hold him in her arms. Although she had work and the children to look after, her only concern was for her highly vulnerable son.

"You had a nightmare . . . It is OK." She said caringly.

"I know... I am sorry for waking you up." He said.

"Son you are home now; Sophie isn't going to do anything now." He then told his mum everything about Sophie, this was to a mother, who although she never went to church led a life of great piety. "Let me tell you this, if I were in your shoes, I hope I would have run off just like you did. Of course, you love your daughter, but this has nothing to do with Sophie. Your father has never hit me, never threatened to kill me, what right has anyone to threaten you with violence? You can't keep blaming yourself all the time." Although he certainly gave no impression of feeling any better, he appreciated his mother's words, but at the same time he felt that he had to pull himself together from within, even so deep down he felt that his mother was helping him somehow.

The next day and feeling a little stronger, he decided to go off in search of work in the Lake District. It was the wrong time of year to find work, but he knew that there were organizations looking for volunteers. One had a head office based at Ambleside. He called in and was advised to go and stay at Watendlath Barn where he could help with working on the footpaths. During this time, he was signing on at Lancaster at what was known as the Job Centre at that time and given his parents address was more than 6 miles away and he had no car, he signed on by way of post. This made claiming benefits easier for him. Every morning after breakfast, he would walk down into the valley meet up with his colleagues who were paid to fix the path leading up to Watendlath, but close to the valley down in Rosthwaite. There was plenty of walking involved and plenty of time to admire the views and equally the barn itself was in a very romantic location and had a sweet orchard with many kinds of fruits: apples, berries, damsons, pears, mulberry and of course he enjoyed some of them during his time spent there, in this beautiful part of Borrowdale.

Karen's mind was frequently concerned with Mark. Although he was nothing like her sister Amy, enjoyed the simple things in life, she was worried about him taking his own life. She herself had never suffered any physical violence and knowing that Sophie could have killed him, sent shivers running down her spine. It was still September, so she hadn't gone back to university proper and one mid-morning when she was thinking to herself that it was time for her to go out, the doorbell rang. A badly bruised and beaten Louise arrived with Sarah, "Come in." She said after trying not to stare at Louise in shock. They then walked inside to her living room where she then took out some toys and placed them on the living room floor for Sarah to play with. Karen then burst out crying.

"I can leave if you want." Said Louise and then Karen put her arms around Louise and she too sobbed like a baby, as both were consoling the other. Before they had a chance to analyze what might have been going on in their heads Karen began, after wiping her tears and moving away from Louise as to be in view of her.

"Sophie, tried to kill Mark." Louise almost collapsed. "Don't worry, he is Ok, he is back here." She said trying to smile. Louise then had tears once more running down her delicate face.

"Can I see him?" She said somewhat desperately.

"Yes of course you can, he would love that." Said Karen.

"Where is he?" She asked worried and less nervous.

"He is in the Lake District . . . what did your parents say about the bruises, they must have had a fright at first?"

"They don't know, and I couldn't face telling them everything . . . I only just arrived back now." She said desperately and hoping for some sanctuary for a night or two.

"Why don't you stay here for a few days and then go and visit Mark, do they know about you, Mark and the baby?"

"No," she almost wailed. "They are devout Catholics they simply wouldn't be able to understand my actions . . . To be honest although they would never say this, they probably think that I brought all these things on myself." She said tearfully.

"Come and look at his bedroom." Louise then followed Karen upstairs into Mark's bedroom. It was large, bright although a little masculine with books and papers lying all over the place, but even so it had a warm and welcoming feel about it.

For Karen having Louise staying over was no big deal for her, and she never asked for any help from her guest, since she understood that Louise was in trauma and needed to be given some space, Karen and Louise got on very well together anyway and of course her child was of mutual interest for both of them and Louise insisted on doing her fair share of housework.

Louise was of course very thankful for the small mercies in her life, thanks to Karen, and simply hoped that no one from her school would see her bruises and decided to venture outside at first only at night and not for long since she was a mother and wanted to look after her child. Karen simply gave Louise use of

Mark's bedroom at least until she was to meet up with him, but nothing had been agreed as to how long she should stay, or when she should visit Mark. After a few days, Louise felt that she would leave Sarah behind with the Taylors and go off on in search of Mark.

The barn where Mark was staying had no telephone, but he had received a letter from Sophie, which read:

Dear Mark,

I told my father everything, he said I need help and that I treated you terribly, please can I visit you with Axelle just for one week, let's say the 21st also if you are afraid of me coming over, my father has offered to come over too, so as to keep an eye of things.

Love,

Sophie.

Mark was numb, being alone wasn't good for him, he missed his daughter and equally he was missing the touch of a woman as well as the thrill and excitement of making love. Despite his needs and desperation for a woman, Sophie wasn't in his eyes a female anymore, for him women were, soft, gentle and peaceful beings, while Sophie was some evil Medusa for him.

The following day Mark posted a letter to Sophie agreeing to her proposal but without her father coming too. This letter was most welcome for Sophie and she was pleased that he trusted her, and she promised herself and him that she would do everything to make it his worthwhile for him to come back to her.

Louise's bruises had subsided, and she arrived at the barn one afternoon. Mark wasn't there, but as she was waiting, she walked around the settlement caught the eyes of a local Tyson son. "Hello, I noticed that you seem to be looking for someone." Given that the hamlet had very few inhabitants it was always an occasion when some unknown offcomer came around to visit a neighbor.

"I am, Mark if you know him." She said smiling at him.

"Indeed, I do . . . Why don't you come in for a brew?"

● ● ●

"I will just write him a note first." She smiled and then took out her pen and notebook, jotted some words down and after dropping a note off for Mark she then went back for her afternoon tea with the young Tyson and sat in front of his house waiting.

"He hasn't been hitting you, has he?" Poor Louise, there she was thinking that her horrific bruises had somewhat completely healed, but instead for those who had seen her after the attack it was plain to see for anyone that she had been physically beaten.

"I might had been attacked because of him." She said.

"But he would no way do such a terrible thing, would he?"

"My husband found out that Mark is the father of my child." Originally, she wanted no one to know and seeing how protective this Cumbrian was of womenfolk she was satisfied that she had given an answer, which would basically close the matter, and anyway what she said was in fact true. As for young Tyson he was simply shocked to the core, and relieved that Mark was a good guy. They continued sitting and drinking tea and eating scones. Mark arrived a couple of hours later and he noticed a note on the floor.

Dear Mark,

I am at the Tysons waiting for you.

Love,

Louise.

His heart started beating he then opened the barn door and Louise grabbed hold of him from behind, she had seen him walking to the barn from the Tysons and ran quietly up to him. At first he was in shock and almost jumped out of his skin and then he looked down at the body he hadn't seen in nearly five years, she was holding onto him like a little child holding on to its teddy, and was crying, he felt and smelled so different to any man she knew, he was the man who had stolen her heart, the one whose touch could never have been bettered. Tears ran down his face too, he sensed from her that she had suffered too, it was as if

• • •

they had been at war, and although he sensed she had been badly injured, both mentally and physically, like him he felt that she was still full of love and wanted to put the past behind her, and at that moment he knew that she was his, as he was hers, and that they were forever together.

Mark produced a simple but healthy dish for them both and during a quiet cooking moment Louise took out of her jacket pocket the black pebble he had carried all the way from Austria for her, which she carried everywhere with her ever since, and walked up to him, kissed the pebble before placing it onto his lips and in turn he too kissed the pebble. She then walked off placing the precious stone inside her jacket before returning to him and kissing him on his lips. For her this was significant, since as he was close to the pebble, he was close to her too and that he should stop being all over the place and simply stay put in Lancashire with her.

That evening they wanted to confess everything to each other, they wanted to cleanse each other, and simply told each other about the pains they had been through and both knew that they had been damaged, but not destroyed. Had they made love, Mark would had slept like a baby, but instead there was a moment when he sounded as if he was howling like a wolf through a nightmare related to his ex. Louise felt so useful to be there helping him, especially since she thought simply of him being just a very strong and independent guy, but now she knew she needed to mother him and she didn't mind, since she knew Sophie had tried to kill him.

The following day a new dawn had broken, there was calm in the air and after breakfast she went with him to work. She knew that Sophie was coming around to visit him, she wasn't pleased at all about this, but she understood that he was doing this for his daughter, and given she too was a mother her patience, love and understanding would spell no bounds for the man who was simply her soulmate. There were of course times when everything was all too much, since she carried his child before anyone else had done, and all the pain and misery, which they had gone through could have simply been avoided, as being together was testament to that. As for work, she was very happy to help on the paths that day. His colleagues were of course pleased to have an onsite beauty that day, as well as being of course slightly jealous of Mark.

Back at the barn, there wasn't much food, but something was better than nothing and although neither of them was overweight, they still had some fat reserves left to help them get through the barren times, which had been caused by her unexpected arrival, meaning that the food for one had to be shared.

That night they made love together, but both felt as though they were on the run. With Sophie coming in a few days' time, they felt that they were unable to enjoy their time a hundred percent together. Equally, given they had no home of their own, it was best for Sophie to face the music with him and not with his family. They both decided that she should stay with him until the day before Sophie would arrive. The next day Louise would go and do the shopping, at least they both had some money, and although there was a shop just 30 minutes away after a walk which went between two fells and down into the valley, there was basically nothing other than sweets there. As such the next day, Louise walked the 5 miles down into Keswick where she filled up his rucksack with plenty to eat and arranged with the Tyson boy that he would pick her up at 4 in the afternoon so that she would arrive back in time for Mark.

Meanwhile Karen on Louise's behalf went around to see her parents. "Hello, Mrs. Jones I am Karen Taylor, a French lecturer at Lancaster University and we have something in common, which I would like to discuss with you." She said firmly but friendly.

"Please come in." She said a little fearful as well as curious. They then walked inside, as Mrs. Jones sensed that this had everything to do with her daughter. "I will take you to the living room . . . Can I get you something to drink?" She said a little confused.

"Yes please, a tea would be nice." Said Karen appreciatively and Karen once in the lounge was able to sit down on the sofa while Mrs. Jones was busy with the refreshments. As Mrs. Jones walked in with the refreshments and sat down waiting in great anticipation Karen began, "It turns out, that we are both basically the grandmothers of Sarah." She said to a shocked Mrs. Jones.

"Please Karen, before you continue, I want you to know my name is Denise." They then smiled at each and Karen continued.

"I only found this out recently, and Louise is staying with me, until both she and my son can sort things out together."

"Why didn't Louise come to me with her problems?"

"I think she felt that she had let you down." Said Karen

"Louise, let me down, never!" She said almost shaking.

"My son went to Belgium and had no idea that he was going to be a father, and Louise took in Peter as a father figure for her child, and now she is back with my son, after basically living a lie regarding her child." Karen then felt pleased with her speech.

"I see, so my daughter feared that my strong Christian principles regarding marriage and family, the views of her father too, meant she felt that she had let us down." She said pensively.

"I am afraid that it is so in a nutshell." Nodded Karen.

"We would never in a million years turn our own daughter away . . . How do you feel about everything, Karen?" She asked.

"It is simply my wish to see Mark and Louise together."

"This is exactly how I feel . . . I just want the parents to be happy, and as for the Bible it is just a guide, and very few of us can live up to its expectations and that includes myself, it is just an example for us to follow, all I want is for them both to be happy."

"Oh! They are, they really love each other . . . As far as I know they are together in the Lakes and discussing their future lives together and have been the last few years missing each other."

"What more can a loving parent ask for?" Said Mrs. Jones.

"I am sorry that Louise sent me on her behalf, but I think she was overwhelmed with events." The conversation continued with them discussing that society needs rules and regulations to

• • •

follow, but not the ones that were then in place and Karen promised Denise that once they came back, she would meet Louise and Mark.

Sophie came over with Axelle to visit Mark while Louise was going back to Karen's, who had been relying on the village childminder whenever she needed to go to work. Karen was a little frightened of what Sophie was capable of and decided that she wanted Louise to stay at the youth hostel at the bottom of the valley where she could keep a close eye on things but knew that instead Louise would be going back to Garstang, later that day. Fortunately, Louise telephoned, and it had been agreed that Karen would call the hostel and pay for accommodation.

Sophie had already arrived with Axelle at Keswick Bus Station and Mark walked them along the shores of Derwentater carrying her large rucksack while she had a smaller one on her back. Sophie was so glad to get away from the hustle and the bustle of Brussels and was simply admiring the views of the lake, and the mountains as well as the walls made of slate, while inside she had a pain in her heart, since although he was delighted to be with Axelle there, Mark seemed so cold and distant towards her. As they reached Barrow House, they then followed the country lane up to his barn. They hadn't spoken much, but Axelle had been singing. While Axelle was delighted with the barn, Sophie was a little shocked and horrified, since although they had been happily staying in rather dirty places together when they were in love, now that they were full of hatred, she felt that the place was simply too disgusting to spend a night in. Mark cooked the three of them a meal and then Axelle was put to bed on a floor inside a sleeping bag.

With Axelle asleep, Sophie then kept speaking about her plans for them both, but it fell onto death ears when he spoke about Louise and how she was already expecting when he met

Sophie. "But Sophie it is over between us." He said after the umpteen time.

"You have known about this for years." She said angrily.

"I tried, I tried." He pleaded in vain towards her.

"But you met her before you met me, this story is so disgusting, you brought a bastard child into this world, well OK the child was adopted by the mother's new partner, and now you want me to simply walk away and say fine... I am Axelle's mother and she needs us both together." She said with all her angry energy.

"Well, you can't exactly move in with Louise and me." With that she was incensed, but luckily, she had already decided what she was going to do, and this kept her calm and she was so proud of herself for organizing every eventuality before she arrived.

It was a long night for them. Mark couldn't take his mind off Louise, while at the same time he couldn't cope with Sophie and tried to block Axelle out of his mind, since for him the only way he could be truly happy would be if Axelle lived with him and Louise, and this was simply a pipe dream.

During his restless night with Sophie not far from him and sleeping in the same room as him, he prayed that Sophie would accept that it was over between them both, and in the interests of their child come to some arrangement so that Axelle could see him and his family frequently. As for Sophie she felt ashamed of the way in which she had behaved, but equally she felt that he had provoked her, since he was the one who moved away from the love, which she believed in for both of them and for the protection of their precious daughter, so that she could grow up in a loving environment.

The next morning Mark went to work, and Sophie put some mysterious drops into his milk, she then went off with Axelle and their luggage down into Barrow House, where Louise was walking in the grounds. When he came to the barn later that day as expected he drank the milk, and within 15 minutes he collapsed and was alone. The timing was perfect; Thursday afternoon, he only worked 4 days a week so that meant Friday, Saturday and Sunday before anyone would notice him and hopefully, he would be dead within one hour of drinking the poison, at least that was what Sophie understood. When Louise walked up to Watendlath that lunchtime she told the Tyson boy that she would be waiting for Mark at his parents, since Sophie was still there for a few more days, and she wanted to go back home as such she went back to the youth hostel and packed her belongings. She then started walking through the valley towards Keswick and once she arrived in the town Tyson invited her for a brew and told her that Sophie had left that same day. With that she panicked, and Tyson took her as quickly back as possible in his car to the barn. As a Cumbrian he was used to the windy Lakeland roads, but this wasn't quick enough for Louise who was in fear and once at the barn they saw him lying on the floor.

Of course, they were both shocked, luckily the door was open and for the next few moments she had no recollection of what happened next, still in no time he was rushed to Lancaster Infirmary via helicopter with Louise by his side. She was at his bedside when he came around full of wires and tubes all over his body and realized that Louise had saved his life and knew that he had to listen to her, and that somehow, they had to get Axelle.

As soon as Mark was allowed home back in Garstang a worried Frank and Karen gave Mark and Louise 1,000 Pounds to help them bring back Axelle, that is if she was still alive. As for hardly seeing his other daughter, Sarah, that wasn't a priority for the time being. They arrived at Hull the following day, and back in those days they could simply book sailing just before the ships departed. Of course, they couldn't enjoy anything since their only concern was for Axelle, and they hoped that she was still alive.

Sophie was sat in her living room looking demonic while Axelle was playing when Thierry came in after being away visiting some of his friends in France. "Did you have a good time?" He asked.

"No, it is over with us both." She said somewhat robotically.

"In time you may get him back." He said kindly and sensing the atmosphere was lethal but had no idea how to reply.

● ● ●

"He is dead . . . I poisoned him." She said and was too proud to tell him the truth that she made no mention of his other love child.

"You are going to end up in jail, why did you kill him? He was not so bad." He then looked as though he was starting to cry.

"You always stick up for him, he is terrible, he has finished with me . . . Tomorrow Axelle is staying at the nursery school, and I would like you to pick her up." She said completely uninterested at all with the fact that she had killed the love of her life.

"Well, it looks like that I will be picking her up more often." He said as he was gaining his authority not that that mattered now.

"You, that's all you ever think about, yourself, she is your grandchild, what about poor me?" She then started wailing and was acting as though the emotional pain was killing her, and worried about Axelle, Thierry took his grandchild upstairs with him. He wanted to send Sophie onto the psychiatric ward, but he was worried and given she had killed Mark he simply didn't know what to do and hoped that things would sort themselves out. After taking Axelle upstairs he then called his landlord who lived on the floor below and together they carried Sophie upstairs who seemed to be in a very deep sleep. She was placed onto the four-poster bed, and poor Thierry who worried that it would be the last time that he would see his favorite child alive, placed Axelle in the middle of the bed with himself at the other side of his daughter.

During the night, Sophie had the most beautiful of dreams, she was walking around some exotic place full of waterfalls and turquoise pools, she was there with Mark and Axelle and awaiting the child she had so badly wanted to have with her family. They all looked so happy, loving and tender together. An hour or so later she had another dream and in it she was in the country with her man and two children picking fruits from their orchard. A while later she had yet another dream, and in the dream, she was on a desert island with Mark where they were simply making love inside a simple seaside log cabin. Sophie was so happy and the energy around the four-poster bed was one of a soothing heaven.

Sophie woke up and had no idea where she was; it was getting light and then the sad reality sank in. Thierry cooked an English breakfast and was happy to see Axelle enjoying the meal. After Sophie and Axelle were walking to the nursery school and looking very sullen. "What your father has done is unforgivable, a child needs both its parents . . . I really loved him, but now my life is broken. Your father killed me, but the day we left I poisoned him, as such you will now live with your grandfather, he will pick you up later." Axelle then burst into tears. "I have to go now." Just as she was about to run off Axelle then pulled at her mother's clothes in order to save her mother's life. For the moment the earth stood still, as Sophie imagined that Mark had arrived and that they were going to live happily ever after, away from the hustle and bustle of city life, they could all be so happy. She then kissed Axelle and picked her up into her arms. Everything seemed so beautiful and her daughter felt like a baby again and it was as if all the pains and sorrows surrounding her parents' separation were over. Suddenly holding tighter onto her child, Sophie started to cry and to hate herself, as she then thought about Mark's death, which she had caused, and with there no longer being a reason for her to live, Sophie broke free and ran off, while Axelle sensing danger started chasing her, without looking Sophie ran into the path of the bus and was killed instantly. Poor Axelle, she was haunted not only from the death, but also from Sophie's confused and schizophrenic drama.

As for Axelle, all she could do was lie next to her beloved mother. Her mother was still warm and curled up close to her soothed Axelle. Her mother wasn't screaming or going hysterical as she had been the past few weeks, and all Axelle could do was to imagine that she would somehow come back to life without turning into the hysterical monster that she was. If only a prince would walk by and kiss her mummy back to life.

Meanwhile Mark and Louise were on their way to collect Axelle and were leaving the train from Knokke Hesist, which had just pulled in at Brussels. Axelle went up to her mother, suddenly a police car pulled up, and a police officer was seen getting out of the car. Axelle then looked at him, the officer's presence had somehow brought her back into reality as she stopped thinking about princes kissing dead princesses. "My father, Mark Taylor killed her." Axelle then ran off before the policeman had a chance for everything to sink in, he decided to run after her. "I am going to my grandfathers." As they continued; she noticed Mark with another woman, inside she was filled with hatred and rage, "There he is!" She wailed.

"Who?" Asked the officer with his heart beating quickly.

"My father, he killed my mummy." Suddenly the police officer messaged for help and in no time Mark and Louise were taken in a police car down to the Station for questioning. On hearing the doorbell ring, Thierry answered the door and was in shock on seeing the police arrive and sensed why the officer came around.

"I am looking for a Thierry Charlebois." The officer said.

"Yes, this is me please come inside." He said politely. They then walked upstairs he then opened his flat and Axelle ran straight inside.

"Would you like a cup of tea?" Asked Thierry cordially.

"Maybe later thanks . . . I am sorry to inform you that your daughter is dead, but we have found the suspect, being Axelle's father." Thierry almost collapsed with the contradictory news.

"Mark is dead." Said Thierry bewildered and feeling sick.

"What are you trying to tell me?" He said suspiciously.

"Sophie told me that she was the one who killed him."

"We have just arrested him on suspicion of her murder." Said the agitated policeman to a speechless Thierry who felt that he had to defend his son-in-law. "I am sorry, I will come back later and keep you updated." He said wanting to deal with other matters.

"No . . . my daughter killed him." Not fully comprehending that the officer had told him that a living Mark had been arrested.

"Look this is a serious case." Warned the officer.

"I know that, but she was the one who killed him."

● ● ●

"This is a serious matter, please go down to the station."

"With my granddaughter?" He said worried.

"No, a female officer will look after her." Said the officer relieved that Thierry was co-operating but was wondering if Thierry was somewhat psychologically disturbed.

After Axelle had been taken care of, Thierry was escorted to the station with the officer. The questioning was tiring with Thierry in one interview room, and Mark and Louise in two other rooms. The police were certain that Thierry was covering up for Mark and Louise who had arrived from England in order to murder Sophie and soon enough they would be able to point the finger towards them. The police then had to decide what to do with the two British suspects who were not allowed to meet up with each other. Meanwhile the officer in charge of looking after Axelle decided to take Axelle back to the scene of the murder inquiry.

On arrival at the scene Axelle burst out crying. "My mother was here, and he killed her in his car." She then dialed the station. The police then pieced together the fact that Louise and Mark had arrived by train, and it was 50:50 as to whether or not they had hired out the car which killed Sophie, since had they arrived just ten minutes later after steeping out of the train as their stamped tickets showed in Brussels, then there was some probability for them to have had enough time to kill Sophie. As such they were released on bail, pending further enquiries and had to hand in their passports.

The following day the police trusted that maybe they were telling the truth, and once again they went to Thierry's home and had a warrant allowing them to take a disturbed Axelle back to the scene. Once there, the patient female officer repeated the same questions, and one word could land her father in jail. "How did you know daddy was driving the car?" She asked delicately.

"Because my mummy told me that he had killed her."

"When did she tell you this?" Asked the confused officer who looked as though she needed some emotional support, since she could feel the suffering that Axelle was going through.

● ● ●

"Just before she ran into the road." The officer, still confused, wondered if Sophie was a very disturbed individual and wanted to put the blame on Mark for her suicide. She then realized quite obviously that things were becoming too much for a small girl to handle and, with it nearing midday, she took Axelle out for lunch.

Axelle and the officer ordered their meal in a fast food where the conversation continued as they sat down eating their meal. "What did you do after mummy ran into the road?"

"I ran after her, the car hit her, and she ran back onto the pavement before she fell." Said Axelle calmly. They continued eating their hamburgers as the officer simply held her breath. "I then went to mummy and cuddled her and was dreaming that my daddy would come back and kiss her." By then the officer was worried that Axelle could permanently be damaged from such a harrowing event, while she herself was starting to crack up under the disturbed event as she dropped the child off at her home. She then informed her superiors that she was going to file a report. Instead, she went to a local shop wanting to drink herself unconscious, but as an officer of law she simply bought a packet of cigarettes. She had given up smoking five years earlier when her father was dying of lung cancer, but now she was buckling from the stress and smoked one cigarette after the other while writing some confused and nonsensical report, before going back to the station.

Meanwhile Thierry was living in fear of the police coming around to take Axelle's only living parent away. On top of that, his daughter, Sophie, claimed that she had killed him, and he wondered what the hell was going on. He then sat down quietly and decided to open up a bottle of wine, he then sat down and thinking that because Mark had been taken into hospital, that at least there was evidence for the fact he had been poisoned and that even if Mark had killed his daughter, she had tried to kill him, but even so he believed that his daughter was insane and he had since heard about Sophie's previous attempt on Mark's life, and Axelle never once said that she saw the face of the driver who ran over her. As such and with a heavy heart, and even though

● ● ●

he felt it was a big betrayal of his to go against his favorite child, he had to help an innocent Mark out.

Eventually the police came to the conclusion that Sophie had simply ran into the car, that the driver had no chance of avoiding her and that the case would be closed and Mark's and Louise's passports would be given back to them, but that it was still 50:50 that Mark had killed Louise, but that neither the defense nor the prosecution were either right or wrong. In total Mark and Louise had been in Brussels for two long weeks. Thierry arranged that he would come over for a visit when things calmed down, and since then he had grown very fond of Louise, he accepted her as family. Both Thierry and Mark agreed that Axelle was too young to go to the funeral, especially under the emotionally disturbed way in, which Sophie had committed suicide. Louise hoped that in time Axelle would be able to remember the happy times, which she had with her parents together since she certainly didn't want to be looking after a child who had been psychology-ically damaged beyond repair and able to destroy the harmony of everyone else around her. As for Mark, Thierry put no pressure on him, but Mark decided that given Sophie had tried to kill him that something terrible might befall him in going to pay respects to the person who had wanted him dead and Thierry soon came round to the idea that it was best for his daughter to lie in peace and think that Mark was no longer alive.

At the funeral, which due to the circumstances surrounding the death had been delayed somewhat took place during early October at, The Vogelzang Cemetery, where two police officers were present, and Thierry gave a speech. "This is the worst day of my life; Sophie was my favorite child, the only one who cared about me, when my wife left me. Of course, I will never under-stand why she believed that Mark had killed her, and I can only imagine that when he left her, as someone who experienced something similar when my wife left me, as someone who felt dead too at that time, I can only imagine that when Mark left her, that her life was simply no longer worth living . . . Finally, I would like to say that for the rest of my life I have myself to blame for

• • •

Sophie's death, she told me she had killed Mark, this wasn't true, and instead of placing her for the night in my room I should have had her sanctioned where she would had been unable to commit suicide as she had the following day." He then walked off and was thinking about his own divorce when he blamed his wife for everything and simply wanted to kill himself. He had been watched, and someone placed an arm on his shoulder, it was a police officer who was involved in the case.

"Don't worry Mr. Charlebois, the case is closed." Said the officer who then walked off solemnly leaving Thierry able to walk up to his landlord and his hairdresser, who both put their arms around him. While his ex-wife and three other children had been informed of Sophie's death and the funeral, only Thierry was present as the only representative of the family for Sophie.

September had certainly been an unpredictable month and Mark and Louise were worried that they and their pebbles would in October still be all over the place. Despite their pretty much messed up lives, both were enjoying the love which they gave to each other, they were still enjoying being with each other every heartbeat of time, which was simply the best medicine for them.

● ● ●

Chapter Eleven

November: Pebbles Staying Put in Lancashire.

Back in Garstang, Karen had been almost out of her mind with worry, and when Louise arrived back with Mark and Axelle she almost passed out when everyone sat down in the living room. "It has been such a terrible time, an unimaginably bad experience for everyone . . . . Luckily, we have four bedrooms here . . . And both Amy and Kerry have decided themselves to share a bedroom so that Axelle and Sarah can have a room together." She said motherly.

"Thank you, Mrs. Taylor." Said Louise as she simply put her arms around Karen as they hugged each other, with tears running down their faces, in what was a truly an emotional display.

"Thanks mum." Said Mark, who although he was distraught that Sophie was dead; he was now able to grieve for her instead of living in fear and even hatred of her, and to simply get on with his new and beautiful life. With that, they all simply hoped that things would simply sort themselves out. Once again Karen's life had been blighted with an untimely death, but luckily for her it didn't touch her direct household, and even though she was deeply bruised by the tragedies, having eight people living in her home would keep her very busy indeed. On top of that, Mark had hardly had time to meet up with Sarah, who hadn't even fully realized that he was her father. One thing he made sure of was that he had two pebbles for his daughters. He had specially bought for Axelle an emerald gemstone from a shop in Brussels, while he gave to Sarah the other black pebble, which he had been keeping, while for himself he was still carrying Mireille's blue slate pebble, which he simply called the Lake District Pebble and Louise simply took him for his word.

Louise and Mark walked round to visit her parents for dinner. Louise, although she had a key, rang the bell out of etiquette and her mother opened the door, and as soon as she saw the light coming out of both the two lovebirds together, she was simply spellbound. Mark came up to her and she almost melted in him as she saw such a positive difference with him than with Peter, the man Louise had basically taken advantage of when she was on the rebound with Mark. For Louise it was simply emotional, her mother had shown her that she simply approved of her daughter's decision, and after embracing Mark, it was Louise's turn. Inside the house and into the living room, her father, Ted greeted them. The two young lovebirds sat in the same place as they had done previously, on that fateful first day of spring, five and a half years earlier. Ted wanting to break the ice began- "So; tell me how it all began with you both." Mark and Louise looked at each other and almost burst out laughing since, they were at the exact seating places of when they first French kissed and then they explained how they got together, without going into the sensitive bits and so the ice was completely broken, and Mark was feeling very welcome.

The dinner was vegetable soup with brown rolls and butter followed by trout, potatoes and three veg, while dessert was strawberry cheesecake. By then and after the meal, Denise wanted to speak alone to her daughter, and she knew that her husband would want to show Mark his video collection. While downstairs the two ladies were busy clearing up the dishes and discussing Louise's love triangle, which was a hot topic of course for them.

"What about Pete's parents, are they still in touch?" Asked Denise since she didn't wish to offend anyone.

"Well, they never made much a fuss about Sarah," She said with a hint of defiance, since they were no longer important.

"Well, that is just as well don't you think?" Denise said sounding somewhat relieved and smiled.

"It is, but they are welcome to carry on as before." Smiled Louise as her mother just looked at her thoughtfully.

"What about Peter did he ever discuss this with you?" She asked as though Peter was important in their lives.

"Nothing but . . ." Louise was suddenly lost for words.

"I am sorry, maybe we shouldn't be discussing these things with Mark around, we don't want to make him ill at ease."

"No, it is okay, he is with dad so there is nothing to worry about. Anyways Peter told me that he never wants to see Sarah again, so I am not chasing him, but I posted a polite letter through his parents' door and left them with your address."

"How long ago was this?" She said relieved.

"Well, it is early days, just the other day they haven't posted anything yet and maybe it is better this way anyway." She said without realizing that they had simply not had long enough to reply.

The boys came back down just as the girls had finished with their slow washing up and everyone sat down for a cup of tea, before Mark and Louise went back home. As for everyone, the visit was very positive for all concerned and while Mark felt very welcome in her parents' home, both parents felt very relaxed in his presence, and the evening was a great success.

For Mark being back home with his other daughter Sarah whom he didn't know very well was a very humbling experience for him, this was the daughter produced out of love yet he almost let her mother get away, while for Axelle seeing her father with another woman after he had in her own mind killed her own mother was a disgusting sight for her. In Axelle's disturbed mind he was a reminder for her as to why one of her parents had been taken away from her and she wasn't going to allow her daddy to get away with this crime.

At first Sarah and Axelle, who shared a room together, were happy. Sarah spoke about how she missed Peter, while of course Mark felt uncomfortable with the fact that his own daughter had stronger feelings for someone else other than him. To make matters worse Axelle would make fun out of Mark, and at times he wanted to simply run away from both of his daughters, but thanks to the love of everyone else in the Taylor household he felt strong enough to keep to the faith that it would all work out in the end, but was a little worried all the same, just like the other family members.

It was during these emotionally charged and disturbing times for Mark, Axelle and Louise, Thierry came around for a visit. He slept on the floor downstairs in the living room, and even met up with Louise's parents along with the Taylors, and seeing as Ted, Denise, Frank and Karen got on so well they started seeing more of each other and would meet for walks sometimes or simply call round when out walking. The Joneses had a car but didn't use it very much. Seeing Mark happy was a lovely sight for Thierry, and he hoped that this secure background of his would rub off on Axelle and that she would love not just her daddy but the new environment of Lancashire too. There were times when he wanted to simply move to Garstang, but then he wondered if he could get used to the strange cuisine, the language and of course the weather. Equally he hoped that Axelle had listened to him when he spoke of his desire that she would make peace with her father and of course as a romantic man he was able to listen to Mark's and Louise's story without any bitterness, but because of Louise there was no mention of Mireille since Mark wanted this dark tale of his to lie dormant in his memories with just himself, his mother, and his father.

Louise never once during these shaky times doubted that Axelle would come around to love her, and that equally Sarah would accept Mark as her real father, who after all was her biological dad. As for Karen, who was the gentle matriarch sitting quietly on the sidelines, she was proud of both Mark and Louise and their love for one another and had dreamy expectations for them.

Of course, both Mark and Louise were thankful for his parents' support; her parents would never have taken them all in.

Her parents' house being a semi was too small and as for taking on Axelle this would have been clearly out of the question. Back in 1992 with both being out of work they could have easily not just claimed social security benefits but a flat too in either Preston or Lancaster, but for Karen it was family first. Louise and Mark were both recovering from the traumas surrounding their violent ex-partners. Peter could have unintentionally killed Louise during one moment of anger, while Sophie tried to kill Mark three times, with the final time being organized in advance, and in cold blood.

As a devoted father he was most concerned about Axelle and with her not wanting to move on, she was slowing down the healing process for her daddy, which had of course an effect on Louise too and everyone around him, when they were confronted with her unpleasant behavior towards him. For Mark it was almost as if Axelle was carrying on with Sophie's vendetta, and he was scared that eventually she could create a rift between him and Louise. For him his dreams of being a parent turned out differently to how he had imagined, since although he did his best, was a full time dad, the most important for him was that the children were conceived out of love and brought up into a world full of harmony, and it was devastating for him to think Sarah knew nothing about him during those early formative years of her life, still he wanted to move on, and simply get on with his family concerns.

Mark was worried about how he would provide for his family, he could easily have got a job at W.H. Smiths in either of the local stores at Lancaster or Preston, but for some reason he saw this as being too much of a connection with Sophie. Sophie had initially visited his former workplace with the intention of learning English for him; the manager of the store although Flemish, spoke English almost as a native, and Sophie right from the beginning respected him. He was a few years older than Sophie, and thanks to his dealings with feisty Mark he viewed for some reason her to be a shy, sweet and submissive partner, who was hopelessly devoted to a man who didn't deserve her, since

Sophie knew how to play on this bachelor's sympathies in being the poor baby as she liked to portray herself, and he kindly gave her books for free under the impression that given her partner worked there that it was simply a nice gesture from him, and nothing more.

Sophie never once had the intention of having sex with him, but with the inevitable and the unconditional love, which they had for each other, the guides for her learning, combined with the romantic novels, which were a part of the recommended reading of English, went in tandem with the kissing and the sex of which they were both as thick of thieves behind Mark's back. Never once did Mark suspect Sophie of sleeping with his boss, but equally he knew deep down that his colleagues felt very sorry for Sophie and wondered how she could live with such a difficult man, who lived such a simple and uncomplicated life.

Little wonder that Mark the former bookworm couldn't bear to pick up a book and read about anything, since any literature, which even if it hadn't been taken home by Sophie was in his mind still a part of her; and something which she noticed when she had passed through the aisles of one of the world's largest bookshops outside of London. Like Sophie, Louise loved reading books, but luckily her chosen genres were more akin to Karen's: food, health, gardening and travel and of course romance. Sophie's choices had been crime, the occult and philosophy. Even so all it took was for Axelle to move on, and the often imaginary and paranoid demons playing tricks running through her dad's mind would have vanished, and so long as Axelle was nasty to him, he was afraid that Sophie even after her own death was looking up at him from hell, and that she still wanted to kill him.

Very soon people were gossiping all over Garstang. As such Louise decided to walk into the local newspaper office and to offer them an exclusive story. It being a small newspaper meant that they wouldn't get much in the way of royalties, but Louise was tired of wagging tongues and as such; both she and Mark gave an interview together for the Garstang Courier. After being paid the princely sum of just 50 pounds for their exclusive, they decided to look around the town and to see what they had in stock regarding Christmas presents and decided that although they didn't have much money, they had plenty of love and planned to have their best Christmas.

One week later the parent newspaper, the LEP based in Preston, wanted to take on their story and they took the bus down into the town and received a further 200 pounds. This time they felt more confident in visiting the shops, and with more choice the prices were lower too, so they bought some small things for all the children back home. Their story as soon as it was published became an instant hit and given their second interview had been more revealing than the first one, the national dailies wanted to get hold. For this they then had to go to Manchester and there they received two grand. Louise was by this time gob smacked, and once again they looked around the shops, but decided that after spending 200 pounds enough was enough since they wanted to go away together on holiday in the sun.

One evening as she lay in bed a little traumatized about her previous life with Peter, Louise thought about the lifestyles of both Mark's and her own parents' habits, which had been passed onto them. As such she appreciated not only his parents, but also those of her own, which was a recipe of love for the life of which she was leading then. True they were from the same culture and even town, but for her it was simply about time. While modern life had brought about equality of the sexes, any differences existing between a couple were put down to sex, but for her feminism hadn't touched her brute of an ex, who preferred the pub to his wife, the TV and watching other people's lives to tender nights in bed with Louise, while Mark the most caring partner she could had wished for, hadn't been touched by the sex wars either, he was simply a gentleman from a previous and forgotten century.

As for herself, she had friends who loved the bright lights of Blackpool, and the holidays on Tenerife, which meant that the idea of swimming in the Wyre wasn't for anyone other than a Russian Bear, but for Louise as a girl close to nature, she knew that she would never get bored of Mark. Of course, the houses she lived in were centrally heated, but at just 65 degrees, which meant that there wasn't the coughing and sneezing which her friends complained about; who worked in the public offices heated to around 80 degrees. Louise was sure that the beautiful complexions of Karen and her own mother were partly as a result of living in a house which didn't dry out the living feelings of every living thing with its humidity of a desert; she was after all a girl who enjoyed swimming in her cool and local River Wyre. Previous generations were similar, but as the times went by the likes of the Taylors would look increasingly anachronistic as society moved on. As such she felt more and more apart from the world, but with Mark she had her own universe, and one, which her parents understood too.

At times she found things a little boring with the Taylors, at times she felt bored with Mark too, but these were times for reflection, and whenever she felt a little bit cold wearing her nightie, she always knew that Mark was always there on standby and ready to give her a hug and to enjoy the tangible things together. Equally during one of her moments of reflection she decided to get out of bed and to write him a message, since unlike those with non-stop television she was able to think and to use her own mind actively, and like Mark wanted to make their lives a success.

Who needs a radio when I love the sound of your voice?
Who needs TV when I love the beauty of your face?
Who needs a car when we can walk together hand in hand?
Who needs a fire when we can blanket each other?
Who needs a light when we can all through the night?

Later the following evening as they got inside their bed Mark was given an envelope and inside her message decorated with her own symbols of love through her pencil work. "You know darling, the excesses of the consumer society are making men and women more equal and more independent on an another and are actually creating a society that is more sexist and lonelier than ever." He said, he then went up to kiss her, but she gently resisted.

"For both of us, it is the simple life which keeps our love for each other burning." She replied, they then looked at each other, turned out the lights and started to kiss, and continued in doing what made their life one of pure ecstasy, and both enjoyed the night.

By Christmas, Sarah was starting to become very fond of her daddy and had stopped saying negative things about him, while Axelle who stopped loving him, the day he left, since Sophie fearful of him kidnapping Axelle and taking her back to live with him in England wanted Axelle to be suspicious of him and to understand that unlike her daddy who had left her; she stood by her own daughter, and that was the best love a parent could give to his or her child. Even so, one evening Axelle needed her daddy and came and sat with him in his arms. Mark was of course delighted, finally for the first time since those ultra-tempestuous days, which she had to endure, Axelle was now calming down, serene was too strong a word to use, but at least Mark was hopeful. "Daddy, I want to show you something." She said sweetly to him.

"Please do my little darling." Said a delighted daddy.

"I want to show you in my bedroom." She then took him upstairs away from the prying eyes and then looked at him.

"Daddy, I want to go back to mummy." He then went up to his daughter picked her up in his arms, was feeling very sad for her, and wanted to show his empathy to her, while at the same time he was scared, scared that eventually Axelle could tear the family apart, since Louise was only human and he worried about how much more she would be able to take the horrible atmospheres which Axelle was unfortunately generating to those around her.

"Darling, mummy is no longer with us." He said dolefully.

"You killed my mummy." She then bit his hand, he quickly moved it away, but was too late since her jaws had already dug deep into his skin and he was bleeding. He then ran downstairs to his mum and showed her his hand, as Frank shook his head.

"She bit me!" He said Karen froze and after a moment of shock, she was angry and ran upstairs in a state of fury to Axelle.

"Don't you ever do that again Axelle, next time you are going to live in a zoo with the crocodiles." She then left the room, and Axelle stayed behind on her own sulking.

Later that evening when Mark and Louise were in bed together after putting a terrified Sarah to bed, although appalled and disgusted with Axelle, Louise had no intention of being the instigator of a rift between the father and daughter. As such she simply supported Axelle and told Mark to simply grin and bear it, while in vain Mark wished that Sophie would somehow come back to life and take Axelle back to Belgium for everyone's sake.

Like a whirlwind their story was being read in the millions and then came a big television exclusive of which they had been invited. This time the sums they were able to command were truly mind boggling for this country couple. While they had good intentions and merely to put the record straight in their home-town, with an attempted death and actual suicide surrounding the sleepy market town of Garstang they became national celebrities, until of course they had to travel for interviews on the continent since their story was spreading. All this happened in the run up to Christmas.

While the proceeds from their interviews were giving Mark and Louise plenty to celebrate about, the interviews were having a negative effect on Axelle who didn't approve of the publicity, which involved her mother after all. By then her animosity towards her sister was becoming palpable and during the night she wanted to scream and shout until one night she decided to get out of bed, go to one of the dolls and throw it on Sarah's head. Sarah woke up crying and ran out into her parents' bedroom. Axelle was relieved and immediately fell asleep. Mark was slower at waking up than Louise, who was pleased to be in command, and not wanting things to escalate she simply took Sarah back into her bedroom and heard Axelle snoring. The following night, a repetition of the drama the night before was played again. This time Louise was convinced that Axelle was simply a victim of being out of favor with the others. Mark was not so convinced and the next night he took a sleeping back with him late one evening and slept on the floor in his daughters' room. Nothing happened, Louise was relieved, but Mark wasn't. A second night on the row and nothing happened, and Louise was starting to become annoyed with Mark.

On the third night, Axelle got out of bed and went looking for her doll and just as she found it and was about to throw it at Sarah, Mark quickly grabbed her arm and took her out to Louise, "I am sorry, I am, but daddy killed my mummy and I want to hit him." She said and started to cry while Louise had by then had enough.

"Axelle tomorrow you will sleep in the garage if you do this again." Said Louise, and by then Axelle simply wanted the whole world to swallow her up, while Mark felt safe with Louise.

Fortunately, Mark and Louise were united and as such during the coming days, Mark and Louise looked around the state agencies as a matter of greater urgency and decided to buy a semi-detached house in Scorton. Until they moved into their own place, Sarah would sleep in Mark's and Louise's bedroom, and Axelle started to hate her father more than ever for no longer caring about her, and would seek more and more attention, if she could get away with it, but simply didn't know where to begin.

Another person who wasn't too chuffed about the media interviews was of course Hugh. By then he had a family of his own in the Netherlands, and his partner Antje enjoyed the interview of Louise and Mark and knowing that it was not so far from Manchester meant that Antje was following the story of her partner's region. Of course, Hugh remembered Garstang, and when Amy from Calder Vale had been mentioned in the interview, he wanted to send out a hit-man to Garstang, but of course he was no longer rich and powerful and luckily for him the trail never got any closer than Amy during the interviews.

In February 1993, Mark, Louise and Sarah had a wonderful holiday in the sun on Tenerife, where the weather was perfect. This was the perfect antidote to the interviews, which had at times brought back their past traumas. Sometimes people would even recognize the couple, but they did their best to distract people. Their hotel room was very large, with two double beds several feet apart from each other. So in love with each other were they, that they could always be healed between the sheets, and while Mark had lost one child he gained another, his love child with Louise, and they one more together, which they were to find out about that she was carrying, since here on this two week holiday during valentine without anyone else around other than their sleeping daughter they were making love most naturally without any care in the world, that their second child without any fuss was conceived. It was there too on this romantic holiday that had the simplest of a wedding ceremony by, simply writing their own certificates of love on scented papers, since Louise was still officially married to Peter.

Amy and Kerry were in the third and first year respectively at Garstang High School and would generally walk along the river to the end of the town since for them the route from then on was less interesting, and after school they would take the bus back to the same bus stop and walk back from there since for them a little stroll made the day simply more pleasant. Louise too, was born and bred in Garstang, had lived almost all her life just over 30 miles (50km) from the Lake District, which she surprisingly hardly knew. As such she was looking forward to the Taylor's summer fortnight and they arranged to go to Austria too, which was to Louise's delight.

June came, and the young lovers moved into their new house, and Mark found it so interesting the way in which the place had been decorated and installed in a way which was; like his mother's. Simply put, Louise was in fact very similar to Karen, and Mark like his dad, just wanted his woman to feel at home in her bespoke nest. Thanks to Mark, they had the special, "Lake District Pebble," secretly known as Mireille's Blue Slate Pebble, as well as his black pebble for her, which was placed onto their window ledge since he no longer wished to carry it around everywhere. Equally had it been Sophie living there with him and bringing in some continental hues, Mark would have accepted that she simply needed to feel at home, but as in the case of Louise he felt that the best things were often to be found on one's doorstep. June was also the time when she midway through her second pregnancy and like Karen she dressed modestly, was herself very feminine but was less into dresses; apart from during more special occasions even so her style was to Mark's liking and whenever they went round to visit his parents and even to her parents, that she had more of a tendency to wear a dress than before, and Mark would also compliment and tell her how beautiful she looked in her frocks, which he often said made him want to passionately rip the dress off her sultry body.

The house itself was a semi-detached house just like that of their parents when they were young, they couldn't believe their luck. Now living in a house in Scorton, yet just several months earlier Louise was trapped far away from her family in the wilds of Scotland, while Mark felt trapped in Brussels. What a turn-around in their lives, which had gone from rags to riches, of course both grew up in a sheltered background and as such they weren't used to real hardships in life. Obviously for anyone to have suffered under the hands of a partner who either could or planned to murder the mother or father of their child was a most terrifying ordeal, but both Louise and Mark had healthy and relatively young parents who could look after them during hard times.

The Lake District holiday was a success. The eight-berth log cabin was full, with the whole family and Axelle was nice to her father, and in turn he and Louise were delighted with her and were showing her pleasant displays of love. No one recognized that Axelle still hated her father, but at the same time she was enjoying the way people treated her when she was being nice to all and sundry and was starting to wonder if things were better this way. Louise, like Mark, enjoyed swimming in Blea Tarn, it was bracing as they got into the water, but very quickly they got over it and were proud of each other. Walking in the rain was no problem either, they had waterproofs and Sarah whether she was with her parents or grandparents it made no difference she would have to explore the hills come what may and simply enjoyed the freedom of the place.

In August they went on Mark's tour of the Austrian Alps, with Axelle and Sarah, Louise was six months pregnant and wasn't the only mother to be sleeping in a tent, since back then there wasn't the money to throw around which a future generation would have. They visited the same places Mark had been shown through his parents and later shown to Axelle's mother, but he saw no reason to go into this, and in his thoughts his mind was simply on nothing else other than Louise, and their family, which they produced together. In fact they did more or less the same walks he had done with Sophie, and while his mind would take him back to those blissful days, he was poignantly reminded that while then he was waiting for the arrival of Axelle, Sarah, his other daughter was a baby growing up without him because of his own lack of diligence and while this gave him pain in his heart, as he looked at his love, his passion for Louise soothed him just like all the waters around them whenever they went walking around Schwarzensee, Krottensee or Zinkenbach whose streams would flow into the waters of Lake Wolfgang where their tent was pitched close to her banks. The tent was large enough and had two rooms, one for sleeping and the other for their luggage, where Louise and Mark would visit together for some privacy when all was quiet.

Back at Garstang Axelle settled down happily without her father around after what had been for her the holiday of a lifetime, and she loved her grandparents and aunts dearly. Karen found being responsible for her granddaughter so easy, she was only 41 when Axelle was born, and she still had young daughters to look after anyway. Even so not everything was plain sailing.

Axelle had been trying to turn both Amy and Kerry against their brother, and for that reason Karen was none too pleased.

One evening Frank was to play the bad cop, while Karen the good cop. The setting was in Axelle's bedroom, with Axelle smiling at her grandparents, who were basically her de facto parents. "How would you like your bedroom to be?" Asked Karen.

"I am happy with it, it is beautiful." Said Axelle happily.

"Oh, but this is a princess room." Said a seemingly concerned Frank, who then continued. "I wanted to paint it black with monsters, witches and devils for you." He said calmly, as Axelle started to cry, and Karen knew his game fully well.

"Grandpa you wouldn't do that?" Said Karen trying to provoke a verbal response from Axelle, as Frank remained silent.

"Please grandpa, please, please!" She begged desperately.

"Daddy is my son, and if you say or do any nasty things to anyone who is a Taylor, I will turn this room into a witch room." He said staring into her eyes before he stormed out. Axelle then started screaming, and Karen then put her arms around her.

"Don't worry, you are a good girl, your daddy loved your mum, but sadly she walked into a car." Goodnight darling. She then kissed her goodnight and left the room, while Axelle cried herself to sleep alone in her room. Karen felt very guilty leaving Axelle on her own, but with two young daughters to look after as well as her husband and career there was only so much, she could take.

On November 15th, 1993, Louise gave birth to a healthy boy weighing 8 pounds (3.6 kilos) and they named him Benjamin. They had wanted a complete family unit, Louise would from then on often mention that he had three children, which although she was right, for him it took more than just producing a child to be a father, and for him he was faced with the sad reality that in many ways Axelle wasn't his, since apart from being a biological father to her they didn't really have much of a connection. Of course, prior to Sophie's hateful crusade he and Axelle were simply two peas in a pod, but what was the use for endless tears, his life was now complete with his one and only love, his darling Louise. One thing for certain was that Sarah and Benjamin were lovely together and Sarah wanted to help her mother and being six years older she felt as though she was a very big older sister. As for Mark, whenever he looked at the pebbles that November, he felt sure that they were staying put in Lancashire, with him and his family.

One evening while thinking about her mother, Sophie's words in which she explained to Axelle that her father was dead, and that he had killed the mother were starting to make Axelle's disturbed mind go into overdrive. What did her mother mean that both Sophie and Mark were dead? The night of March the 22nd the second one of the Spring in 1994 was nothing out of the ordinary where Axelle was concerned, but when what seemed to an apparition of her mother appeared, this was in her disturbed mind simply a night to remember for the rest of her life.

As for the other family members, the year was just an ordinary but magical year for the rest of the Taylors. Amy took her GCSE's and gained straight A's before moving onto Lancaster Sixth Form College, while Kerry was doing well at school. Mark had started working at Booths and was responsible for visiting the farms and checking the produce and mingling with the farmers as well as giving a hand at the Garstang Store, while during his free time with his immediate family they would spend a lot of time playing in the river and swimming, especially during July which was one of the hottest on record. As for Louise, she was so thankful that she had a good honest and traditional family, especially since it was almost never going to happen because of her carelessness with Mark who at the time was lost and off on his travels. Now of course together and with each other, these romantic lovers were now safe and sound regarding the paths that they would take as one heart.

• • •

Exactly one year later to the day and hour on March 22nd, 1995, and, as if by magic, her mother appeared as though she was sitting on the bed next to Axelle. "I'm always here for you." Said her mummy looking so serene, beautiful and like a queen.

"Mummy I love you." The ghost-like image started fading.

"Please don't go." Said Axelle sadly and feeling lost.

"I will be back." Said the diminishing voice and image of her beloved mother. For the next few days Axelle could think about nothing else so deeply as her mother and was in her own world.

Once again 1995 was just a normal year in the households of both Frank and Mark. Karen was by then truly at home in Garstang and was pleased that all three children had a bedroom of their own. Mark and Louise were leading similar lives to their parents in that they were devoted spouses and parents but there were of course some differences. Louise like her mother stayed at home looking after the home, her husband and their children since she didn't want to pay for child minders, take days off from work when the children were sick, while at the same time she was happy so long as Mark loved her and they had a roof over their heads, good food, heating and clothes, for the rest, her life was simply being with her family and enjoying the beauty of her hometown and its surroundings. Of course, with one salary they had to make sacrifices, they had no family car, Louise often made do with the local village shop, but of course with Mark working at Booths it made sense in him helping with the shopping.

As for their holidays, well unlike his dad who had much of the summer off, they had just one fortnight's holiday at a family run campsite near Keswick and that was during one of the many and long heatwaves of the summer. They were there during late July and early August, this time without Axelle, who apparently hated the Lake District, in fact it was her way of not being with her father for two weeks. Sarah was then 7 and a half, while Benjamin was 20 months and Derwentwater was the perfect setting for an aquatic family. Sarah, like Karen, was adventurous and wanted to see as many things as possible, as such Benjamin was carried in a sling, and many places which Mark had seen in

PEBBLES: LOVE ACROSS THE MORECAMBE BAY

his youth with his parents were shown to his Louise, Sarah and Benjamin to the delight of all concerned.

Amy, as in traditional Taylor fashion went onto sixth form that autumn, while Kerry kept her head down, especially when one of her classmates told her about some of her older brother's antics, since all families knew each other, and many were linked. When Kerry came home that evening and told her parents Sarah was amused, even Frank chuckled but Karen froze. She certainly didn't wish for her own dark past to be revealed or Frank's for that matter, and merely looked straight into his eyes as she spoke. "It is all very well people making fun out of your brother over something he did when he was your age, but time is the best judge and I am very proud of him." She said calmly, as Kerry was red in the face.

"I am too." Said Frank, who knew what his wife meant, and he too of course wanted the matter closed and forgotten.

On the 22nd of March 1996 Axelle had been waiting the past few days for her mother to re appear, but this time a man about 50 years of age appeared, in other words one like a grandfather. "This is your husband." Said the voice of Sophie.

"But mummy I am only 7 years of age." She said.

"It is perfect." Said the ghost staring into her wild eyes.

"Mummy you are right." She said completely frozen and scared. "I am dead." Said a confused Axelle, hiding the fears of the fact that her mother wanted her to be with an old man.

"What do you mean?" Asked a seemingly concerned ghost.

"I am half you, so without you I can't be alive too." She said.

"Don't worry my little angel, your daddy who killed me is dead too." And once again Sophie disappeared but remained in Axelle's completely tortured and battered mind as always.

Karen had often wondered if in choosing the name of her younger sister for her older daughter might have spelled a bad omen, but at the time of the christening, Amy's death was still raw in her heart. Amy, like all the other members of her family, was romantic, but equally she wanted to do well in school and it was becoming increasingly obvious that she was in many ways

● ● ●

just like her own mother, and now aged 17 she was thinking about her future career. Kerry, she was simply doing well in school and relied on Amy's old notebooks when the homework got too difficult.

With Benjamin from the spring two and a half years old, as with Sarah they no longer used the pram, but would carry him on their shoulders if he got too tired, and whenever Mark was around the carrying would be left to him. In fact, Karen and Denise had done things very similarly, but then in the latter half of the 90s more and more children would be seen sitting in prams after their third birthday, while Benjamin without too much trouble was managing the Nicky Nook walk, to the pride and delight of the others. Walking along the road from their house was a little boring for him, but as soon as they reached the stile and would walk up the muddy path either next to or covered in the stream he was entertained. It being steep, his adrenaline was pumping and when the pond was reached, he wanted to admire it and then knowing that the sandwiches were to be eaten at the top simply helped to keep any of his moans at bay. From there the walk was downhill with sheep everywhere and then through the woodland he would look for twigs and use one as a walking stick and keep on going with the promise of an ice cream at, "The Barn," in their village.

Axelle, however, became more and more obsessed with modern life, but she was of course living in some time warp, with her family having no TV although they did have a radio. She did, however, have friends and she often went around so that she could see some two-dimensional entertainment. There was also a local amateur dramatics society and she had Karen's consent in taking part. Axelle was turning into a right little actress, and her family members enjoyed the performances, where she would play many of the darker characters, which other children found too demanding.

As such the latter part of the 90s continued with basically the families living the lives as they had ever since Karen and Frank became an item, with Mark and Louise being a younger version of both. In 1997 Axelle seemed more settled, and that spring no apparitions appeared. Of course, nobody was a clone, even the angelic Amy and Kerry were testament to this, but it seemed that although they were both traditional girls and had male friends both seemed very focused on their studies. As such after the summer holidays Amy went onto Myerscough College in order to study to become an assistant vet, and when the weather wasn't icy or too rough the 10 miles round trip did her a world of good. 1997 was also the year in which Karen celebrated her 50th birthday at her home and close family members, which coincided with Booths being 150 years old, and Frank was proud to tell all and sundry about that.

Louise had been quietly negotiating a divorce and given she had been separated from Peter for five years, her divorce was finalized at ease. The following year in 1998 Thierry spent much of the summer in Garstang and attended the rather quiet wedding of Mark and Louise, which was attended by just the immediate families, including Louise's older brother who came down from Edinburgh with his wife and son. Thierry was satisfied with the way things were turning out with his beloved grand-daughter but the summer that year was a washout and he seriously wondered how people could survive with so little in the way of sunshine.

While being married didn't change anything between Mark and Louise, she had after all already been married, there was no doubt at all that had Mark not continued for Belgium 9 years earlier, that just as with both of their own parents a shotgun wedding would have been arranged. Of course, with all couples so madly in love, it was of course simply a wedding ceremony for these families concerned and most importantly of all just like their own parents they were made for one another and simply happy.

• • •

The final year of the 90s ended with Karen as usual looking back on the decade and with her youngest child starting university in Paris and she could see Axelle too was a testament that the world was becoming more global. Equally she felt at little sad that nearing 53 that her exciting days with her family adventures were over, while at the same time, Axelle, although she would never reveal this to anyone was discontent in her home and there simply because there was nowhere else for her to go. Axelle was 11, and while she was tamed under the watch of herself and Frank, she felt less at ease with her than with any of her other family members, but she was family after all. Even so having Axelle at home who spoke French with Karen when the others were not around and having someone who took a great interest in the cooking kept the soft spot, she had for this grandchild intact and in turn Axelle felt secure.

As for Mark and Louise, they were proud of their children, who like their parents were simply used to walking and both children enjoyed bike rides as well as swimming with their parents. One difference was the holidays, Mark had less time off work than his father had, and Louise stayed at home, so as much as Mark missed his holidays, he was thankful for the fact that he had a wife who was devoted to him and their children. As for Louise, she wasn't impressed with diamonds and pearls, but sometimes she would work in the local village store, and simply felt that The Forest of Bowland was simply the best place in the world and that they simply didn't need any holidays abroad.

The Millennium came in, and the Taylors didn't understand what all the fuss was about, while Axelle the more consumerist member of the family was impressed with the landmarks such as: the giant hand and depictions of animals along the river footpath trail, on top of that she wanted to become an actress. Karen and Frank were completely against the idea but didn't take her seriously, as such she was heartbroken, since seeing all these pretty girls with incredibly wealthy men in the films who in many a case looked like an Adonis made her mind set up aged just 11 years.

The following year, 2001 came in, both the parents of Louise and Mark would often meet, since they all enjoyed eating, walking and having a laugh together, while their son and daughter were simply getting on with their lives. Amy had completed her 4-year veterinary studies program, found a job in a surgery in Kirby Lonsdale on the edge of the Yorkshire Dales and wished to qualify through part time studies. As such she rented a room and aged just 22, she would often visit the local Booths and it was there she met and fell in love with one of the duty managers and very quickly they set up home together, while Kerry was still in France studying.

As such their lives were pretty much very peaceful, but with the angry general election campaign of 2001 it was obvious that life around them was pretty messed up. The conservatives were not offering anything new, and looking around Garstang they could see that people were generally doing their best, but when it came to the interests of the farmers, neither of the main political parties really cared, since most people lived in the towns, but many from the villages around often wondered who would feed the nation if there was a war and the British farmer had been forced off his land due to the foot and mouth epidemic. In the end their views on politicians were none too positive, and they had other concerns of their own.

More important was of course, their own personal lives, which in both Karen's and Mark's households functioned very well. While Axelle with her occasional black moods and tantrums was at times a little tiring for Karen, luckily, she was just as much in love with Frank as he was with her and was often looking at her photographs with such delighted sentiment. As for Louise, there would always be a scar, the one of her wasted years bringing up her love child with a man who wasn't worthy of her love, when quite easily she could had played her cards a little differently just before she gave birth, but she wasn't alone in this stupid mistake and Mark like she, who was also reckless, knew that the happiness which they were giving to each other was genuine and that the most important thing in their lives was their love for each other.

It was during, one evening just after the 9 11 bombing of twin towers when Axelle, then aged 13, went around to visit her father unexpectedly after rowing with Karen and Frank. She then, as she arrived in front of his house, rang the doorbell. A surprised Louise opened the door, Axelle walked in and kissed them. It was just after 9 in the evening, so her half siblings were already in bed sleeping. Then she sat down looking tense for anyone with open eyes to see. "Would you like a hot chocolate?" Asked Louise.

"Yes please." Axelle then sat down after taking off her coat while Louise was making a hot chocolate drink, which was becoming her trademark, to Mark's pleasure.

"What's wrong Axelle, you look very sad?" Asked Louise as she came over with the three drinks, while Mark was sitting on the floor relaxing and all ears, with his chocolate drink.

"It is my grandparents, I want to study to become an actress, but they are dead against this." She said despondently.

"Why don't you before you start sixth form, go and spend a year in Austria, with a family and improve your German?" Said Louise, who had already been discussing the idea for her own children recently with Mark and Karen as well as her own parents.

"Axelle love, I know people there." Said Mark helpfully.

"Or you could go to France, grandma has contacts there." Said Louise, while Axelle, although she was looking very sweet, this was often when she was at her most dangerous and felt that for her to get what she wanted, that she would have to drive a wedge between her parents and her grandparents. She had simply put: one dream, one goal, one aim in life, and that was simply to become a Hollywood star and that nobody was going to stop her.

"Daddy, I would love to go and improve my German in Austria." She then, after some more pleasantries between Mark and Louise, spent the night on their sofa downstairs.

• • •

Within the next few days Louise had found out; that teen-agers as young as 14 were taking part in exchange programs and Axelle had been doing her research too. As such Axelle then told Karen about her news, but her grandma was in shock, for Karen she simply felt that her granddaughter wouldn't be old enough at 14 to spend a year away. In the end Frank disagreed; Karen was a university lecturer and the perfect person to solve this. She recommended Thierry, "No grandma, I have too many memories there." She lied, because the capital of Europe would have been perfect for her, and how could she betray her beloved grand-father, the father and connection of her own beautiful mother?

Karen then wanted to sleep on this issue and after a few days she came up with Colmar, Nantes and Lyons since she had reliable contacts there, but Axelle wasn't impressed with any of them, although she knew that these choices were her only escape.

2002 was the year when France would be very strongly etch-ed into the hearts of the Taylors. Kerry was still in Paris studying, while Axelle would as soon as somewhere suitable be found, be planning for her French exchange later that year. As usual during the weekends Sarah then 14, and Benjamin 8 enjoyed with Louise walks, as well as sometimes cycle rides and swimming, but when Mark wasn't at work, during the weekends, they would find themselves doing bigger walks, more adventurous rides and more swimming. Sometimes his days off would be during the week, and if Louise wasn't working in the local shop where she had a very flexible contract, they would certainly enjoy their time alone together while their kids were safe in school.

During August of 2002 Axelle was 13 years and 11 months old when she settled in with the caring family whom Karen had already had some contact with. They lived in a nice old house, which had at one time been a country house, until the town sprawled out in all directions and over the years local shops had been built on their doorstep. Being in France she was certainly taken care of with the food and basically enjoyed everything served on the table. The family had a dog, an Alsation, and very quickly Axelle got into a routine of going on walks with Timmy. One day after a few weeks and while walking a little further towards the city, she noticed a sex shop. With its bright lights, beautiful women and men, she was a little bit mesmerized. She then, after staring in awe for a few moments, and a little bit afraid of who might have seen her, went back home where she felt safe and sound once more.

For the next few days, she simply couldn't stop thinking about the shop. She knew it would be difficult to go on a walk without Timmy since it would arouse the suspicions of the others, equally she was only going there out of curiosity, since deep down she wanted movies rather than sex movies. On the front door a sign said, nobody under the age of 18 is allowed entry. As she entered the boss a man around 50 years of age, didn't wish to overpower her, especially since she had never been there before, but for him there was something about this Lolita, something mysterious, which for him meant that she was the master of his destiny. She then picked up a video and started to stare at it. Although she had never met Amy, something was telling her that this lady in this old video might have been her. She then walked out, thinking to herself, that either Amy had been crazy in making herself famous in such a way, or that it wasn't her, and if it were, she had somehow metamorphized herself into a French lady, but anyway it didn't matter, Axelle was now 14 and could easily pass for 17.

That night she went to bed thinking about how pure the other members of her family were, her older sister Sarah, was such an innocent child next to her and her father was of this kind in many ways, and this was one reason why she hated him, especially since in her still disturbed he had sent her mother to suicide. She went back to the sex shop a few days later, the person on duty was a youngish woman who simply asked Axelle her identity and her age. Axelle was relieved, it was a slight brush with the law, which she needed before she would go into permanent decline and after blushing slightly, she walked out with her head low and decided to do something once and for all about her immoral behavior.

Around this time Mark's children with Louise aged almost 15 and 9 were basically happy with each other, played games together and while Sarah was academically years ahead of Axelle, she was, as all the Taylors knew smaller and, in many ways much more naïve and in keeping with the rural life of Wyreside.

September came in and for the next few weeks Axelle settled down in at school, celebrated her 14th birthday and was starting to enjoy domestic life in France for the first time. It was after all something and exciting to be living in France, and she was starting to think more and more about her grandfather. Maybe she should have gone to Brussels after all! Her new plan was to simply finish the term in Colmar, and then move on. At first, she was a little scared of upsetting the family who were being so kind to her, and simply went out walking with Timmy as usual. The family were pleased since the previous two days she hadn't taken the family pet out on a walk. While walking a man walking in her opposite direction smiled at her. She had no idea who it was, but after a few moments she realized it was the male assistant from the sex shop.

Bernard was a rather strange man both inside and outside probably as a result of his lifestyle. He had never married, never fallen in love, and would make love to anything that moved, mainly human of both sexes and for money. Sometimes his partners would confuse his desire with his love for them, but with his lack of morality he wasn't someone who could ever give anyone love for more than the next occasion when he would be able to move on. There were times when he would stay longer with his prey, but that was usually business related, since all he understood was money.

The next few days she simply spied on the shop, with the intention of working out when he was there. It wasn't so easy and then she thought; on Thursday the shop opened at 18.00 in the evening, and dinner was usually served at 19.00. At around 5 PM that evening she went out on a walk with Timmy, came back and had dinner. Of course, being in France dinners are not over with in just 5 minutes, and as for the sex shop, she had no idea as to when it closed. The dinner that evening was her favorite: spaghetti, fried vegetables and Parmesan cheese with Bolognese sauce. After it she then left the house discreetly and ran as fast as she could to the sex shop. As she walked in, the owner played it cool, he wasn't sure of her real age, but given he was almost ejaculating in his pants he simply had to help her. "If you need any help, just ask." She then looked at him, totally frightened and disappointed. "I was just offering to help you and look after you in this business."

"Please cut the crap, what do you want from me?" She asked and by then she was very curious and looking like a hot kitten.

"I want to fuck you." He said little scared in case she was some undercover juvenile police officer.

"How much are you offering?" The last thing he was going to offer a minor was money, especially if it looked like prostitution.

"A partnership 50:50." He said which in court could have amounted to a long-term prison sentence unless he could persuade the jury that his business was merely harmless glamour shots.

"You want 50 percent of my earnings?" She said defiantly.

"No, we can make films together." He said he was no longer able to hold back his desires. His talk had simply taken her breath away, and after a few moments she had decided that this was maybe a great deal, but she wanted to keep him guessing. He was a little scared, since although his intuition told him he would be fine how could he be so sure? He had already been imprisoned for having sex with a 12 years-old girl while in Paris twenty years earlier when aged 30 and didn't wish to lose his new safe and relatively clean and comfortable new life. "Look before you want to think about it, let's go out for a drink." He said he was expecting a later rendezvous and by then wishing that he had waited for an older client, while at the same time he knew that they were more difficult for him to catch into his net, while she was expecting to strike the iron while it was hot. "I'm closing the shop in half an hour." His answer was not direct but implied that he wanted to take her out as soon as possible, was exactly the way in which she wanted, and made her feel so excited.

A few hours passed and of course her host family were out of their mind with worry. They contacted the police, but given that she wasn't a French national, the local station was less concerned, since she wasn't someone that they had some close connection with. As such the family had to come and remind the station about the seriousness of the suspected disappearance, which could turn out bad for them after all.

During her host family's misery, she had been out with Bernard wining and dining, and he gave her a present. It was a rather unusual one, but one in which her desire for material possessions would grow as would her dependence on him. The present was a book, a fashion book, and at first, she was a little intrigued as to his choice of literature but was too afraid to ask since he had something of an air of arrogance about him, but seeing models wearing expensive clothes and jewelry was enough to whet her materialistic appetite even further. A while later he took her back to his flat, she was still a little merry. "Have you ever had a massage?" He asked her since he was more than ready for her.

"No." She looked at him and before she had a chance to think, he simply did what he had done to so many of his previous virginal conquests, and that was to start of massaging her so innocently and to flatter every inch of her skin as though he had never seen a naked body before, while his slow and deep voice was hypnotic for her. Eventually they caught each other's faces and started to move their faces closer and kissed. While he was her first, she thought that it was love, while for him he had some sixth sense telling him that there were many francs to be made from her.

A few days later for the first video as soft porn video was made with him on top of her, it wasn't a video which he wanted to use, he just wanted to get her in the swing of things, but paid her something as a sweetener, which his distributor had sent onto him, and was within three days of her disappearance. They were for his own safety reasons now in Germany, since his bosses had the best lawyers around and with her being a foreign national; with many of his key clients working for the judiciary he was safe. Of course, with the open borders it had been so easy to just sneak across as they had done during the evening when September became October.

During this time, Mark was devoting his life to his wife and their two children, while he often went swimming as a complete family unit, he was proud to see Sarah training Benjamin with his own personal swimming techniques and he was happy to leave them alone so that he could coax Louise into swimming more and more. Their evenings were relaxed too, without Graham Norton and Dani Behr appearing in front of their faces, they simply had to make their own entertainment and would often play family games such as monopoly together or make jigsaws. On top of that, the icing on the cake was for him Axelle, the one he had no power over but was posting letters to him, this was a little bit strange for her, but her bitterness and hatred of him had now been replaced with that of a teenage girl in pilot mode, as she wasn't sure of herself.

After Bernard's bosses had seen the first video which was too soft for commercial purposes, they were satisfied that Axelle had great potential, and while she could had passed as being just under 18, they were satisfied that she had just celebrated her 18th birthday and would never in a million years have guessed that she was only 14. The next video was a little rougher and would be used commercially, more positions took place, such as oral sex and he ejaculated all over her face. Bit by bit he wanted her to get used other kinds and desires to suit all the tastes of the clients, which included: local politicians, lawyers and judges but of course the videos could be bought all over the world, and not just in Essen where they were then based. Of course, if they could make something special then they would need to draw in the attention of the entertainment mogul: Winston Harvey, politicians William and Helen Busby as well as financier Simon George.

For the third video he introduced his gay partner to her and her enjoy-ed having a threesome, he could then, as she became more adventurous move onto a threesome with another girl. All this happened during the month of October and she had lost count with the number of partners of both sexes she had had, one thing was certain she fell pregnant during the month since November was when she realized that she was in the family way. When the crew found out, one of the videos was edited as the impreg-nation video. During the next few weeks cats and dogs were introduced into the scenes, as well as strange and weird masks as well as sadomaso-chism and whipping, as tastes of almost every sexual perversion were carried out increasingly during her pregnancy.

By this time, she was living in a luxury suburban house with its own hi tech private security and some of the partners from the early days would come back for more videos to star in with her and of course she had lost track of the countless men who might had been the father of her child, still everything seemed exciting. She was making good money, but decided that straight after the birth, and feeling scared for her own safety that she should come back home in Lancashire to a shell-shocked family with her baby. For the time being at least she was living in some hospital, where there was plenty of money around, with state-of-the-art equipment. Equally being paid for sex, she was always fulfilled. She did attend the odd visit to the doctors regarding her pregnancy and was given vitamin and mineral supplements, since the foods she ate weren't highly nutritious, but for the rest she had no responsibilities, and was exhausted from making so many videos.

During one of her quiet moments, she would write, and Mark's most prized letter from his daughter, which would always remain in his heart, was the one she wrote to him below and was around the start of the New Year, which she wanted to make good.

Dear Daddy,

My studies are very intensive, and I hope that you understand my move to Germany. Not a lot to write about, other than that my French and German have improved, and I am a changed person, who is no longer angry with the world. I realize although I wish that I had somewhat earlier, that what happened in the past is no longer relevant to me now, and that I want to build a new future, full of happiness.

Finally, I am so sorry, for the pain that I have caused to you daddy, looking back I never thought that you killed my mother, sorry for such a short letter, but once again I have so much to concentrate on at school ETC. Looking forward to seeing you all soon.

Lots of love,

Axelle.

When Mark received the letter, he was absolutely convinced that he was blessed, and found himself writing poems and singing more to Louise than was usual. In turn her sky-high amorous feelings towards him knew no bounds.

What had changed Axelle, maybe fear, she certainly hadn't come to France to become a mother, and at the end of the day she was receiving no emotional support from any of the men in her circle. When she got involved in the porn industry, she was proud of the way in which she had shown herself how she didn't need any help from her murderous father, even so, she got involved in the industry simply by chance. Her former feelings for her father whom she loved as a small child were growing as fast as the baby inside of her, and in the end, there was no place like home, Brussels for her was a distant memory, while Garstang was where her heart lay.

Back in the immediate world of pornography, whenever Axelle was hungry there were fruits lying around everywhere, chocolate bars and if she was hungry plenty of deep freeze pizzas ready and waiting to be cooked in the microwave. Cleaning wasn't so simple, but with so much money there was never a problem paying for a cleaner. What was complicated for the couple or trio was the routine; the sex, which during the filming was dependent on the camera crew such as when they could assemble and the demands that they would require. Of course, with more money coming in thanks to the great success of the videos, the investors agreed to round the clock-crews on standby. Sometimes the camera crew would wake up the actors, other times the actors would be waiting for the director to surface, and of course the roles would often change, since piecing together the shows was often done on impulse with there being no set rules. In fact, there was little in the way of any routine regarding the times to wake up, start filming, in many aspects there was nothing but chaos. In the end they decided to have a cleaner every Wednesday and Saturday evening, this tied in with their plans to go out to the restaurants.

There were times when Axelle hated herself, and with her mind elsewhere she wasn't always the best when it came to personal hygiene. Sometimes while in the middle of preparing something to eat, she would run out to the toilet and then back to preparing the food without washing her hands and continue with handling the food. One day when she wanted to cook for everyone and had been all by herself in the kitchen and microwaved and placed 6 pizzas in the grill, she was very proud of herself. A few hours later, to her shame the whole pornography crew were feeling sick and vomiting. "Axelle, I have noticed that you don't always wash your hands before preparing food." Said a junior model gently as he had a tender moment thinking about the child, which he hoped might have been his, which was growing inside of her.

"I know because you don't always clean your hands after going to the bathroom." She screamed at him. One thing he felt sure about was that before he prepared anything to eat, he always washed his hands, and expected others to do the same too.

"Before I eat or prepare something, I always wash my hands." He left it alone since he knew that he wasn't able to get anywhere judging by the terror in her eyes and was terrified of what she was capable of doing during the filming, which was about to take place between them both with her as the leading partner.

One evening during filming part of the script involved two of Axelle's partners, and after 30 seconds of heavy breathing, the director was going to direct the male star to spray himself all over Axelle's breasts, instead the director's phone rang and without the director there the male actor impregnated the girl, the third member of the acting crew trio, who was on crack, and totally unaware of what was happening around her. Even so as he pulled out the cameraman continued with a wonderful moving shot of her creampied vagina, at least she was 18 years of age. The director then came back. "Axelle and Richard, here is 1,000 euros, this should keep you for some time out of hunger, the place is yours until we get back, but we are needed to do some work connected with Winston Harvey and there's some big money involved." Said a delighted senior female crewmember.

Axelle and Richard were impressed, one of the most powerful movie moguls was going to collaborate with Germany's most powerful pornographic industry. Richard was just two years older than Axelle; he too grew up in a dysfunctional family, and like her was searching for love. She was at first delighted to be alone with him and hoped that she could focus her mind on him. She had never had any tender moments since her only connection with making love was in this dirty business. Looking back, she knew of course that it had never been sweet, and that Bernard was simply coaxing her to the route, which she regrettably encountered.

While left on their own together, Richard and Axelle spent some time in the sun together outside on the apartment balcony relaxing and sleeping off the exhaustion from the recent film-making. She then wondered what it would be like to make love without the crew around, maybe it would have more depth, maybe they could run away together. As such she enjoyed the more natural stress-free way of making love, but then she became confused about his intentions, her own lust for money and her cynicism of him.

* * *

As a part of her necessary education, she had been encouraged to watch at least one pornographic video each day, and seeing other young girls doing this made her feel more relaxed, while seeing more daring styles would prepare her for something new. After several weeks it had all become the same and she had learnt something much quicker than most modern people could ever learn in a lifetime. She had had so many different men going inside of her, as well as all the different styles and toys, but the thing that she realized was twofold; it didn't matter who, it didn't matter how, the simple loving tender and passionate positions were the best, and if only she had realized that with just one man, just as in the old romantic movies of those she imagined her grandparents mirrored, since they were probably themselves by way of their loving tenderness to everyone around them gentle lovers, and it was after dozens of partners and when she compared Richard to the others that this painful reality set in. It was in moments like these when Axelle felt so ashamed of herself. Fortunately, she had the feisty spirit in her and planned to wipe out France from her mind forever when she arrived back in England. True she was pregnant but wanted to return as the virgin she was as she left home and find love with just a man, the first man who would love her for who she was, all she wanted was to forgive her father. Knowing that families came first, then surely Louise owed Axelle a favor for being a part in the death of her mother, and that she would simply look after Axelle's baby. Simply put she felt that; as a born-again sweet girl she could be the child who would have made her mother, Sophie, proud so that she would be free to find her sweetheart. As such when her days in the porn industry finished, a new dawn begun, and she became in her mind a young maid once more.

Financially she had received around 20 thousand euros in cash, as well as plenty of gifts and just before she gave birth, she gave up her career while keeping mum, and her employers paid for her hospital care in a private hospital in Essen, and on the 20th of July 2003 she gave birth to a baby boy. A week later she had already left the hospital and checked in at a hotel close to

Frankfurt Airport a few days earlier, ready for her return flight home. On the day of her departure, she checked in at the check-in desk with her unidentified baby whom she loved, and simply stated that it was an early birth and that she would register the baby at home in the UK. Fortunately, at the customs it was a middle-aged man, and he believed in the story that her 9-pound (4 kilos) baby was born a little earlier than expected, hence the reason for the unexpected birth in Germany. Once the plane took off, she felt free, a new life was dawning, with her baby sleeping in her arms her emotions came back and she couldn't stop the tears running down her face as she simply felt so cheap but was looking forward to going home to her safe Garstang.

And so, it was she wasn't even quite 15, yet in the summer of 2003 when her aunts hadn't even got married, she was already a mother. There had been no mention of her situation, she had even thought of placing her baby in a baby box but luckily, she decided against that, and while at first the Taylor family were completely shocked, they were all as lovers of babies and starting to coo over the baby. Axelle lied about the conception, and it was of a great relief to the Taylors that the father was an innocent boy two years older, who like Axelle was from another country, and they decided to separate since she had no intention of moving to Moldova, and although shocked at first, they believed her story, which although heartbreaking sounded at least some-what romantic.

One evening Karen looked after the baby, her great grandson and Karen was only 56. One of Axelle's female classmates from school who was dressed up and not in her school uniform spotted her in the Wheatsheaf, she wasn't sure if she recognized her or not as being someone, she knew and decided that she would remain discreet. As Axelle left the pub, she decided to venture out admiring the hedgerows in the gardens, since she knew that England was famous for this. In fact, along the country lanes one could for miles and miles see a chain of this beautiful man-made flora all over the bay and Bowland areas.

The next day she went out with her baby in his pram, and was simply proud of her Lancashire origins, the wholesome local shops delighted her, as did the rain, which she found so pure and refreshing as she had finally decided to wash away her sorrows. Axelle was also delighted that the continental pornography connections couldn't trace her, but sometimes she would try to guess who the father was, and although she had no idea, she hoped that it wasn't Bernard, since he was the one who introduced her to vice. If only the young man she got to know more than the others had been the father of her child, but he was simply one of the twenty men who had filled her up for the videos and the only one who had been introduced to her when she was already pregnant. He was the only one who had any feelings for her, yet she couldn't even remember his name, that being of course Richard. For now, at least she was away from her sordid past.

Later that evening on the last day of July she went out again to the place she had been the night before, that being the Wheatsheaf, there were plenty of young country gents and the girl spotted her from the night before, her male friend was pretending to masturbate over a picture of Axelle in a sex scene from a porno mag and her schoolmate smiled at Axelle. Axelle then went over and as soon as Axelle noticed the boy holding a picture of Axelle on his crotch, she went crazy, and simply ran out. Feeling so humiliated, especially since they were friends of friends connected with Sarah, her own sister of all people, she felt as though she was sinking into the gutters. A moment later and while walking outside she was in fear of someone else spotting her as: Grating's Porn Queen. Memories came running back to haunt from the death of her mother, until she could bear no more and she ran straight in front of a bus on the way back home, in order to protect her son from humiliation, since she knew how much she herself had been traumatized over the death of her own mother, while her baby was still too young to have become emotionally attached to her.

Chapter 12

That evening Mark and Louise found themselves looking after the baby longer than they expected, and simply put it down to a wild child, Axelle running away from her responsibilities. During the morning of the next day, Karen came round, and before Louise had a chance to offer her a drink she began, "As you know, I'm involved with students, many of whom will become influential people, and I never thought I would be discussing what I am going to tell you right now." Mark and Louise looked on tensely, wondering what was going on, if it were Axelle why hadn't she told them what could possibly be more important than that concerning a missing child, and above all her granddaughter? "Before I begin, I want you both to be prepared for an emergency crisis meeting this evening . . . First, I want you to read this when I have left the house." She then handed them a book, and left as quickly as she came in.

Both Louise and Mark almost collapsed with fear. Mark's mother, the beloved soft and gentle feminine beauty had given them something, which would have made any extremist proud. It was simply a book about how unconventional families were taking over and that the state would no longer allow people to be in control of their own lives and above all their own families. Both felt sick, equally she had given so much to Louise let alone as to what she had done for Mark. Still in shock, both knew they

• • •

had to get through with the rest of the day and spent as much time with their children, including Axelle's baby together.

When Karen came around with Frank who simply understood that he was going around to discuss something important, a shell-shocked Mark and Louise as well as Frank were about to receive an earthquake. "When I fell pregnant to your dad and was expecting you, my parents wanted me to give you to my parents so that they could bring you up as your parents." She said this as she had her hands on Frank's knees. "So that I could be free from the chains of poverty and study at Cambridge or Oxford University." In shock everyone sat around moving closer to Karen, and they were all numb, waiting in great anticipation for her to continue. "I am not an extremist, but I have always known that modern technology is going to destroy the very fabric and structure of love. My whole and Frank's life has been devoted to bringing up our family together, and I'm scared about the future of our kids."

"You mean the LGBT, Feminist agenda, which wants to bring up children under the property of the state, and that those who produce children in a natural way will no longer be the norm?" Asked Louise as she was gaining her inner composure while Mark's jaws dropped. Karen was satisfied that she didn't need to continue.

"Louise, you are only a sweet and innocent country girl, who has everything that nature has provided us with, as such you are now the baby's mother and you will go with me to the registry office in Preston. You have just arrived back from France. No one will check the hospital where you gave birth. Nobody watched TV today, but this morning I read in the newspapers that Axelle committed suicide." She then handed the newspaper report to them. At first, they thought the reason for this change of parental guardianship was as a result of Axelle's irresponsibility, but now they were having to take in new and unwelcome mysteries, as everyone present looked on as though they were about to be sick. Karen, who had basically in her own way taken over the hearts, minds and souls of her terrified family, was sitting as

● ● ●

though she was Boudica. Everyone sat in the room had children, as a part of the survival of themselves in the image of their offspring and felt that they were not simply mass produced goods in a factory such as Ford or Sony ETC but simply of a man and a woman who would die for each other, who valued the touch of their skin, the look of love they saw in their eyes, resulting in the fruits; their children as well as the sounds which distinguished Frank's stomping from Karen's gliding, to Mark's smells of an animal to Louise's aromas of blossom. They could have been beauties and the beasts, and their kids were simply theirs, and theirs alone.

"Are you asking us to fight against this?" Asked Mark a little frightened but equally in awe of his mother.

"Of course not, we have no reason to. So long as we live our lives in peace, then that's the best thing that we can do . . . But it has been written in the Bible that money destroys the soul. Look what happened to Amy my sister, swapping her kids for a man in a sports car." She then thought about Sophie, who was a victim of life in the lonely city of broken hearts but didn't wish to hurt Mark and to embarrass Louise. "As for Axelle, she got involved with the oldest profession in the world . . . She became addicted to the money she could earn. In the end she wasn't any different to Amy . . . Just forget the misery and love each other till death do us part, and so long as you stay together, the outside world can't touch you." She then felt confident that she had done her duty to everyone present.

"But what about the fluoride in the water, all the injections we are meant to poison our kids with?" Asked Louise, Karen looked at her proudly thinking there was no better wife for Mark.

"One hundred years ago people were dying in the smoke caused by the factories, then we had cigarettes, there is always something, just don't be paranoid, live your lives with love, and you will be free." She said with the strongest of conviction. As for the porn, they had all suspected this, but didn't wish to discuss it.

● ● ●

That same weekend Karen met up with her old schoolmate, Heidi, for a coffee at the church in Calder Vale, where her husband Peter sometimes helped her. After discussing everything, it had been agreed she could come the next day with her daughter-in-law and sort out the bureaucracy. As arranged, Karen and Louise went to the registry office in Preston. The clerk there was a young lady several years younger than Louise, Karen smiled at the assistant and then Karen's old time friend came and took them both into her office, and she herself was helping a traditional Christian politician, her husband Peter, who was fighting in vain to bring back traditional family values, as such all the important documents had been according to law dealt with in a way, which placed family values first and foremost.

After being in shock at the start of August, Mark had to work with Louise and his mother in getting the legal rights for the baby sorted out, that included the name, since Axelle hadn't thought of that, and in honor of the mother the baby was christened Alec. Sarah and Benjamin agreed that Alec was their little brother and that Mark and Louise were the rightful parents.

Of course, things were a little strange regarding the anomalies with their third child who had been registered and the reality, but in knowing that previous generations had done exactly the same convinced Louise to keep the faith that she was doing the right thing for her man, and that the world outside was less stable than the walls outside of their house which in turn were a part of an increasingly unstable world, where the winds from the south east would blow the air from the sewers of the House of Lords with their plans to destroy a thousand years of Lancashire Life with the PC culture from Brussels and beyond. With their whole family they would be able to connect with the right people in the appropriate offices, they were able to save their own family themselves without any governmental interference, while the horror stories about micro chipped human beings were still only to be found in science fiction books and of no concern to Louise in any shape or form.

September came, and with things settling down Mark went into a depression regarding Axelle, at least though, he was able to grieve. "This is all my fault, I failed her!" He wailed to Louise.

"You can't blame yourself for her death." She said tenderly.

"Had I not got any further than Garstang, this wouldn't had happen-ed." He then completely burst out crying. She had never seen him so sad and felt that she had to help him get through this as much as possible. There were times when she felt that he simply didn't care about Axelle and this side of him she didn't like, but now of course she was relieved that he had such strong feelings of love for his second daughter. Sadly, Louise hadn't experienced the feelings of mutual love and respect this father and daughter had for each other before he left Sophie. "Do you think if she knew how I am feeling now that she would still be alive?" He said in desperation. She agreed with him but tried not to express her views with her body language and just wanted him to somehow recover.

There was nothing that you could have done. As soon as her mother accused you of murder the die had been cast . . . Just remember that the children and I need you, and the best thing you can do right now is to sleep in my arms. Streams of tears ran down his face, she wanted him to know that she was behind him, and took out a tissue wiping the tears, which she knew were running down his cheeks, since she could feel them on her wet hand, which contained her own tears of sadness too, and they simply nodded off to sleep.

As for Karen, the death of Axelle triggered off the silent wounds of the untimely deaths of her parents, and even worse those of her younger sister. She even cried for Sophie, despite that she tried to kill her own son. The funeral of Axelle, which took place on the 5th of August in the grounds of St Thomas's church made Karen proud. "I would like to thank the lord for blessing me with such a beautiful family, but once again we have been touched by the power of the dark forces, which pushed my daughter into taking her own life. May the Lord have mercy, her legacy, the one being of her memory, which will never be taken away from us amen." Said a Mark with a touch of defiance as he thought about all the people, he knew who were stressing about their mobile phones and cleaning their cars on a Sunday. The legacy was of course her baby, but no attention was to be drawn to this and luckily once the tormentors found out about her death, the former schoolmates, so ashamed and disgusted with themselves, had no intention of seeking malice, and automatically assumed that Axelle's family would take care of the baby, and that this was simply none of their business, since although they had been nasty and cruel, they were still country boys at heart and the inner city gangs of teenagers were simply something, which they were not a part of.

With Axelle now gone, life for Frank and Karen was quiet, calm and increasingly predictable, also both of their daughters had left the nest. Amy although she wasn't married was in a stable relationship, still living in Kirby Lonsdale, in a house with her partner, while Kerry seemed settled with her student life in France. As such Karen and Frank were pleased that three of their children were settled in a relationship. Matthew although he hadn't moved very far just the next village but one, he hadn't been in much contact with his parents since working on the farm kept him busy from dawn till dusk, and with his four children his wife was busy, even so all four children would often visit on their bikes Frank and Karen. As such although she had grown very fond of her house, with Mark and Louise suddenly gaining a baby, of which she felt partly responsible, she felt that Mark and Louise needed some support since they were undoubtedly under some form of stress and needed to speak with Frank. As usual he came home placidly and pleased to see his wife. "Shouldn't we swap houses with Mark and Louise?" She asked as he walked in through the door happy as usual.

"Sounds like a nice idea, but I am worried about them as a couple, I mean he always looks so dour, before we can offer them the house, I would like to have some guarantees that their home isn't broken." He said as he was taking off his coat.

"I know, he looks so distraught all the time I call into Booths, and as for Louise, she has lost her sparkle." She said a little worried.

"Look, if they are strong; they can survive a rabbit hutch together, and if they are, I will gladly let them have some extra space, but I don't think that now is the time." He said dolefully.

"Neither do I, you have just confirmed my feelings too." She said as they were both looking into each other's eyes.

Losing a child for any parent is a tragedy of a most horrendous kind and while Louise understood this and was worried about her beloved, who was obviously racked with guilt since he had over the years been estranged from his daughter, he had for the first time since they were together stopped making love, and instead of visiting the doctor she decided to confront him in the bed, since it had been 3 months since his daughter's death and while she was never a fan of November, this 11th month seemed to be more horrible than she could ever had anticipated.

"Darling if you don't love me, I can leave." She said meekly.

"I love you more than anything, but I feel like nothing." He then started crying. "It is all my fault, I should never have gone to Belgium when I met you, because all I ever wanted was you, and looking back who cares if I had broken the law by one month because you Louise are simply the best." She then went down with her head and buried herself into his chest, he then started to become aroused and she being of a sensitive kind simply got on top of him, and he enjoyed looking at her breasts and just before it was time to ejaculate he ushered her onto her back and knowing that he had within the space of several minutes proven to her that he loved all of his children equally, and, that there was simply no one else like her, was enough to turn her on so much that in the heat of the moment she let herself go completely and was ready for another child. As such she fell pregnant in no time and looking forward to another baby freed Mark from his sorrows over Axelle and the warm and loving tenderness of this couple in love kept their relationship safe and sound. As such for the rest of November they were making up for the lack of inti-

● ● ●

macy he had for her recently, and by Christmas it came as no surprise when they realized that their baby number three was on the way and were happy once again.

It was then over the festive season, boxing day, in fact that Mark and Louise invited both of their parents over. All four parents couldn't help but notice the sparkle in both the eyes of Louise and Mark, and a rhubarb crumble with local ice cream was served with a bottle of Champagne. "I thank you in coming here today, I know things have been rough, but thanks to my darling Louise, I have got through this. Losing one's daughter, one's child is the worst thing to happen to a parent, but Louise has without any complaint taken on the responsibility of Axelle's son, Alec. I would like to say she is the best person in the world, so true, so loyal, and I was too much wrapped in my own sorrows regarding Axelle, and I am sorry, I must have simply been a black hole, but Louise helped me get through those dark days, and now the light has returned once more into our lives and we are having a baby." He said proudly. Louise then stood up, put her arms around him and then they kissed lovingly. Frank then looked at his wife and saw her looking delightedly at the two lovebirds and then he stood up and walked towards them both, proudly.

"Karen and I had such lovely times in Scorton, we always pre-ferred the village to the town, even so Garstang was great when we had four kids, but now with the place empty since they have all fled the nest, and with the young ones here about to have four kids of their own, your mum and dad are offering to swap houses." Karen was delighted since he had read her so well and acted like a man in dealing with such an important family matter.

The house swap was very quick and took place during the rest of the Christmas season, and with them being family, they basically went around taking whatever they needed. As for the furniture and beds, they left everything as it was, so mainly they had to sort out the clothing, books and children's toys. With Karen and Frank on their own, three bedrooms were plenty, while for Mark and Louise they had four bedrooms, one for themselves, one for Sarah, one for Benjamin, and one for both

Alec and the baby when he or she was born. Of course during the moving process Frank had been busy with Mark going through with him the pebbles, which had been accumulated over the years, and knowing that Sarah and Benjamin were fond of these gemstones he went around the garden with his son making sure that the memories of the pebbles could be passed onto the next generations, as such December was the month of the pebbles shifting homes, but gently like ripples since the Taylors would go backwards and forwards between the two houses without any hurry whatsoever.

The following year 2004 came in and Amy got engaged and married in Kirby Lonsdale in the spring, while Kerry now back from France and working in the sports center in Garstang was going steady with her French partner Louis who was working in Lancaster in the information center, and they were sharing a flat there in the city together. Sarah too was turning into adulthood, had done well with her GCSE's, and was after the summer moving onto higher education in order to become a lawyer and to Karen's joy.

As for Louise's pregnancy, everything was running smoothly, but for Mark things were a little bit creepy. The reason being that exactly 16 years earlier he and Sophie were going through a pregnancy together, and this baby was due around the time of Axelle's birthday. He never once mentioned this to Louise, but obviously she had thought about this too, but while he never mentioned this so as not to make Louise jealous, she never mentioned this to him so as not to make him grieve over Axelle. As to be expected, they were active together during the pregnancy, they had three children to look after, went on their walks, bike rides and swims together, while making sure that they were happy at home with family life, the food, as well as the icing on the cake, which was simply the tender times they had for each other.

On August the 20th and exactly 16 years since Axelle's birth, Louise gave birth to another healthy baby girl. Louise was then 36, Mark 41 and their children were Sarah 16, Benjamin aged 10 and of course for the new edition well the name Alec was out, but Claire was in and not forgetting that they were the legal parents of Alec too aged only 1.

Louise had always wanted three children and felt blessed, especially since many of her school contemporaries, although they hadn't had such a traumatic end to their teenage days as she had, since then women were having babies later in life. Equally she knew that very few were in happy and traditional families and as a teenager she remembered girls speaking about lovely guys, and then the stories were about terrible husbands and she blamed the soap operas on television and the celebrity programs in brainwashing people into behaving so badly. As such she was happy that she had her own family and was living in her own world and bringing up her children without worrying about modern society.

Louise wasn't tired of looking after four children now, and the stress, which was a result of the way in which she had acquired her third was a distant memory. Mark was still working as a duty manager at Booths as usual and when he came home, he wanted to devote his life to his family. In bed that night and when everything was quiet. "I think we are fine with three kids." She said but was unsure and wanted to know what Mark really thought.

"It was always our desire to have three children and instead of speaking about the what ifs and possibilities, we are just live!" As such she understood, like him she was content, and she too deep down so very much wanted the passion rather than of the pain regarding his daughter and grandchild. As such, in between the cries and the breast feeding of Claire they simply couldn't get enough of each other after she had recovered from the birth.

Autumn 2004 and nearing 17 Sarah would take the bus to Lancaster, where she was taking Politics, Law, Sociology and French. While there, her views were considered moderate, since she kept her head down and wanted to take in as much as possible, analyze and formulate her own understanding as opposed to her own views. As such, she was able to convince the others that she agreed with everyone while at the same time she understood how and why people have different perspectives. It was there at 6th form that Sarah fell in love with Daniel, he was a little different to the others. Friendly but never loud and wanted to be an economist while Sarah wanted to be a lawyer and they studied different A-Levels but as time went by and they saw all the other university couples breaking up, they decided that given they loved each other that they needed to treat the matter of university very seriously. As such instead of simply going their own ways regarding their choice of study, they decided to work out some compromise. Both had a multitude of different courses and universities as well as desires to get away from their parents and to live together. They spent a lot of time researching. In the end they both decided to study at Lancaster and to work at Booths part time but would continue staying with their parents until 6th form was over.

Daniel grew up on the Morecambe bay in Flookburgh, a small village a few miles west of Grange-over-Sands. From his home with the family dog, he would sometimes walk to Humphrey Head, a limestone outcrop, where he would often think about his life and there, he could easily make out the area around Silverdale, and the landscape was similar his territory. Perhaps this was one of the reasons why as time went by, she found him to be not so dissimilar to Grandpa Frank. For some reason, like Frank he went to Lancaster for his A-Levels, Ulverston was much closer, but part of the attraction was the university. For Sarah, it was simply their fate.

As for Mark, he knew how lucky he was, and his life was around Louise, he didn't go out to the pub much because he didn't drink, but for him the tales were incredible whenever he visited, usually less than once a month. One of his schoolmates from Garstang High was very beautiful, she looked like his mum, but Mark wasn't ready to settle down at the time, and she found an average man who would stay with her, because she wanted love so much. She went to the same sixth form as Mark where she was expected to achieve much more than Mark and in her second year after dating a few men she fell pregnant to a plumber. They had 6 children together were still living together, she had never worked while he had no respect for her whatsoever and the open secret was that if any woman was bored, he was the man to fix her needs. She knew everything that was taking place behind her back, but with six children she had no intention of leaving him. While she came from a loving family, he came from a broken one, and had no confidence in himself. While he was just an ordinary man, his partner was very beautiful, intelligent and good inside, a devoted wife and mother while he felt inferior to her. Louise knew of many stories around her Garstang like this and wasn't surprised with any of the news he relayed to her, and simply put her own family first and basically outside of her own family, like Mark she had very few friends, and wasn't in the slightest bit concerned about that.

2005 was a calm year for all concerned in the world of the Taylors. Frank was planning to retire but wanted to wait until Karen had, as such with plenty of money they decided to hire out an 8 berth-log cabin once again in Langdale for two weeks. There were only 6 but Amy and Kerry came over separately with their partners, and Sarah also came over for a few visits. As for the walks, well, it was business as usual and it was Benjamin aged 11 who thoroughly enjoyed all the walks with his grandparents, while his parents seemed to have their hands full with Alec aged just two and Claire not quite one. Even so Mark and Louise managed plenty of swims and enjoyed every minute of the holiday.

During the first few years of Alec's life, Mark couldn't help but to compare similarities with Axelle, who too had had what seemed to be a perfect bond with her father. Thinking about this was of course enough to send him into moments of despair but being the kind of man who simply wanted to be happy and live his life beautifully with the woman he loved was enough for him. On top of that, this child had a very different situation to Axelle's, which stared at Mark, whenever he was around Louise. Simply put, while the previous relationship was one of love, it was also combined with many problems, since the foundations had never been pure, Mark knew deep down from the beginning that Sophie wasn't the one for him, while Louise was simply his other half in his mirror of love, both equal but both different, as he respected her as a woman, she respected him as a man and their harmony protected all the children around them. Both had and accepted each other's faults. On top of that, Alec had a baby sister, Claire, of course biologically the relationship was of an uncle and a niece, with Claire being the senior and Alec being the junior, and with everything being so absurd, having them simply as brother and sister saved a lot of confusion for everyone around them, which in the "Brave New World of Aldous Huxley," was in some ways becoming a sad reality.

Mark and Louise had by the time of their fourth child a good solid collection of children's books, they didn't need DVD's since they both enjoyed interacting with their children and wanted them to draw instead of listening passively to some loudspeaker. Beatrix Potter went down well, while for Alec he was more of a Winnie Pooh listener, and sometimes Benjamin, and even Sarah would join in and read. Of course, living close to nature, the children loved to collect leaves and place them inside a book, while Benjamin would sketch animals, and collected Beatrix Potter memorabilia. In summer they enjoyed the confluence of the Wyre and Grizedale, where they would spend a lot of time in the water and Sarah and Benjamin would find themselves swimming there too, so long as the young rams were not lurking around. Alec and Claire enjoyed looking for leaves together as that autumn Claire was gaining confidence on her own two feet. Most importantly of all was that Louise loved Alec as much as her own children, while Mark played the father role as opposed to the grandfather role to him very naturally. As such for them, life in Garstang was simply beautiful, and their happiness put smiles on the faces of many who saw them.

When 2006 came in Benjamin was just finishing with some success his first term at Garstang High, where to Frank's delight he was a better budding sportsman than his sons. Mark and

Louise were enjoying themselves more as a family, since their two small children were starting to walk more, and of course they often went out cycling with Alec on the back of Mark's bike and Claire on the back of Louise's, along with their packed lunches.

Sarah was inevitably a hard working scholar and got 4 straight A"s at A-Level in the long hot summer of 2006, and with her boyfriend Daniel as a tip from her father they spent the summer as assistants working at youth hostels in the Borrowdale Valley, where Karen and Frank now without children at home and still fit were able to cycle up from Scorton 65 miles (105KM) the same day and stay over for a couple of days before the cycle back home on the same day of their depart when they would call in for dinner at Silverdale. Of course, her parents stayed over with her siblings since as with all the Taylors they didn't need much of an excuse to visit the wonders of The Lake District, and for the small children it was their first time in a youth hostel and even toddler Claire seemed to enjoy the bunk beds along with Alec while both for safety reasons and due to their ages slept on the lower bunks. The view from the room overlooking Derwent-water, Skiddaw and the islands close to Keswick was of course simply breath-taking and they wondered in awe and curiosity about the kind of Victorians who must have lived in this truly elegant and grand building.

Back in the Autumn, Karen was still teaching for one more year when Sarah arrived at the university where she was sharing a student's house with Daniel and sometimes without him, they would meet up for lunch, and many believed that they were mother and daughter. Sarah was talk of the campus, a typical Taylor brunette, with long legs, and was 173cm around 5'8" and turned the heads of many at the campus, which was a common feature in her family.

The following year was much the same, but Frank organized some-thing special for Karen's 60th birthday and together they went away on a camping holiday during the summer for six weeks with their bikes on the continent. They cycled down to Switzer-land along the French and German borders, so they were able to enjoy The Black Forest, as well as the Vosges region of France near Alsace. After going through Switzerland they managed to spend some days walking in their own memory lane around Lake Wolfgang where they holidayed 29 years earlier with their boys, before taking a night train back from Salzburg to Brussels, where they paid their respects to Sophie, and since they were still in touch with Thierry, they were welcome to spend the night with him, and luckily for him his fridge had been stocked up fully for him to cook and entertain his guests who had arrived unexpectedly.

Louise and Mark were quietly getting on with their beautiful lives, while Sarah had spent the summer in The Lake District, this time as a relief warden along with her partner Daniel. That autumn Frank went back to school for his final year, he was approaching 65 and it was time to retire the following year.

The following year arrived Sarah spent a year abroad in Strasbourg starting at the end of her second year at university in the summer of 2008 and Daniel came over to visit her. It had been a difficult year apart, for both of them, but Sarah's eyes had certainly opened and it was there that seeing that city life wasn't for her, not that it ever had been, was enough for her to see how Garstang had to remain cut off from everywhere else, since this small market town with its close knit communities and local businesses was in her view a much more humane society than that of the ever increase-ing centralized super-state of Brussels.

At the end of the first decade in the new millennium, Karen had reach-ed almost 63, Frank nearly 67, and both were enjoying their lives together. With four children, they had plenty of visits from their children, along with their many grandchildren. Matthew and Mark had been parents for nearly a generation, while her daughters who were both by then married were settled too. Amy was 30 and had two children one boy and a girl in Kirby Lonsdale while Kerry then 29 had returned back to Lancashire after her studies and was working in Garstang Sports center but was now working at Oxenholme working as an executive officer for the national park and living in Ambleside with Louis and their daughter, by this time he was then her husband and working in a Kendal museum as a curator.

This was also the decade in which Mark and Louise had fully settled down too. Sarah was of course becoming fully independent, was hardly ever at home and in a serious relationship as well being in her final year of her bachelor's course and this meant her room in Garstang was now used for just Claire who no longer had to share with Alec. Benjamin had just reached 16 and was getting ready for his GCSE's while their babies Alec and Claire were aged 6 and 5 and at the local primary school. In short, the next and final decade was their eldest child's time, since Sarah was the embodiment of all the goodness of her mother, as well as both of her grandmothers combined, and was about to cause quite a stir in the city of Lancaster for several reasons.

The summer of 2010 was a time of celebration for both Sarah and Daniel as he passed his economics with an upper second-class degree, while she passed Law and French with a first. Also, she entered a beauty pageant contest and came first, where she was offered to enter the national contest but dropped out, since she merely wanted to make a point against the feminists running the local council, and what was more although nobody knew this at the time, she looked like Amal Alamuddin who would later on get married to George Clooney. That autumn, Daniel started work and ironically enough he jots a job as a civil servant at the same office where his father-in-law had been working 24 years earlier, and it was just as well that his name was Metcalfe and not Taylor since Mark had developed an unflattering reputation there, but of course it being a generation later very few of his colleagues were still there. They never ate out, spent a night away in a hotel and as such after their studies they had managed to save up enough money for a deposit so that they could get a small flat close to the marsh in the city. Their neighbors were usually dysfunctional, violent, alcoholic single mothers whose husbands lived close by in either Lancaster or Preston and were often detained at her majesty's pleasure, usually for something drugs related. As such, in for them to escape from the estate they never bought anything expensive.

As with all the other Taylors, Sarah and Daniel although he wasn't a Taylor, understood how important it was for their bedroom to be a place to sleep and a place for them to be intimate with each other with no TV, just a radio which went off at the time they needed, but usually with them in bed by ten, they often woke up before the alarm clock went off at 6, so that they could start the day with love and passion just as their parents still did.

That autumn Sarah went on for her masters and in 2011 she graduated and after the summer went straight into a local law firm run by a traditional gentleman based in Lancaster who took her on as a trainee solicitor and with her traditional views on marriage she was a close confident of her boss Tony, and very sorry when he was going through a difficult marriage with his wife, Gemma, who was also a city lawyer, but in Preston.

The following year in 2012 aged 24 just like Daniel they both got married and Sarah wanted everything to be romantic and chose Calder Vale, in memory of her great grandparents who were the parents of her wonderful grandma Karen. This was also the time when Benjamin started his studies to become a sports teacher at Aberystwyth University.

Alec and Claire were certainly no longer small children and would still often take part in outdoor activities, and whenever Benjamin was around, they were so happy whenever he came home and organized trips for them, which whenever his mum and dad were both at work meant that he simply enjoyed playing the father role. It was then 2013 and both Mark and Louise felt that with Benjamin away a lot studying as well as the fact that Sarah had fled the nest that their house was starting to get a little bit too big, and both wished at times that they were living in Scorton, but would never of course mention this to his parents, while life passed by as usual for their parents and their children.

In 2014 there was simply nothing worth writing about, since most of the characters were simply going on the same walks and trips around the Forest of Bowland and holidaying in the Lake District as usual, and were either normal children in school or parents just getting on with their loving and peaceful lives, while Sarah had a most eventful year, which was significantly more of a landmark than the year she got married in.

Daniel had been working for just over three years and Sarah for just over two and still aged only 26 they viewed a house up for sale at the start of the year. It had all the mod cons with sensors and switches all over the place, as they left, they looked at each other, "What do you think?" She asked, waiting for his reply.

"I found it awful clinical and with too many choices."

"Actually, you are right, I would be redundant there, with everything being programmed." She said somewhat relieved.

The next house that they viewed the following evening had curtains, one light switch in each room and had a much cozier feel to it. As such they decided that this semi was the one they wanted to move into and was on the fringes of the city, near Williamsons Park and overlooking the Forest of Bowland. Sarah was proud that she had her degree, her career, and now she had found her house. The end of the month ended with them both expecting their first child together, and Sarah wanting to get the hell out of the Marsh Estate, quickly, and since the house was empty, they were able to move into it during the second month of the new-year, thanks to help from both of their families.

Thanks to having a steady boyfriend, her husband, she didn't need all those massage therapies since her healing was love, and while her peers were still enjoying the single life, she knew that ten years down the line that they would either be running around like headless chickens as their biological clock was ticking or simply married to their work. One of the bedrooms faced Garstang, it was south facing, and this was to be their room, and on the window ledge, where it could attract the sun's rays the black pebble from her father was placed where it could heat up very quickly. This same pebble had been carried with her to university when she lived in Scotforth near the university and then onto the Marsh Estate but now it was resting in more homely surroundings.

As they moved into their new home that February, all the eyes of the neighbors were on them. The couple next door had two children on the left side. Julie was the breadwinner, she worked hard, while her partner Christopher stayed at home looking after their two small children, the house and the family. He also believed that he was getting the best deal, since he always wanted a family of his own. Both were happy with this arrangement, but she was leading a double life and was having secret affairs with junior male members of staff. On the right side lived another family. Lori stayed at home bringing up two children and Sarah knew about Julie's double since it was common knowledge on the estate, equally Christopher knew that Julie's partner was cheating on her, and she like him was simply, so family orientated.

If only Lori could meet Chris, one reading this woeful tale might be thinking, if only given they were two of a kind and both romantic. Sadly neither of them were the type to earn money but that wasn't the only problem, Lori was like her partner Trisha a lesbian, but outside of the home Trisha was like Julie and having affairs with her male subordinates, since there were times when she wanted to be treated like a lady, while in the home she was the dominant partner, but outside at work the stress from the job and domestic duties simply made her seek the release and frustration by way of just flittering her eyelashes, lying on her back in her office and ready for the missionary position and this was better than the drugs and anti-depressants which had helped her get this far in life, and unable to find one special man who was good enough for her to leave Lori, this for her was the best way in dealing with this toxic and compromising situation.

Sarah's personal life was on the up, and although they were well off, and would have quite honestly enjoyed luxury holidays together, they kept their leisure to simply going on day trips around the Forest of Bowland and, Silverdale and Arnside as well as the odd camping trip in the Lake District. Even so they were romantic, and on Valentine's Day they cooked for each other, opened-up a bottle of wine and shared chocolates as they watched "Les Miserable," starring Liam Neeson, her favorite actor. While her career was important, she had her marriage, her house, her career and without a care in the world about the problems in the city or the expectations she had as a career woman, she was simply looking forward to parenthood with her man.

As for her boss, his wife had basically gone off the rails and was living with her new partner who had also left her husband, but Sarah had the feisty Taylor blood inside of her. As such she represented her boss in the proceedings that spring and being only 26 beautiful and pregnant and standing up for family values and making mincemeat out of his wife, the press wanted to get onto the story. Equally in the courtroom seeing a rather heavily pregnant female lawyer that June who was sincere in her views on marriage shook the other members of the judiciary to the core, who were only interested in business and money while at the same time they had no morals or respect for anyone. In the end his haggard-looking wife could take no more and on the verge of a nervous breakdown ordered her counsel to stand aside for a bit and she asked Sarah what she should do. "You fell in love with your husband, marriage is for life, you went off the rails, and my advice is simple: go back to him, go to church and seek redemption and look after your family." Sarah herself didn't go to church, but considered herself a good Christian all the same, and as a lawyer knew how to play with words in order to destroy her opponents, while in fact she didn't trust any institution out-side of her home. Politics was also an area she steered well away from, since living in Lancaster she knew council members from every political shade and simply didn't trust any of them and decided to simply be on friendly terms with all of them, but behind her back very few people loved or even liked her, not that that at all mattered to her one little bit.

Gemma went back to her husband and he made sure to keep her busy so that she would have another child. At first, she would-n't let him go any-where near her, but each time he found out about lesbian domestic violence from a magazine he would leave a copy on the dining room table semi-discreetly as if it was a part of his cases. At first, she had been utterly provoked by what she saw as his arrogance, especially since her lesbian partner had started laying her hands on her violently, due to her jealousy. As such she soon got the message, her husband had never once lifted his finger against her and after nearly ending up with nervous breakdown she started to get close to him physically and before she had a chance to take in her pleasures properly, which she had spurned from him for years, she fell pregnant and was simply relieved.

Sarah herself gave birth on September 25th to a healthy girl called Emma and thanks to the support of both her husband who was able to work flexibly and her boss she was able to work part time and this her husband fully supported, since she started representing male victims of domestic violence, and in many cases she was contributing to a fall in the divorce rates in certain circles, since the women knew that if Sarah was on the case she would do everything to make sure that everything was split 50:50 and so in many cases the bored housewives decided that it was more in their interests to simply get on with their husbands than to go on a crusade in the courts and to destroy them, since if Sarah was on the scene the wives would have their reputations destroyed instead. What was interesting was the fact that Gemma was helping Sarah, since she decided to take a long break and had by this time forgiven Sarah for the humiliation, she had done to her, since at the end of the day she realized that her family was more important, than people she didn't know to be thinking how nice she was.

The following year, and despite working many less hours than Daniel, Sarah was looking for every bit the breadwinner, while at the same time she felt that she was a good mother too. They paid for a cleaner, and for meals they both worked together on this depending on their schedules, both could cook, and both were flexible enough in meeting the needs of the individual tastes of the other. On top of that they would go out with Emma in a sling. Also that year Benjamin started work as a sports teacher at Garsting, and decided that he wanted to settle down after a few more years, since being the energetic sportsman he was, he would need a younger partner when the time came to settle down, until then he had girlfriends but didn't rate their chances in being able to keep up with him ten years down the line, since his plan was to do plenty of sport with his partner and to go wild camping with his grandchildren, as such his expectations were very high. Meanwhile he was back with his parents, who were naturally delighted that the house no longer felt empty in any of the four bedrooms.

Even in 2016 Mark and Louise were living inside their own world, which hadn't changed much since George Michael was born. They had no internet at home so their children had no access to modern ills such as play station, that had helped to destroy the lives of so many single mothers the world over, when their children without their permission could run up debts against the unsuspecting parent who had no idea her underage son was able to run up a fee of 1,000 pounds or more. Equally they had a local Furness building society account run by people who cared for their people, and as such their hands were not tied up to unsavory businesses globally. While the Taylors were proud of their genes, which they passed onto their children, they cherished the fact that with Alec now being already 14 that he was a clear example of hope since he was doing well in school, and was popular with the girls, but didn't take that too seriously to the relief of both of his parents.

Sophie's traumatized mind, which was the result of the high conflict divorce of her parents led her to becoming a highly deranged psychopath, in turn Axelle's mind had been poisoned from her mother, who had brainwashed her into believing that Mark had killed her mother before Sophie took her own life, this had destroyed the innocence of Axelle an otherwise sweet girl.

Later and after being desensitized and the willing partner in depraved sexual acts, which took place under the most artificial of environments, Axelle's child was conceived.

Fortunately, with love, even though his start in life began in the bowels of hell, Alec thanks to his closest family members of his mother took over his wellbeing and he enjoyed the Forest of Bowland, was just as Lancastrian as George Formby and Eric Morecambe. Maybe Nicky Nook, whose presence imposed above the Taylor's bedrooms among others was protecting all of those who cared to look at her, the small hill where thousands of locals have seen the sunsets over the Morecambe Bay on her soil. In turn Alec was very caring towards Claire, who he treated just as any brother would be expected to look after a younger sister. Claire too was a very sweet child with a vivid imagination and loved family pets, which had a habit of going to and fro between the houses of the two Taylor families in Garstang and Scorton. Generally, they also had one dog and one cat, but of course there were two Taylor homes, and new family pet addi-tions.

When Mark read that George Michael had been arrested in a toilet in Los Angeles in 1998 he burst out laughing, but 18 years later and nowhere near as wealthy as the former singer, he fully realized how lucky he was to be Mark and to be in a loving and modest family, who understood him so well and was starting to feel sorry for his own personal previous so called nemesis.

On the 26th of December 2016, Mark went to work as usual at Booths, and the atmosphere was a little strange. The day before the radio at home had been off as the Taylors were in their own world with their family. Now back in the modern world, one or two of his colleagues had been crying; George Michael was dead. He then, during his coffee break, went to read the obit-uaries and as such was himself sad. As he read through the obituaries, he couldn't understand why this man had chosen his alternative existence apart from a few years with Kathy Jeung. Mark felt that George wasn't so glad to be gay as he made himself out to be, but simply became a lost and disturbed soul of the material world. Unlike his colleagues, Mark, who wasn't texting all the time and surrounded by radio waves like many others he knew even when they were in the company of their loved ones, saw things differently. For him, George Michael had been des-troyed psychologically due to fame and fortune, and of course the choices in every aspect of his life, which were based on living for the moment and nothing more. Mark then walked home to Louise and was feeling low, since he had once again been reminded of both his aunt Amy and Axelle as being testament to this. As usual without the distractions of modern life, he made love to Louise. "All the money in the world can never replace the heavenly beauty of you, which I see with my own eyes, the touch of your skin and the feeling of being at home with you and especially when I am deep inside of you, since the money and the material things we have, without you, mean absolutely nothing to me."

It was Sunday morning, and Daniel woke up as usual at 6 and made love to Sarah. Their lovemaking was for many predictable, they didn't wear anything special, since all that they wanted was for skin to skin, tongue to tongue, hand to hand to touch each other, simply put they loved being naked. On top of that she was all woman and didn't need any toys for her to take the lead, she would simply submit, while he would make sure in the most passionate way, just like in the days of old of previous genera-tions of romantics, he knew how to send her to heavenly highs with him. He then went downstairs and made three packed lunches with all the trimmings before getting breakfast ready for 7.30. He had plenty of time and at 7 he dressed their daughter Emma and she was approaching 2 and a half as was the coming spring of 2017, before they would both jump on their resting mummy, who would then give everyone a hug before they would all venture downstairs and be served cereal and a full English breakfast made and served by her husband who loved to serve her with food at weekends.

Then it was time to get ready and Daniel placed into his 40 liters rucksack three packed lunches as well as 3 bottles of fluid. Then it was time well before 9 to set off slowly and to go up

Clougha Pike, on the northern fringes of the Forest of Bowland. On the walk Emma did her best, and sometimes Daniel would carry her along with the rucksack, and sometimes Sarah would. Of course, Emma as many were on a winter's day was shivering on the summit as they rested, but as they tucked into the food made with love and with the flask of hot-chocolate they very soon all warmed up as their child benefitted from the warm environment, which both parents had created between each other for all three of them.

In summer things were not much different with the shivers during the cool wet and windy nights, as the rain tried its best to encroach into the sleeping area of their tent, even so they made sure that even during the typically infamous British summers that they swam in the lakes and that their hearts were beating with excitement as they pushed themselves and would whenever they met up with their parents simply speak about their wonderful trips, which the family on both sides could relate to.

In short it didn't matter to them how society was progressing, they had each other, their love of all things simple, which modern life could never in a million years take away from them. While in Cumbria on their camping trips, they did the same walks as Louise and Mark did, who had followed in their own parents' footsteps. As such with the Weetabix, Hovis Bread and milk for breakfast nothing had changed in their families, and in knowing this they felt so comfortable and grounded.

Sarah had certainly made many enemies. She was perceived as a woman hater and was reviled by the feminists as someone who wanted to enslave women. As such when a very traditional woman came into the law firm fighting against a divorce, her boss knew that Sarah was the one. In theory this was exactly the case to prove to the local press that Sarah was no misogynist and her client was a very soft-spoken young lady. The high-light of the court proceeding was thus: "Her husband married her under the false pretenses of love, when deep down all he wanted was a baby-maker, so that he could have children of his own. And look, he is a wealthy man, and thinks that the law can be used to his advantage. Let me get one thing clear, you married and took God's vows until death do us part, when secretly you were making love to other men. Your wife stayed at home looking after your children, protecting them while you were taking part in acts, which had nothing to do with bringing up a family and were simply for your own hedonistic pleasure. You created your children together, and you will bring them up together, since to decide one day you want to sleep with men and walk away from your marriage when your wife is standing by you, shows how weak you are." After this monologue the whole courtroom was shaken and silent. Honesty in this room full of liars and professional perverts wasn't something, which the members of the judiciary were at all comfortable with.

A few more proceedings took place, and when Colin her closet gay great uncle found out he was incensed. As a solicitor himself he warned her, about how she was becoming a hate figure in Lancaster, of course she knew that she had gone from being anti women to homophobic, she merely could not win, but she didn't care since the case proved that she wasn't against women, but even so many local councilors, smelt blood and wanted to destroy her reputation once and for all, and to wipe that smile off her face.

Nothing could be found against her, but then one day the husband of her client, simply went into his garage while his wife was visiting her parents with their children in Milnthorpe and simply ran the exhaust of his car and fell asleep and died in the toxic gas of carbon monoxide. When the press got hold, Sarah was berated in the local Lancaster papers as being the cause of his death, and when asked for a comment she simply expressed her wish to see all parents together so that children could be brought up in safe homes, and that she supported all men and women who kept their marriage vows. Eventually she was reviled throughout the whole of the city and under pressure from her husband she gave an interview on the radio. This came as a shock, since the media had been happy to depict her as the most-evil woman from the Morecambe Bay, who was too scared to speak to the people of North Lancashire, now though they had a real problem, she wanted to talk to the Lancastrians while the media now wanted her quiet.

In the end, given she was a famous lawyer the local media felt obliged to give her some airtime, and during the interview, she simply said. "As a woman there is no one more than my Daniel whom I would like to thank, my partner who has supported me in my career, but above all is a wonderful husband and father to our children, and that my heart goes out to all of you, mothers or fathers who are no longer with your children thanks to a system, which values divorce more than marriage and the money in the form of alimony as being of a greater value than the needs of a child who simply loves both of his or her parents."

With that the press were still on her back, she had won one battle and now it was time for the journalists to get their own back on her. As such she was invited to Manchester the home of the most liberal newspaper north of London when suddenly the presumptuous female journalist began, "What do you think about Muslims?" She said as she was waiting for some racist remark.

"I work in Lancaster, there are many people of Pakistani origin, and while I feel that the Burka and terrorists are not in keeping with British values, I am not anti-Muslim." She said.

"Well, I think you have just half-admitted to being, a white supre-macist." Said the delighted journalist, who grinned at Sarah.

"Quite the opposite, many people of Middle East origin want to know why the west is supporting ISIS and destabilizing their countries. You know, they have leaders who are protecting their people from extremists and we are saying, you can't do that, they have their human rights. What we are doing is helping the shariarists in gaining control of the Levant and this is contempt-uous. As for the Burka, if I were to tell my secular friends of

Pakistani descent that I want to see them all dressed in black and covered from head to toe, they would simply call me a racist since many have fled these countries in order to escape the oppression of the mullahs." She said to a completely shell-shocked journalist.

The interview carried on a little more, and then the journalist admitted that she had been sent to damage Sarah's career but could now see that she had a heart of gold. As such in the press she was described as the Amal Clooney of the north and as a great representative and emblem of emancipated women the world over, fighting for women, mothers and wives.

At the time of writing, Frank's parents Jack and Betty were already 96 and 94 and still in relatively good health and helping on the farm. The daughter aged 76 had already retired, but with her husband they would help. Simon hated cleaning, so he cooked for his wife and her parents, while she made sure that their place was clean. Never once did they think about sending them to Grange- Over-Sands in what was locally known as the waiting room, simply the place where one went while waiting for his or her death. Instead, they preferred to receive some home help so that they had the chance to get away on a break. Neil the youngest son had taken over the farm with his wife, he was perfectly happy, life though hadn't always been so stable for him, since his first wife from Silverdale ran off to Cornwall to be with her lover and took the three children with her, on the grounds that he beat her up, and had incestuous relationships with his son eldest aged 6 at the time of the separation, but the united and strong force of the Taylors helped him into getting full custody of his beloved sons back to their home in Lancashire and the au pair girl from Turkey had since become his wife and mother of another 3 children of their own together.

For some unknown reason to him, each time Mark heard a George Michael song; he then simply felt remorse and sadness. His views on marriage values hadn't changed, but for some reason he saw George as someone like his darker twin. As such with Louise, they were organizing a big event and with their previous experience with TV they were working on a big event for Mark's 54th birthday. 2017 was also the year when Karen was 70 years of age, while Sarah would become 30. In the end it turned out less to be an event for Mark but one instead for the whole family. The event was to be called, "In the Shadow of George Michael," and money raised would go to local animal charities. The children Claire and Alec drew pictures along with help from their parents. Mark compiled events from each decade of his life, while Louise did the same around George Michael and with help from the children.

On the big day at Mark and Louise's home in Garstang, that midsummer the children Claire, Benjamin and Emma held up their artwork of their colored sketches of Frank, Karen with baby Mark and Matthew, with other members of the family. Frank spoke about the 1960s from his perspective and Louise finished the decade off surrounding the pop stars' infancy. They then covered the 70s and a minute's silence was held for Amy and her parents. For the 80s they continued with the sketches, which had been influenced from the photograph albums, and Louise enjoy-ed telling everyone how cool George was as a singer, and why aged 14 he was her first love, while Mark was feeling sorry for himself at university for being a loser, this of course sent every-one into wild laughter. The 90s came, but Sophie and Axelle were omitted to the dismay of certain members, but equally in order to protect Alec. Then came the decade 0, where Louise described George's decline while her own life was one of joy and finally the decade 10, which spoke much about the fame of Sarah. There were times like these, when Mark and Louise were glad that they had their big house close to the river, and they still had three children living at home. After the celebration, Mark and Louise were thinking how they like, Frank and Karen, didn't enforce their views on their children, but it seemed that the stable calmness surrounding the parents rose the expectations of what their children wanted for themselves too.

All the Taylor children, who had been brought up in the close-knit family, knew of nothing else other than a stable family. Of course, Axelle was one of Mark's failures, but then again, she became disturbed since she only saw conflict between her parents. Of course, nothing is ever quite so black and white, Amy grew up in a loving household, but the swinging 60s and 70s consumerism helped to lead her astray. In the end most of the Taylors felt that by living by example that that was simply the best that they could do, that their children were never too old to be dependent on them, and that Louise's parents although brought up in the Christian world of piety, were at the end of the day just as forgiving and tolerant as the Taylors since the one thing which connected the in laws generally was that while men and women were equal they were both different and like a stalk with two leaves, both on two different sides, with the children snuggly in the middle.

For her 30th birthday Sarah on the 19th of December 2017 she wanted to follow in the footsteps of her heritage. As such two nights were spent in Garstang where she walked with Louise, Mark and her three siblings as well as of course her immediate family members along the river to Scorton where her paternal grandparents joined in before walking over Nicky Nook into Calder Vale where they paid their respects before walking down and past the Kenlis Arms where Frank continued the chit chat about his romantic days of old with Karen. Then they moved onto Bowgreave for dinner with Ted and Denise before going onto Garstang where Frank and Karen would continue with their walk back into their home, while Sarah, Daniel and Emma would spend another night with her parents.

While millions of people worried about Brexit or whether a cyber-attack would take out their networking all over the world they themselves like the family members they were visiting, felt that their own lives would be left untouched in and around, the Forest of Bowland and the Morecambe Bay, where they could enjoy walking along the river, swimming in a pool, picking berries and most importantly of all making love to each other.

The next day after breakfast Sarah, Daniel and Emma drove up to Silverdale where they rested and ate with her paternal grandfather's roots. The following day they walked along the bay to Arnside and then went up the Knott before going back via Eaves Wood where they watched the sunset over the More-cambe Bay and made their wishes privately just as her grand-parents had done.

It was also during those days away from home, and especially away from work when Sarah was in tune more with her body, and was convinced that she was with child, and with Daniel being of a caring nature and discussing everything together they both knew that sometime in August that they would be expecting their second child. For Sarah this was a dream come true, since there were times when she was younger and with her careerist ambi-tions that she was scared that she would never become a moth-er, and her original aim was to fall pregnant by her 30th birthday, and with this being her second pregnancy she was of course delighted, but wanted to keep it between her and Daniel and that Emma would be the first to know after they could celebrate the news together privately, but not for long, since they planned to spend much of the Christmas period over at his parents in Flook-burgh.

While away they also wondered if two years down the line baby number three should come, Sarah was aged 30 and a very contented mother. She decided that they would carry on living simply so that she could take a break from work or given she could earn much more money than her husband who hated his job anyway that they would decide things for themselves. As such she decided that in four years" time that she planned after her maternity days were over, to take over as being the breadwinner, in the meantime she planned to continue with part time studies and part time work at the practice. Anyways this was all simply detail for this uncomplicated lady, since just like Karen and Denise, her grandparents and Louise her mother, she felt that there was no place like love for her, and the pebbles she had were as far as she was concerned just as much a part of the view of the Forest of Bowland from her back garden as they were for her husband and child.

As for Sarah, her husband Daniel and the rest of the family, they didn't really have any strong opinions about anything, they simply wanted to be happy with their families, and whenever they could, they would support anyone suffering from a family crisis.

Sarah also came home from Garstang on this trip with a beautifully framed picture and poem. It had its origins in Garstang and had been written and drawn with help from Karen along with her granddaughter Sarah herself when she was aged just 5 as a present for Mark, her father on his birthday, and Louise and Mark wanted it to be passed on as an heirloom in order to inspire their daughter's children. Just before she put her child to bed, she showed to her the picture from her poem, which she had written before reading it to her darling Emma, while Daniel was sat with his arms around them.

Find me a pebble on the riverbed.

One with a smooth and shiny head

Take me home and make her colored and red.

Don't leave her brown and looking like bread.

Might be a piece of rock with a heart of stone.

Or as good as gold and something to hold.

During 2018 Sarah decided to piece together the diaries, which Karen, Louise and herself had written. Some things were so revealing that she kept mum about what she had read. She had told both of those concerned that she was going to one day write a novel, and that she wanted to learn more about her own background. While Karen initially went red in the face, since although written in French and away from Frank's prying eyes, there were many embarrassing secrets. Louise's diary was revealing too, but none of her stories would have shocked Mark.

● ● ●

Sarah's aim was simple; she wanted to help bring back love between men and women. She had seen the wonderful photo albums from those of her ancestors and wanted to become a writer in support of traditional family values. Still very young, she felt that time was very much on her side.

As she looked around and saw that people were willingly destroying their families like lemmings jumping off a cliff, she believed that people were not ready to listen to her, she decided to set out on a long-term plan. At first, she would write about truly romantic tales and step-by-step as her stature grew, she would warn people about the dangers in allowing the New World Order to continue with its genocide against families all over the world.

In the meantime, she learnt a thing or two from Karen and Louise through reading their diaries, while Daniel her devoted husband couldn't believe how lucky he was, since as much as he wanted to make her happy, she was simply his boomerang when it came to love. On top of that: he wanted his wife to spread her message of love, to become some leader and help bring back family values. For Sarah, although flattered, she would have none of this. For her it was her own family first, and all she wanted to do with her books was to inspire others, since she believed that the most important things in her life were Daniel, her children and her home.

Much of her literary inspiration came from following in the footsteps of her parents and grandparents, and for her, going on walks down memory lane around Garstang was lovely. She borrowed books from the library about bygone times and found members of her family taking part in local events, and in turn she felt as though she was blessed. For her there was no place like home. With her now living in Lancaster, home also included the area around Silverdale. One place missing in the diaries was Heysham, whose cliffs were marvelous. Those Easter experienced days: which were ones of summer, and a few days away from the diaries, yet just a few miles from home, Heysham, was the perfect getaway for this down-to-earth lady. The sandcastles she made with Daniel and Emma were testament to the deep bond that existed within this family. While there was a view of the nuclear power station, Sarah felt that her body longed for a swim, and ran into the sea where the salty air and water rejuvenated her mind, body and soul. As she got out, her two loves were there, and Emma placed her head on her mother's growing belly, as Daniel looked on lovingly.

With Emma not yet in school, and the baby on the way, on the final week of June and the first week in July, they camped at Loughrigg tarn. They couldn't have chosen a better time, with the days being as warm as one would expect on the continent. The area was fertile for her research, but also poignant. It was here that she was studying the messed-up days of her parents and had to endure the times when Sophie and Axelle rather than her own mother and herself, were being warmly entertained by Grandpa Frank and his tales. It wasn't right for Sarah that she had missed out on such a wonderful holiday, and for a brief moment she was jealous of Axelle before feeling disgusted with herself. The sun was shining, the waters were inviting, Emma had her armbands on, while Daniel and Sarah went for a swim around the tarn with Emma holding onto them as she was between the two of them. As they got out of the water, other families saw them, and many other mothers wanted to shed tears, since the happiness from Sarah and her world was captivating, and poignantly for them, who were mostly in patchwork or broken families, they wished that they were blessed and stoical just like Sarah who was loved by her man and child.

And so, it was, on August 24th, Sarah gave birth to a healthy baby boy, and along with Daniel, felt that their family was more or less complete, and that life without each other and their children was unimaginable, since their world was their family.

Ironmantle Books

An Imprint of **DonnaInk Publications, L.L.C.**
17611 Aquasco Road
Baden, MD 20613

Special Markets: donnaink@gmail.com
https://www.donnaink.shop